THE JUDAS

Also by Steve Jackson

The Mentor

STEVE JACKSON

The Judas

HarperCollins*Publishers*

HarperCollins*Publishers*
77–85 Fulham Palace Road,
Hammersmith, London W6 8JB

www.harpercollins.co.uk
1

Published by HarperCollins*Publishers* 2007

A catalogue record for this book is
available from the British Library

ISBN-13: 978-0-00-721212-5

Set in Meridien by
Palimpsest Book Production Limited, Grangemouth, Stirlingshire

Printed and bound in Great Britain by
Clays Ltd, St Ives plc

For Mum and Dad

Acknowledgements

A big thank you to the following:

Karen, my soulmate and best friend – the journey wouldn't be half as much fun if I didn't have you to share it with.

Veronique Baxter and Wayne Brookes . . . my guardian angels in the publishing world.

Betty Schwartz is a one-off. Thank you for all your support and encouragement.

Fellow author, Rosie Goodwin, is an inspiration. It's good to have someone who understands only an email away.

Greig Stewart does a fantastic job of looking after my website. He also checked through the final draft to make sure the technology used in the book was bang up-to-date. His insights were invaluable.

Rob Coe of ESFAC Ltd gave me the perfect assassination technique. All well and good except I was on one of Rob's First Aid courses at the time, and was supposed to be learning how to save lives! I should point out this is more a reflection on the way my mind works than on Rob's skills as a trainer.

You can't do this job without the support of your friends and family. In particular I'd like to thank Mike, Karen and Amy Jackson; Paul, Dawn and Ruth Jackson; Anne Jackson and Mark Green; Simon Harding and Clare McMillin; Ian and Cath Springate; Nikki Searle; John Connolly and Karen Mardle; Candice Williams, Paul Ingram, Cindy Brown, Annabel Montgomery and Nikki Thompson.

And last but not least, a huge thank you to all the readers who got in touch to tell me how much they enjoyed *The Mentor*. Writing is one of the most rewarding jobs you can do, but it can be a lonely old business at times. Your comments and warm wishes have been much appreciated.

Steve Jackson
March 2007

PART ONE

Watching The Watchers

There are no facts, only interpretations.
Friedrich Nietzsche

Heads turned when Kestrel entered the bar, then quickly turned away. Even the squat bull of a doorman sneaked a glance. Kestrel knew he looked good. The faded blue 501s had a cheeky rip just below the left back pocket; the skintight white Calvin Klein T-shirt showed off his tight pecs. He had spent ages fussing gel into his hair, playing with it until he had that just-got-up look. The finishing touch was the pair of Armani shades propped on top of his head. Today he was blond, because the gentleman preferred blonds.

Kestrel chose a booth with a good view of the entrance and ordered a bottle of red. The air was warm and moist, heavy with cigarette smoke and alcohol fumes. Candlelight splashed the crimson walls, and the gothic feel was enhanced by the arches and low ceiling. This bar didn't advertise. You either knew it was here, or you didn't. Understandable for this most Catholic of cities. Four pretty boys were giggling and conspiring at one end of the bar, talking in rapid-fire Italian. The centre of their universe was a large man

3

with a greying ponytail and a face that suggested he'd been there, done it, got the T-shirt. The ponytailed man dragged himself away from the attention and came over, made himself at home on the other side of the table. He was older than Kestrel, pushing fifty. The first facelift was beginning to sag; no doubt he'd already booked in for the second. The Marlboro between his thumb and forefinger signed the air with lazy trails of smoke.

'What's your name?' The English was accented, fluent enough to indicate time spent in Britain.

'James.'

'And I'm Luciano. So, James, what brings you to my humble establishment?'

'I'm looking for work.'

The mouth stretched into a sly grin; Botox kept the eyes and forehead frozen in place. 'I'm guessing you're not talking about bar work.'

'You guess right.'

Kestrel turned away while Luciano checked him out. He could feel those frozen eyes crawling all over his skin, studying him like he was a piece of meat. One of the pretty boys slinked into a booth. Thirty seconds later he was winding across the room with a middle-aged man in tow. They disappeared through a doorway hidden in the shadows at the end of the bar.

'Okay, here's how it works.' Luciano took a final drag and folded the half-smoked cigarette into an ashtray. 'The customer pays me, I pay you. Weekly. On a Friday. That way you won't be tempted to rip me off. That's the deal. Take it or leave it.'

Kestrel considered this for a moment. 'Okay, you've got a deal.'

They shook hands, and Luciano kept hold. A finger stroke along his palm, a lingering look, then a nod towards the darkened doorway. 'I could give you a tour of the back rooms . . .'

'It'll cost you,' Kestrel deadpanned.

Luciano laughed as he stood up. 'Ah, the English sense of humour. Don't you just love it?'

The target appeared ten minutes later and made a beeline for Luciano. He bought him a drink and they chatted like old friends, laughing and joking. Luciano nodded in Kestrel's direction and the target turned slowly. He gave Kestrel a predatory once-over then turned back to Luciano. Business talk judging by the body language. Money changed hands and the target walked over. He lowered himself into the booth, put his wineglass on the table and offered his hand. While they did the whos, whys and wheres, Kestrel went with the flow. The target was fifty-eight, but looked seventy. He was overweight with thick, saggy jowls. There was a yellow tinge to his skin – an alcoholic's complexion. He had dark bags under his eyes, nicotine stains on the thumb and fingers of his right hand. Kestrel reached under the table and laid a hand on the target's thigh. Squeezed. Moved an inch higher. The target smiled, his bloodhound eyes twinkling in the candlelight. He nodded towards the back room. 'Shall we?' he suggested. His accent was bland and middle class.

Kestrel shook his head. 'Why don't we make a night of it?'

'I've only paid for an hour.'

'You'd better go talk to Luciano then.'

The target got up and headed for the bar. More money changed hands. Less than a minute later the target was leading the way up the smooth stone steps, on a promise and in a hurry. They stepped out onto a narrow street with a slim pavement lining one side. The city hummed quietly in the background, a low rumble creeping over the tops of the high rooftops, sneaking in through the gaps and cracks. There was a news-stand on the corner, the bright glossy magazine covers standing out against the dull chipped paintwork. The owner was flicking through a newspaper and smoking a cigarette, minding his own business.

'My place isn't far from here,' the target said.

'You're not suggesting we walk, are you?'

'Good God, no!'

A Fiat turned into the street, the taxi light on its roof lit up. The target waved it down. Playing the gentleman, he opened the back door for Kestrel who climbed in beside him. While the target gave the driver directions, Kestrel reached into the side pocket of the door. The syringe vibrated in his hand as though it was made from electricity. He jabbed hard, stabbing the needle into the target's thigh. The eyes widened for a moment, then softened as the drug took hold; his head slumped onto his chest. The lookout walked over from a doorway on the other side of the street and climbed into the passenger seat. Without a word, the driver put the car into gear and pulled away from the kerb.

They drove out of Rome, careful to keep to the speed

limit. Forty minutes later they turned onto a dirt track, the Fiat bouncing over the ruts and dips. The farm-house was hidden in a valley. Deserted and rundown. The engine died, the mechanical rumble replaced by insects and birds and the wind in the trees. The driver slipped his hands into the target's armpits, his partner took the feet, and they manhandled him into the farm-house.

Everything had been provided as per Kestrel's instruc-tions: the tent pegs, the mallet, the tarpaulin, the white forensic suit, the axe. The target's unconscious body was placed carefully onto the tarpaulin, arms spread out at shoulder level. Kestrel removed his denim jacket and climbed into the forensic suit and checked the boots and gloves were secure.

The first tent peg went through the right hand, driven between the bones into the wooden floor. The target awoke immediately, howling in agony, His screams seemed to go on forever. This wasn't how Kestrel usually did business, but the customer had been very specific. The two Mafia men held the target down while Kestrel did the left hand. The target was crying between the screams now, blubbing like a baby, begging to know what he'd done. The trick with the feet was to put a bend in the knee so the soles lay flat. As the peg was hammered in, the target passed out. Kestrel did the left foot then pulled up a wooden chair. When the target regained consciousness, he instinctively pulled his hands back. Skin and gristle ripped, and this set off another bout of screaming. Kestrel waited for him to settle.

'Look at me,' he said softly.

The target's wet bloodhound eyes met his and Kestrel said one word:

'Judas.'

Realisation dawned on the target's face. His body sagged. All hope gone.

Kestrel picked up the axe and hefted it in his hands, feeling its weight. The first swing severed the target's hand, blood spraying from the open artery and painting the bright forensic suit with abstract patterns. He swung again and the axe crashed through the target's ribcage, destroying his heart.

1

The sign on the door made Paul Aston smile – no mean feat, the way his life had been going lately. Anything that steered him from under that black cloud, even for a second or two, was a welcome distraction. The doorway in question was certainly sturdy enough – if he had to guess he'd go for oak; that would be appropriate – and the masonry surround was tidy, good solid blockwork. The sign, however, was another matter altogether. It had been bodged together and hung crookedly on the doorknob. Plywood and string and an A4 sheet informing him that the public gallery would be open at 9.30. It was all so typically English. The Old Bailey was the highest court in the land and this was the best they could do. It was pathetic. No wonder the woman with the scales on the roof wore a blindfold.

He checked his watch. A couple of minutes to go. Quite a crowd had formed on the pavement, a real mixed bag. American tourists, Germans,

Italians. The Japanese couple looked completely lost – cameras and camcorders were banned from the court and they didn't know what to do with their hands. The students were trying to be mature and ending up with the giggles, while their stressed teachers attempted to keep them under control. And then there were the journalists, a whole snarling pack of them, most trying to squeeze in one more cigarette, puffing away as though their lives depended on it.

'So, who do you work for?'

Aston turned towards the voice. The suit had seen better days, as had the body inhabiting it. The journalist's nose was an explosion of capillaries, his complexion the colour of cheap red wine. His shoulders were hunched from crouching over a keyboard and he held his head to one side, as if the wind had changed direction while he was in the middle of a telephone interview.

'Freelance.' Aston injected the word with as much 'fuck off' as he could.

'Hey, only asking.' The journalist flicked his cigarette into the gutter and lit another. He turned away and struck up a conversation with the poor sod standing on his left.

At exactly half past nine the door opened – the sign might have been crap but at least it was accurate. The journalists surged forward, pushing the tourists and students aside, making sure they got in first. While the security guard checked his press pass and patted him down, Aston fought the urge to fiddle with the moustache. If it came off in his hands, that would lead to a few awkward questions. The rest of his disguise consisted of a pair of thick rimmed glasses, the same black wig he'd worn for the pass photo, and a charity shop suit. He'd even asked one of the girls from the typing pool to fill the first dozen pages of his notebook with shorthand notes. Fuck knows what she'd written, probably something obscene.

The journalists passed through the metal detector in single file. Aston kept close to the one in front, not wanting to lose him. There was only one story here today, and it would be best if it looked as though he'd been here before; standing around like a lost tourist was not going to give the impression he was a shit-hot reporter.

The trial was being held in Court Two. No surprises there. This was the high security court, fully kitted out for terrorists and monsters. According to the media, Robert Macintosh was both. The press box was a squeeze, but gave a better view than the packed public gallery way up there with the gods. Conversation was muted, everyone mumbling in whispers. With its stern wood panelling, green leather and high glass ceiling, the old courtroom demanded respect. Aston glanced over at the empty dock – the perspex lining the top looked so out of place against all that ancient wood. In one corner was a seat for the guard; next to that was a big red panic button. Directly in front of him, the lawyers were preparing for battle, sorting through paperwork and making space on the desks for their boxes. They were wearing their best wigs, black robes pressed and swishing. The jury box was empty today. Aston elbowed himself some space, earning a couple of scowls from his fellow journalists. He crossed his legs and placed the notebook on his thigh.

The last six months had been hell. He'd never expected a medal – you didn't join MI6 for the fame and the glory – but then he hadn't expected a right royal fucking over, either. The backslapping lasted a whole week, and then things had gone downhill. Rapidly. Colleagues began treating him like a leper, and all because he'd worked for Mac. It hadn't taken them long to forget who'd put their neck on the line to catch the bastard. No, memories were short indeed at Vauxhall Cross.

His last performance review was a complete joke. From Box 1 to Box 3 in six months. An ambush was what it was. Plain and simple. The message was clear: They wanted him out. And if further proof was needed, three weeks later he had found himself in a windowless room far below street level analysing data on a forgotten corner of Africa. Africa, for Christ's sake! The dark continent was so far off the map, it didn't even merit its own controllerate. It was like being sent to Siberia. The whole Mac affair had been an embarrassment, and the Powers That Be had gone into serious cover-up mode. It was the only explanation. And hadn't that always been the Six way?

Sweep it under the carpet and pretend it never happened?

He'd considered quitting. Even got as far as writing the resignation letter. His finger had hovered over the print button for an eternity, then, at the last second, he'd hit delete. All that stopped him was stubbornness. Why the hell should he quit? He hadn't done anything wrong. In fact, his only crime was doing his job. Up until last September his career had been on the fast-track; he'd been doing fine, thank you very much. Anyway, what would he do? Disappear without a fuss and go back to working in a bank? No, if they wanted rid of him they'd have to do it the old-fashioned way. Assassination. Stabbed with a poison-tipped umbrella or taken out by a sniper.

Today was a prime example of how bad it had got. Nobody knew he was here . . . and nobody cared. Certainly not his new boss, who was counting off the seconds until his retirement and spending more time at Vauxhall Cross's bar than his desk. Last night Aston had taken the shoebox containing the bits and pieces for a new journalist alias he was working on home with him. This morning he hadn't bothered showing up for work. Mac would have crucified him if he'd pulled a stunt like that.

Mac turned up at five to ten. The room fell silent and everyone turned towards the dock to get a better look at the monster as he was led up from the cells. This was the first time Aston had seen Mac since that September night all those months ago. He still wasn't sure what had drawn him here today. Curiosity was part of it, but that wasn't the whole story. Not by a long shot. Katrina, MI6's caffeine addicted shrink, would no doubt have told him he was looking for closure. If he believed in all that psychobollocks it would have provided a tidy reason. However, sitting here now, staring at the man who'd fucked his life up, closure was the last thing he was feeling.

Mac was smaller than Aston remembered, somehow diminished, older. Prison life obviously didn't agree with him. He was limping heavily, his right knee giving him gyp; his face tensed with pain whenever the bad leg went down. Then again, this was Mac. How much of the pain was real and how much was he playing to the gallery? Mac's hair used to be corn coloured, not a trace of grey. There were definite streaks of grey in there now, and the cut was cheap, prison barber cheap. The face was thinner, the waistline, too. His eyes were as sharp as ever, though, scanning the courtroom and taking everything in. Mac's expensive lawyer flashed a sympathetic look at his meal ticket. Another obvious play, and it made Aston's skin crawl. The tail ends of Charles Wainwright's hair contrasted against the dirty ivory of his wig – his hair was so white it practically glowed. He was the top defence lawyer in the country, charging God knows how much an hour. That he lost more cases than he won was no reflection on his skills.

You only called on Charles Wainwright when you were in deep, deep shit.

Judge Charles Staunton was five minutes late, just late enough to show who was boss. The defendant might have had more column inches lately, but this was his court. His face was long and angular, the nose pointed; deep lines were buried in the leathery skin, carved out by years of stress and worry. There was a definite no bullshit aura about him. He had to be tough – this case was going to be a bitch. Mac had been with MI6 forever, and Aston was certain he would take the stand. No way would he miss his chance to cause as much mayhem as possible. The Powers That Be back at Vauxhall Cross were terrified of what he might say, and the Six lawyers were pushing to have as much of the trial heard *in camera* as possible. Wainwright wanted everything heard out there in open court. In the interest of free speech, of course.

Mac was guilty. Everyone knew that. The police, the media, the public. The fact the Crown Prosecution Service had got this to the Old Bailey so quickly meant they were convinced of his guilt; if Mac got off on a technicality, heads would roll. Finding twelve people good and true who could view the trial with an impartial eye would be impossible.

Today was the first round. The charges were read out and Mac was asked how he pleaded. The body might have been frailer than Aston remembered, but the voice was as strong as ever. To each charge Mac uttered two words – 'not guilty' – his rich baritone reaching into every corner of the courtroom. Over the years, Aston had come to dread that booming voice. Even now, the sound of it still made him shiver. The plea was no surprise. Mac was going to spend the rest of his life in prison and this trial was a distraction, something to amuse him. If he could spend the next few months shuttling back and forth from Belmarsh Prison, having the opportunity to taste free air a little while longer, of course he was going to protest his innocence. What did he have to gain from pleading guilty? That there was the potential for Mac to cause maximum embarrassment to MI6 was a bonus.

It was all over in less than five minutes. Judge Staunton adjourned the court until a trial date could be set. Wainwright flashed a reassuring look at his client and Mac rose unsteadily to his feet. Aston noticed the guard wasn't offering to help, wasn't getting too close. Wise man. Mac hobbled over to the top of the steps. Before disappearing back down to the cells he paused for a second, hand on hip as though he was catching his breath. He turned slowly and looked straight at the press bench, straight at Aston. A smile and a wink and then he was gone.

Judge Staunton stood, and there was the noisy thump and shuffle as everyone followed suit. The judge left and the press bench started to empty.

Aston stayed put, pushing himself into his seat to let the other journalists through. He stayed there until he was the only person left. That bastard had got one up on him again! Unbe-fucking-lievable! The wink and the smile had been meant for him. No two ways about it. He'd seen through the disguise. Must have clocked him during that quick scan of the courtroom when he first came in. Mac's powers of observation had always been spectacular, honed through years of practice. Looked like he'd lost none of his edge.

Aston got up slowly and retraced his steps through the corridors. There was a spook waiting for him outside. Definitely a rookie. He was dressed in regulation black with the shades to match. That brought back a memory of the first time he went walkabout with Mac. Like this rookie, he'd been dressed in black. As soon as they got outside Vauxhall Cross, Aston had fished out a pair of Ray-Bans and put them on. Mac had leant across, whipped them off, dropped them on the ground and crushed them under his heel. Aston had been speechless. The sunglasses had cost a fortune. 'And another thing,' Mac had said. 'Lose the black clothes. They make you look so fucking obvious.'

'Come with me, Mr Aston,' the rookie said.

'Why?' He was definitely going to have to do some work on this alias. If a rookie could see through it no wonder Mac clocked him so quickly. Some latex prosthetics might help. A new chin, a different nose . . .

The rookie appeared flustered. 'Orders.'

'Whose orders?'

'Need to know.'

'Feels good saying that, doesn't it?' Before the rookie could answer Aston added: 'Okay, let's see your ID.'

The rookie passed his card to Aston. A quick check before handing it back. 'Where are you parked?'

'This way.' The rookie headed for the kerb and waited for a gap in the traffic.

'Mind telling me what this is all about?'

'Need to know.'

'Thought you might say that,' Aston replied. 'Word of advice: Lose the shades . . . and the black clothes. They make you look so fucking obvious.'

2

'So you currently work for the Foreign Office, Ms Strauss.'

'That's correct,' George replied.

'And what exactly do you do there?'

'Administrative work, mainly.' The lies flowed easily, as she'd been trained. She shifted in her seat, uncomfortable within the confines of her suit, but trying not to let it show.

'And what do you think you can bring to Goldberg, Levinstein and Samuels?'

Bloody good question. She could bug your house, organise a dead drop, pick a lock, pick your pocket. She could take on a new identity: become a journalist, a waitress, a secretary. She knew how to recruit a foreign agent, could put a bullet between your eyes from a hundred yards, could disarm you if you charged her with a knife. But when it came to working in a solicitor's office she didn't have a fucking clue.

This was all her mother's fault. The battle had

19

been long, but her mother had won in the end. Again. She'd seen George was miserable at work, and played on it mercilessly. Sympathy to start with, then slowly, slowly chipping away. A throw-away comment here, a subtle suggestion there, put-downs disguised as concern; when it came to psych-ops, her mother was in a league of her own. Timing it to perfection, waiting for that moment when she sensed the prey was exhausted and ripe for the kill, she'd struck. A friend of a friend had a small legal practice, mainly conveyancing work, with a bit of personal injury. Anyway, they had an opening for a secretary and – if you're inter-ested, but only if you're interested, mind . . . don't feel as if there's any pressure – she could put in a good word and get an interview arranged. No pressure! That was a laugh. The pitch was deliv-ered with the skill of a veteran salesman; the hidden implication was that this was George's last shot at respectability. This was a proper job, not like that spying nonsense. Blow this one and you're going to burn in hell for all eternity.

Yes, the pitch had been impressive.

George looked across at Goldberg. He was waiting patiently, an earnest expression on his face, elbows on the desk, fingers interwoven and prop-ping up his chin. The overhead fluorescents reflected off his bald patch. George leant forward and picked up the cup and saucer, she sipped dain-tily like a lady, weighing her options. The coffee had been brought by a mousy secretary. Cheap shoes, a polyester suit, and completely in awe of Goldberg. She'd practically curtsied when she'd put his cup down. A couple of stolen glances, then she'd darted from the office before the blush took hold. Goldberg had watched her go – a twist of his wedding ring, and another – his eyes fixed on the secretary's arse. George wondered whether Mrs Goldberg knew what was going on, or whether she was the sort of woman who would turn a blind eye for the sake of the two kids with the beaming smiles in the photos at the side of the monitor.

Goldberg looked perfectly at home behind his wide antique oak desk, surrounded by mementoes of his success, shelf upon shelf of heavy legal tomes climbing the walls all around him. Could she find a space to call her own in this place? Could she play the role of the dutiful secretary? Fending off the advances of over-enthusiastic partners at the office Christmas bash? It was a no-brainer.

'So what can I bring to Goldberg, Levinstein and Samuels?' George mused.

Goldberg smiled encouragingly for her to go on.

'Well, Mr Goldberg, to be perfectly honest there's absolutely fuck all I can bring to your firm. I'm sorry, it seems I've wasted your time here.' George got up to leave and Goldberg just sat there with his mouth hanging open, too stunned to move. 'Have a good day, Mr Goldberg.'

She kept her smile in check until she was out

of the office. This was the most fun she'd had in months. Her mother would go supernova when she heard about this. And hear about it she would. Goldberg was probably on the phone to her already. Oh, to be a fly on that particular wall.

So what now? She was in no hurry to get back to Vauxhall Cross. As far as her boss was concerned she had a hospital appointment. 'Women's problems,' she'd whispered when he'd asked. Typical bloke, he'd gone bright red, huffed and puffed a bit, then quickly changed the subject. It was only biology, for God's sake; it wasn't as though she had the plague. The NHS being what it was, she estimated she could justifiably bunk off for the rest of the morning and nobody would raise an eyebrow. A glance at her watch. A couple of hours to kill. She headed for the nearest tube station. A spot of retail therapy wouldn't go amiss. She wasn't big on clothes, however, shoes were another matter altogether.

So where had it all gone wrong? She'd had her six month review the same time as Paul, back in November. The result had been the same as his, a Box 3. A fucking Box 3! She deserved better than that. She knew it, and the simpering little shit from Personnel who carried out her review knew it, too. Perhaps she should have taken more notice of the signs. The assignments she'd been given after the Mac fiasco hadn't exactly been taxing; it was the sort of work she could do with her eyes shut. Then there was the way she'd been gradually edged out of the loop. Her security clearance hadn't changed, not according to the computer, but she was no longer getting access to the juicy stuff. Her boss had still been his usual polite self; in hindsight, perhaps a bit too polite. It was during the week before Christmas that the world ended.

Jeremy Gaskin, the Middle East controller, had called her into his office. He told her to close the door and take a seat, and there was something in his voice she didn't like one bit. Gaskin came from the Oxbridge side of the family, an old Etonian through and through. By the time he'd finished, all George wanted to do was ram that silver spoon down his throat and watch him choke on it.

'Can't help noticing, but you don't seem your usual self,' he'd begun, reasonably enough. 'Anything the matter?'

George put on her best 'everything's A-OK' face, a face she'd had a lot of practice with lately. A shake of the head. 'Nope. I'm pretty busy, but aren't we all? Looking forward to going to Cairo, though.'

'Ah,' said Gaskin, and he didn't need to say any more.

'Is there a problem?' George managed to ask. Her stomach was churning and she suddenly felt light-headed. Cairo was her first overseas posting; she'd been working towards this for the best part of a year. They couldn't take that away from her.

'Well . . . for the time being, we think it might be best to postpone. Just for a few months.'

23

'Why?'

Gaskin's answer was vague, all padding and no substance. He mentioned budgets and cutbacks, but George wasn't listening. Her mind spun as she tried to work out what was really going on here. Gaskin's delivery gave the impression he was relaying a message. If that was the case, who was the message from? There was only one person with the clout to push Gaskin around: Anthony Heath. But why would the new Chief be interested in her? George doubted he knew she even existed.

Gaskin had dismissed her with a: 'Sorry, I know how disappointed you must be.'

'And merry fucking Christmas to you,' George had hissed under her breath as she ever so gently closed the door behind her.

Her mobile vibrated and she pulled it out, checked the caller ID. Looked like mother had heard the good news. She let the call go to voice-mail, noticed there were a couple of texts. A flick of the thumb and the first one flashed up. George didn't recognise the number. She read it, stopped dead, read it again. According to the message, it would be in her interest to go to an address in Camden. If it had just been the one text she probably would have dismissed it as an error. However, the second message convinced her this was for her eyes only. And she knew who it was from. Paul.

```
go on u no u wnt 2
wot u got 2 lse ;)
```

George glanced at her watch and did the calcu-
lations. She was twenty minutes from Camden
and her curiosity was killing her. Once a spy,
always a spy. The shoes would have to wait.

3

Aston settled into the passenger seat and watched the streets and buildings go by. They were heading north, which wasn't what he'd expected. His money had been on Vauxhall Cross. The rookie wasn't giving anything away; he had his orders and was following them to the letter. Aston had given him the third degree, but it hadn't done any good. They turned into Camden High Street, drove past the tube station and pulled up by the black metal sign for the Inverness Street market. The market consisted of a couple of shabby stalls selling designer knock-offs and tourist bait; the fruit and veg didn't look particularly fresh. The most impressive thing about this market was the sign: stylish and rust-free with a lamp curving up at each end. Compared to the colourful main market on the other side of the canal this one was thoroughly underwhelming.

The rookie fished a key from the pocket of his black jacket and passed it to Aston. He pointed to a doorway next to a second-hand record store. 'You need to go in there and wait.'

'Wait for who?'

The rookie said nothing, just stared stony-faced. This was pretty much what Aston expected. He got out of the car and slammed the door shut. 'Have a nice day,' he mouthed through the window. Not so much as a smile from the rookie as the car slipped away from the kerb. Aston threw the key into the air and caught it one-handed. *Okay, let's go see what this is all about.* He walked through the market, dodging between a pile of empty boxes. Rubbish spilled out from a green wheelie bin, the damp, fetid stink hanging heavily in the air. Yup, definitely the posh end of town. A couple of cops in bright yellow fluorescent jackets turned into the street, walking towards him. Without breaking stride, Aston swiftly side-stepped and got interested in the candles on a nearby stall; the survivor from the Summer of Love who ran the stall got all interested in him. She had dirty greying dreadlocks and the complexion of someone who spent their life outdoors. She jammed a half-smoked roll-up into the corner of her mouth, flicked a Zippo and launched into her spiel. Aston feigned interest until the cops were out of sight.

The shop front was painted bright purple, and had VINYL TIMES scrawled in large funky lettering above a window filled with faded LP covers. Bob Marley, The Velvet Underground, The Sex Pistols.

The glass rattled under the onslaught of something electronic that had too much bass, too much drums, too much everything. There was a two-floor apartment above the shop, the brickwork dirty and worn, the windows on the top floor were boarded over. Aston did a quick 360 degrees. Nobody watching. He twisted the key in the lock, stepped inside and quickly closed the door.

The smell hit him straightaway. New woodwork and fresh paint. He flicked on a light and climbed the narrow stairs, shoes snapping on the bare wooden boards, the bass boom from next door vibrating through the wall. There was a locked door at the top of the stairs, a numeric keypad with a fingerprint scanner attached to the wall beside it. Curiouser and curiouser. Aston typed in his MI6 PIN and pressed his thumb against the scanner. A gentle click and a whirr as the invisible bolts withdrew. The door moved easily but was much heavier than it appeared. Aston took a closer look. Brushed steel, two inches thick – the pine panelling attached to the front made it look like a regular door. He stepped inside and pushed it shut. The bolts slid back into place with a barely audible thunk.

The office had no character whatsoever. White walls, three black veneered desks with chrome trim, a matching bookcase; ergonomically designed chairs and keyboards, and a scratchy hard-wearing navy carpet; wooden venetian blinds covered the windows. He tapped one of the panes with his fingertips. A dull thud rather than a sharp ting. Bulletproof. No noise leaking in from the shop downstairs, which meant a floating floor and serious amounts of sound-proofing. Aston made himself at home behind the biggest desk. Spread out in front of him was the flotsam and jetsam you expected to find: a ruler, hole punch and stapler, all lined up nice and neat; a desk tidy loaded with brand new pens and pencils. The flat screen monitor was bang up-to-date. He reached down and switched on the computer. While it booted up, he went through the drawers. All empty. The computer had a copy of Microsoft Office installed, but this was a virgin machine: no personal files on the hard-drive, no saved messages in Outlook. He rocked back in the chair, hands behind his head, fingers laced together. There was no year planner pinned to the wall, no pictures, no clues as to what business might be carried out here. There was a white plastic clock on one wall, the bright red second hand ticking loudly in the stillness. And that new smell everywhere.

A completely blank canvas, but what was the picture?

Aston got up and went through the rest of the rooms. They were all as characterless as the main office. The kitchen was kitted out with a fridge, cooker, microwave, all brand new. The other two doors led to a tiny bathroom that had a shower cubicle fitted in one corner, and a bedroom with a couple of army cots pressed up against the walls.

And then there was the third door.

It was only when Aston got back to the office he realised something was missing. The apartment had two floors, yet he hadn't seen any stairs. He found the door on his second pass. It was at the far end of the hall. There was no handle; when you were right up next to it you could see the thin black line where it fitted into the wall. Aston spent ten minutes trying to get in before admitting defeat. Back in the main office, he settled down behind the big desk and waited.

The buzzer made him jump. He'd been staring at the screensaver, following the ribbons of coloured lights as they snaked across the screen. The buzzer sounded again and Aston went to investigate. There was a small monitor next to the door: three inches square, the image sharp and definite. Even if the screen had been totally low-tech, the face nothing but a blur, he would still have recognised it. Aston buzzed his guest in, listened for her footsteps on the stairs, but couldn't hear a thing because of the heavy steel and the soundproofing.

The door swung open and George came in wearing a puzzled expression, her kinky black hair held in place with a red scrunchy. 'Okay, Paul, mind telling me what the fuck is going on here?'

Aston shrugged. 'Your guess is as good as mine. There I was minding my own business. Next thing

I know I was bundled into a car and driven here. What about you?'

'I got your text telling me—'

'Not my text.'

'Okay, I got *a* text, telling me to come here.'

Aston went over to the big desk. He sat down and rolled back till the chair hit the wall. 'Here's what I know. Somebody's gone to a lot of trouble – not to mention expense – here. Everything is brand new and the paint's barely dry. The security's state-of-the-art.' He nodded to the door. 'Those don't come cheap. It would stop an army of mujahidin armed with rocket propelled grenades.'

'Tell me something I don't know.'

Aston grinned. 'Well, there is the secret doorway that leads up to the second floor.'

'Where?'

'End of the hall.'

Without another word, George headed for the door.

'You can't miss it,' Aston shouted after her.

Twenty seconds passed, thirty. 'Where?' George hollered. 'I can't see anything.'

'You will.'

Another ten seconds then: 'Ah yeah, I got it.'

George came back in. 'So, how do you open it?'

'Good question.'

'Well?'

'Fucked if I know.'

'So what's this all about, Paul?'

Aston opened his mouth, stopped dead. He nodded to the brushed steel door. 'My guess is we're about to find out.'

4

The door opened in slow motion, and it wasn't until it was fully open that Aston realised he was holding his breath. The man in the doorway stood about five-eight and was meticulously turned out: bespoke charcoal grey suit, expensive Italian leather on his feet, a shiny black attaché case in his hand. His back was parade ground straight, and there was a quiet confidence surrounding him. He was well into his forties, probably hitting fifty. It was difficult to say for certain since that point was open for debate . . . as Aston had found out. When Anthony Heath was announced as Grant Kinclave's successor, he had hit the computers looking for bio-data on the new Chief . . . as had everyone else at Vauxhall Cross. Despite the servers running red-hot for the rest of that afternoon, nobody came up with anything particularly interesting.

Heath was squeaky clean, a safe bet. Married for the past twenty years, he had two kids, girls, both at university. The marriage had been uneventful, no away games on either side. The only blip was the date of birth. August 12, 1957, according to passport and birth records; August 12, 1959, according to the taxman. Probably an admin error, or maybe a small vanity. Whatever the reason, it was the only discrepancy, and it was nothing to get excited about. Heath was from the Sandhurst side of the family, and had risen to the rank of Major in the SAS. He joined MI6 in the late Eighties and had progressed steadily upwards, eventually being promoted to the Director of Security and Public Affairs. As D/SPA, his fiefdom included security vetting, counter intelligence and I/Ops, the propaganda department. His speciality was old school paranoia. In light of last September, the general consensus at Vauxhall Cross was that his promotion to Chief wasn't necessarily a bad thing.

Playing it cool, Aston swung back in the chair and put his hands behind his head. George found a space on the edge of the desk, her intelligent brown eyes fixed on The Chief. This should be interesting. Heath walked over to the window and peered around the blinds, gave the market the once-over.

'So, what do you think?' He addressed the question to his reflection in the bulletproof glass.

Aston caught George's attention and gave her a look. Neither of them jumped in with an answer.

'Well,' Heath said, turning and looking at them

both in turn. 'I asked you a question. What do you think?'

The silence went on for a long second, then Heath grinned broadly. 'Okay, Mr Aston, shift your arse. By my reckoning, that's my chair. Last time I looked I was still your boss.'

Aston got up and Heath slipped into the big chair. He laid the attaché case on the desk and placed a hand protectively on top. A little satisfied nod to himself as he looked around, taking it all in. George rounded up two chairs and wheeled them over. She rolled one to Aston then sat down.

'You know,' The Chief said, 'it's amazing what you can do with an unlimited government budget and a little imagination. Take this place, for example, from conception to realisation in just four months. That takes some doing. Not to mention a shed-load of cash.'

'And what exactly is this place?' Aston asked.

'Why, Mr Aston, this is your new home,' Heath replied simply.

'Do you mind explaining?'

Heath didn't answer immediately. He leant forward, elbows on the desk, index fingers tapping out a tattoo on his lower lip. 'Do you know how MI6 is viewed by the rest of the intelligence community at the moment? We're a joke. Hell, even the ASIS out in Australia are more respected than us. The bloody Aussies, for Christ's sake! What the hell do they know about spying? Okay, so one of our top men went AWOL, ended up switching sides. That never goes down well. But if that wasn't bad enough there's a rumour flying around that he managed to detonate a bomb at Vauxhall Cross. A completely unfounded rumour, of course. Everyone knows it was a fire. But you know how it is with rumours – once that genie is out of the bottle it's almost impossible to get him back in again.' A sigh. 'And that's the shit-storm I walked into. Once upon a time, MI6 was one of the most respected intelligence agencies in the world. The way I see it, my job is to get the respect back.'

'Fair enough,' Aston said, 'but what does that have to do with us.'

'Any organisation is only as good as the people who work for it. You two happen to be among the best I've got.'

George gave a sarcastic little chuckle. 'Have you seen our personnel files lately?'

'Seen them, Ms Strauss?' A checkmate smile. 'I helped write them.'

Aston caught George's eye, desperate to know what she was thinking.

'To defeat your enemy,' Heath said, 'you have to understand him. However, that in itself isn't enough. You have to adapt to take advantage of that knowledge. A level playing field is for losers. You want to make that playing field as uneven as possible – sloped to your advantage, of course – and then take the bastards out.'

'The lousy personnel reviews,' Aston said, 'the way we've been edged out of the loop. You set us up, didn't you?'

'One way of looking at it, Mr Aston.'

'There are others?'

The Chief ignored this. 'Since the Berlin Wall came down, MI6 has been struggling to find its place in the world. During the Cold War we knew who the enemy was. MI6 was a huge dinosaur of an organisation, and that was fine because the enemy was a bigger dinosaur. And then the wilderness years. Those long, lonely days of accountability and crippling budget cuts. 9/11 saved us. We have a purpose again, a new enemy. The problem was that MI6 was still a dinosaur, and this new enemy was no bigger than a mouse. That's where we came unstuck. That's why the London bombings happened in the first place.'

'You haven't answered my question,' Aston said. 'You set us up, didn't you?'

'Yes.'

'Why?' George asked. 'Do you know how hard I worked? Do you have any idea how much of a slap in the face it was to be edged out like that?'

'Unfortunately it was necessary. You fight fire with fire, right?' The Chief waited for nods from Aston and George before continuing. George gave hers reluctantly. 'Terrorism is cellular by nature, the organisational structure loose and flexible. You have a couple of people at the top, but for the most part you are dealing with small self-contained groups. And because they're so small, these cells can move around easily. Turn and look and they've already gone. Terrorists have no respect for borders. They can be in Spain one day, the UK the next, back in Syria or Iran or wherever before you know it. MI6, on the other hand is rigid. Look at the way we're set up. Controllorates defined by region. It's so out of date.'

'And the only way to fight terrorism is to take a cellular approach,' George said.

'Not just terrorism. Drug dealing, money laundering, you name it. To deal with the demands of the modern world MI6 needs a precision weapon . . . that's where you come in.'

'Don't the SAS employ a similar philosophy?' Aston asked.

'Where do you think I got my inspiration?' Heath said. 'By the way, your remit also includes internal security.'

'You mean spying on the spies.'

'As the Ancient Romans were so fond of saying: *quis custodiet ipsos custodes*. Who watches the watchers? If we're going to regain our respectability, we cannot afford another Robert Macintosh.'

'So, it's me and George against the rest of the world?'

'Oh, no. You'll have some help.'

Heath pulled the attaché case towards him and thumbed the combination tumblers. He lifted the lid and pulled out two thin brown files. Leaning

across the desk, he handed one to Aston, the other
to George. Aston flipped his open and lifted out
the photos. Black and white surveillance shots
taken with a zoom lens, grainy and raw. In the
first photo, the girl was looking to the left, getting
ready to cross a road. In the second she was staring
straight at the camera, caught unawares. She had
a pretty impish face, dark spiky hair, a slight boyish
build and a 32A chest. A quick scan of the accom-
panying report, and Aston put a name to the face.
Jemima 'Jem' Russell was twenty-three years old,
not long out of Oxford where she'd got a first in
Computer Science. Her parents had split when she
was twelve and she'd gone off the rails for a while.
Minor flirtations with the law for underage
drinking and smoking dope. At fifteen she was
raped. To add to the trauma she fell pregnant.
Having the baby was not an option, so she had
an abortion. This was the wake-up call she needed.
Russell went to the police and the bastard got ten
years. She gave up drugs, cut back on drinking,
managed to get straight As in her A-levels and a
place at Oxford. Aston noticed her professor was
Charles Devlan, the same talent spotter who had
recruited him. A separate sheet contained a refer-
ence from Devlan. In his opinion Russell was
unconventional but brilliant. She had a MENSA-
level IQ and could hack into any computer. On
one occasion, she used the university's system to
penetrate the White House's computers. Once in,
she got hold of the president's personal email

address and signed him up to a couple of dozen porn sites. What particularly impressed Devlan was the way she hid her tracks. She'd routed through servers across the world, laying down a complicated web the Secret Service had no chance of untangling.

'Meet your new computer expert,' Heath was saying.

'Are you sure about this?' Aston said, flicking between the sheets. 'The last time we used an outsider it didn't work out too well.'

'Believe me, Russell has been thoroughly checked out.'

'Even so.'

'This was one vetting I oversaw personally. Russell is clean. A couple of minor infractions when she was younger, but we all did stupid things as kids. Isn't that right, Mr Aston? Stealing cigarettes from a newsagents and selling them to your mates. Sound familiar?'

'You've looked at my file, then?'

'Gone through it with a fine-tooth comb,' Heath said. 'Yours, too, Ms Strauss. Mistakes might have been made in the past, but not this time. Not on my watch.'

'Does Russell know she's going to be working for MI6?' Aston asked.

'Not yet. You'll need to recruit her.' Heath widened his gaze to include George. 'Look on this as your first assignment.'

'You still haven't told us why you set us up?'

'I want this op kept completely secret,' Heath said. 'Your resignations have already been written and accepted. As far as anyone at Vauxhall Cross is concerned you'd finally had enough. No surprise there. You haven't exactly been discreet about your feelings on that particular score, have you?' He homed in on George. 'Incidentally, how did the job interview go this morning?'

'How did you know about that?'

'All-seeing and all-knowing, Ms Strauss. You'd do well to remember that.'

'And what if we decide we don't want to do this?' Aston said.

'What you want or don't want is irrelevant. You work for MI6, which means you work for me. I say jump, you jump. Got it?'

'Yes, sir.'

A quick glance at his watch. 'Okay, any questions?'

'Just one,' Aston said. 'How do we get up to the second floor?'

'The second floor?' Heath asked, all innocence.

'There's a hidden door at the end of the hall.'

'Afraid that's a Need To Know, Mr Aston.' Heath smiled. 'The good news is that this time you're in the loop.'

5

The coffee was black and sweet, three sugars and thick enough to stand a spoon in. Jem took a sip and felt her teeth dissolving. Last night had been a killer. Kathy had persuaded her to go to a new club in Soho . . . not that it had taken much persuading. The tunes had been mental and she'd danced forever, losing herself in the beats. She'd eventually crawled into bed at two, just wanting to sleep. Kathy had other ideas. Not that she was complaining. Lie back, think of England, and melt into the mattress. Heaven.

Another slurp of coffee. Only half-nine according to the clock in the corner of the screen. Today was going to be the longest day of her life. Forget twenty-three, right now she was feeling a hundred and twenty-three. The office was open-plan and filled with losers. Elite Personnel was *elite* in that it found work for secretaries and white collar workers rather than truck drivers. What a laugh. Her job was to make sure the computers kept grinding away. Taxing it wasn't. Mostly she dealt with bozos who were having trouble remembering their passwords, or where they'd saved their Word documents. The job was meant to be temporary. At least that's what Jem told herself when she started here. The plan was to get her debts under control then go travelling. Great in theory, but six months had passed in a flash and she was more in debt than ever. Living in London had taken its toll on her university-battered overdraft; she was so far in the red it didn't bear thinking about.

Fingers click-clacking on the keys, Jem worked on autopilot. This machine was fine. She'd fixed the problem in five seconds flat, but she had to make it look like she was earning her money. To distract herself from the tedium she thought of Kathy . . . her soft mocha skin, the things she could do with that pierced tongue. They'd been together almost three months, which had to be some sort of record.

'You going to be much longer?'

Jem turned and gave a well-practised smile. The man standing behind her looked completely defeated – that was what working for Elite Personnel did to you. 'Almost done,' she said.

'When you're finished, Einstein wants to see you.'

Jem shuddered inwardly. Great. Just what she needed. She made a play of doing important computer things. A virtuoso pianist flourish on the keyboard and she was done.

'You should find it's working fine,' she said as

she got up. 'Any problems give me a shout, yeah?'

Jem picked her way between the losers. The older ones were speaking into mouthpieces with quiet assurance; the younger ones were talking ten to the dozen. Tortoises and hares doing their deals, both heading for the same finishing line. Einstein's lair was a rectangular box that had been partitioned off in one corner. The walls were made from flimsy plywood and the blinds were drawn. She knocked once, a light knuckle rap on the glass, and was told to come in.

'Close the door and take a seat,' Einstein said in his nasal whine.

Jem closed the door and took a seat. She placed her hands demurely in her lap. Einstein was no Einstein. He had a wide Neanderthal forehead and a monobrow. If you got too close you couldn't miss the dog breath. He glanced up from his paper-work, trying to look important. Peered across the top of his glasses, eyes undressing her.

'Six months,' he said. 'Doesn't time fly. Tell me, do you enjoy working here?'

Jem gave another of those well-practised smiles. 'Very much so.'

'We've been impressed with the way you've integrated into the workforce. The quality of your work has been exemplary. We'd like to offer you a permanent contract.'

'Thank you,' Jem said.

Einstein pushed the contract across the desk and placed a pen on top. 'Read this and, if you like what you see, scribble your name at the bottom of page three.'

Jem read without taking in a single word. She was aware that Einstein had moved around to the front of the desk and was now sitting on the edge; aware of him watching her; aware of the pen in her hand, and the sudden urge she had to ram it into his eye. He was too close for comfort, and she could smell the stale sweat of someone who showered every other day. This was an off day. Jem was hit by the sudden realisation she wanted out, wanted out now. Another six months of this and she'd be completely Loony Tunes. She flipped over to page three and scribbled the first name that came into her head – Marilyn Monroe – dated it and passed it back. Einstein witnessed both copies without looking, eyes on her, pen scratching on paper.

Holding out his hand, he got up. 'Let me be the first to congratulate you,' he said.

Taking hold of his hand was like plunging her arm into a barrel filled with eels. He held on longer than necessary, kept holding on. Jem tried to pull back, but he tightened his grip.

'You know,' he said, 'I'm glad you've decided to stay. It's going to be fun getting to know one another better.'

'Please let go,' Jem said.

Einstein pulled her closer, hands slipping around her waist, fingers exploring lower. 'Come on don't be like that.'

Jem couldn't believe this was happening. What the fuck was he playing at? She looked around desperately. All the blinds were shut tight. It was just the two of them. Jem had a sudden flashback to that terrible afternoon all those years ago. She was fifteen again, thinking she was so grown-up, so cool. She'd been to the house before to score dope, but this was the first time she'd gone alone. There had been no-one else there, just him, and she'd thought about making an excuse and leaving, but that would have made her look like a pathetic loser. So she'd stayed and he'd made her a cup of tea and let her have all the dope she could smoke. And then he sat beside her, pressing up against her leg. He was so close she could smell his musty clothes, the stale cigarettes on his breath. She told him no and she meant it, but he wasn't listening. The more she struggled, the more he got off on it, so in the end she had lain there until he finished. It had crossed her mind he might kill her. At the time, she believed it was nothing less than she deserved.

Jem felt Einstein's thick, cold lips on her neck, and the rage took over. She stamped hard, driving her heel into his foot, putting everything into it. He gave a yelp and let go. Pushing him back onto the desk, Jem grabbed hold of his tie and pulled his face towards hers.

'Now listen carefully,' she hissed into his ear. 'If you so much as look at me the wrong way, I'm coming after you with a machete. Got it?'

She stepped back, straightened her clothes, and turned on her heels.

'Don't think about suing me,' Einstein said quietly. 'Nobody would believe you.'

Jem stopped at the door and turned to face him. His tie was squint, his face beetroot red. He looked pathetic. He *was* pathetic. Jem stormed out, slamming the door behind her, not caring that everyone was staring. She made for a workstation manned by a spotty student and told him to move. Fuming, she sat down and began typing. She hooked up with her computer at home, accessed her toolbox and found a suitable virus. It took less than five minutes to adapt the program. She hit enter. Seconds later there was a burst of laughter from the middle of the office, then another from the far side. She looked at the screen. The grotesque charicature of Einstein – facial features stretched and contorted, that single eyebrow even bushier, the forehead wider – had his trousers around his ankles and was going at a confused cartoon sheep like there was no tomorrow. Jem watched Einstein's door and counted down from ten. She got to six before he came out demanding to know what the hell was going on. He marched over to the nearest workstation, took one horrified look at the screen then started hammering at the keyboard. Everyone was watching him, laughing and whispering and shaking their heads. Einstein shoved the keyboard away in disgust and stood up to his full height. He scanned the office, looking for her. Jem waved and this just wound him up even more. Face twisted with rage, Einstein stomped towards her. Deciding it was time to leave, Jem grabbed her denim jacket from the coat rack. She could hear Einstein getting closer, ranting and raving like a lunatic. Jem wasn't particularly bothered if she never worked here again. And as for being a 'stuck-up little cunt' . . . well, she'd been called worse and survived. She took one last look at the sorry bastard, then gave him the finger. Grinning, she pushed through the double doors and headed for the stairs.

6

'Got her,' Aston said into his mobile.

'I'm in position,' George replied.

'Good. And George . . . try not to get too pissed, eh? It's only lunchtime.'

'Nothing stronger than soda water will pass my lips. Promise.'

'Yeah, right!' Aston killed the call and dropped the phone into his pocket. Jem was coming out of her basement flat, climbing the steps wrapped in a thick red duffel coat, eyes hidden behind sunglasses. Her skin was student white, and she was prettier in the flesh; the surveillance shots hadn't done her justice. They'd been following Jem for a couple of days now, getting a feel for her routine, and today they were going to make the approach. Aston still wasn't convinced. He would rather have someone tried and tested, someone from Vauxhall Cross. But as George pointed out, when it came to computers Six's people were way too conventional; they needed someone who wasn't afraid to go out on a limb. This had echoes of Mac's justification for taking on Mole, and did nothing to ease Aston's concerns. A few discreet enquiries, and they discovered Jem had recently been fired. On the plus side, that would make the pitch easier. However, the way she had gone out showed she might have a problem dealing with authority. Then again, who was he to talk? She'd be in good company.

At the entrance to Highgate tube, he pulled out his mobile and updated George. Through the ticket barriers and down to the platform, the butterflies were with him every step of the way. Six months on and he still hated using the tube; just one of those things he had to learn to live with. Like the nightmares. Not so frequent now, but every once in a while he'd have a real video nasty.

Aston leant against the wall, far enough from Jem so she wouldn't get spooked, close enough to keep tabs on her. A glance at the sign. The next train was due in two minutes. He pumped some coins into the chocolate machine, keeping Jem in his peripheral vision. The train arrived on time and she climbed aboard. Aston jumped into the adjoining carriage, squeezing in as the doors closed. At each station he checked she hadn't got off, and those butterflies got ever more frantic.

The train stopped at Leicester Square, and it all came flooding back. The claustrophobia, the heat, the wailing and screaming, and all those dead bodies. When Jem got out here the first day, Aston couldn't believe it . . . when she did the same thing yesterday, he seriously considered staying on the train. Why the hell couldn't she have got off at Piccadilly Circus? It wasn't that much further to walk.

Aston waited for Jem to reach the exit before following. A deep breath as he stepped onto the platform. This was where a suicide bomber had ended her life, and the lives of 262 innocent men, women and children. As the train pulled away, he told himself this was no different from any other tube station. Yeah, right. Who the hell was he trying to kid? They'd done a good job of disguising the evidence of the attack. Replacing the broken tiles, hiding the scars with fresh paint. But that in itself was telling. Everything was too clean, too new. It would take more than a lick of paint to erase the memory of what happened here. A shiver touched his spine as he stepped onto the escalator. He remembered what it had been like to climb down those still steps into the darkness. The heat hitting him like a brick, claustrophobia crushing his lungs. For the last six months he'd avoided this station. Given the choice, he would have kept it that way.

Aston let the escalator carry him, distracting himself by reading the posters. The sooner he got out of here the better. Jem was three-quarters of the way up, a couple of dozen people separating them, head nodding in time to a tune on her iPod. He waited until she disappeared over the top, then moved to the left and started walking. Oystercard in hand, he joined the shortest queue. Jem was three machines to his left, passing her card over the sensor. She passed through the ticket barrier and headed for the nearest exit, dodging between the tourists and suits. Outside, the sun was shining, but there was a bite in the air. Aston zipped up his coat and took a quick look around. There. On the other side of the street. He dodged behind a bus and pulled out his mobile. George answered on the first ring and he told her Jem would be there in five.

7

Vega was busy, the clientele one hundred per cent female. It made a change to sit in a bar where there was no testosterone flying about. No lads hitting on her and getting lairy when she told them to piss off. Not that she couldn't handle that sort of attention. She'd come top in the self-defence classes during training, even beating Paul. No, she could deal with those wankers – she knew a dozen ways to put them in casualty. The bar had a pleasant vibe, comfortable and chilled out. It was tastefully furnished, the décor modern: lots of soft Scandinavian wood and softer lighting. And she was being paid to be here. Bonus. Life could be hard sometimes. George sipped her drink. Jack Daniels and Coke. A couple were reflected in the mirror at the back of the bar. She watched for a while, slightly envious of the casual familiarity between them. There were lots of little touches, plenty of eye contact and secret smiles. No two ways about it: definitely in love.

George had already been hit on. The girl doing the hitting was oriental, androgynous and gorgeous. She had a pierced eyebrow, pierced nose, half a dozen rings in each ear; a nipple ring was visible through her skimpy top. Heroin thin, but the look was cultivated rather than inherited from the needle. Her eyes were too bright, too knowing. A tattoo dragon climbed across her shoulders and breathed fire down her arm – the artwork was exquisite. The girl hadn't been offended when George said she was waiting for a friend. She'd smiled and said the offer of a drink would still be open if her friend didn't show.

For the past six months George's love life had been a disaster zone. There had been a couple of dates where she'd rather have been anywhere else. Even having dinner with her mother, which was saying something. They weren't bad people, her heart just wasn't in it. She was kind of seeing someone at the moment. An accountant, but at least he wasn't married – she'd finally learnt that lesson. Paul didn't know about Alan, and it was going to stay that way. She doubted he'd approve. An accountant . . . no, he wouldn't let that one go in a hurry. She'd met Alan about three weeks ago. The sex was adequate. If nothing else, she was saving money on batteries.

Jem turned up six and a half minutes after Paul's call. He was slipping. He'd said five minutes. George watched her chat up the barmaid. She had the body language of a serial flirt, someone who didn't have to try. Flirting came as naturally as breathing, and George guessed she wasn't even aware she did it.

During their investigation they'd discovered Jem had signed on, and didn't seem to be in any great hurry to find a new job. She had an interview lined up for next week, but that was it. George had gone through her financial records and couldn't believe how relaxed she was being. Totalling up her student loans, bank loans and overdrafts, Jem was the best part of twenty-five grand in debt. If she'd been in Jem's shoes she would have been frantic, lining up interviews left, right and centre. Not that she would ever have got so far into the red in the first place.

Jem paid for her drink and found a table with a good view of the whole bar. George had noticed her do the same thing yesterday. Positioning herself with her back to a wall so she could see all the comings and goings without being obvious. Good spy behaviour. This could actually work. Jem took off her big red duffel coat and hung it on the back of the chair. She sat down and glanced around, taking it all in.

Where you made an approach was almost as important as the how. The golden rule was to choose somewhere the target was comfortable. The more relaxed they were, the more responsive they were likely to be. Jem had been making pilgrimages to Vega every lunchtime since losing her job; her bank statements had backed this up. This was obviously a regular haunt, somewhere she felt at home. Perfect for the approach.

Once you'd decided on the where, you had to work out the how. In this case, it was a no-brainer. A nice big cheque to clear off the debt, and then a salary that was double what she'd been earning at Elite Personnel. They rarely bothered to read the small print. If they did, they'd discover the deal was something the devil would be proud of. MI6 wanted nothing less than your soul . . . as George had discovered. The idealism lasted for all of three seconds, and by the time reality hit it was too late. She almost felt sorry for the girl.

George sipped her drink and glanced over at Jem. Their eyes met briefly – long enough for George to signal her intent, not long enough to pose a threat. She put her glass down and looked over again, catching Jem's eye. This time they exchanged smiles. The girl couldn't help herself. George picked up her glass and walked over.

'Mind if I join you?' she asked.

'Knock yourself out.'

George settled into the chair opposite. They traded names and handshakes, drifted through some small talk. George thought it was going well until Jem started giving her funny looks. The first one she ignored, and the second. 'What?' she said the third time. 'Have I grown an extra head or something?'

'Just wondering when you're going to get to the point, that's all.'

'I don't understand.'

'Well, for starters you're not gay.'

'What are you talking about?'

'I'm talking about the fact you're not gay. If you had STRAIGHT in neon letters on a sign above your forehead, it couldn't be any more obvious.'

George opened her mouth, but Jem steamrollered on.

'I saw you in here yesterday. Checking the place out. Watching everybody. Your hair was different, and you were wearing a different coat, but it was definitely you. So what's the story? No, don't tell me. You've got a boyfriend and he's talked you into a threesome. So you head down to your nearest neighbourhood gay bar and pick someone up. Anyone, doesn't matter who. That sound about right? Well, I've got news for you: you're wasting your time. First off, I've got a girlfriend. And secondly, it's not like those movies your boyfriend makes you watch. Believe it or not, lesbians don't just hang around waiting to jump into bed with the first straight couple that comes along.'

George laughed, and Jem's face fell. Obviously this wasn't the reaction she expected. For a moment Jem looked like the person she was: a young girl who wasn't quite as cocky as she made out.

'You're so far off the mark you wouldn't believe,' George said. She took a sip of her drink and smiled. 'How would you like to earn twenty-five grand?'

8

'Okay, drink up,' said George. 'We need to talk, but not here. Somewhere more private.'

'This doesn't involve drugs, does it? No way am I getting involved with that shit.'

George laughed. 'I can assure you I don't represent any Colombian cartels.'

It crossed Jem's mind not to go. She had met a few psychos in her time, had learnt to spot them a mile off. This George person didn't look like a psycho. Even so, she knew nothing about her. Jem weighed up the pros and cons. There was no choice really. When you're completely skint and someone offers you a serious wedge of cash, it would be rude not to hear them out.

They took the tube to Hyde Park and found a bench overlooking the Serpentine. A mother and toddler were standing at the edge of the water throwing bread for the ducks. It was chilly, and Jem was glad she'd worn her duffel coat. 'So, this is your idea of private,' she said.

'It'll do.'

'Twenty-five grand. That's a lot of money,' Jem mused. 'Twenty-five . . . the magic number. Just plucked that one out of the air, did you?'

'Kind of.'

'Who do you work for?' Jem stared into George's big brown eyes. They were the sort of eyes she could lose herself in. The rest of the package wasn't bad, either.

'Would it surprise you if I told you I worked for the Government?'

'No. I'd just want to know what branch of the Government has the right to go snooping around in my bank accounts.'

George reached into the inside pocket of her coat. She pulled out a sheet of paper and a pen. 'Read this and sign it.'

Jem read through the extract from the Official Secrets Act then looked up at George with an is-this-for-real expression. She glanced around for the hidden cameras, read through it again. The letters made words, but the words made no sense. Twenty minutes ago she'd been enjoying a quiet drink, and now this. It was like *The Matrix* or something; completely surreal. She hesitated with the pen hovering above the page, reluctant to scribble her signature.

'And what if I don't sign?'

'In that case, I disappear and bang goes your best chance for getting out of the shit.'

Jem shook her head. She held out the paper and pen.

'Look, if you sign all it means is you can't go blabbing about anything I tell you.' George shrugged. 'Anyway, sign or don't sign – it's your call. I'm not about to be evicted.'

'How do you know that? Actually, don't bother. You're from the Government, right? Big Brother's watching and all that! MI5, wasn't it?'

George smiled. 'Nice try.'

'Whatever. But I'm not signing.'

'Fair enough. If you don't, I'll find someone who will. There are plenty of people out there who'd jump at an opportunity like this.' A nonchalant shrug and Jem found herself staring into those big brown eyes again. 'Last chance . . . you sure you want to be living in a cardboard box under Waterloo Bridge? The nights get pretty chilly this time of year.'

Jem snorted and shook her head again. She laid the sheet of paper on her leg and signed, then handed it back to George.

'Don't look so worried,' said George. 'There are no strings attached.'

'And I'm supposed to take your word for that, am I? There are always strings attached.'

'And when did you get to be so cynical?'

'I was born that way. Okay, I've signed, so when are you going to tell me what this is all about?'

'I work for MI6,' George said. 'Well, at any rate I used to work for MI6.'

'And what's that supposed to mean?'

'It means that the world isn't quite as black and

60

white as we'd like it to be. There's a huge grey area, and that grey area is getting bigger all the time. That's where we exist. In the grey.'

'And that paranoid shit is for freaks. Next you'll be telling me you work for some *secret* Government department. Working outside the law, and all that.'

'That's about the long and short of it. Except for the "working outside the law" bit. We're not allowed to break the law.'

'This is a joke, right? Someone put you up to this.' Jem got up to leave. 'Nice meeting you. Have a nice life.'

'Please sit down.'

'Why? So I can turn on the telly in six months time and see me being made a fool of? Not going to happen.'

'There are no hidden cameras, and this is no joke.'

'Yeah, right. Someone appears offering you a big wad of cash and claiming to be one of the Men in Black . . . don't know what planet you're from, but that sort of thing happens to me every day. Put yourself in my place, George – or whatever your real name is – what would you be thinking? It's got to be a set-up, right? Now I've no idea how the hell you got into my bank accounts, but I'll tell you what: when I do find out . . .'

9

George zoned Jem out. She inhaled, exhaled slowly, paused. Patience, she told herself. Paul was much better at this. The problem was, he would have stood out like a sore thumb in a bar full of lesbians, probably would've ended up getting lynched. So she'd drawn the short straw. Normally when you recruited you did it over a much longer period, months rather than days. Plenty of time to wine and dine. When the approach was finally made everybody had a pretty good idea of who was who and what was what. With crash approaches, you were walking such a fine line. Disbelief and mistrust were common reactions. And you only got one shot.

'Please sit down,' George repeated.

'Why?'

'Oh, for fuck's sake just sit down!'

Reluctantly, Jem sat down.

'That's better.' Another deep breath. Appeal to the ego. 'You're not stupid. If you were, you wouldn't be here now. I understand how weird this must be.'

'Understatement of the century.'

George looked Jem in the eye, flashed her most disarming smile. 'This is not some reality TV show, this is real life. I'm not a TV presenter, I'm a spy. That's the truth.' A pause, and the smile widened. George felt like a shark going in for the kill. 'And we both know you're not going to leave until you've heard what I've got to say. You're in no position to turn your back on twenty-five grand.'

'Cards on the table,' Jem said.

'Cards on the table,' George agreed. 'We need a computer expert and we've heard you're one of the best.'

'One of the best . . .' Jem snorted. 'Try the best.'

There was an echo of Mole in that statement, and it made George uneasy. What was it about computer experts that made them so arrogant? 'Professor Devlan speaks highly of you.'

'You know The Dev?'

'Not personally. He's one of our talent spotters.'

'And when you say "our" you're talking about MI6?'

'Yes.'

'But you don't work for MI6 any more.'

George took another deep breath and made an executive decision. This *so* wasn't working. They were going around in circles and she was just getting more and more wound up. She'd wanted to do this in Camden; Paul had wanted it done in

Hyde Park. He really got off on all that James Bond spy crap. George stood up. 'Come on,' she said.

'Where are we going?'

'Camden. There's something I need you to see.'

10

Jem had asked a few questions ... and got no answers. In the end she got the message and shut up. For the rest of the journey she sat back watching the charcoal walls whizz past from the tube train window, lost in thought. Jem was no stranger to Camden; the market was one of her favourite shopping haunts. The clothes were cheap and lasted until fashion moved on to the next big thing, which was about long enough. They came out of the tube station and waited for a gap in the traffic. On the other side, George led them through the Inverness Street market to a doorway next to a secondhand record store. She unlocked the door and pulled it open.

George stepped inside and Jem hesitated. The building was rundown, the top-floor windows boarded over. The doorway was dark and not particularly inviting. It was the thought of the money that got her moving. She shrugged to herself and followed George up the stairs, noting the smell of fresh paint and new wood, the bass rumble coming from the record shop.

Surprise number one came at the top of the stairs. A numeric keypad and a fingerprint scanner. George wasn't as careful with her PIN as she could have been: 5-7-4-8. Still, unless she was going to snip George's thumb off, that info wasn't any use. Surprise number two was the door itself. Two-inch thick steel. George disappeared inside, but Jem stayed where she was, frozen to the spot. She suddenly felt like Alice. Any thoughts that this might be a joke quickly evaporated. What the hell had she got herself into?

A man's voice filtered into the stairwell: 'Didn't expect you back so soon. No problems I hope?'

'Not quite,' George replied.

Jem could hear the inadequacy of the reply. There was a problem, and that problem was her. It crossed her mind to sneak quietly back down the stairs. Twenty-five grand or not, coming here didn't seem such a good idea any more.

'You can come in,' George called out.

'If it's all the same, I think I'm going to make a move.' Jem's voice was much smaller than usual. It wasn't often she got broadsided like this. She generally took life in her stride – right now that stride had been reduced to baby steps.

'You brought her here!' the man was saying. 'I thought we agreed not to.'

'It's easier this way. Believe me.'

George poked her head around the door. 'It's okay,' she said, 'his bark's worse than his bite.'

Jem didn't move.

'Come on.'

Moving on autopilot, Jem followed her inside. George pushed the door shut and there was a dull thunk as the bolts slid home. No going back now. The mystery man got up from behind his desk and walked across, arm outstretched. She shook his hand.

'Aston,' he said. 'Paul Aston. You don't mind if I call you Jem?'

'Whatever.' Jem turned to George. 'Okay I believe you. You guys really are the Men in Black.'

'Men in Black!' Aston laughed. 'Is that what you told her?'

'Of course not.'

'The fingerprint scanner,' Jem said, 'you don't expect to see those in Camden. Then there's that steel door . . .'

'That's nothing,' George said.

'George, I don't think this is a good idea,' said Aston.

'Why not?'

'We need to talk. In private.'

'No we don't. We tried it your way, and your way didn't work. Now we're going to try it my way. A tenner says we'll have this signed, sealed and delivered in five minutes.'

Jem watched them trade verbal volleys. They were acting like she didn't exist. Finally they seemed to reach an agreement and turned to face her.

'What we're about to show you goes no further than these four walls,' Aston said. 'Do you understand?'

'Paul,' George said. 'Stop playing the heavy, eh? You're impressing nobody. Anyway, I've already been through the OSA stuff with her.' A soft smile and a confidential whisper for Jem: 'He loves getting all melodramatic.'

Jem let out a nervous chuckle that sounded so fake. She choked it off in mid-flow. Why was she acting like a dork? This was totally uncool. She watched George go over to the computer. A flick of the mouse, a couple of keystrokes, then she inputted her PIN number.

'This way,' George said.

Jem followed her into a hallway, Aston tagging along behind. She headed straight towards the far wall and for a moment Jem thought she was going to walk into it. At the last second she stopped, put her arm out at shoulder height and placed her palm on the wall. A barely audible click, and the wall swung away to reveal a well-lit stairway. Going with the flow, Jem climbed the stairs. And just when she thought she was beyond surprise, she walked into a large open room and it was all she could do to stop her jaw hitting the floor.

There was plenty of light, all of it spilling from the halogen bulbs sunk into the ceiling. The smell of newness was everywhere. Outside, she'd noticed the windows on the top floor had been boarded up, but up here there was no indication they ever existed. A room built within a room. There was a large metal cube in one corner, each side measuring about eight feet. She wasn't a hundred per cent sure what it was, but she'd seen enough spy films and programmes on Discovery to hazard a guess. A secure room. A place to talk when you didn't want anyone eavesdropping. The main workstation was against the far wall; it had three twenty-inch LCD flat screen monitors arranged like dressing table mirrors. Very cool. Dotted around the room were half a dozen lesser machines. There was equipment everywhere: a tall glass-fronted steel cabinet filled with servers, communications gear of all shapes and sizes, a fax machine, a photocopier, a shredder, even a coffee percolator. A bank of sixteen flat screen TVs in a square formation were fixed to one wall, each one tuned to a different station: CNN, Sky News, Al Jazeera . . .

Wherever she looked there was hi-tech gear. All of it state-of-the-art, all of it brand new. Toys for her to play with.

'So, what do you think?' George asked. 'Impressed?'

'Where do I sign up?'

The flat wasn't the Ritz but it served Kestrel's needs. It was damp and musty with mildew on the carpets and curtains; there were things growing in the kitchen and bathroom. Like most rentals, the furniture was nasty and past its sell-by date. There was a saggy mattress on the bed, a sofa with a well-worn Homer Simpson groove. And all this for seven-fifty a month. The main selling points were the bay window that gave an unrestricted view of the street for a couple of hundred yards in either direction, and the fire escape leading down into the wilderness that was the back garden. The rusty fire escape had creaked and groaned when he tried it out, but it held his weight. You had to be able to get out in less than thirty seconds. With this flat it had taken 23.8 seconds. Well within established parameters. His neighbours caused him no trouble. They kept themselves to themselves and, apart from the occasional polite hello on the stairs, he never spoke to them. There was a family on the floor above. Indians with a couple of kids. The scampering sounds of tiny feet could often be heard through the ceiling, heavily accented shouts to keep the noise down and play nice. The couple below occasionally had their music too loud, and got a bit carried away when they were screwing, but he wasn't about to make an issue out of it. He was definitely not a neighbour who complained.

To practise taking on different personalities, Kestrel visited chatrooms. Some days he'd be a rock fan raving about the latest band, or a schoolgirl bitching about her boyfriend, or some moany old bastard whinging on about everything and nothing. Cyber-schizophrenia on a grand scale. Whatever the role, he worked hard to get the appropriate level of authenticity. There were lots of people out there pretending to be someone they weren't. Most of them he could sniff out a mile away. There'd be something that didn't quite add up. Whenever he uncovered a pretender, it reinforced the importance of taking care of the details.

The Internet was multi-layered. The top layer was the Internet of the people . . . Yahoo and Google, horoscopes and weather reports. Dig deeper and you found yourself in the Internet of the perverts and deviants. And right down at the bottom, like some subterranean world, was the level where Kestrel carried out his business. A level where you could buy whatever your heart desired – guns, explosives, a murder – a level where one of the most valuable commodities was information.

Kestrel worked in darkness, his face streaked with the colours leaching from the monitor. Without taking his eyes from the screen, he reached for his vegetable smoothie. He took a sip and licked the green froth from his lips. The body was a temple and his was in first-class condition. No alcohol and definitely no cigarettes; daily workouts to keep *him toned and tight; constant training to sharpen his reflexes; mind puzzles for the brain. Right now he was in the best shape of his life, which was just as well because his current assignment was the most challenging he had ever faced. It was also the most satisfying.*

He left a message on a particular notice-board: **charly knows nuthing**. *In bold, all lower case, the misspellings deliberate. Three words that would mean nothing to the casual surfer, but everything to the information broker. The broker went by the handle Spinny. Male or female, he neither knew nor cared. What mattered was that they came up with the goods. That said, Spinny was having a few problems with his latest request. He clicked to another site, moved the mouse to the far left corner and pulled the arrow out of the screen. He clicked again and the screen went blank, the arrow froze in the middle of the page. Anyone getting this far accidentally would assume their machine had crashed. Kestrel drank his smoothie and waited. Exactly two and a half minutes later a message appeared:*

the price is £10,000 sterling

Kestrel felt his heart beat a little faster and willed it back to its normal rate. This was more expensive than usual, which meant . . . well, he wasn't sure exactly what it meant, but it had to be a big deal. Spinny wouldn't stay in business for long if he ripped his customers off. He typed one word:

agreed

72

Three seconds later a name appeared on the screen:

edward coulson

Kestrel smiled to himself. This was a big deal. The information was worth every penny. In this business the client often went to extreme measures to retain their anonymity. Understandable. The client had as much to lose as he did. And because of the nature of the business, Kestrel had long ago made it a rule to find out who he was actually working for. The last thing he needed was to take on a job for some joker who might do something stupid and end up dumping them both in the shit. Usually he got this information before he did the hit, but on this occasion the information had been harder to get so he'd gone ahead without it. The move was a calculated one. Three hits, a hundred thousand a pop and a two hundred grand bonus for completing all three. With money that serious on the table, it was unlikely the client was an amateur.

Face lit up by the screen, Kestrel tapped his lip and considered how this information might benefit him. Edward Coulson . . . Sir Edward Coulson. He already knew a fair bit about Sir Eddie – everyone did; Sir Eddie wasn't exactly media shy. But there was always more to learn. Moving up to the top level of the Internet, he typed the name into Google and went to work.

11

'I don't think I'll ever get used to this.' Aston's voice was dull and flat and completely lifeless. He clapped his hands. A single crack and then nothing. There were no echoes whatsoever inside The Cube. The mountain ranges of charcoal grey foam underneath the floor grill were scientifically designed to soak up the sound. More mountain ranges on the walls and ceiling. The brain was used to dealing with aural reflections, and when they were taken away it struggled to cope. 'Pretty freaky, huh?'

'The sooner we get out –' George began in a voice that sounded just as alien.

'– the better,' Aston finished for her. 'No arguments here.'

'Hello.'

They both looked up towards the speaker hidden in the roof. This voice sounded even more peculiar. Filtered through the latest crypto software, fired up to a satellite, bounced back and decrypted by the computers on the other side of the lead-lined walls, it possessed all the charm of a robot. There were no dynamics, no inflexions, just words delivered in a passionless, androgynous monotone. Aston made a mental note to ask Jem if there was anything she could do about that.

'Before we go any further, I need you to identify yourself,' said Aston.

'Of course. JKY47LOY9.' Each letter and number was delivered with crisp, android-like efficiency. The code had been randomly generated by a computer at Vauxhall Cross, and would be changed for each communication. Aston checked it against his laser printout.

'Confirmed,' he said.

'So, how are you settling in?' The Chief asked.

'Still early days, but so far so good. Everything seems to be working okay.'

'I hear there were no problems with the recruitment.'

No names, security first and foremost. 'She seems to be settling in. Definitely knows her stuff.'

'Good,' Heath said. 'I need you to look into a murder. One of ours. Retired a couple of years ago.'

'And you want to know if this has any connection with anything he did while working for us.'

'Got it in one. Maybe he was in the wrong place at the wrong time, but I'd like to be sure.' A pause. 'I have to say, I'm not a great believer in coincidences. They don't sit well.'

'I know what you mean.'

'Like I said: we can't afford another scandal. If anything suspicious is going on I need to know.'

'What level of authority have we got?' George asked.

'*Carte blanche,*' Heath replied. 'Do whatever you need to do to get the job done. Any questions?'

Aston could think of a dozen questions, but they could wait until he had more information. A glance at George, who shrugged and shook her head.

'No questions, sir,' he said.

'Good. Keep me posted.'

Aston waited a few seconds in the unnerving silence to make sure The Chief had actually gone, then hit the button. The door sucked open and he hurried out into a world of noise and echoes: computer fans and the quiet buzz of electricity, the static crackle from the sixteen TV sets, the gurgling of the coffee machine, Jem humming along to a tune on her iPod. The sounds were much brighter than he remembered.

'Hi guys,' Jem shouted. 'You have *so* got to see this.' She popped her earphones out and her voice dropped to a more normal level. 'This goes beyond gross. I tell you, I haven't seen anything this nasty since *Dawn of the Dead* . . . and I'm talking the remake, not the cheesy Seventies version.'

Jem was at the main workstation. It hadn't taken long for her to make herself at home. Two days into the job and her desk looked like a bomb site. A scattering of pens, a coffee mug displaying signs of new life-forms, and paper everywhere. There was a tasteful black and white print of a naked woman stuck to the wall next to the monitor: back arched, a study of soft curves and dips, the play of shadow and light making it erotic rather than pornographic. She handed a bundle of printouts to George and flashed her a smile; gave another bundle to Aston.

Jem was right. It was gross. The top sheets contained close-up shots of a dismembered hand. Lots of different angles, lots of detail. The first picture showed the hand *in situ*. The police had drawn a crude chalk circle around it and placed a one Euro coin beside it for scale. It took Aston a second to work out that the small stripy tubes covering it were maggots. The hand was in an advanced state of decomposition, puffy and bloated, skin looking like stilton. Another picture, another angle. The hand was now resting on a steel tray, brightly lit from the side. From this angle you could see the small navy blue cotton bag clenched inside the fist. Another shot: a close-up of the bag – again, well-lit on a steel tray. The bag was open, the contents heaped in a small pile. Silver coins.

'What did Heath have to say for himself?' Jem asked.

'Need to know,' Aston replied without looking up.

'Oh come on! That's not fair.'

'Get used to it.'

From the corner of his eye, Aston saw Jem swivel around in her chair. She scrubbed the mouse across the mat, a couple of clicks and a game of solitaire appeared on the screen. He laughed to himself and shook his head. Christ knows how many hundreds of thousands of pounds worth of computer equipment, and she was playing solitaire. Aston flipped to the police reports. Jem had run them through a translation program – a pretty good one at that. There were the occasional grammatical blips, but they more or less made sense.

A couple of tourists had found the hand near the Spanish Steps in Rome. At first they'd thought it was made from rubber; then a pigeon swooped down and had a chew. Forensics had ascertained the killer had used an axe; with one swing, he – or she – had sliced through the lower part of the radius and ulna. They had also salvaged a couple of fingerprints, and this led them to the hand's owner. Gary Hathaway had been with the Foreign Office, stationed in Rome. He had liked the city so much he'd decided to stay when he retired. He'd had a two-bedroom top-floor apartment in the Trastevere region of the city. The rest of his body was still unaccounted for. Hathaway hadn't been seen at his apartment for about ten days. His neighbours said this wasn't unusual. Hathaway often disappeared for days at a time.

The police investigation had turned up very

little. Forensics estimated the hand had been without a body for at least five days. However, this was a guess. It was possible the hand had been kept on ice for a while, highly probable in light of the fact Hathaway hadn't been seen for the best part of a fortnight. Reading through the reports, Aston saw the police's main concern was that there might be a serial killer on the loose. A severed hand clutching a bag of silver coins . . . this had all the hallmarks of a serial killer's signature. Aston understood why the police were panicking. Rome was gearing up for the main tourist season. A maniac running around cutting off people's hands didn't look good in the brochures.

The biggest problem the police faced was that the hand was so old. Best estimates put the murder at five days old; worst, ten to fourteen days. In a murder investigation, forty-eight was the magic number. If you didn't find anything within the first forty-eight hours, you might as well give up.

'Are you thinking what I'm thinking?' George asked.

'He did say *carte blanche*,' Aston replied.

'It would be rude not to.'

'It certainly would,' Aston agreed.

Jem spun away from her game of solitaire and looked at them with a curious expression. 'You sure you guys aren't married?'

'Okay Jem,' Aston said. 'We've got an assignment for you, something that's going to push you and your machines to the absolute limit.' He found an edge of desk on one side of Jem; George perched on the other side.

Jem's eyes lit up. 'You mean I get to do some real spy work.'

'In a manner of speaking,' George said.

'What?'

'We're going to need two airline tickets to Rome,' Aston said, face straight and serious.

'First class,' George added, and Aston looked at her. 'Well, MI6 is paying, and The Chief did tell us to do whatever needed to be done.'

'First class,' he said to Jem. 'Do you think you can handle that?'

Jem rolled her eyes and turned back to the monitor. 'Be nice to me,' she muttered under her breath, 'or I'll have you travelling with the bags.'

12

Jem booked them a lunchtime flight. BA from Heathrow, travelling at the front of the plane with the rest of the beautiful people. From the airport, it was a half hour taxi ride to the hotel. The room was pleasant enough. It was tall and airy with generic black and white prints of the city on the whitewashed walls. Clean and fresh, it smelled like an orange grove. There was a double bed and a sofa, and they'd already flipped a coin. Best of three. As usual George won in two, and Aston wanted to know how she did it. Witchcraft was the only explanation.

The hotel was in Trastevere, a couple of streets from Hathaway's apartment. As far as reception was concerned, the couple in room 24 were Mr and Mrs Sharp. Aston and George even had the passports to prove it . . . passports provided by Central Facilities . . . who'd got them from Peterborough. A flick through the pages showed that Mr and Mrs Sharp were well travelled:

Singapore, Australia, the USA. They definitely hadn't been to the Middle East, or Northern Ireland, or anywhere else that might set alarm bells ringing at passport control. Mr and Mrs Sharp was a favourite alias, as comfortable as an old pair of shoes. On this occasion the Sharps were returning to Rome for a second honeymoon. They'd been married for five years, and the first honeymoon had been so, so special. This time, however, they wanted to get out and see the sights.

April in Rome, and the daytime temperature was hitting twenty degrees, a little higher when you got out of the shade. Britain was currently under a big grey cloud that had taken up residence last November and showed no signs of moving any time soon; it was good to see the sun again. They had the windows open and a light breeze rustled through the room. The bed had been turned into a makeshift desk. Pictures and papers lay scattered across it, like a three dimensional mindmap. George sat cross-legged at the head, her back resting against the wall. Melissa Sharp was a touch new-age, so George was wearing a floaty, purple ankle length dress and a simple white cotton shirt . . . which she hated; all too girly for her tastes. The trademark red scrunchy was gone, her hair hanging long and loose. A pair of sunglasses was propped on top of her head. Peter Sharp was wearing faded jeans and a well-worn Hard Rock Café T-shirt, which didn't cause Aston a problem. Comfortable and casual, that pretty much covered his entire wardrobe.

Aston pulled his chair closer to the bed. He picked up the closest photograph and wondered where the rest of the body was. The pictures of the dismembered hand were still gross, but he'd seen them often enough now for the shock value to have worn off.

'So, what's the motivation?' he asked.

'Wrong time, wrong place?' George suggested.

'Not buying.' Aston shook his head. 'There's no way this was a random killing. Look at the way it's been staged. This has premeditated written all over it. Whoever did this *targeted* Hathaway. Why?'

George shrugged. 'Beats me.'

'Not the answer I was hoping for.'

'Perhaps we need to try a different angle,' George said. 'Rather than looking for the motivation, maybe it would help to look at the message.'

'Message?'

'Like you said: this killing was carefully staged. Everything the killer did, he did for a reason. I mean, what was that bag of coins all about?'

'The thirty pieces of silver . . . the police tied that into the story of Judas.'

'Of course they did. It fits in with their serial killer theory. Everyone knows serial killers love their religious symbolism.'

'Not buying the serial killer theory, then?'

George made a face and shook her head. 'I'd be very surprised if there's a Ted Bundy loose on

83

the streets of Rome. If Hathaway hadn't worked for Six then it might be a different story.'

'Well, for starters, it wouldn't be our problem.'

That was worth a smile.

'Hathaway spent his whole working life with MI6,' Aston said, 'chances are he made an enemy or two. It goes with the territory.'

'My thinking exactly,' George agreed.

'Okay, Sherlock, so what's it all about, then?'

George reached for the thickest file and tossed it to Aston. 'No idea, but my money's on the answer being in there.'

Aston picked up Hathaway's MI6 file and flicked through the pages, stopping occasionally when a paragraph caught his attention. He'd already been through this with a fine-tooth comb – so far nothing – but that didn't mean there wasn't something in there. Answers were always so bloody obvious when you knew they were answers.

Hathaway was born in 1948 in Brighton. Educated at Cambridge, he had gone to work at Century House straight from university. He started as a gofer in the Soviet department and steadily worked his way through the ranks. He had a knack for the language and this resulted in a posting to Moscow in 1972. From then on it was three years in London, three years in Moscow, all the way through to the end of the Cold War. He never headed the station, but during his last posting there in 1990 he was promoted to MOS/1, the second in command. In 1996 he became H/ROM, his final overseas posting. The city must have made an impression; since his retirement he had been living *la dolce vita* in Rome. That he was gay only came to light in the late Nineties, and by then it wasn't an issue. These days MI6 was an equal opportunities employer . . . black, white, yellow and red, gay or straight. That said, it didn't do your promotion prospects any harm if you happened to have an old school tie hanging in the wardrobe; revisionism only took you so far up the ladder. During the bad old pre-PC days, the fact Hathaway wasn't married and had never had a girlfriend no doubt raised eyebrows. Of course, there had always been homosexuals working at MI6.

The problem with personnel reports was that they only gave the bare bones; you didn't get any substance. Hathaway's personnel reports were unspectacular. His journey through MI6 had been storm-free. He was never destined for greatness, but from what Aston could see he understood the game and had played it well; he'd known which egos to massage. Heading up a European station like Rome was no mean feat. But what had gone on behind the scenes? If he got Hathaway alone in a bar, what stories would he tell? And how much truth would there be in those stories? That was the problem with this business. There were too many lies and half-truths – stories based on fiction became the truth because they were recounted so often. George was looking at him

expectantly. Aston shrugged and shook his head.
He closed the file and tossed it over to her.

'Your turn,' he said.

George picked up the file and started reading.

13

They had a late dinner in a romantic little restaurant hidden down a narrow alley. It was off the beaten track, making it easy to spot a tail . . . and small enough so they could keep an eye on the other customers. They were both dressed in burglar black: Aston in black 501s, a black T-shirt and a black leather jacket; George in black trousers, black shirt and a black coat. The restaurant was picture postcard perfect: tiny square tables with red and white checked tablecloths, a waiter who couldn't do enough, and candles everywhere. Lightweight operatic arias played gently in the background. They washed their meal down with half a bottle of a substantial red. A glass and a half each; enough to glow, but not enough to dull their reactions. There were lots of long lingering looks and soft caresses and all done without a hint of self-consciousness. Mr and Mrs Sharp were deeply in love, no doubt about it. The act was as natural as breathing.

The meal paid for, the tip left wedged under the candle holder, they walked from the restaurant hand in hand, heading for Hathaway's apartment. It was a little before ten and there was a big, bright Hollywood moon in the sky. An airliner flew overhead leaving cobweb slivers of silver vapor in its wake. With no sun and no cloud cover the temperature had dropped. Aston zipped up his leather jacket and noticed George buttoning her coat. Bang on ten, he pulled out his mobile and checked in with Jem. She was pissed off about working late, but Aston couldn't care less. MI6 wasn't a nine to five option. The sooner she worked that one out the better.

They headed up narrow mediaeval alleyways, the old stones worn smooth over the centuries, through a piazza and past a fountain. An occasional surreptitious glance to check no-one was following. It was hard to relax when you were in a strange city and about to break the law. They turned down a side street and Aston was hit by the sudden certainty someone was watching them, a feeling that was too strong to ignore. Another fleeting glance behind, searching the shadows. No-one there. He wasn't convinced. He tried to shake the feeling, but couldn't – there were ice-bugs crawling all over his skin, hundreds of the little buggers, thousands of them. The Glock dug re-assuringly into the small of his back, and he resisted the urge to pull it out. Heath had arranged for the gun to come over in the diplomatic bag; it had been delivered to their hotel earlier that evening by an agent from the Rome station who'd posed as a flower delivery man . . . Peter Sharp could be so romantic when he wanted to be.

'What is it?' George said.

Aston took her hand and picked up the pace. 'Keep walking. We're being followed. Don't turn around, and don't run.'

'What do you think I am? A rookie?' George whispered. 'Anyway, are you sure? I didn't see anyone.'

'Pretty sure.'

'Did you actually see anyone?'

'No.'

'So this could be paranoia getting the better of you.'

'That's a possibility. Or how about this one: maybe we *are* being followed?'

'A gut feeling?' George said.

'A gut feeling,' Aston agreed.

'Okay, that's good enough for me.'

'Down here.' Aston led them under an archway into a narrow alleyway. They were moving away from Hathaway's now. He'd memorised the street plan of Trastevere and there was a large, open piazza a couple of streets away that would be perfect. Whoever was following would be forced to break cover or risk losing them in one of the dozens of alleys and streets that led away from the piazza. Aston wanted to run, but forced himself to walk. Not too fast, not too slow. George was doing the same; she was like a racehorse waiting to explode from the starting gate. They stepped off the kerb and squeezed between a couple of parked cars. Aston chanced another glance behind. Still no-one there . . . at least, no-one he could see.

The alley was narrow, a couple of yards wide, ideal for an ambush. Aston considered heading further up the road and finding another way into the piazza, but that would look suspicious. This alley was the most direct route. He didn't want the shadow to realise he was on to him. Ditching a tail was easier when you had the element of surprise. Fighting the urge to jog, he headed into the alley, pulling George along with him. If the shadow wanted them dead, they'd already be dead. Buildings towered on either side, a gash of night sky high above. Aston could feel the old stone pressing in on him as they moved deeper into the blackness. It was too dark in here; they were too vulnerable. George looked over at him. Her face was a silhouette but he could tell she was thinking the same. This had been a serious mistake. The scream froze his blood. High-pitched and horrible, it was the sound of someone being murdered.

George stopped dead, her hand crushing his. 'What the hell was that?' she said her voice a panicked whisper. She let go of his hand and fumbled the Maglite from her pocket.

'No!' Aston hissed, grabbing her hand. 'Too suspicious! How many tourists wander around Rome at night carrying torches?'

'Fuck that!'

George lowered her hand, though. Stuffed the torch back into her pocket and pressed in closer. Aston peered into the gloom, trying to pinpoint the source of the sound. It had come from up ahead, near where the alley took a ninety degree turn to the left. He saw nothing except shadow layered upon shadow. Listening closely, all he could hear beyond the booming of his heart was the faraway rumble of the city.

'Let's get out of he—' George began.

Another scream . . . only now Aston could hear it for what it actually was. The screech of arguing cats. He honed in on the sound and saw a shadow streak towards them, a blur of grey. It brushed his ankles, and then disappeared into the night. A second shadow slinked victorious towards the turn in the alleyway.

'Like I was saying,' George said. 'Let's get the fuck out of here.'

They walked quickly to the corner and Aston was relieved to see the piazza less than twenty yards away. He breathed easy again and walked into the large square. There were restaurants on all four sides, apartments piled up on the floors above. The umbrellas on the sidewalk tables were folded down, the tables empty – it was too chilly to be eating outside. The restaurants were still busy, though, candlelit faces smiling on the other side of the windows. The angels and saints in the fountain glowed silver in the moonlight, the dancing water sparkles making them look alive. Aston led them over. From here they had a good view of all the streets leading into the piazza.

'Okay,' he muttered under his breath, 'I'm thinking "the argument".'

'Works for me,' George agreed.

'Okay let's make this look good.' Aston put on his angry face and pointed a finger at George's chest. 'What are you talking about?' he said loudly.

'Keep your voice down. There's no need to make a scene.'

More pointing. 'Who's making a scene?'

'You're making a scene.' George pointed back. Jab, jab, jab. She moved to his left so she could see behind him.

'No I'm not.' Aston was almost shouting now. A couple of passers-by glanced over, then quickly walked away, giving them a wide berth. Aston danced around George getting the full 360 degrees. No shadows lurking in the alleyways.

'Why are we fighting?' George said in a resigned voice. 'This is supposed to be a holiday . . . our second honeymoon. We should be enjoying ourselves.'

'You're right. This is stupid.' Aston pulled her close, brought his lips to her ear. 'See anything, Mrs Sharp?' he whispered.

'The coast's clear, Mr Sharp,' she whispered back.

'See that restaurant straight in front of you? We'll take the alleyway on the left.'

They untangled themselves and walked quickly towards the alley. As they turned into it, Aston took one last look at the piazza, at the streets and alleyways on the far side. No-one was there, but he still had the strongest feeling he was being watched.

14

It took less than thirty seconds to get inside Hathaway's apartment. A quick glance up and down the street to make sure it was empty, then they ducked into the doorway. Quickly past the door for the ground floor flat, the sound of a TV blaring away on the other side of the ancient wood. Up the narrow stairs, past the door for the first -floor apartment, then on up to Hathaway's floor. George already had the electronic picklock in her hand. While Aston kept watch, she pushed it into the lock, pressed a button and the pick did its magic. A flick of the wrist and she was in. Aston scanned the stairwell one last time and ducked inside, closing the door gently behind him. He flicked his torch on; George did the same. Pocket-sized Maglites, small but powerful.

George's cheeks were flushed, her eyes wild. She was breathing fast, each breath rapid and shallow. Aston thought she looked gorgeous. So alive and vital.

'What?' she whispered.

'I didn't say a word,' Aston whispered back. The people on the ground floor weren't a concern; the TV was so loud World War III could break out and they wouldn't notice. However, he didn't know if anyone was in the apartment below. Best to veer on the side of caution. Fairy steps and whispering.

Aston played his torch over the room. There was evidence of the police's visit everywhere. Forensics had gone overboard with the finger-print powder and it was as dusty as a tomb; it looked as though it had been a century since anyone had been here. Unsurprisingly, seventy per cent of the prints had belonged to Hathaway. A further twenty-seven per cent belonged to his cleaner. The other three per cent belonged to three other people. Two were unidentified, but one set rang bells on the police computer. Luciano Valerio had been convicted on a minor drugs charge eight years ago. He currently ran a small bar ten minutes walk from here, and a visit was definitely on the cards.

The Maglite clamped between his teeth, Aston pulled on a pair of latex gloves. The front door opened straight into the lounge. There was a battered sofa and a couple of matching armchairs; faded rugs, chipped wooden furniture, naked floorboards. Comfortable rather than condemned – it cost money to get this level of worn. The ceiling was high, a large fan hanging limp in the middle.

There were two tall windows overlooking the street below, the heavy curtains closed. There was no TV, no stereo, no telephone; the most modern items in the room were the light bulbs. The bookcase was crammed to bursting, the creased spines indicating the books weren't there for show. Dickens and Graham Greene, Tolstoy and Dostoevsky . . . spy books by Ian Fleming and Tom Clancy for lighter moments. There was a lot of non-fiction – a ton of history. One whole shelf was devoted to books chronicling the rise and fall of the Roman Empire. The well stocked drinks cabinet came as no surprise. Hathaway had worked for Six, after all.

They combed the lounge, covering the same ground as the police and finding just as little. It was still a useful exercise, though. It enabled them to get a feel for who Hathaway was. Mac had always been dismissive of secondhand information, and Aston understood why. A report, whether verbal or written, was no substitute for getting in there and getting your hands dirty. Working *in situ* got all five senses going.

On to the kitchen, which told the story of a single man who either couldn't cook, or couldn't be bothered to cook. Probably the latter. Why cook when you had so many fine restaurants on your doorstep? Hathaway's kitchen reminded Aston of his own. The cooker looked as though it had never been used. Apart from a few essentials, the cupboards were bare. There was a spice rack, but all the jars were sealed and well past their sell-by date. The only appliance that looked used was the kettle. The police had interviewed the cleaner, but got nothing useful. She came in once a week and often didn't see Hathaway for months on end. He left the money in the same place each week, on the third shelf of the bookcase. Last week he had forgotten, which wasn't unusual. Whenever he forgot in the past, she left a note and he had paid double the next week.

The smaller bedroom was filled with junk: old clothes and old books, discarded furniture and other oddments bought on a whim. The police had given it a thorough going over and come up empty handed. Aston and George were content to wave their torch beams over the clutter. A quick look before heading along the hall to the main bedroom.

Aston went in first. Fingerprint powder covered the furniture, the windowsills, the lampshades. Once again, the theme in this room was designer worn. All the woodwork looked as though it had come from the nineteenth century, but Aston reckoned it was probably only a couple of years old, a decade at most. An old-fashioned Big Ben alarm clock sat on the bedside table, a dusting of powder on the hammer and bells. The bed had been stripped bare, the linen removed for examination. According to the police, traces of semen from two different men had been found.

They went through the drawers, the wardrobe,

the cupboards. The police had taken out all Hathaway's clothes and put them back any old how. The only incriminating evidence was the stash of pornographic magazines hidden in the bottom of the wardrobe ... hardly a hanging offence. There was a small empty safe in one of the cupboards, the door open. It had been locked when the police found it. A locksmith was called in, but all it contained was a passport and a couple of hundred Euros.

George straightened up, hands on hips. She moved her head from side to side, the vertebrae in her neck cracking. 'I don't know what I was hoping to find, but I thought we might find *some-thing*.'

'Not true,' Aston said. 'We've found plenty. For example, we now know that he had an aversion to the twenty-first century, he liked books, didn't like cooking, and had a preference for men who are shaved and oiled. None of that was in the police reports.'

'And how exactly does that help us, Paul?'

'Well, it doesn't *not* help us.'

'Come on, let's get out of here. It's been a long d—' George didn't get any further. A noise from the other end of the apartment. They both froze. 'Did you hear that?' she whispered.

Aston nodded and pressed a finger against his lips. He pulled out the Glock and listened hard, focusing his attention on the sound. There it was again. The unmistakable creak of the front door slowly opening. Aston tiptoed towards the bedroom door and gently pushed it closed, praying it wouldn't squeak, praying the click of the lock wouldn't be too loud. He lifted his Maglite and made it obvious he was switching it off, then shoved the torch into a pocket. With the lights out, it was as if someone had turned the volume up. Another creak, and for a few moments they heard the distant echo of the television from the apartment on the ground floor. A final creak and a click, and the TV faded out. Aston moved closer to George, felt her hand searching for his arm, fingernails digging in. Footsteps in the lounge, more than one set, maybe as many as three. Possibly even four. Fuck! Not good. The only way in and out of the apartment was through the front door, which meant getting past whoever was out there. And it got worse: if there were three of them out there, the Glock was next to useless. He was good with a gun, good enough to take down two armed men so long as he had the element of surprise on his side. But three or four, forget it.

'What now?' Aston whispered.

'Fuck knows,' George whispered back. Her face was right up next to his, her breath tickling his cheek.

The footsteps were moving through the lounge. Slowly getting closer. Whoever was out there was acting as though they had all the time in the world. Aston fished his mobile out and flipped it open.

The light was too bright, a beacon advertising their existence. No signal. He shot a panicked look at George. All the colour had drained from her face. He shook the mobile . . . still no signal. Of course, there was no fucking signal! Anyway who the fuck was he going to call? The police! He snapped the phone shut and jammed it into his pocket. The intruders were going through the other rooms. Bathroom first, then the kitchen. Footsteps in the hallway. Heavy feet on hard wood. It was only a matter of time before they reached the bedroom. Aston pressed his lips to George's ear.

'When that door opens we rush them,' he hissed.

'You've got to be fucking joking,' George hissed back. 'No, I'll tell you what's going to happen, Paul. When that door opens you're going to shoot the bastards.'

'Who do you think I am? Billy the Kid?'

'Well, give me the gun. I'll shoot them.'

'If we start shooting, chances are we're going to end up dead.'

'At least we go down fighting.'

'And that'll look great carved on your grave-stone.'

The footsteps stopped on the other side of the door; wisps of torchlight stole underneath. Breathing, whispering, the shuffling of shoes. The sound of the door being kicked in was like an explosion. The wood around the handle splintered and the door slammed open crashing against the wall. Torchbeams fired into Aston's eyes, momentarily blinding him. As his vision cleared he could just about make out three shadowy shapes. George launched herself at the nearest shadow. A mutter of surprise and then an *ooph* as her knee found its target. The lead figure sank to his knees, clutching his groin. She linked her hands together and smashed them down on the back of his neck. All three men were dressed entirely in black, ski masks hiding their faces. They were carrying submachine guns – snub-nosed with silencers – and one of them was pointed at George's head.

Acting on instinct, Aston charged. At the last second, he knocked the gun to one side. A *psst* and a puff of plaster and masonry. He brought his head back and rammed it into the hooded face. Bone smashed against bone with a sickening crunch. Grabbing the gunman by the hair, Aston smashed the Glock against the side of his head, knocking him out cold. The man slumped to the ground and Aston brought the Glock up and sighted along the barrel, looking for the third intruder. For a moment he thought they might pull this off. One on one . . . now that was more like it. Aston turned, and found himself staring into the cold black eye of a silencer. He froze. The intruder said something in Italian, and Aston shook his head. Another rapid-fire burst of Italian; an order judging by the tone. Aston shook his head again. From the corner of his eye, he saw George step back warily, showing her hands.

The masked man didn't ask a third time. Aston saw the butt of the gun rushing towards him, and the world went black.

15

Jem checked her watch for the umpteenth time, then glanced at the clock on the screen to make sure it hadn't stopped during the last twenty seconds. 10.02. Up until a couple of minutes ago she'd been in an absolutely foul mood. Stuck here in the middle of the fucking night! It wasn't like she couldn't do this anywhere, which, of course, she'd suggested. Listen up people: that's what mobiles were invented for! But no, they'd wanted her here. Some crap about secure Comms.

To make matters worse, she was supposed to be going out with Kathy tonight. Understandably, Kathy wanted to know why she was being blown out, which led them into murky waters. Aston had been very definite on what outsiders were allowed to know: i.e. nothing. She'd argued that Kathy was her partner, not an 'outsider', but it made no difference. Nobody could know she worked for Six. Not a soul. So she told Kathy she wouldn't be coming out to play because she was working late, which went down like a lead balloon. Kathy had pointed out – rightly so – that Jem had never worked late in her life, and that led to a big argument where Kathy convinced herself Jem was having an affair. They'd moved from DEFCON 5 to DEFCON 1 in a heartbeat – neither was prepared to back down. In the end Kathy had said 'well, fuck it, I'm going out anyway', and then hung-up. Jem had stared at her mobile for a full five minutes, willing it to ring; Kathy had hung-up therefore she had to make the first move. Those were the rules. Jem then spent the next hour fighting the urge to phone Kathy. That had all happened at five. For the last five hours Jem's imagination had been working overtime. Jealousy was a new emotion, and she didn't like it one bit.

George and Aston had been very clear with their instructions. They would be in touch every hour on the hour. If they failed to contact her, she had to let The Chief know. Immediately. So far that's exactly what had happened. Every hour on the hour they'd called in. As it got later, Jem had become increasingly uncommunicative. The last call had been at nine – ten p.m. in Rome. By that point, she'd wound herself up into such a fury she'd answered with a 'yeah, whatever', and then hung up. She couldn't get off the phone fast enough.

The irony was that she'd now do anything to talk to them. Either of them. Her anger had completely dissolved, replaced by fear. She checked the time again – 10.03 – looked at the dead phone. They were three minutes late, and those three minutes had been the longest of her life. Jem glanced at the street map of Rome on the big screen. At least their tracking devices were still working. The two flashing red dots were moving away from Hathaway's place now, going fuck knows where. The simple thing would be to call them. Find out what the hell was going on. But she'd been given her instructions on that one, too. Strict radio silence, Aston had said, and she had pointed out it was a phone, not a radio. George had grinned, the grin turning to a frown when Aston looked at her. Radio silence! Bollocks to that! Jem snatched up the phone and dialled George's mobile. It went straight to voicemail. Aston's, too. Slowly, without realising she was doing it, she put the receiver back into the cradle.

Jem watched the red dots move along streets with unpronounceable names, the feeling that something was very wrong increasing with each passing second. She felt sick and useless, completely ill-equipped to deal with this. She had been working for MI6 less than a week. This was all too real. George and Aston were stuck in a strange city, thousands of miles away, and she was their only link to home. Yes, maybe the mobile battery had gone flat, maybe they were having difficulty getting a signal. Jem had enough imagination to think of a hundred good reasons why they hadn't called. She also had enough imagination to think of a thousand bad ones. Like maybe they were in trouble.

Or maybe they were dead.

All too real . . .

Another glance at her watch. Five minutes past ten. Jem picked up the phone and called Anthony Heath.

16

George emerged from the fog slowly, disorientated and confused and convinced she was drowning. There were iron bands around her chest and they were getting tighter and tighter. She couldn't breathe. Panic gripped her and she tried to kick for the surface, but she was paralysed, legs and arms useless. And then she realised she wasn't wet. How could you drown without water? She forced in a breath, exhaled, forced in another. The air was hot and rancid – thin and there wasn't enough – but it was air rather than water. George remembered being knocked unconscious. Then nothing until a few seconds ago when she'd come back around and thought she was drowning. She took another gulp of warm, fetid air and opened her eyes. The world in front of her was a soft golden blur. She tried to focus and the world sharpened. She could make out the individual strands of the bag now, the light seeping through the weave. The bag smelled of old animals and oil.

She tried her arms and legs again. They still wouldn't move, but that was because they were tied. She could feel the ropes digging into her wrists and ankles, compressing her chest. A light breeze blew in and touched her naked skin. Fuck, no! Oh, this couldn't be happening! Apart from the stinking bag, she was completely naked. It was too much; she felt so vulnerable. While she'd been unconscious someone had removed her clothes, her underwear. It was too creepy for words. But she was alive, she told herself, clinging on to the positives. Naked, being held prisoner with no idea why, but most definitely alive.

She took a deep breath and forced herself to concentrate. There was nothing she could do about being naked, or the fact she was tied up, however, she could still do what she was trained to do. Collect information and analyse it. Stepping from the internal to the external, George went to work. She was tied to a wooden chair with a smooth, hard seat. The air in here was warm, comfortable against her skin. Below street level? A basement of some sort? Like a lot of cities, space in Rome was precious. It made sense to convert basements into rooms – make the most of what you've got. A pipe rattled there was a whoosh of water. She focused on these sounds, listened hard. The thump of feet on wood above her head sealed it for her. She was in a basement . . . and she'd put money on still being in Rome.

A noise on the other side of the room made

108

her heart race. The brittle sound of her hurried breathing was loud inside the sack. Shit, she wasn't alone! Someone was here. In this room. Watching her and getting a voyeuristic kick. The idea made her squirm. She wrestled her imagination under control. It couldn't be one of the gunmen. If that was the case, they'd have said something when they noticed her struggling, maybe even tried to stop her. She listened more closely. Whoever it was, they were breathing irregularly. The sound was laboured and wet, like someone with a bad head cold.

'Paul?!?' she whispered urgently.

A grunt and a snort.

'Paul!' she hissed again.

Another unintelligible series of guttural noises. And then the fierce sounds of struggle, the legs of a chair scratching the floor like nails on a blackboard.

'Paul, stop it! It's okay.' *Okay!* This situation was far from okay. The noise gradually lessened. A final scratch and then nothing.

'What's going on, George?' The words were puffy.

'They took my clothes, Paul. All of them.' She didn't mean to whine but she couldn't help it.

A pause. 'Ah fuck. They've taken mine as well.'

A door opened behind her and they fell silent. One set of footsteps, a second, a third. Heavy male feet slapping against hard tile, no effort being made to keep quiet. Not a good sign. They were being held somewhere where noise wasn't an issue. Blind inside the stinking sack, George felt three sets of hostile eyes exploring her naked body. Goosebumps erupted across her body and her bladder shrank to a fraction of its normal size; it was all she could do to keep control of it. Pissing herself would be the ultimate humiliation. During training, they'd been interrogated by the SAS, and that had been horrendous. Forty-eight hours of having your senses stretched and warped in every direction while desperately trying to keep a hold of your cover story. She'd got through the ordeal by telling herself it was just an exercise. The interrogators were allowed to go so far, and no further. But this was real, and George doubted these guys would be working within such carefully prescribed limits. The Geneva Convention . . . not a hope in hell. Whatever happened next, it wouldn't be pleasant. George was sure of that. For a brief moment she wished for the darkness of unconsciousness again. Anything but this.

17

Two of the men stopped walking, one a couple of yards in the direction Aston currently thought of as north, the other south-east. The third man was making slow circles around the room, his footsteps ebbing and flowing. In his own time he stopped directly in front of Aston. *Calm, calm, calm,* he told himself. It took all his willpower to stop himself struggling against the restraints. That would make him look weak. He might be seriously disadvantaged, but that was no reason to make the situation worse.

'Who are you?' The words were ice coated and delivered with a heavy Italian accent.

Aston said nothing.

'Who are you?'

Still Aston kept quiet. The blow took him completely by surprise. It wasn't hard, an open-handed slap, but it was shocking nonetheless. The skin on the upper part of his left arm throbbed. Another loud, stinging slap. This time the right arm. The third slap caught him on the left cheek, thudding dully against the sack. Aston bit his lip and refused to make a sound. *Say nothing, give nothing away.* Strong hands grabbed his bare shoulders, and then he was tumbling backwards. He tried to move, desperate to regain his balance, but the ropes held firm. The back of his head cracked on the floor and he saw stars. Something hard pushed against his forehead and he knew immediately it was a gun.

'I'll ask one more time. Who are you?'

'Untie us and give us some clothes, then we'll answer your questions.' He pronounced each syllable carefully, trying to disguise the fear in his voice.

'You really don't get it, do you? You're in no position to make demands.'

The gun was removed, and the interrogator walked across to George.

'So, are you going to be more helpful?'

Don't hurt her, Aston almost blurted out. He managed to stop himself at the last moment. That would have been a big mistake. Begging was a sure sign of weakness.

'Look,' the interrogator continued. His tone was confidential, reasonable, one friend to another. 'I don't want to hurt you – come to that, I don't want to hurt either of you – it's just that I need to find out more about you both. If that means hurting you then I will. But I'd rather we kept this civil.'

Say nothing, Aston thought, beaming the message telepathically to George. Name, rank, serial number. No more than that. Remember your training. Training . . . that was a laugh. Nothing the SAS had dished up could compare to this. Now the focus had moved on to George he was suddenly all too aware of the danger they were in. The interrogator would keep going until he got his answers, of that he had no doubt. But where would he draw the line? So far he'd dished out a couple of slaps. Shocking, yes; life threatening, no. His imagination threw up scenario after scenario, each one more terrible than the last – torture involving water and electricity, power tools – and there was nothing he could do to stop it. Of course, that's what the interrogator wanted. A practised interrogator knew that psychological torture was far more effective than physical torture.

'Well . . . ?' the interrogator said.

'Fuck you,' George whispered.

The sound of the gun was huge in the room. It took a second for Aston to realise the anguished strung-out '*nooooo!*' was coming from him.

'George!' he cried out. '*GEORGE!*'

'I'm all right,' George said in a small voice.

Relief washed through Aston. She was alive. His hands trembled from too much adrenaline and he gripped the hard wooden seat, hoping the interrogator hadn't noticed. Being blind was a bastard. Spying was all about seeing, all about watching. What people did, how they did it, told you more than their words ever would. Aston was fluent in body language; so was George. But what good was that when you were blind inside a sack?

'Next time one of you will die,' the interrogator said. 'Do I make myself clear?'

The rational part of Aston's brain was telling him the interrogator wouldn't carry out the threat; he needed them both alive so he could play them off against one another. The irrational part of his brain wasn't listening.

'What do you want with Hathaway?'

George said nothing and Aston wondered how much longer she could hold out for. How much longer *he* could hold out for. The interrogator was quickly losing patience. He could hear the tension creeping into his questions. The footsteps moved closer again, stopped in front of him. An immense pain in his stomach, and Aston was suddenly coughing and gasping and fighting for breath. He tried to suck on the stinking air inside the sack, but his lungs wouldn't work. The tiniest breath reached his chest, a slightly larger one. He forced a mouthful of air down, feeding greedily.

'What do you want with Hathaway?'

Got to buy time, Aston told himself, *weave a story, any old bullshit.* 'He owes our boss money,' he said.

There was a long silence, and Aston braced himself for another kicking. Eventually the interrogator said: 'I'm waiting . . .'

'A lot of money.' Aston hurried on, making it up as he went along.

'Almost four hundred grand,' George added.

'Why?'

The question was aimed at George, but she didn't answer. Had she blanked? Was she expecting him to pick up the ball? What if he said something, and then she said something at that exact same moment? And what if they said something different? Then the interrogator would know they were bullshitting, and they'd be royally screwed. One wrong move and it was all over. Seconds stretched out, time unravelling as surreally as a Dali clock. The tension was unbearable. No more than thirty seconds passed before the interrogator spoke, but it felt like forever.

'Please answer the question.' The interrogator didn't raise his voice, and this made him sound all the more menacing.

'Drugs.' Aston blurted the word out before George had a chance to open her mouth.

'Go on . . .'

'He was one of our couriers,' Aston continued quickly. He forced himself to take a breath and slow down. Sound too eager, and the interrogator would know he was lying. He needed to drip-feed the story, tease it out while maintaining an appropriate level of reluctance. Bullshitting was all about striking the correct balance. 'It was supposed to be a simple exchange. He delivers the cocaine, picks up the money, brings it back to us.'

'But he didn't show up,' said the interrogator.

'No, he didn't show up,' Aston agreed. 'Our

boss doesn't like being fucked over . . . he likes losing money even less.'

'So you were sent here to get the money back. Then what? You were going to teach Hathaway a lesson?'

'Something like that.'

'I heard Hathaway was dead.'

'We want to be sure he is actually dead.'

'The police are saying he was murdered.'

'And you believe them?'

'You've got a point. Until I see Hathaway's body with my own two eyes I'm keeping an open mind.'

This was delivered with a snake-like smile. Aston heard it loud and clear. It was as obvious as if he'd been staring the interrogator straight in the eye. A draft whispered through the basement and he shivered. He was getting a sore neck from the way he was lying. An egg-sized lump was forming on the back of his head, the skin taut and stretched.

'Did you find anything in Hathaway's apartment?'

'No.'

'You wouldn't lie to me?'

'We didn't find anything.'

Aston heard the interrogator move away. He stopped by the gunman standing due north.

'Kill them,' he said.

18

Aston's face was burning inside the sack. If it came down to it he would beg for his life. This had nothing to do with a lack of self-respect, and everything to do with staying alive. Okay, it might only buy them another couple of seconds, but every second was precious . . . even more so when there appeared to be so few of them left.

There were still three bad guys in the room. No-one had left; no-one had entered. There was no point appealing to the interrogator – the man was soul dead. The best they could hope for was to wait for the interrogator to go and then try and bargain with the two goons. Thinking it through, Aston realised how flawed his logic was. The basic premise was that the interrogator *would* leave – an assumption of the highest order; perhaps he was one of those sick bastards who got their kicks from watching. Secondly, neither him nor George spoke Italian, and he doubted English was on the curriculum at goon college.

And thirdly . . . they had absolutely fuck all to bargain with.

But there had to be something they could do. He twisted his head in George's direction, imagined her sitting there, as terrified as he was. Unless things improved in the next few seconds, they were going to die. Aston heard a round being chambered and his head snapped towards the sound. He wanted to swallow, but his mouth was dry. He was breathing rapid, shallow gulps of superheated air that seared his lungs.

'Wait,' he said.

'Something you want to add?' the interrogator said.

'You don't have to kill us.' Aston hurried the words out.

'He's right,' George said. 'We don't know you. We've never seen your face. Let us go and we'll catch the first flight back to England. You'll never see us again.'

'If only it was that simple,' the interrogator said.

'It *is* that simple.'

'Let me tell you something: if the roles were reversed, if it was me sitting naked on that chair with a sack over my head, then the first thing I'd do when I got out was kill the person who put me in that position. How could I hope to get my respect back if I didn't?'

Aston opened his mouth to speak, and then everything happened at once. The scene was played out in detached fragments. Disorientated

118

and blind inside the bag, he tried to make sense of what was going on, but it was impossible.

A door opens. The whisper of a silenced automatic. A big handgun booms a reply. Ears ringing. George screaming his name. 'Paul! Paul! Paul!' She's been hit. She's dying. A thud like meat being slapped onto a chopping block. The smell of cordite. A sharp intake of breath to his left. Another of those stomach churning thuds. Screaming. The high-pitched keening of a wounded animal. Waiting for the bullet to smash through his brain. Through his heart. A tiny metallic messenger of death. A toxic inhalation. George has gone quiet. 'George!' No answer. 'GEORGE!' More sharp inhalations. The sound loud in the bag. More screaming. Male rather than female. George is dead. This time it isn't an act. It isn't a game. The bastards have killed her. A voice. Irish. 'You okay?' His chair is pulled upright. The bag is ripped from his head. Bright light assaults his eyes. A silhouette hovers above. A black cut-out with a gun hanging from his shoulder. Smoke everywhere. The bitter taste of cordite finds his tongue. The silhouette moves towards George. In the chaos her chair has tipped over. She's lying on the floor. Face turned away. Not moving. Dead.

And then stillness.

No more than ten seconds had passed, the longest ten seconds Aston had ever known. His vision slowly clearing, he watched the man in black kneel down. Ever so gently he removed the bag from George's head, as if he were performing a religious ceremony. It was done carefully, with so much respect, and Aston had seen enough death to know she was gone. He would never see her again, never hear her laugh, never see her smile. They'd put her in a coffin, put her in the ground, and that would be that. She'd be confined to memory, and with every passing year that memory would grow fainter until she ceased to exist altogether.

Grief-stricken, he offered a deal to any God who might be listening: my life for hers. But his heart kept beating, his lungs continued to pump. Aston's head slumped to his chest and he stared past his naked body, seeing nothing.

From somewhere deep in his memory George called out, asked if he was okay. 'Of course I'm not,' he snapped, uncertain whether he'd spoken out loud. And then she was saying thank God, over and over – *thank God thank God thank God*. The words tumbled together, and the voice in his memory sounded so real. Then the Irishman was talking, his accent warm and musical. He was telling George to take it easy, telling her not to get up too quickly. Aston lifted his head and saw George coming towards him. She smiled, and with that smile he knew it really was her – this wasn't some trick of his memory. Aston slumped with relief, the ropes around his chest the only thing holding him up. George suddenly remembered she was naked. She stopped dead and covered herself self-consciously with her hands, blushing. The man in black walked up to her holding a leather coat. His face was hidden by a balaclava. George snatched the coat from his outstretched hand and slung it on. It came down to the top of her thigh, just about long enough for modesty. There were two bullet holes on the left breast, directly above the heart.

'You're alive,' he whispered.

'Your powers of observation astound me sometimes,' she whispered back. 'They really do.'

The man in black used a flick-knife, to make easy work of the ropes. Aston shook them off and rubbed some life back into his wrists and ankles. He did a quick 360 degrees. There were two corpses lying in crazy piles on the floor. The third man was still alive, sprawled out in a pool of blood, mewling and spluttering. The Smith and Wesson Magnum was well out of reach, kicked away, a red skid mark leading to it.

'Don't suppose you've got another jacket knocking about?' Aston asked. Now the initial shock had worn off, he was suddenly conscious of his own nakedness.

The man in black knelt down beside one of the corpses and wrestled the jacket off. He tossed it over. Aston caught it one-handed and slipped it on. There were two bullet holes on the left breast of this one, too. Whoever the Irishman was, he knew how to shoot. Aston went over to the larger of the two corpses and started removing the trousers. They were too big, but they'd do. The dead man's shoes more or less fitted.

Aston turned to the man in black. 'Who the hell are you?'

'John Priest.' He rolled the balaclava up, revealing a well-used face. His eyes were bright green; tufts of jet black hair snuck out from under the balaclava. He was about five-eight and in good shape. There was a quiet sense of contained energy about him, like a bomb. Aston put Priest in his early forties. The gun hanging from his shoulder was a Heckler and Koch MP5, the version with the built-in silencer – a serious piece of hardware that had don't-fuck-with-me written all over it.

'Okay,' George said as she pulled on a pair of trousers that were so big they looked like waders. 'Now, I'm going to go out on a limb here, but I'm guessing you're on our side.'

'Heath asked me to keep an eye on you.'

'So what kept you?' Aston said.

'Well, there was that little stunt you pulled after the restaurant . . .'

'That was *you* following us.'

'Guilty as charged. Nice move, incidentally. By the time I worked out what you were doing, you were long gone. Jem was able to help me out . . . once she'd confirmed that I was who I said I was . . . which all took time, of course.'

'The tracking devices were in our shoes, though.'

'And your shoes are upstairs with the rest of your clothes.'

George looked herself up and down, not bothering to hide her disgust. 'So why the fuck am I wearing a dead person's clothes?'

Priest shrugged. 'You seemed in a hurry to get some clothes on and those were closest.'

'And why all this cloak and dagger stuff anyway?' Aston asked. 'You could have joined us for dinner and saved us a whole load of trouble.'

'You know what Heath is like. My orders were to stay in the background unless I was needed.' Priest grinned. 'Now, unless you've got any further questions, I suggest we find out what these bastards are all about, then get out of here pronto.'

Priest went across to bad guy number three and crouched down beside him. He pulled him upright so his back was flat against the wall. The man's face was ghost white, pain etched into every line and wrinkle. His hands were pulled tight across his gut, blood seeping through his fingers. There were dark wet shadows on his black silk shirt and he was sitting in a pool of red. Aston walked over, George clomping behind in shoes that were far too big. Aston hunkered down at eye level. The injury looked bad. If he got to a hospital he'd probably survive, but he needed to get to one quickly.

'Can you hear me?' Aston said.

The answer was muttered in Italian, low and threatening, unmistakably a curse. Although the voice was barely a whisper, Aston placed it straight-away. The interrogator.

'I'll take that as a yes,' he said. 'What's your name?'

'Fuck you.'

'Look, if you help us, we'll help you. You need

to get to a doctor. If you don't you're going to die. Do you understand?'

The man looked at Aston, then George, then back again. 'I'm telling you nothing,' he said weakly. 'Do you understand *that*?'

'All we want are the answers to a couple of questions.'

'And then what? You take me to a hospital? Do I look that stupid? Whatever I say or don't say, you're going to kill me . . . so I'm saying nothing.'

A polite cough made them turn. Priest was standing there holding a flick-knife. Light glinted off the razor-sharp blade. 'Do you want a hand?'

George and Aston stepped aside, and Priest moved in. He got up close, moving the knife slowly from side to side. Tick-tock, tick-tock, like a pendulum. Rhythmic . . . hypnotic. 'You know,' he said, talking as though he had all the time in the world, 'I spent a lot of time working undercover in the IRA. Now they were vicious bastards. When they wanted to get someone talking, they used bolt-cutters. They'd start with the baby toe of the left foot and sever those little-piggies one at a time. Do you have any idea what that sounds like? The crunch of bone. The screaming.' A pause. Tick-tock, tick-tock with the knife. 'Actually, I reckon you probably have a good idea what I'm talking about. Anyway, they'd start with the left foot and if that didn't work they'd move on to the right foot. Still no joy, well, then they'd start on the fingers. Most people lasted a couple of toes before talking, but there was a story did the rounds about one grass who lasted all the way to the end. Took two days. Anyway, there he is, no fingers and no toes, so what happens now, eh? Well, basically they cut his bollocks off, which did the trick. After that, they couldn't get him to shut up. That wasn't the end of it, though. Oh, no. Once he'd told them everything, they doused him in petrol and torched him. See, because he'd wasted their time they didn't see why they should make it easy for him. Can you imagine that? Being burnt alive . . .'

'You don't scare me,' the interrogator said.

Priest didn't answer. He clicked the knife shut and moved the interrogator's hands out of the way. The interrogator tried to resist but there was no fight left in him. Priest gently unbuttoned the shirt. There was a sticky tearing sound as silk parted from skin. He pressed his thumb into the wound.

'Why are you so interested in Hathaway?' Priest was talking loudly so he could be heard over the screams. 'Talk to me and I'll make the pain stop.' He dug his thumb in deeper, and the intensity of the screaming notched up another level. 'Tell me about Hathaway. What do you want him for?' The interrogator glared, eyes beginning to glaze. Going into shock. He was one small step from uncon-sciousness. Priest twisted his thumb and the inter-rogator howled. The sound was horrific, but Aston didn't look away. Sometimes the direct approach was the only way.

'Okay, I'll talk.' The interrogator pushed the words out through clenched teeth, his voice barely a whisper.

Priest wiped his bloody hand on his trousers and stood up. 'You should find him a bit more co-operative,' he said to Aston.

The interrogator shot a wary look at Aston and George, then said: 'I want him for the same reason as you. Money.'

'How much?' George said.

'Half a million.'

Euros presumably. Aston did a quick calculation. Around one third of a million pounds. People had been killed for less; people had done all sorts of things for less.

'Hathaway was a gambler,' the interrogator went on. 'He'd had some big losses and tried to gamble his way out. He laid bets all over the city. And lost. When people worked out what he'd done they called me in.'

'Why you?'

'I collect debts.'

'Go on.'

The interrogator coughed and his eyes flickered shut. Aston thought that was all they were going to get, then the eyes opened again. 'I had Hathaway's apartment watched. Just in case he came back. You two showed up. I figured you might know something.'

Aston studied the interrogator's face, searching for any sign that he might be lying. He wasn't.

Nor was he behind Hathaway's death. With half a million Euros at stake, he would want Hathaway alive. 'Heard enough?' he asked George.

'Yeah,' she said.

The interrogator had dropped his head and was staring at his bloodstained hands. They were clasped together, fingers interlocked. Lips moving, he muttered a prayer in Italian. Too little, too late, thought Aston. It was going to take more than that to get him past St Peter.

Priest picked up the Magnum and flicked it open, checked it was loaded. 'You two go on ahead.' He spoke quietly, his eyes locked on the interrogator. 'I'll catch up in a second.'

Aston and George left the basement room without looking back. Halfway up the stairs, a single shot boomed out. They paused for a moment then carried on climbing.

19

Jem answered with a tense 'yeah' on the first ring, and from the relief in her voice Aston could tell she'd been worried about them – or, to be more accurate, she'd been worried about George. Aston was under no illusions there. Hopefully, the computer expert would mellow with time. Working together on a long-term basis would be a pain in the arse otherwise. He pressed the phone to his ear and settled deeper into the back seat of Priest's rented Alfa Romeo. The city flew past on the other side of the glass, a blur of coloured lights and bustle. Aston barely noticed.

'Thank God you guys are okay.' Jem spoke in a rush, like a hyperactive kid who'd had one Pepsi too many. 'I did everything you told me to. When you didn't call in, I phoned Heath. He told me not to worry, said he had everything covered. He wouldn't say any more than that, though. A couple of minutes later I get a call from this Irish bloke. He wants my help tracking you two down. At first

I'm thinking it's some sort of a crank call, but how the hell did he get this number? He won't give me his name, but he tells me Heath will vouch for him. So I check him out because that's what I'm supposed to do, right?'

'Right,' Aston said even though he wanted to say 'wrong'. She'd wasted valuable time there. If Priest had got there sooner, he wouldn't be aching so much now. Still, he could forgive her. She'd done her best. And it had worked out okay in the end. The bruises would heal.

'He checks out, so I tell him where you are and he hangs up without another word. Then it's like I don't fucking exist. Nothing from Heath; nothing from our mystery Irishman; nothing from you guys. Until now that is.'

'We were kind of tied up,' Aston said.

'Whatever.'

Aston glanced over at the driver's seat. Heath might have vouched for Priest, but the jury was still out. The Irishman didn't give much away. He was friendly enough, however, Aston had noticed that when he spoke he didn't actually say anything. Forget keeping your cards to your chest, Priest's cards never left the table . . . bend them up at the corner, take a peek, then sit back all enigmatic and keep everyone guessing. What unnerved Aston the most was that in the short time he'd known Priest, the Irishman had killed four men – in addition to the three in the cellar there had been a guard at the top of the stairs with his throat slit. What's more, he'd done all this without any emotion whatsoever. Just another day at the office.

'I'll check in with you on the hour,' he said.

'You'd better do,' Jem said. 'One heart attack a night is enough.'

Aston hung up and shut his phone. Their clothes had been left in two neat piles in one of the upstairs rooms. Watches, phones, jewellery, shoes on top. He'd changed in record time, trying to ignore the dead-eyed gaze of the guard with the slit throat. It had been good to get back into his own clothes again.

Priest glanced over his shoulder. 'Well?' he said.

'Looks like you are who you say you are.'

'That's good to know.'

Aston tried for a smile, but it wasn't easy. The shock still hadn't worn off, if it had worn off at all. There was a good chance he was indulging in a serious dose of denial right now. He didn't want to think too hard about what had happened back in that basement. No, denial was the only way. The full horror would hit later, probably when they got back to the hotel. The last of the adrenaline would finally seep away and he'd start to relax. Then he'd start thinking. Generally speaking, it was when you started thinking that things fell apart. Thankfully, George would be there. They would help put each other back together again. Wouldn't be the first time; wouldn't be the last. As they drove on in silence, Aston kept glancing across at George. She was dealing with things her own way, no doubt indulging in her own brand of denial. She hadn't said a word since they got in the car. Understandable. Being stripped naked like that would have been tough on her. Come to that, it hadn't been a bundle of laughs for him.

They parked in a side street near the Tiber and walked to Luciano Valerio's bar . . . except the bar wasn't there. The street was filled with apartment buildings. Not a single bar in sight. Aston checked the address. They were in the right place, so what was going on? The three of them crowded around a map none of them were paying any attention to, and did their best to look like lost tourists.

'Maybe the police got the address wrong,' George suggested in a whisper.

'Maybe,' said Aston.

'It has been known for them to fuck up,' Priest added.

Aston looked around, taking everything in while trying to keep it casual. Tall buildings crowded around a narrow rutted road that was just about wide enough for two minis to squeeze past each other. There was a thin pavement on one side. The news-stand on the corner looked like it had been there forever. Frozen supermodel faces stared out from the magazine covers, head-lines blared in 72 point. The owner was watching them, but pretending he wasn't. Three lost tourists standing scratching their heads – the highlight of his day. Aston double-checked the address, triple-checked. Definitely the right place. The building had three floors and white shutters that were folded back from the windows. The paintwork was starting to blister and crack. Not completely rundown, but some TLC wouldn't go amiss. The owner of one of the apartments turned up. A furtive look around, then he disappeared through the door. Aston was about to suggest having a word with the owner of the news-stand when a second man turned up. He did the same as the first. A quick look-see, and then he pushed the door open.

'Ah,' said Aston.

20

Aston wasn't sure he liked this; George, of course, loved it; Priest didn't seem to have an opinion either way. The bug was microscopic, hidden in a ring on his right index finger. George and Priest were only a street away, sitting in the Irishman's Alfa Romeo. At the first sign of trouble they'd be there in less than a minute, Priest had assured him. But a lot could happen in a minute – a thousand lifetimes lived and lost.

The door opened into a small, dark reception hall. Stairs led up, stairs led down. There was no choice, really. He kept one hand on the banister as he made his way down the steep, smooth steps. The door at the bottom was closed. He knocked once and the Judas-window snapped open. Aston tried to look relaxed as a pair of hooded eyes gave him the once-over. The Judas-window snapped shut and the door opened.

He walked into a small, sweaty cellar room and within two steps had seen everything worth seeing, just like Mac had trained him. As he walked, he scratched his upper lip and whispered into the ring, hiding his mouth with his hand. The walls were painted crimson, and a thick fug of tobacco smoke hung at head level. Privacy booths were fitted along one wall. A bar reached out from the far corner. There were candles on every table, every shelf; tealights in small glass holders lined the bar like runway beacons. Golden light and shadows conspired to turn the bar into a church. All eyes were on Aston as he walked towards the bar, checking him out with stolen glances. There were a dozen people in total. The doorman, who looked like a muscled-up version of Danny DeVito, and half a dozen punters. Luciano Valerio stood with his boys at the bar, making no effort to pretend he wasn't staring. He was wearing a loud lemon coloured shirt, and his skin was facelift smooth. His long grey hair was tied back in a pony-tail. He was holding a cigarette between his thumb and forefinger like the Chinese do, taking little puffs. In the dim light of the bar the years had peeled away, making it look as though he'd found the secret of eternal youth.

'Do you speak English?' Aston said.

'A little,' Valerio replied. 'I'm out of practice, but I know enough to get by.'

The response was too quick, too fluent, the Italian accent exaggerated. Valerio was obviously comfortable with English.

'How can I help you?' Valerio asked, crushing the half-smoked cigarette into an ashtray.

134

'I need five minutes of your time.'

'Why?'

'Can we have some privacy?' Aston glanced at the boys at the bar. All of them had fresh skin, deep tans and tight muscles. They radiated with health. Three of them were under twenty-five; one looked no older than eighteen. The fourth was in his early thirties, but even to Aston it was obvious why he was here. He was as perfect as Adonis, all sleek lines and testosterone. Valerio waved the boys away, and Aston waited until they were out of earshot before fishing the photograph of Hathaway from his pocket. He laid it on the bar without taking his eyes off Valerio.

'Ah, you're a policeman.' Valerio didn't look at the photograph, just kept staring at Aston. The false friendliness had completely gone now, replaced with a colder, darker attitude. Aston didn't bother correcting him. If Valerio thought he was a cop that could work to his advantage.

'Should have guessed,' Valerio went on. 'Must be losing my touch.' He flipped open an antique silver case, took out a fresh cigarette and lit it with a gold Dunhill lighter.

'Have you seen this person?'

'You know, you're a long way from home.'

'Look at the photograph.'

Valerio smoked, holding the cigarette between thumb and forefinger. In his own time he glanced down – briefly, no longer than a second. 'No, I've never seen him before.'

'Your fingerprints were found in his apartment.'

'There must be some mistake.'

Aston felt his patience ebbing away. The atmosphere in the room had become heavier. The punters had shrunk into the security of the booths, making like they were invisible; the boys were huddled around a table, watching intently and pretending they weren't. 'There's no mistake,' he said. 'They're your prints.'

'Okay, so my prints were in his apartment,' Valerio said. 'What are you going to do? Arrest me?'

Aston looked slowly around, taking in every single face. This wasn't going well. Not well at all. Before he knew what was happening, the interrogator's Magnum was in his hand and he was pointing it between Valerio's eyes. He was aware that the room had frozen. Nobody moved; nobody breathed. The boys were sitting with their mouths open, and the punters had made themselves so small they'd virtually disappeared. Danny DeVito over by the door didn't know what to do with himself. The colour had drained from Valerio's face, and the cigarette drooped between his finger and thumb.

'I want you to listen to me,' Aston said very quietly, 'and I want you to listen good. I am having the day from hell. You can't even begin to imagine. Now, I'm going to stand here while you have a good long think about things. All I'm asking for is a little co-operation. I don't think that's too much to ask.'

Aston stood in silence, pointing the big Magnum at Valerio's head and counting off the seconds. He reached forty-three before someone hammered on the door. 'Let them in,' he shouted, and the squat doorman practically tripped over himself to oblige. Priest entered first, closely followed by George. 'I'm having trouble getting him to co-operate,' Aston said.

'We gathered that.' George stood with her hands on her hips, getting her breath back.

Valerio looked from George to Priest. An inch of ash was hanging precariously from the end of his cigarette. 'Get him to put the gun down and I'll tell you what you want to know.'

'Paul, put the gun down,' said George.

Aston lowered the Magnum and thumbed the safety catch. He tucked it into the back of his jeans and pushed the photograph across the bar. Valerio crushed the half-smoked cigarette into an ashtray and took another one from his silver case. He lit it with a shaky hand and looked at the photograph.

'This is Greg Hathaway. He's a customer here.'

'A regular?'

'As clockwork. When he's in town, that is.'

'Any idea where he goes when he's not in town?'

'What do I look like? His keeper?'

Aston took a step forward and Valerio stepped back. Fists clenching and unclenching, he came within an inch of punching Valerio out. He really didn't need attitude right now. Some days were bad, some were *really* bad. Today had hit an all-time low. It was slowly sinking in how close he'd come to dying in that basement . . . how close both of them had come. Priest was owed a drink, that was for sure.

'I've got this, Paul.' George turned back to Valerio, who was nervously eyeballing Aston. 'When he's in town, how often does he come in?'

'Every day.'

'And how long has he been coming here for?'

Valerio puffed on his cigarette while he thought about this. 'That's a tough one. I don't know. Three years, maybe four. Quite a while.'

'So, you know him well?'

'Yes and no. Hathaway's from a different generation. Once you've led a secret life, it's difficult to shake that off completely. Old habits, and all that.'

Ain't that the truth, Aston thought. 'But you knew him well enough to visit his apartment?'

'We socialised from time to time. There's no law against that.'

'What do you mean "socialised"?'

'We were friends, that's all.' A shrug and a sigh. 'Look, I know he had money troubles. Is that what this is about?'

Aston nodded.

'Thought so. Last time we talked, he reckoned he had the situation under control. He said he was expecting a big payout any day soon. Told me it would be enough to get him out of the shit.'

138

'Where was the money coming from?'

A grin and a drag. Valerio folded the cigarette into the ashtray. 'Well, that's the thing, isn't it? There was never any big pay day, was there? He was trying to buy time . . . looks like time finally caught up with him.'

'Why didn't the police speak to you?' Aston asked.

'Who says they didn't?'

'There wasn't any transcription of an interview—'

'Of course there wasn't. I have an understanding with the police, and that understanding doesn't come cheap. They came to me, asked a few questions. I told them I knew nothing and they went away again.'

Aston sensed he was holding back. Find the right question and he'd get the right answer. Valerio wouldn't give something for nothing. 'Just like that,' he said.

'Just like that,' Valerio agreed. 'Nobody wants to rock the boat. I'm sure that's as true in England as it is here.'

'When did you last see Hathaway?' George asked.

'A couple of weeks ago.'

Aston studied Valerio carefully, noting his body language, what he was saying and how he was saying it. Valerio was getting cocky, the balance of power shifting. Not good. He glanced across at Priest – the Irishman was smiling serenely, seemingly

139

disengaged. Looks could be deceptive, Aston thought, wondering what was going on in Priest's head. The punters and the boys were pretending not to watch, the act so obvious. The soap opera happening at the bar was far too interesting.

'What aren't you telling us?' Aston said quietly, and Valerio's head snapped towards him. He held the Italian's gaze, demanding his full attention.

'What do you mean? I'm co-operating.'

'You might be answering our questions, but I wouldn't say you're co-operating.'

Priest moved so fast, all Aston saw was a blur. One second the Irishman was standing there doing a good impression of a Tibetan monk, the next he was clicking an empty clip from the Heckler. Shattered bottles lined the back of the bar, the stink of spirits and cordite hung sharp in the air. The three bottles directly behind Valerio were still intact. Valerio was rooted to the spot, his face drained of colour. The punters and the boys had dived for cover, hiding beneath tables, behind chairs. Danny DeVito had his hand on the door handle. Priest snapped in a new clip and aimed the Heckler. 'Get away from the door,' he warned, and the doorman slowly made his way to an empty booth.

'There was a man came in here the last time I saw Hathaway.' Valerio was speaking quickly now, eager to please. 'He was looking for work. Handsome. Talked the talk. Called himself James. I'd recently lost one of my boys so I was looking for a replacement. I didn't think too much about it at the time, but thinking about it now it was a bit of a coincidence. It certainly saved me a load of trouble. Hathaway came in at his usual time, and I pointed out James. He was Hathaway's type. They chatted for a while, and then Hathaway took him home. I never saw either of them again.'

'Can you describe this man?' Aston asked.

'I can do better than that. I've got him on film.'

'Where's the film?'

Valerio nodded to a door at the side of the bar that was hidden in the shadows.

Aston pulled out the Magnum and pointed it at the Italian's head. 'Show me.'

Valerio magicked a key from his trouser pocket and unlocked the door. He made an 'after you' gesture and Aston waved him on with the gun; George brought up the rear. The passageway was narrow and noisy. At first, Aston thought someone was being tortured, then realised these weren't cries of agony. Half a dozen doors lined the passageway, most closed; grunts, groans and squeaks behind some, silence behind others. A door at the end of the passage was open and Aston glanced in as he walked past. The room was no bigger than a broom cupboard, with a padded bench and a single unshielded red light bulb. A one way mirror was fitted into the wall; beyond the mirror was a small room with a bed.

The passageway veered left. Six foot and then another door. Valerio conjured up another key and let them into a windowless office. The room was four yards square and spotless: whitewashed walls, an empty wastepaper bin, the ashtray wiped clean. A large desk with a leather office chair was pushed up against one wall. On top of the filing cabinet was a document shredder and a fax machine. A mix of ylang ylang and patchouli hid the smell of stale tobacco. There was a bank of black and white CCTV monitors fitted to the wall above the desk, each one labelled with a hash sign and a number, the numbers running sequentially from left to right. VCRs hummed underneath. Three rows of shelves circled the room at head height, crammed with videos, each one dated and titled in the same precise handwriting. An intimidating safe sat in one corner. Aston glanced at the monitors. Shots of the bar, shots of the rooms. He could see Priest from two different angles, and on three of the monitors he saw more than he wanted.

'I'm going to want all of today's tapes,' Aston said, glancing at Priest on monitor #6. The Irishman was behind the bar helping himself to a drink from one of the bottles he hadn't blown apart. A good sized measure of Smirnoff, by the looks of it. 'As far as you're concerned, we were never here. Understand?'

'You're not with the police, are you?'

'No,' Aston agreed.

'Hathaway was a friend. Do you think you can find the bastard who killed him?'

'Yeah, we'll find him. Okay, let's see this tape.'

Aston expected Valerio to go for the shelves. He didn't. Instead, he knelt down in front of the safe and spun the knob: left then right, left then right. He pulled down on the handle with both hands and the door clunked open. Valerio took out a video and plugged it into one of the machines. Out of the snow on monitor #1, a picture appeared. The bottom of a stairwell. Grey and black shadows. There was a door in the middle of the shot, a Judas-window at head height. The entrance to the bar. Filmed in time-lapse, the frames appeared at two second intervals, juddering like an old black and white movie. The time was displayed in white at the bottom of the screen: 19:53.

At 19:54 a man appeared in the stairwell, the back of his head to the camera. He was well-built, amply filling the corners of his denim jacket. In monochrome his hair appeared silver. Little teases of a profile. Not enough, though . . . never enough. Aston willed the man to turn around, but he kept his eyes on the door and his back to the camera. The frames flicked forward, strobing. Arms by the side, knuckles hovering over wood, back to the side again, no movement in-between. The Judas-window closed, the Judas-window open. And closed again. Door shut, door open. Aston was convinced he wasn't going to get a face shot, but at the last moment the man glanced over his shoulder. A spy glance to make sure he wasn't being followed. Aston dived towards Valerio.

143

'Pause!' he shouted. 'Pause the film!'

Valerio was way ahead of him. The picture froze. Grainy and blurred, it was difficult to make out much on the small monitor. Aston smiled to himself. The image enhancement software they had was state-of-the-art. Once Jem had done her thing, they would have a picture good enough to hang in the Louvre. He stared at the face, and the face stared back. There was arrogance there; confidence, too. Catch me if you can, the killer seemed to be saying to him.

Catch me if you can.

PART TWO

The Long Time

This only is denied to God: the power to undo the past.

Agathon

The target had a detached house in Chesham. At least half a million pounds worth of bricks and mortar – nothing particularly grand. It was mock Tudor, built sometime in the Fifties. The street was full of them. There was a medium-sized garden with a hedge, a shed and a small pond . . . and every house in the street had those, too. There were 3 series BMWs in the driveways for the husbands, SUVs for the wives and kids. The trees were healthy, the verges well maintained. The client wanted this hit done softly, softly. No headlines, try and make it look like an accident, better still make it look natural. They had spoken on a secure line, encryption software doing its thing, and Coulson had sounded like an alien.

Kestrel was last here a month ago. Dressed in black, he'd come in the early hours, that time of the day where the world slowed to a sigh. Breaking in hadn't posed a problem. He'd taken a large stone from the garden and wrapped it in his jacket. It took two attempts to smash the glass panel nearest the lock. Then it was a simple matter of reaching in and unlocking the door. Like most houses, the intruder chain was dangling loose, an orna-ment rather than a deterrent. The alarm system made a soft, insistent beep – loud enough to remind you to

147

punch in the code; not loud enough to be heard upstairs. It took less than ten seconds to plant the miniature camera. And then he was out and running, the sound of the alarm chasing him down the street.

The police turned up eventually, had a quick look for the sake of public relations, then left. It was obvious what had happened. A junkie had broken in – no doubt looking for a DVD player he could sell for a rock – and been scared off by the burglar alarm. In the end nothing was stolen, and no-one was stabbed while they slept. The attempted break-in hadn't merited so much as a single paragraph in the local paper.

The alarm company arrived around eleven the next day to check everything was working fine. A glazier came at lunchtime to fix the window. The target returned from work at seven. He punched in the code to deactivate the alarm system: 723995.

Kestrel had watched all this from his flat in Hendon, the kids upstairs running riot. Over the next month he checked daily to ensure the target didn't change the code. The target left the house at a quarter past seven each morning, arriving home bang on seven. No doubt he was feeling a little vulnerable these days, a touch paranoid even. Understandable. His personal space had been invaded. Kestrel reckoned a month was long enough for the target to start relaxing into his old ways again.

The street was quiet and still as he walked up the path to number 11. The skeleton keys were in his hand when he reached the doorstep. The lock was a simple Yale and took five seconds to pick. Kestrel said a quick prayer as he leant against the wood. His luck held. Not *so much as a single squeak. And there was the chain, made from dirty brass and dangling uselessly. That had been his biggest concern. He couldn't exactly use bolt cutters. Even the police, overworked and apathetic as they were, might have noticed that one.*

Quickly into the porch. Three soft beeps before he punched the number in: 723995. The flashing red lights immediately turned green. Kestrel paused and listened for any movement upstairs. Nothing. Good. Moonlight streamed through the quarter windows of the front door, silver and ethereal. Enough light to see by – he didn't need the torch. He took the SOCOM from his backpack. The gun had been commissioned by the American military; designed specifically for Special Ops. It was considered the world's first offensive hand gun. Interesting choice of word, Kestrel thought. All guns were pretty offensive when used right. The SOCOM was basically a Heckler and Koch USP. What made it special were the added extras: a silencer and a laser sighting system.

The target's wife had left two years ago. The only surprise was that she'd hung around so long. Presumably, she did it for the sake of the children. They'd had three – two girls and a boy. The youngest had flown the nest a couple of years ago. There was evidence of the wife everywhere. From the choice of carpets and wall- paper to the framed photos decorating the hallway. More pictures lined the stairs, children and grandchildren staring from behind a layer of glass. Kestrel recognised the target in a couple of them. A floorboard squeaked, the noise immense in the silver silence. He stood stock-

still, holding his breath as the house creaked and groaned all around him like an old sailing ship. No going back now – he was past the point of no return. This job would be carried out one way or another.

Satisfied the target wasn't about to appear at the top of the stairs brandishing a sawn-off shotgun, he continued climbing. Slowly, carefully. One heart attack per job was more than enough. Kestrel stopped on the upstairs landing to get his bearings. The main bedroom was at the back of the house. He could see the door. It was open a crack, dense darkness beyond. Kestrel edged along the landing, the SOCOM leading the way. He reached the door and gently pushed it open. The target was cocooned in a duvet, a tangled mass of shadows in the middle of the double bed. He was sleeping the sleep of the truly righteous: dead to the world, snoring and snuffling. Kestrel swapped the SOCOM to his left hand. The EpiPen was an over-the-counter injector that he'd modified to deliver a 1 milligram hit of adrenaline. Without taking his eyes off the target, he walked over to the bed and made his way along the side. He felt calm, relaxed. These were the moments he lived for. Closing in on the target, easing nearer, taking his time. He could see the head poking up from the covers, the thick dark hair. Closer, closer. Kestrel brought his leg to within a millimetre of the bed, careful not to bump it. Slowly he extended his arm. The target slept on, oblivious. Kestrel's hand hovered above the target's scalp, the end of the EpiPen almost touching. He brought his hand down and the spring-loaded needle released.

The target awoke instantly, eyes huge. He saw Kestrel

at the end of the bed and began wrestling himself from the duvet. Kestrel swapped the SOCOM back to his right hand and aimed. 'Not a sound,' he whispered.

The target stopped struggling. He scratched his head, momentarily confused. An insect bite, perhaps? He noticed the dancing red dot on the front of his pyjama top, just above his heart, and looked up, terrified. That little red dot did the trick every time; it was better than any verbal threat. Everyone had seen enough movies to know what it meant.

'What do you want?' The target spoke as though he was used to being in charge. Even now, that was evident.

Kestrel said nothing.

'Who sent you?'

'Judas.'

Realisation stretched the folds of the target's chubby face. He suddenly looked even more terrified.

'You killed Hathaway.'

A statement rather than a question, a note of uncertainty creeping into the voice. The target started to get up and Kestrel made a show of reaffirming his grip on the gun. The target slumped back against the headboard, that little red dot dancing mischievously on his pyjama top.

When it happened, it happened quickly. The target began scratching his left arm, shaking it as if there were bugs trapped under the skin. Seconds later, he was clutching his chest and gasping for breath, pleas in his whispers, pleas in his eyes. Kestrel watched impassively as the target crawled to the edge of the bed and crashed to the floor. A big man, it was an effort to drag himself

151

along the floor. Fingers digging into the carpet, he managed a couple of feet before going still.

Kestrel took a moment to admire his work. Looking but not touching. The target was lying in a heap and his pyjama bottoms had ridden down to his knees. No dignity in death here. Most heart attacks happened in the early hours; there were statistics to back that up. And the target was a prime candidate: overweight and in the right demographic. Any overworked medical examiner would be more than happy to sign this off as a Myocardial Infarction. If they chose to investigate further, not a problem. Adrenaline was produced naturally by the body; there would be nothing in the bloodstream to indicate foul play. The likelihood of them examining the scalp for the needle mark was next to zero. As far as hits went, this was even tidier than the assassination of Georgi Markov, the Bulgarian dissident who was stabbed on Waterloo Bridge with a ricin-tipped umbrella. That one was widely recognised as a classic. Shame nobody would ever know about this one.

Kestrel stayed another five minutes to make sure there were no miracle resurrections. Before leaving, he removed the camera and punched in the code to reactivate the alarm.

21

Belmarsh Prison, last September

The cell door clanged open and Mac just stood there for a moment, psyching himself up, the greasy stink of school dinners surrounding him. The prison overalls the medics had found for him fitted like a clown suit. Someone's idea of a joke. Ha-fucking-ha! If things weren't bad enough, he now looked a complete twat. In Belmarsh, that wouldn't pass unnoticed. Like the new kid at school, you really didn't want to stand out in here. Mac had done his best to get the overalls to look halfway accept-able – he'd rolled the trouser legs up to stop himself falling flat on his face, rolled up the sleeves – but it was a losing battle. He stuffed the mug into his pocket and picked up his tray. Resting heavily on the crutch, he stepped onto the landing, out into a noisy hurricane of banging boots and clanging cutlery. Every step was hell, his knee flaring fire whenever he put any pressure on it. Mac hobbled towards the hot plate, aware that everybody was watching him, checking out the new boy in the clown suit. Nobody stared directly. It was all done through casual glances and sideways looks. He joined the back of the queue. And that was where he stayed. As far as the other cons were concerned, the back of the queue was one foot directly in front of him. Nobody spoke to him, nobody registered his existence; he was just elbowed out the way. The screws kept well back, watching but not getting involved, letting the cons sort out the pecking order for themselves. Reacting at that stage wouldn't have done any good, so Mac just stood there, taking the abuse.

Taking it all in.

The last few cons were the worst. These were the bottom-feeders, and it made a change for them to have someone to shit on. Mac understood where they were coming from. His bruised face was the face of a victim; the crutch marked him as weak. When he finally reached the front of the queue, there was only bread and gravy left. The tea was so stewed it had the consistency of liquid shit. Mac was three doors away from his cell when a skinny guy with tattooed teardrops on his left cheek 'accidentally' walked into him. An elbow in the ribs and he was sent sprawling to the floor, tea and gravy decorating his overalls. With the sound of laughter spinning all around him, Mac grabbed his tray and mug, the crutch, and struggled to his feet. He didn't hurry to his cell, just walked at a casual pace, ignoring the looks and the jibes while trying to keep hold of what little dignity he could. He'd known it would be bad, but this took the piss. Cockroaches demanded more respect. Mind you, it could have been worse. If that elbow had been a shank . . .

His cell was worse than grim. Dirty walls scribbled with graffiti, a metal bed bolted to the floor, and a toilet that was a health inspector's dream. The plastic shaving mirror above the sink gave a warped reflection, like a fairground mirror. The toilet was positioned so he had a modicum of privacy when the screws slid back the inspection flap, although whether this was done for the benefit of the screws or the cons, Mac wasn't sure.

He'd only been on Houseblock Four for three hours, and already that was three hours too many. Before moving across from the hospital unit, the Governor had come to see the latest addition to his collection of monsters. He had introduced himself, and Mac got the distinct impression he didn't make a point of welcoming every new con. The governor was a tall man, permanently weary. He had a slight stoop, as though he'd been carrying the weight of the world far too long. Even his voice sounded worn out.

'Macintosh, a word of advice: do your time quietly and with the minimum of fuss, and we'll get on fine.'

'You're talking like I'm going to be here a while,' Mac replied. 'Like I've already been convicted. What happened to innocent until proven guilty?'

The Governor almost smiled. 'Looks like you're going to fit in just fine. Everyone in here is innocent. At least that's what they keep telling me. All a big misunderstanding, Your Honour, it was someone else what done it.' The almost-smile disappeared. 'Oh, and one more thing, Macintosh, just in case you're under any illusions: escaping from here is impossible. Even thinking about escaping is an exercise in futility.'

Mac had been welcomed on to Houseblock Four by Mr Grover, the head screw. He was a hard-looking bastard with a boxer's nose. Black, six-two, and as serious as a heart attack. His uniform was immaculate, giving the impression that this was someone who most definitely gave a shit. He gave Mac the pep talk, told him he'd no doubt work it out as he went along . . . most did. Mac reckoned Grover would be decent enough so long as you didn't cause trouble. Do that and he wouldn't think twice about using his retractable baton to carry out some cosmetic surgery.

'And Macintosh . . .' Grover was hovering by the door. 'I don't give a fuck who you are; don't give a fuck what you're supposed to have done. While you're here, you belong to me. Understand?'

'Yes, sir.'

'Glad we got that sorted out.' Grover turned and left, slamming the heavy door behind him.

Mac put the dinner tray and mug on the table then leant the crutch against the chair. He hadn't been hungry anyway. Out on the landing, he could still hear a few stray laughs being aimed in his direction. He stripped off the dirty overalls and laid down on the hard bed in his boxer shorts and T-shirt. Staring at the walls, Mac tried to tune out the noisy bang and rattle of the prison. It was impossible – Belmarsh infected all the senses. Time passed, the minutes crawling by. Mac got up and took a piss, then did a circuit of his cell to stretch his stiff limbs. He hobbled over to the tiny window and stared through the thick bars at the litter strewn exercise yard. Like an animal in a cage, he wanted to understand his new surroundings. He finished a second circuit and sat down on the bed. The mattress was flimsy and he didn't want to think about who'd used it before him. How *many* had used it. He bashed the pillow into shape and stretched out. Behind closed eyes, pain numbed with medication, he did his best to block out the grim reality of that tiny cell. He imagined himself floating on a perfect Caribbean sea. High above, birds swooped and dived, circled and called, crying out their freedom. A banging on the door and the daydream dissolved. Mac looked over and saw Grover peering through the slot.

'Up and dressed, Macintosh. You've got a visitor.'

22

'Give me some space, for Christ's sake.' Jem pushed back in her chair and put her hands up. 'You know, I could do this a lot quicker if everyone just left me alone for five seconds.'

'Someone got out of bed the wrong side,' Aston muttered.

Jem made a face and Aston fought the urge to throttle her. He was tired and headachy, and today was going to be a long one. They'd got the early flight from Rome, leaving at some ridiculous time of the morning, and come here straight from Heathrow. For the first five minutes Jem had been all smiles . . . now it was business as usual. She was going to have to watch her step today. He was sorely lacking in the patience department. 'How long's this going to take?' Aston said.

'It'll take as long as it takes,' she said. 'If you think you can do it any quicker, be my guest.'

Aston glanced at George, glanced at Priest. They were staying well out of it and he didn't blame them. Rightly or wrongly, Jem now thought of the upstairs room as hers. Her influence was everywhere, little territorial touches. From the chipped Simpsons coffee mug with the missing handle she used as a pen holder to the black and white erotic photos on the walls. Her first big change had been to fix the lighting, dim it down to the levels of a bad sci-fi movie. Aston had overheard her telling George how she loved the twilight feel of the place, loved the way night and day had no place here. What was it with computer experts and gloom? Were they all vampires? Was that it?

'What?' Jem asked, all suspicious. 'Why are you grinning?'

'I'm not grinning.'

'Yes you are. George, is he grinning?'

'Like a Cheshire Cat.'

She turned to Priest, who raised his hands and backed away. 'Don't bring me into this.'

'The picture,' Aston said. 'Can we please keep our minds on the job?'

Jem rolled up to the desk and began typing ferociously, her face tight with concentration. A still from Valerio's security video appeared on the middle monitor: grainy, black and white, the usual crap you'd expect from a cheap CCTV camera. She drew a box around the face on the screen and double-clicked to zoom in. The source material was nothing special, an abstract collection of black, white and grey shapes that had been thrown together loosely to resemble a face. It could have been anybody, male or female. Jem pulled down a menu from the top of the screen and selected a filter, which helped a little. A second filter removed the background.

'Okay,' Jem muttered, 'here's where the real fun begins. What I'm going to do now is get rid of all the extraneous detail so I can isolate the key anatomical points. I'm after the underlying bone structure.'

Aston watched in fascination as Jem systematically worked her way around the head, drawing boxes around each feature she wanted the computer to analyse: forehead, cheekbones, eyes, nose and chin. A couple of mouse clicks and a 3D wireframe representation of the assassin's skull appeared on the screen. Next, she began adding muscle and tissue, painting it on a layer at a time, slowly fleshing out the skull.

'Anthropologists use similar computer modelling software,' Jem explained. 'You must have seen the programs on Discovery where they're working on Egyptian mummies and the fragmented skulls of Neanderthals. It's so cool. They start off with a pile of bones, and before you know it, some ancient Egyptian princess has been brought back from the grave. Of course, the software we use is way better than theirs . . . don't you just love those unlimited Government budgets? I mean, do you really think that the NSA and CIA are going to be happy using the same software as the bearded hippies who present those shows? I don't think so.'

160

Once the skin was on, Jem took a moment to admire her handiwork. She pushed back in the chair, tilted her head to one side and studied the screen. Nodding pretentiously to herself, she rolled back to the desk. Aston had to smile – it was such an obvious display of showboating. For the final touch, Jem went back to the filtered CCTV image on the left-hand screen. She twirled the mouse and clicked. Within seconds the computer had analysed the various shades of grey, compared the result to a vast digital library of facial structures and colour permutations, and made an educated guess as to what each one represented. Another couple of clicks and the 3D head on the main screen burst into colour.

'Impressed or what?' Jem said.

'Yeah, I'm impressed,' Aston heard himself saying. He wasn't really aware he was talking. All that interested him was the face on the screen. It stared at him, taunting him. *Catch me if you can.* The confidence was more apparent than it had been in the original picture; if anything, the assassin looked even cockier. In 3D, he was practically sneering. This was someone who was under no illusions that the universe did indeed revolve around him. Physically, the assassin's face was unremarkable. No scars or distinguishing marks; neither handsome nor ugly. If you wanted to go into the killing business it was the perfect face. Mid-thirties, maybe younger, maybe older. His blond hair was designer mussed, fussed and teased into a mess. The software had given him hazel eyes.

'Beats the shit out of those old-fashioned Photofits you used to get on *Crimewatch*,' Priest said.

Aston had to admit that the SAS man had a point. Jem was twirling the mouse, changing the viewpoint – they could see the head from any angle they wanted. It really was quite remarkable.

'Definitely chemical blond,' said George.

'What makes you say that?' Priest asked.

'I'm a girl. I know these things. Jem, can you change the hair colour? I'm thinking brown.'

'No problem.'

From the corner of his eye, Aston caught the shy, quick smile. Looked like George had a fan club. A couple of clicks and Jem was done. The screen changed in an instant, and even Aston could see the result looked more natural.

'Not quite there yet,' said George, 'a little bit darker than that, please.'

They went through half a dozen shades of brown before George was satisfied.

'What about the hairstyle?' Jem asked.

'Something a little less trendy,' George said.

'That's what I was thinking.'

'What do you reckon? Short back and sides?'

'Give it a go.'

This took a little longer. Menus flashed up on the screen as Jem went to work. She had a couple of runs at it before they were happy. Aston got in closer for a better look. 'So this is our man,' he said.

'All well and good,' said Priest, 'but who the fuck is he?'

Aston and George turned together. They smiled at Jem.

'And for my next trick . . .' the computer expert said, and went to work.

23

Belmarsh Prison, last September

The interview room was a windowless concrete box with a wooden table bolted to the middle of the floor, and a couple of red moulded plastic chairs. There were cigarette burns on the table; black melt marks like scar tissue on the chairs. The man sitting opposite in the crumpled Oxfam suit looked like a cop. Smelled like one, too. A bald-headed bouncer wearing a sovereign ring any chav would be proud of. Mac had met enough bastards in his time to recognise one on sight.

'I'm Detective Superintendent Harry Fielding, and I'm with Scotland Yard's Anti-Terrorist Branch.'

A proclamation of intent rather than an introduction. Mac wasn't even remotely impressed. As for being intimidated – forget it. 'I want a lawyer.'

'I've already sent for one. While we wait for him to turn up, why don't you and me have a little chat?'

'Get me a lawyer, than maybe we can talk.'

Mac refused to say another word for the rest of the afternoon. Like he guessed, no lawyer had been called. Fielding tried bullying, tried cajoling. One second he was Mac's new best friend, the next he was ranting, the veins in his neck bursting, eyes popping. The detective could have saved his breath. What did he think was going to happen here? A tearful breakdown and a full confession? That'd be fucking right. Mac just sat there in his stained overalls, counting off the seconds and staring at the graffiti tattooed onto the table.

Fielding kept him until after dinner. Did it on purpose, too. At five-thirty the stink of school dinners wafted through the interview room. Mac could smell it, which meant the detective could smell it, too. His stomach grumbled. Although the detective's face didn't change, Mac could have sworn the fucker grinned. Fielding had no doubt heard what happened at lunch.

'We could stay here all night. Makes no difference to me.'

'Where's my lawyer?'

'On his way. He must be stuck in traffic.'

'For the last three hours?'

'You know how it is with the roads these days. Too many cars, not enough tarmac.'

Fielding stuck it out for another hour before calling it a day. A new shift, which meant a different escort on the journey back to his cell. The screw on his left was practically albino – the only thing missing were the red eyes. Mac had never seen skin that pale on anyone before . . . anyone with a pulse. According to the name badge, his surname was Carp. Edwards was on his right. He was built like a mountain, six feet two and not a single ounce of fat. There was a stink of steroids about him. Carp and Edwards weren't big on conversation. If they had a combined IQ that hit treble figures Mac would have been amazed.

His first night on Houseblock Four was horrendous. The only silver lining was that he had a cell to himself. Category A prisoners had very few privileges, but that was one. He'd also been given some heavy-duty painkillers. Mac was under no illusion whose benefit that was for. The more compliant the cons were, the better. On the whole, the screws were looking for an easy life. Mac lay there with his hands behind his head, staring at the ceiling and trying to ignore the wailing from a couple of cells down. Not easy. The wailer had wound himself up into a right state. Crying, ranting, sobbing his little heart out. People were telling him to shut the fuck up, disembodied voices floating in from all points of the block. Someone piped up and told him that if he didn't shut the fuck up he was going to get his motherfucking throat slit. Someone else started up with some pretend wailing, and before long there was a whole discordant choir going at it. This was the sound of madness. The wailer ignored them all, kept right on sobbing deep into the night. Mac had no idea what time he eventually fell silent – one o'clock, maybe two. His Tag Carrera had mysteriously vanished. That night was long and hard. Even after the wailer shut up, it was still noisy. There were almost two hundred cons on the block, snoring and farting, tossing and turning. Then there was the constant sound of the prison breathing all around him. It was like trying to sleep in a hospital. Too many distractions. Mac lay there on that hard mattress with the prison screaming all around him and waited for morning, knowing what he had to do and not looking forward to it one bit.

Knowing he had no option.

24

Two hours in, and all George was getting for her troubles was eye strain. They'd tried MI6's database first. Nothing. Jem had grinned wickedly as she let herself into Scotland Yard's computer system via the deputy commissioner's account. The username and password had came from a secretary who was on Six's payroll. Unfortunately, Scotland Yard were unable to help. Playing the long shot, George had settled down at another machine and gone through the FBI's Ten Most Wanted. The long shot didn't pay off. Jem saw she had the FBI website up on screen and rolled across. Their chairs bumped together.

'Shove over,' she said. 'Let me show you how it's done.'

Jem was so close their legs were practically touching. Without making it obvious, George pushed her chair an inch to the side. The computer expert's eyes were glued to the screen, fingers tapping. Jem was suddenly oblivious to the rest of the world, and George was reminded of Mole. She had that same focus, that same intensity. Jem had slipped into a Matrix-like world of dripping green numbers and symbols, and nothing else mattered.

'There we go,' she was saying. 'We're in. Piece of piss, really.'

'Yeah,' George said distantly.

The computer expert spun her chair around. 'You okay?' she asked.

'I'm fine.'

'Thinking about what happened in Rome?'

'No,' George said, a little too quickly.

Jem looked at her for a moment, then went on, 'Okay, I've sent the pic to the FBI's computer. Let's see what they have to say on the subject.' She hit enter and the screen split in two. The enhanced photo taken from the video was on the right; on the left, pictures flashed past in a blur of noses, mouths, eyes and hairstyles as the computer searched for a match.

'You know,' Jem said, 'if you need someone to talk to, I'm a good listener. I'm not saying you do, but . . .'

'Thanks, but I really am fine,' said George, uncertain who she was trying to convince.

Jem leant over and squeezed her arm, then wheeled back to her own workstation.

It was Interpol who eventually came up with the goods. The computer's eye was better than hers, George thought. If she squinted she could see the resemblance, but it was like one of those puzzles where you had to stare at the dots until your eyes watered before you got it. All four of them were crowded around Jem's computer. The face on the screen was another monochrome still originating from a CCTV camera.

'Are you sure this is our man?' Paul was saying.

'The computer says it's ninety per cent certain,' Jem said.

'Only ninety per cent?' said Priest.

Before anyone could stop her, Jem launched into an explanation on how face recognition software worked. She made it sound simple, until George listened to the actual words and realised the computer expert was speaking a foreign language. From what little George understood, the computer analysed the face and turned it into a string of numbers. Once the computer had created a mathematical description of the face it ran this through the database and played the percentage game. According to Jem, ninety per cent was as good as it got.

'So who is he?' Paul said. 'And why is Interpol so interested in him?'

'One second.' Jem pulled up the relevant files and rolled out the way to let George and Paul in.

Interpol had a name – Luke Sanderson – but George would have bet that was an alias. Sanderson, or whatever his real name was, probably had a ton of passports. Different names, different countries. The Interpol records dated back to the late Nineties and the Sanderson legend would be long buried by now. Interpol wanted him in connection with a hit in Munich. The target was a Colombian druglord called José Sanchez. His death was no great loss to anyone. Unknown to Sanderson, the German police had Sanchez under surveillance from the minute his Learjet touched down in Munich. Interpol had got a tip-off that Sanchez was putting together a hundred million dollar deal and they'd been following him as he toured Europe, trying to work out where the shipments were going to come in. The hit was made from an empty office five hundred yards away. The bullet had drilled into Sanchez's chest and shredded his heart. The druglord was dead before he hit the pavement. By the time the police reached the office, the assassin was long gone. They had one piece of luck, though. A secretary working in a solicitor's office opposite had seen a man go in carrying a large case, and come out again thirty seconds after Sanchez was shot. With typical German efficiency, the police had the poor secretary going through airport security camera footage for almost a fortnight before she ID'd the gunman. Two days before the hit, Sanderson had arrived at Hanover airport on a flight from Amsterdam. They never discovered the flight he went out on. He was either travelling under a different name, a different face, or he'd driven to a neighbouring country and flown from there. Interpol had left the investigation open, but nothing had been heard from Sanderson for almost a decade. Until now.

Jem's screens suddenly flashed red and the sound of an old World War II air-raid siren blasted from the speakers. Instinctively, George looked over at the door, half expecting to see an army of masked terrorists come bursting in.

'What?' Paul said, the panic evident in his voice. 'What's wrong?'

Jem swivelled the chair around and burst out laughing. 'You should see your faces,' she said.

'What's the alarm for?'

Jem nodded to The Cube. 'The Chief wants a word.'

25

Belmarsh Prison, last September

Eight-thirty came and went, and the door remained stubbornly closed. The banging and jeering started almost immediately, intensifying quickly as more and more cons joined in. The cacophony was enormous and all-consuming, anger and hatred pouring from the cells. It was as if a valve had opened and high pressure steam was hissing out.

'Hey cripple!' A sharp Liverpudlian voice cut through the din and Mac tried to pinpoint where it came from.

'Hey! Down here!'

Heating pipes passed through the cells, and there was a small gap where they went through the wall. The gap was no bigger than the width of a little fingertip – large enough to pass wraps of drugs, notes, and whispered messages. This was Belmarsh's version of the Web. Mac knelt down. 'What?' he shouted into the gap.

'Ball's topped himself. Pass it on.'

'Who's Ball?'

'Just pass the fucking message on!'

Mac followed the heating pipe to the opposite wall. 'Hey! Ball's topped himself,' he shouted through the gap, not caring if anyone heard or not. He'd done his bit.

The noise reduced by degrees as the news filtered through the block. And then silence. It was hard to believe two hundred men could be so quiet.

Mac's door finally opened an hour later. As he passed Ball's cell he noticed the lingering smell of disinfectant and caught sight of the bare mattress. The cell had already been cleared. There were no books, no clothes, no pictures. It was as if Ball had never existed. Mac hobbled to the end of the breakfast queue, his tray tucked under one arm. He leant on his crutch and tried to look even more pathetic than he had yesterday. And like yesterday, the other cons kept pushing in front. Today his existence was recognised. There were quite a few 'wankers', one or two 'motherfuckers'. And from his Liverpudlian neighbour, a whole sentence, hissed and full of gangster menace: 'Okay, cunt, I tell you to pass on a message, you just do it! No arguments! Got it?' Mac ignored them all. He was more interested in the two groups at the front of the queue.

Playing it casual, Mac checked out the main players. The first group was led by a small man with white hair who was in his mid-forties, fifty at a push. Snowy looked like he'd just stepped out of a gentleman's club. Clothes pressed just so, not a single hair out of place. He didn't look particularly dangerous, but looks could be deceptive. He was right at the top of the tree, and he hadn't got there through charm and hard work.

Bluto, in charge of the second group, was the polar opposite of Snowy. Six foot tall and six foot wide, he had the overdeveloped muscles so many cons had. The sleeves of his shirt had been crudely hacked away to show off his tattoos: the multicoloured full sleeve covering his right arm, and the red and gold serpent snaking down his left. Bluto was a thug who'd sell his own mother for a rock. Mac's assessment of the situation was that there was a major power struggle going on here. Bluto was waiting in the wings just gagging for an opportunity to take Snowy down. Play this right and his time would go easy; get it wrong and he'd be a dead man. Snowy was first in line, a flunky holding his tray while he pointed out what he wanted. It looked like he was choosing chocolates at Fortnum and Mason. Bluto and his cronies were behind Snowy's entourage, keeping a respectful distance.

Mac did a surreptitious 360, noting where the screws were. He hoped they were halfway competent. He wasn't getting any younger and, as he'd discovered lately, he didn't heal as quickly any more. This was going to hurt – of that he had no doubt – he just wanted to minimise the hurt as much as possible. The nearest screw was over by the wall, roughly ten strides away. Mac estimated he could reach him in a couple of seconds. Unfortunately, he would want back-up. The screws never went one-on-one against the cons. Snowy breezed past without so much as a glance in his direction. Mac kept his gaze down. Absolutely no eye contact. He could sense the flunkies checking him out, but he just kept staring at the scuffed linoleum.

The last of Bluto's crew got served, and the group started towards him, the big man leading the way, sharing a joke and a grin with the syco-phant on his left. This was it. Mac focused on keeping his breathing easy, his muscles loose. Projecting an aura of complete defeat, he stared at that piece of lino as though it was the most interesting thing he'd ever seen. He was looking for a Hangman's Fracture – smash that C2 verte-brae and you either end up disabled or dead. Bluto was only a dozen steps away, ten steps, eight. Timing was everything. Another easy breath, and all Mac could hear was the dull echo of Bluto's feet. Out of the corner of his eye he watched Bluto getting closer, closer, closer. At the last moment, Mac dropped his tray and flipped the crutch over. He swung like a baseball player, giving it all he had, going for a home run and wanting to knock that ball right out the park. The head of the crutch hit Bluto square in the face, the force of the blow rattling through Mac's arms and down into his legs. He swung again, smashing the crutch under his jaw. Bluto sank to his knees and tipped forward, his forehead cracking against the lino. Mac stamped on the back of his neck with his good leg, stamped as hard as he could, putting all his weight into it. He stamped again and, in his mind's eye, saw the vertebrae overextending, saw them popping and separating. Saw the fragile spinal cord snapping.

A millisecond of stillness, then everyone was shouting and moving all at once. Bluto's cronies were on Mac in an instant. He dropped to the floor and curled into a ball, his bad leg trailing behind. The first kick caught him in the small of the back, the second and third took the wind out of him. By the fourth the pain had taken on a surreal, detached quality. He brought his arms in tight to protect his face. Where the fuck were the screws? An alarm went off, distant and muffled. Mac felt the darkness closing around him, greying the edges; voices turned into faraway whispers from the bottom of a mineshaft. The blows were coming fast and furious now. And still no screws. Where the fuck were they! His beautiful Sophia appeared out of the darkness, alive and healthy and smiling that strange little half-smile. She was dressed in her blue silk wedding dress, a tiara of wild flowers wound into her long, golden hair. Sophia held out her arms and Mac went to her.

26

There were mountains of grey foam above his head, mountains of foam on the walls, more mountains below his feet. Aston checked his watch – again – and wondered if the hands were going backwards. Heath said it was urgent so where the hell was he? His heart rate was almost back to normal after being shocked to twice its normal speed by Jem's war siren. 'Bloody hackers! Why can't they grow up?'

'I'm guessing it's something to do with their DNA.' George's voice sounded eerie and still, the words dying the second they left her lips.

'You know, she reminds me so much of Mole sometimes. Should we be worried?'

'Of course we should.' A small cynical laugh. 'After all, that's what we're paid for. Remember the mantra: trust no-one.'

'Any idea how paranoid that sounds?'

'Any idea how paranoid *you* sound?'

Aston shook his head. 'With Mole, we should have seen that one coming a mile off. If only—'

'If only what, Paul? He always seemed harmless enough to me. Anyway, she's not going to do a Mole. No way.'

'Yeah, you're right. Paranoid with a big old capital "P", eh?'

'You said it.' George gave him an indulgent what-am-I-going-to-do-with-you smile. 'I do worry about her, though.'

'Why?'

She hesitated, looking for the right words. 'Because she's so young. I'm not talking actual years. In some respects she acts older than she is, but in other ways she's still just a kid. She seems to think this is all a video game or a film or something, and that's what worries me, Paul. I don't think she understands how dangerous this business is.' George paused. 'Maybe I'm being unfair. I mean, with Rome she did really well. Did everything right.'

'Yeah, she did good,' Aston agreed.

'Fascinating though this is, I'm a busy man.' The disembodied robot voice floated down from the ceiling.

Aston looked at George. How long had Heath been listening in? 'Sorry, sir,' he said. George mumbled an apology of her own. They went through the same security protocol as before and The Chief gave all the right answers.

'With regards to your new colleague, I can assure you he's completely trustworthy. I understand how the events of last September might

179

make you question things, but there's nothing to be concerned about there. I can vouch for him personally.'

Reading between the lines, Priest had probably served under Heath at some point. That would make sense. Aston made a mental note to find out what the connection was. 'Why didn't you tell us about him?'

'Need to know,' Heath replied, opting for that age old Six cop-out.

Aston took a deep breath and blurted out the question that had been bugging him since he got back from Rome. 'Why did you have him shadow us in the first place? If you thought we were in danger, you should have warned us.'

'I sent him along as insurance.' The words were terse, delivered with cold computer efficiency. 'Good job I did. Your reception in Rome was as much a surprise to me as it was to you. If I'd known anything, then of course I would have told you. Okay,' he added, 'why don't you fill me in on what happened?'

Aston did all the talking. Throughout the debriefing he stuck to the facts, neither sensationalising nor trivialising. Heath interrupted occasionally to ask lawyerly questions, clarifying the facts, getting him to retrace until he was satisfied.

'Well, I'm glad you're both in one piece,' he said when Aston finished. 'None the worse for wear, I hope.'

'We'll live,' Aston said.

'Good.' There was a pause, the silence in The Cube absolute and unnerving due to the unnatural acoustics. 'I've got another death I need you to look into.'

'Another murder?'

'This one was a heart attack, allegedly.'

'Allegedly?' George said.

'The last time I saw the deceased – which was only a couple of days ago – he seemed healthy enough. Also, he worked for us.'

Aston sensed there was more. 'And?' he prompted.

'This is what really set the alarm bells ringing,' said Heath. 'Back in the Eighties, he worked with our friend from Rome.'

27

Aston wheeled a seat up next to Jem. 'Okay, what have we got?'

'The dead guy's called Bernie Jones,' Jem said, passing around the printouts.

Aston whistled softly. Jones was the Director of Production, a very big fish indeed. The customers – the government, military, whoever – decided what they wanted MI6 to find out for them. This shopping list was then passed down to the D/PR, who was responsible for ensuring the controllerates came up with the goods. The production targets defined each controllerate's *raison d'être*. Bernie Jones had only been a couple of rungs down from The Chief.

'Jesus,' said George. 'And someone's murdered him.'

'Allegedly,' Aston reminded everyone.

'The pathologist thinks it was a heart attack,' Jem said. 'Turn to page eight. That's where you'll find the autopsy report.'

Aston flicked through the pages and speed-read the report. There it was, in the cause of death box: Myocardial Infarction.

'You said "murdered".' Priest was leaning against the edge of Jem's desk. 'Heath doesn't think this is natural causes?'

'No,' George answered. 'There's a connection between Hathaway and Jones.'

'A connection?'

'Page twelve,' Jem said. 'It's all in there.'

Aston looked at Jem. She didn't have a printout and wasn't looking at her screen. The computer expert was remembering all this from memory.

'What?' said Jem. 'So, I've got a photographic memory. It's no big deal. Useful for exams and party tricks, but that's about it.'

'You never thought to mention this earlier?'

'You never asked.'

Touché.

'The pathologist is convinced it was a heart attack,' George said, looking up from the printout. 'So, the big question is: how do you engineer a heart attack and make it look natural.'

'You could scare someone to death,' Jem suggested. 'I saw that in a film once.'

'I can't really see our killer going around in a *Scream* mask,' Aston said. 'Any other ideas? Anyone?'

'Well,' Priest said. 'There is one way.'

'Go on,' George said.

'Adrenaline,' he said.

'What about it?'

'Too much and you'll overload the heart. It's produced naturally in the body, making it a perfect assassination weapon. Better than any poison.'

'But how do you make the body produce too much adrenaline?'

'You don't have to,' Jem said, and all heads turned towards her. 'Remember in *Pulp Fiction* when Uma Thurman ODs on coke and Travolta sticks that huge needle through her chest. That was adrenaline, wasn't it?'

'It was,' Priest said, 'but you don't need a huge needle. You can get small self-administering syringes of adrenaline for treating anaphylactic shock. The delivery device is spring-loaded, like the sort diabetics use. Administered correctly it's a lifesaver; hit a vein and it'll kill you. If you're trying to murder someone, and you don't want anyone to know, then the best place to inject is the scalp. Lots of veins up there. Also, something like forty per cent of your blood supply goes up to your head. From there it's a short trip back to the heart and BANG! A pathologist will take one look and see a heart attack. And that's what they'll write on the form. It's unlikely they're going to go searching the scalp for needle marks.'

The other three just stared at him.

'Is that what they teach you in the SAS?' George said eventually. 'You know, a hundred and one ways to take somebody out without anyone noticing?'

'Actually, I learnt that one on a First Aid course.'

'Yeah, right.'

'I'm serious.'

'Okay, people,' Aston said. 'Let's get back on track. We're all agreed that in theory this is possible.' He waited for nods all round. 'So, what we've got to do now is work out if that's what actually happened here. Which means we need to contact the pathologist and get him to take another look at Jones's body. Jem, can you pull up the details?'

'Way ahead of you,' Jem said, hammering the keyboard. 'Right, it's actually a her, not a him. Dr Belinda Meyer.'

'Print it out.' Aston was already on his feet.

'Are we going somewhere?' George asked.

'Yeah, I think we should have a word with Dr Meyer. See what she has to say on the subject.'

'Sounds like a plan.' George got up and plucked the printout from Jem's outstretched hand. 'Okay, let's go.'

28

Belmarsh Prison, last September

Mac clawed his way back to consciousness inch by precarious inch. Darkness gave way to grey, and was finally replaced by dazzling brightness. Slowly and carefully, he did a condition check. He could wiggle his fingers and toes, move his arms and legs. This was the best news he'd had in a while. His biggest fear was that he'd end up in a wheelchair. Nothing was broken; somehow his fucked-up knee had escaped getting any more fucked-up; in time, the bruises would fade and the swelling would go down. The beating had been bad – worse than he'd imagined – but, all in all, he reckoned he'd got off lightly.

There were no mod cons in the Hole: a bed and a toilet, a rickety wooden table with a single rickety wooden chair slotted underneath. That was it. There wasn't even any bedding. No pillows, no blankets. The screws had even taken the wafer-thin mattress. No way were you going to sleep your time away. Mac hoped they remembered to give the bedding back later. The walls had been white once. Now they were a dull grey and covered with shit streaks that had only been half-heartedly scrubbed off. Illuminating the cell was the brightest light he had ever seen, one thousand watts of pure glare.

The Hole was grim, but it had to be. Belmarsh was short on hope; however, there were degrees of hopelessness. Day-to-day life on the block was a grind, and then you ended up here and discovered the block was a party in comparison. When you were sitting in your cell at the start of a twenty stretch, you looked into the future and saw those years spiralling into the distance; from that perspective it was easy to say fuck it, let's cause a little mayhem. When you'd had everything taken away what did you have to lose? What were they going to do if you had a bad day and decided to stick one of the screws? Hit you with another life sentence? The Hole was a reminder that, yeah, things were bad, but they could be a hell of a lot worse.

Mac wasn't complaining. As he looked around, he wondered if anyone else had ever conspired to get here. He reckoned he could stand a month. That would be long enough to start getting fit again. If he could get physically fit then he stood a chance of surviving Belmarsh. He glanced at the space on his wrist where the Tag had been. Keeping track of time in solitary would be tricky without a watch. He laid down on the hard slats of the bed, hands behind his head, and stared at the door. Five minutes, ten minutes, an hour later – it was difficult to say – the hatch clunked open and a pair of dark eyes peered in, the whites glowing.

'Welcome back to the land of the living, Macintosh.' The voice was flat, the only distinguishing characteristic a nasal West Country twang.

Mac squinted through the glare. 'Any chance of doing something about these lights?'

''fraid not. You're on suicide watch. The light stays on 24/7.'

'You're joking, right?'

'Do you hear me laughing?'

'I'm not suicidal.'

'The Governor reckons you have a death wish, so the light stays on.'

'And that's based on . . . ?'

'Well, you took on Booth. You can file that under suicidal.'

Mac made a mental note of the name. Getting his health back was only part of the game. He needed information, as much information as he could get his hands on. 'How is Booth?'

Dark Eyes blinked, the whites disappearing then reappearing, and said nothing.

'Need to know, I suppose.'

'What?'

Mac could sense the puzzlement. Dark Eyes obviously wasn't the sharpest. 'How long am I here for?'

'No idea. You've got a hearing with the Governor tomorrow. Ten o'clock,' he added unhelpfully. The hatch slammed shut. Conversation over.

After lunch Mac was taken to meet Fielding. The screws didn't trust him with the crutch any more, so it was slow going. Solitary cells lined the corridor, a dozen on each side. Most were quiet. In others he heard the occupants talking to themselves. The guy in the end cell was doing all the different voices – it sounded like he was having a party in there.

The interview room was as grim as his cell, even pokier than the one they'd been in yesterday. Fielding sat on the other side of the wooden table wearing the same navy blue charity shop suit. The top shirt button was undone and his tie hung low; the jacket was slung carelessly over the back of the chair. There was a camera on a tripod to his left, positioned to capture Mac's battered face in all its glory.

'You're looking well.'

'Where's my lawyer?'

'He'll be here in a minute.'

Mac raised an eyebrow. 'Stuck in traffic, I suppose.'

The lawyer turned up five minutes later. Flustered and rushed and red-faced. He was slight and ineffectual, a child who'd been out of law school for all of two seconds. One strong gust of wind and you'd never see him again. Mac looked at him, looked at Fielding.

'You have got to be taking the piss.'

The detective just smiled.

'I'd like a moment of lawyer/client confidentiality. If that's okay with you.'

'Fine with me.'

Fielding made a big deal of turning off the video camera, then left. Before Mac spoke, he got up and turned the camera off.

'Have you got a pad and pen?'

The kid lawyer riffled through his briefcase and came up with the goods. He was all fingers and thumbs as he passed them over. 'So, shall we get started?' he asked in a vain attempt to feign competence.

'Started?' Mac said. 'We're finished.'

'I don't understand.'

'It's simple.' Mac scribbled down a name and tore the top sheet from the pad. He folded it in half and handed it over. 'I'm in deep shit here. What I need is a proper lawyer. Here's his name. You'll find his number in the *Yellow Pages*.'

Fielding spent the rest of that afternoon asking questions. He looked like a bulldog, acted like one, too. The detective was one tenacious bastard. He wanted to know everything. Who Mac was working for. Who he was working with. Where he got the C4 from. Mac told him nothing.

The hearing the next morning was a complete farce. Mac was strip-searched and cuffed and taken to the adjudication room. Flanked by a couple of screws, he hobbled inside and took up position behind the yellow line. Six feet in front of the line was a desk. The Governor sat at the desk looking even more worn than when Mac first met him. Sitting, his stoop had become a pronounced hunch. He picked up a sheet of paper and read it to himself. When he finished, he glanced over the top and shot Mac a disapproving look.

'Prisoner give your name and number,' the screw on his left said.

'Robert Macintosh.' A shrug. 'Sorry I don't know my number.'

'Number 472392,' the screw on the right added.

Mac repeated the number softly to himself, memorising it, and the screw on the left told him to shut up and only speak when spoken to.

In a bland, bored voice the Governor read the charges. Mac didn't listen, just pleaded guilty in the pauses. Kangaroo court justice. He had been pronounced guilty long before he took up position behind the yellow line. There was an assault charge in there somewhere. No murder or attempted murder, though. Examining the available evidence, it looked like Booth was alive. Not good.

'Twenty-one days cellular confinement. All privileges revoked,' the Governor said. It wasn't the four weeks Mac had hoped for, but it would do.

'Is there anything the prisoner wishes to say?' the Governor added. His tone suggested that even if there was, he wouldn't be listening.

'I don't suppose there's any chance of getting my watch back?'

29

The smell of chemicals was horrendous, the lights so bright they were threatening to turn Aston's niggling headache into a full-blown migraine. He supposed they needed the lights on full to keep the ghosts away. It wasn't working. If anything, all that brightness just made the place more creepy. How the hell could anybody work somewhere like this? He looked over at George. She was looking a little green. On the way here, he'd bet a tenner she'd throw up first. Gallows humour . . . he hadn't been looking forward to this any more than she had. The sooner they got back into the world of the living, the better.

Dr Meyer was on the other side of the big window, surrounded by stainless steel. Aston could imagine how bad it smelled in there, and was glad there was a layer of glass between them. Meyer didn't seem to mind the smell or the lights. She was around five foot two and in her late forties. Olive skin, brown eyes and clever hands. Her movements were economical and precise, as though she planned everything well in advance. She was working on a man of about sixty who had skin the colour of old marble. Overweight and with a sheet covering his genitals, he lay stranded on the steel table like a beached whale. Aston wanted to look away, but that car crash curiosity had got the better of him again. Meyer was wielding a huge needle, sewing up the 'Y' incision with big black kisses. She finished the last stitch and cut the thread, snapped off her gloves and smiled at a job well done. That smile was the creepiest thing Aston had seen since he got here, which was saying something.

Dr Meyer pushed through the doors and walked over with her hand outstretched. A chemical cloud surrounded her: soap, disinfectant, and another smell Aston couldn't place but guessed might be formaldehyde. He shook her hand without hesitation, grimacing inwardly. He'd just seen that hand delving into a dead man's abdominal cavity.

'Thanks for seeing us at such short notice Dr Meyer.' Aston held out DI Bromley's ID card and let her have a good look. Like all passport photos, the thumbnail picture made him look like a criminal. Their ID cards had got them this far without any fuss, which was no great surprise. Central Resources got the cards from the same place as Scotland Yard. This was as good as the real thing, because it was the real thing. George was only a

Detective Sergeant, which pissed her off no end. 'This is my colleague, DS Sullivan,' Aston added.

George gave her best smile and shook Dr Meyer's hand.

'How can I help?'

Dr Meyer's voice was surprisingly warm and friendly. Aston had been expecting her to sound like the Snow Queen. 'We need to ask a few questions about an autopsy you carried out recently.'

'Fire away. I'll need a name, and any other details you've got.'

'Bernard Jones. White male. Fifty-three years old.'

'Oh, I remember that one. I did it yesterday.'

George glanced at Aston, eyebrows raised. This was a good sign. For Meyer to remember one particular autopsy out of the hundreds she performed there must be a good reason. 'Why was that?'

'He'd been fast-tracked. Someone upstairs was anxious to get the results. I couldn't understand why. It was a straightforward MI. I couldn't see what the fuss was about. If you don't mind me asking: what's Scotland Yard's interest here?'

In his best police-speak, Aston said, 'We've got reason to believe that it might not be as straightforward as it appears.'

'You think he was murdered?'

'Yes.'

'Impossible. I know a heart attack when I see one, detective.'

'Did you check the scalp for syringe marks?'

'Why would I?'

Aston paused and composed himself. 'We believe he may have been given an overdose of adrenaline.'

Dr Meyer fell silent for a moment. When she finally spoke Aston thought he detected a hint of the Snow Queen there. 'If that's the case, why did no-one mention this earlier?'

'The information has just come to light.'

'Who exactly is this Mr Jones? And why do I feel like I'm only getting half the story here?'

Going down this avenue wasn't going to help. 'We need you to take another look at Mr Jones's body,' Aston said, steering the conversation back on track.

'That could be a problem. I've already released it.'

Shit, Aston almost said. 'So the body's not here?'

'If you're lucky it hasn't been picked up yet. Let me check.' Meyer walked off without another word.

George shrugged at Aston. 'What now?' she whispered. 'Do we go after her or what?'

'Well, she didn't say not to,' Aston whispered back.

They followed Dr Meyer down a corridor and into a room that was filled with more of that bright dazzle. Aston wished he'd brought sunglasses. And a jumper – it was bloody freezing in here. One entire wall was taken up with metal drawers, and

195

there was an orderly sitting with his feet on the desk reading *The Sun*. The orderly snapped the newspaper shut and jumped to attention when he saw Meyer. He was a couple of years off retirement, counting the hours and minutes. Aston half expected Meyer to start pulling drawers open at random until she found Jones's body. Thankfully she didn't.

'Has Bernard Jones's body been picked up yet?' she asked.

'A half hour ago.'

'Damn,' she muttered.

'What?' The orderly looked suddenly panicked. 'Have I done something wrong?'

'No, Pete, you haven't done anything wrong.' Meyer turned to Aston and George. 'Leave this with me. I'll contact the funeral home and get the body returned. Now I know what I'm looking for I stand a better chance of finding something.'

Aston ignored the dig and reeled off his mobile number. If Meyer went straight to Scotland Yard she would discover DI Bromley didn't exist, and that would raise some uncomfortable questions. 'I'd appreciate it if you could get back to me as soon as possible. I don't need to tell you that every minute counts in a murder investigation.'

'I'll do my best.'

'I'm sure you will.' Aston gave a practised smile. 'Thanks for your help, Dr Meyer.'

30

Belmarsh Prison, last September

Charles Wainwright was waiting for Mac in the interview room the next afternoon. He was a large man who wore his success like an aura. Expensive suit and shoes, expensive teeth. A Rolex Submariner peeked out from under the cuff of his silk shirt; the light caught it, reflecting sparkles of gold, silver and blue. Wainwright had a perfectly sculpted bouffant of hair so white there was no way the colour could be natural. When Mac came in, he stood and put his hand out. Mac immediately saw where he was going and was happy to play along. He held up his cuffed hands.

'Get these handcuffs off my client! Now!'

Moses himself couldn't have put on a better display of righteous indignation. The screw who'd brought Mac up from the Hole fumbled for his keys, almost dropping them in his hurry. The cuffs were off in less than a second. Fielding watched this performance with a bemused expression. The screw left and Wainwright turned to the detective.

'I need some alone time with my client,' he said. 'Two ways we can play this. Either we argue about it for the next half hour, and then you leave. Or you leave right now and save us all a lot of heartache.'

Fielding left without a word of argument, and Mac was almost impressed. Wainwright was obviously a complete bastard. Better still, he was his bastard.

'I don't care whether you're guilty or not,' Wainwright said as soon as the door swung shut. 'All I care about is getting paid.'

'You'll get your money,' Mac assured him.

They spent ten minutes haggling over the financial details. Wainwright wanted payment in advance, which was understandable. Most of his clients ended up being found guilty. When you were sitting in a cell looking at a bill that had a telephone number total at the bottom there was a strong temptation not to pay up. The fact that some of Wainwright's clients walked free – and most ended up with greatly reduced sentences – was nothing short of a miracle. Innocent men did not call Charles Wainwright.

'What have you told Fielding?'

'Nothing. Not even my name, rank and serial number.'

'Good. Let's keep it that way. From here on you're pleading the fifth, got that?'

'This isn't America.'

'Ten out of ten for observation, Robert, but you're still going to plead the fifth. I don't want you saying a single word. Okay?'

'Okay.'

'Fielding will try to bully you into a confession. Whatever happens, don't let him rattle you. Can you do that?'

'Yeah, I can do that.'

A digital camera appeared in Wainwright's hand, conjured up from nowhere. The lawyer's grin was filled with shiny white teeth. 'Okay let's get some pictures of those bruises. Just in case there's an opportunity to sue someone.'

The lawyer took pictures of Mac's face from all angles. He even had him strip to the waist for some body shots. Wainwright was someone who covered all the bases. Mac approved. The camera disappeared and Fielding was called back in. For the rest of that afternoon Mac sat in silence watching the second hand of Wainwright's Rolex go around and around, while Fielding got himself more and more wound up. Question after question, and Mac ignored them all. The detective had a pretty good handle on what had happened, a ton of evidence, too. A confession signed in blood would have sealed the deal.

It didn't take long for Mac to slip into a routine. Even with the lights burning day and night, there were ways to track time in the Hole. Meals were a good indicator. Breakfast, so it was between eight and nine. Lunch, therefore it had to be early afternoon. Dinner . . . must be around sixish. Then there were the daily visits from Fielding.

Each day after lunch Mac was brought to the interview room. Wainwright would be there and the drama would play out the same way. Fielding would go through his list of questions, and Mac would blank him. Every now and again Wainwright would raise an objection, but that was more to remind everyone he was still in the room than anything else. Mac wasn't getting rattled; he was more than holding his own; it was unlikely he was going to break down and confess. Wainwright let this go on for a week then started making noises, accusing Fielding of harassment. The detective didn't turn up the next day. Nor the day after. Mac almost missed Fielding's visits. They had helped break the day up.

After three weeks in the Hole, Mac was in much better shape than when he arrived. He was getting three square meals a day; he was exercising regularly; the DIY physiotherapy on his busted knee was starting to pay dividends. Most importantly, he had the time and space to get his head straight.

Mac didn't know what to expect when he got back on to Houseblock four, what sort of shitstorm he'd be walking in to. He hadn't killed Booth, but he had managed to hurt him. He hoped he'd hurt him enough. Mac had tried to get information from the screws, and been met with a conspiracy of silence – they'd obviously put their heads together and decided to make him suffer. Mac had asked Wainwright to find out what was happening. All the lawyer could tell him was that Booth had been taken to the hospital wing – after that nothing. Maybe he'd been moved to another prison, maybe he hadn't. It wasn't much to go on.

His escort appeared after breakfast, and Mac asked for a crutch. The request was met with stony silence. The journey back to the block was a slow one. Mac put on a good show, making his knee look a lot worse than it was. His cell had been tossed. What the hell had they expected to find? Drugs, guns, explosives? He'd come in with nothing, and hadn't exactly had much of an opportunity to acquire anything. He'd just got settled when Grover's face appeared in the hatch.

'Good morning Macintosh.'

'Morning Mr Grover.'

'I trust you'll think twice before pulling a stunt like that again.'

'Don't worry. You'll hardly know I'm here.'

'Make sure that's the case.'

The hatch slammed shut and Mac was alone again. Mid-morning, the door opened and he was allowed onto the exercise yard. Getting outside involved a pat-down and a trip through the metal detector. Early October sunshine filled the grim scrap of a yard, doing its best to bring a touch of optimism to the proceedings and failing miserably. Standing there for a moment with his face turned up to the sun, languishing in the cool heat and imagining he was free, it occurred to him this might be his last day on the planet. Mac walked through the yard, aware that all eyes were on him. Everyone was avoiding him; nobody approached. Something had changed, though, he could sense it in the air. The other cons were now keeping a respectful distance. Mac found a quiet corner and waited.

Two enforcers came for him about fifteen minutes later. Tattooed man mountains. Mac couldn't remember if they'd been part of Booth's crew or Snowy's. He looked around for the two main players. Couldn't see either of them. Standing his ground, he tried to appear relaxed. Someone else's skin, someone else's shoes. He was Brando in *The Godfather*, a God walking amongst men. Mac felt himself grow bigger. If he was going down, he was going down standing tall. No way would he beg or cower.

The enforcers closed in and Mac was reminded of those Westerns he loved as a kid. Everyone watching, but nobody looking. *High Noon*. He could almost see the dusty clapboard buildings lining Main Street, the undertaker skulking in the shadows. The enforcers stopped a couple of feet away, far enough so he couldn't stick them with a shank. These were men who had dished out more than their share of violence. They were both over six foot tall, the smaller around six-two. Despite the chill they wore cut-off T-shirts – the overdeveloped muscles and untidy prison tattoos belonged in a freak show. The smaller one had the smooth shiny stitching of a knife scar across his left cheek; it stopped an inch below his eye. The larger one did all the talking. A whole sentence. He opened his mouth to speak, and Mac felt as if he was in the dock waiting for the jury to deliver its verdict.

Guilty or innocent?

Booth or Snowy?

'Mr Harris wants to speak to you,' he said.

Mac didn't react to this news, not so much as a sigh or a twitch.

31

The company car was a disappointment. A bog-standard 1.6 litre silver Ford Focus with no bells and very few whistles. Bond wouldn't have been seen dead in one. They'd tossed a coin to see who would drive. This time Aston had used his own coin, and he'd insisted on tossing it. Of course, George won. George hated his driving, something she never tired of telling him. So, he liked driving fast. Why should that be a problem?

'What if Meyer can't get the body back?' Jem asked. The call was on handsfree and her voice had a thin AM radio quality to it. 'Maybe Jones has already been buried. Or worse, what if he's been cremated? At least if he's been buried then we can get him exhumed. How gross would that be?'

'Jem, nobody's going to be digging up any dead bodies,' Aston said. 'There's no way Jones would have been buried yet. Or cremated. Or sent floating out into the North Sea on a burning Viking ship.'

'Oh.'

Aston could hear the disappointment in the computer expert's voice. What did she think? That they were going to grab a couple of shovels and go do some digging?

The pause crackled through the confined space of the Focus.

'Okay, boss, what's our next move?'

Boss! Aston couldn't work out if Jem was taking the piss or not. What he did know was that he was getting some funny vibes from George. He glanced over, catching her eye, saw the peculiar smile playing on her lips. She turned her attention back to the road, fingers tapping on the steering wheel.

'Yes, boss,' George said. 'What is our next move?'

Aston couldn't hear any sarcasm in her voice, but it was there. 'While we're waiting for Meyer to get back, what do you say we take a trip to Jones's house in –' he flicked through the printout. '– in Chesham. See if there's anything worth seeing there. Jem, are you okay holding the fort there?'

'Sure thing, boss.'

Aston went to say something, then decided not to. It wasn't worth the effort.

'We'll call in every half hour,' George said. 'If you don't hear from us you know what to do.'

'Don't!' Jem warned. 'Remember what happened last time you said that.'

'We'll be fine.'

'Yeah, you said that, too.'

'Speak to you in half an hour,' Aston said and killed the call. He looked out the window. The part of London they were driving through could have been anywhere in the city. Dirty rundown buildings; a taxi cab office and a kebab shop; stop-go traffic. George gave it almost a whole minute before she spoke.

'So . . .'

Aston looked up from page twelve of the printout. He'd just started on Bernie Jones's CV. 'So what?'

'You know what I'm talking about.'

He did, but he wasn't going to give her the satisfaction. 'I don't have a clue what you're talking about. Despite what you might have heard, I'm not a mind-reader.'

'Good job one of us is.'

'Get to the point.'

'Okay, boss . . .' George chuckled to herself and shook her head. 'You were loving it. Don't deny it.'

'I was mortally embarrassed.'

'Bullshit.'

'You're pissed off about this, aren't you?'

'On the contrary. I think it'll work very nicely to my advantage.' George leant across and patted his leg. 'Just remember who the real power behind the throne is. Do that and everything will work out fine. Okay, boss?'

Aston waited another few seconds to make sure

George was quite finished, then turned back to the printout. Bernie Jones's story wasn't dissimilar to a hundred other people who worked for Six. He came from a middle-class background – mother was a teacher, father an estate agent – and had grown up in Guildford. Divorced, there were three kids: a boy and two girls. The wife waited until the kids had flown the nest before leaving. Jones had been recruited while studying politics at Cambridge and gone to work at MI6's Cold War HQ at Century House in Lambeth. Mac and the rest of the old guard thought it hysterical that drab old Century House had been converted into luxury flats, earning some developer a small fortune in the process. Jones had slotted perfectly into the Six way of life, doing all the right things and getting noticed by all the right people. In addition to the compulsory time spent in London, there were postings to the Far East and Russia. Jones and Hathaway's paths crossed in Moscow in the Eighties. Both had been out there under the pretence of working for the British Embassy.

And there had been someone else pretending to be a Foreign diplomat in Moscow at the same time.

'Fuck,' Aston muttered.

'What is it Paul?'

'Jones and Hathaway worked together in Moscow in 1984. You know who else was there, don't you?'

George shook her head slowly, then went very

still. She slammed on the breaks and skidded to a stop, ignoring the angry horns blaring behind. 'Mac,' she whispered. 'Mac was there.'

32

Belmarsh Prison, last October

Mac did a quick 360 degrees, and saw why Harris chose this spot. They were in a quiet corner of the exercise yard, as far from the screws as it was possible to get. There was a CCTV camera pointing at them, but video surveillance was only effective when it was being monitored – there were thousands of cameras in Belmarsh and they couldn't all be monitored 24/7. Chances were, Harris had made arrangements for this camera to be conveniently forgotten about for a few minutes. The two enforcers were flanking Mac like prison guards, keeping schtum. When Harris finally appeared he was accompanied by a bodyguard who made the enforcers look like kindergarten teachers. This was one of the most vicious bastards Mac had ever seen. It wasn't a physical thing. He didn't have the muscles, didn't have the tattoos; he wasn't even particularly big. Put him in a suit and he would be perfectly at home in a boardroom. It was the look in his eye that unnerved Mac. He'd seen that look before. This was someone who would kill without a second thought and enjoy every moment.

Harris waved the enforcers away. The bodyguard stayed put. Two feet away. Close enough to reach out and rip Mac's heart from his chest. Harris was dressed in grey Nike sweatpants and sweatshirt. The trainers were also Nike – shiny silver and straight from the box. Up close, Harris was smaller than Mac remembered. His hair was a dirty pigeon grey rather than white, a dozen shades down the colour chart from Wainwright's peace dove white.

'I love mornings like this. Sunny with a bite.' The accent was refined East End, all airs and graces. 'Takes my breath away, it does. I think this must be one of my favourite times of the year. So crisp, so fresh. Macintosh, isn't it?'

The question was rhetorical, but Harris was waiting for an answer. He expected nothing less than complete subservience, and that was exactly what he was going to get. 'That's right, Mr Harris.'

'Well you've got balls. I'll say that much for you.'

A statement, therefore no answer was required. The rules of this negotiation were as delicate as any Superpower summit. Mac felt as though he was wading through diplomatic quicksand.

'How's the knee?'

'Not brilliant.'

Mac wasn't fooled by the false sympathy. Harris had made his point: he knew Mac's weak spot and wouldn't think twice about exploiting it. His bad knee was probably right at the top of the bodyguard's hurt list.

'In case you're wondering, Booth is currently residing in Broadmoor. The last I heard, he was wearing nappies and feeding through a straw. Couldn't have happened to a nicer bloke.'

'Thanks, Mr Harris.'

The fact Harris had delivered this news meant Mac now owed him. You didn't get nothing for nothing in here. Unfortunately, the love and good-will was only flowing one way. If anyone was owing anybody, it was Harris who owed him. By taking out Booth, Mac had made his life a whole lot easier.

'I've also had words with Booth's associates, and you'll be pleased to hear their future plans don't involve you.'

'Thanks, Mr Harris.'

Mac did the sums in his head, trying to work out what Harris hoped to get from this. All he could be certain of was that he'd know soon enough. Harris wouldn't go to this trouble out of the goodness of his black shrivelled heart.

'Now you're back with us,' Harris continued, 'you need to be aware of a few things.'

Mac didn't say a word, didn't nod, didn't even blink. He just stood there and listened.

'This is my block, okay? The screws might tell

you different, but they don't know shit. I know everything going on in here. If somebody farts, I know about it. If somebody's in trouble, I know.' A pause. 'And if someone's going to get taken out, I *definitely* know about it. Are we clear on that?'

'Yes, Mr Harris.'

'As far as you're concerned, I'm God. I see everything; I'm everywhere. Pull another stunt like that without my say-so, and it'll be you wearing nappies and feeding through a straw. Do we understand each other?'

'Yes, Mr Harris.'

'Good work, though,' he added.

'Thanks.'

'If you need anything . . .' He let the sentence hang there a moment, his eyes searching Mac's '. . . well, you know where to find me.'

'I'll bear that in mind. Thanks again, Mr Harris.'

'Welcome to Houseblock Four,' he said, deadpan. 'Enjoy your stay.'

With that, Harris turned and walked away. Mac stood there for a minute while his emotions settled. On the outside there wasn't so much as a flicker or a twitch, but inside he was cheering. That had gone better than expected. Much better. For the moment, the pressure was off. Harris had acknowledged him . . . and very publicly. Any of Booth's cronies would think twice before taking him on. Harris was walking laps of the yard, his bodyguard trailing a few steps behind like a faithful Rottweiler. Every now and then, a con would cautiously meander towards him, cap in hand, seeking favours. There'd always be a nervous glance for the bodyguard. Playing the favours game with Harris was dangerous. You never knew when he'd call in the marker. And when he did, you couldn't say no. On Houseblock Four, whatever Mr Harris wanted, Mr Harris got. To survive, you sometimes had to deal with the devil. This wasn't the first time Mac had made such a transaction. He doubted it would be the last.

Harris started his second lap, and Mac had the strongest feeling he was being watched. He turned and saw a small group of Arabs keeping to themselves near the fence. Christopher was standing in the middle of them, holding court. The handsome Middle Eastern face had sunk into something more severe, but it was definitely him. On the outside, Christopher had done a good impression of the successful businessman. Glance his way and you'd see someone suckered by the American dream, a Saudi playboy lapping up all that Western decadence and loving every second. He'd had all the trappings of wealth: a flat in Kensington and a top-of-the-range Jaguar; his golf handicap was twelve. Scratch away at the surface, however, and you'd find someone who made your average extremist look as threatening as a kitten. When they last met, Mac sold Christopher a dirty bomb for thirty million quid. It was a deal that hadn't gone the way either of them expected. Christopher caught Mac's eye briefly, long enough to clock

213

him. Although they'd known each other for over a decade, there was no nostalgic warmth in that look, no friendly good humour. Christopher turned away and carried on talking to the person next to him, leaving Mac with a ton of thoughts tumbling around in his head. None of which were happy.

Looking back, that first kill had been so crude. It was the first and last time Kestrel used a garrotte. He'd had a picture in his head of how things should be, and let his romantic notions get the better of him – getting up close and personal like that had seemed like the right thing to do. That first job had almost been his last. It was amazing the reserves of strength a dying man had access to. A good fifteen years ago and what he remembered most – remembered with a clarity that actually intensified with each passing year – was the feeling of absolute power. He had been judge, jury and executioner.

Kestrel closed his eyes and travelled back to that dingy rain-soaked alley. He felt the smooth wood of the garrotte handles, that tiny knot rubbing the underside of his left ring finger, felt the tightness in his knuckles. He took the target from behind, his body pulled in close, a parody of fucking where death was the object, not life; it didn't matter how much the target bucked and struggled, he wouldn't let go. He remembered the way the rain fell from his hair, washing across his face and dripping from his nose. And that heart-stopping moment when the target summoned up a final superhuman surge of strength that took him completely by surprise. The garrotte was almost jerked from his fingers and he felt himself being pulled forward. At the last second, he dug his heels in and somehow kept standing. He'd gripped the handles as though his life depended on it, his face twisted with the effort. And the rain had washed his eyes clean; he was blind but in some ways he could see more clearly than he'd ever seen. This was the defining moment of his life . . . the only moment of his life that mattered. The target's fingers searched for the wire and desperately tried to rip it away. Kestrel just pulled tighter, imagining that if he pulled tight enough he could decapitate him. Slowly, the target's struggles lessened. One last futile attempt, a gentle caress of the wire, and then his arms fell limply to his sides as the last drops of life drained away. Kestrel stood there for almost a full minute, holding the target up with the garrotte. He stood there until he couldn't hold him up any longer. When he finally let go, the target had dropped like a bag of meat and hit the tarmac with a soggy thump. He checked for vital signs, then dragged the body behind a skip.

Kestrel was paid ten grand for the hit, but would have done that one for free.

The trilogy of hits ordered by Coulson was the most interesting work of his career. The third was the most challenging, and he'd invented a whole new persona. Nothing unusual there; for most of his jobs he used a new alias. This legend needed to be completely bombproof, though.

As always, Kestrel started with the name. Get that wrong and you'd be as well giving up there and then. Rule number one: never use a famous name. Was the bored guard at passport control going to look twice on seeing the surname Cruise? Would a lazy traffic cop do a double-take if the licence-holder was none other than William Clinton? Of course they would. A bland name was almost as bad. John Smith was going to raise as many eyebrows as John Lennon. Never give anyone an excuse to remember you . . . that was rule number two. In restaurants you always tipped; if you didn't, you'd be remembered. However, tip too much or too little and you'd also be remembered. It was all about striking the right balance.

This job was being carried out by Simon Derby.

The next step: Simon Derby needed to exist. That meant acquiring a birth certificate, a passport, a National Insurance number, a driving licence. All these items could be obtained, but not from your nearest Tesco.

Once Simon Derby officially existed, he needed the relevant wallet shrapnel: credit cards, bank cards, a library card, a selection of business cards. The fun photo booth pic of Derby and his girlfriend was a nice touch. It was computer generated, of course; all that was needed was a face that looked like it belonged to Derby's soulmate. Rule number two came into play here. Hanging around photo booths trying to entice strangers behind the curtains was a sure way to draw attention.

Finally, the fun part: working out exactly who Simon Derby was. Where had he grown up? Who were his childhood friends? Did he have a girlfriend? A wife? Brothers and sisters? What was that embarrassing thing

217

his mother did at his eighteenth birthday party? Was it true that his father flew the coop when he was six, only to get mown down by a truck a month later? Or perhaps his father had hit the bottle and drunk himself to death? Was it Stacey or Tracey he lost his virginity to? A legend lived or died by the details. What might seem trivial could be the thread that unravelled the whole persona. This was where most people tripped up. They could do the front story but not the back story. Without a believable back story, any legend had the potential to crumble in seconds.

Getting the job had required some fancy cyber-footwork. He was dealing with a bureaucracy, and that was a major plus; with any bureaucracy, as long as the paperwork was in order, in triplicate, as long as all those Ts were crossed and the Is were dotted, then nobody looked twice. The fact that all the 'paperwork' was on computer these days made it so much easier. Kestrel had got the full service record sorted out, throwing in a couple of commendations for good measure – not so many that he'd stand out, just enough to infer competency. And then he'd worked through all the transfer protocols, backdating where appropriate. The reason for the move from the Isle of Wight was simple. Derby's mother had recently been admitted to a London hospice and he wanted to be nearby to help nurse her through her final days. Kestrel whispered all this to the relevant computer systems, and they took it on board. Lies and truth look identical when reduced to ones and zeroes. When he turned up for work that first morning nobody suspected a thing.

Today he had pulled a double shift. It had been easy

to arrange. More sweet nothings whispered to the computers, job done. He started at two, which meant he'd already had the best part of the day to work through the final details for tonight's hit. The day would be long, but it had to be done; he wanted to keep an eye on the target, try and steer him away from trouble. Kestrel got dressed and admired himself in the tall scratched mirror on the inside of the wardrobe door. He checked his watch: an hour and a half to get across London to work.

33

'What exactly are we looking for?' Priest whispered once they were safely inside.

George shrugged. 'Anything that might be significant,' she whispered back.

'Define significant?'

'I don't know. How about something that might give us an idea of why Jones was murdered. After all, that's what we're here for.'

Two seconds and she was already in danger of losing her rag. That had to be a new record. This would have been so much easier if Paul had been here, at least he knew the score. But, of course, Paul had gone charging off to Belmarsh. Typical fucking Paul! Going in like the proverbial bull! She'd argued that Chesham was closer than Belmarsh, so they might as well check out Jones's house and then they could go to the prison together. Mac could wait – it wasn't as if he was going anywhere. But Paul wasn't listening. It was as though he'd been looking for an excuse to go head-to-head with Mac . . . any old excuse would do. George didn't bother arguing; she knew Paul well enough to realise that when he'd made up his mind there was no point. So she'd dropped him off at the nearest tube station, and wished him the best of luck in her most sarcastic voice. For a nanosecond, she'd considered taking him to Belmarsh. But it was better this way. When Paul was in that sort of mood, she'd rather not be anywhere near him. There was no way she was going to Jones's house alone, so she'd contacted Jem, and Jem had contacted Priest, and, well, here they were. George had wanted the Irishman to keep an eye on the outside of the house and warn her if there were any unwelcome visitors. Better still, take the fuckers down. But he'd insisted on coming inside with her. What was it with men? Why couldn't they just do what they were bloody well told?

Priest asked another stupid question and George pretended not to hear. It wasn't his fault, she realised; he was only trying to help. And he had saved their lives, which had to be worth some leeway. She told herself to chill, but it wasn't happening. Sneaking around Jones's house reminded her of breaking into Hathaway's apartment, and all the memories attached to that evening were still too fresh. She visited that basement room almost every night. To make matters worse, in the nightmares the ending had changed. She was still naked, still tied to the chair with a

221

stinking bag over her head, but there had been no Priest to save the day. Instead, she'd been forced to listen to Paul pleading for his life, screaming and crying and shouting for her to save him. A single shot had rung out, and the silence that followed was the most awful silence she had ever endured.

'Look,' she said. 'Sorry I snapped. I'm not usually such a bitch. Honest. I'm just a bit strung out at the moment, that's all.'

'And the last thing you need is me asking a load of stupid questions.'

That was worth a small smile. 'You must have broken into a house before.'

'No way. My mum brought me up to be a good Catholic boy.'

'Thought you were a Protestant.'

Priest's eyes narrowed, but he was wearing an easy smile. 'Have you been sneaking a look at my sheet?'

'Maybe,' George admitted. 'So, I'm supposed to believe this is the first house you've broken into. Is that it? Come on, Priest, you were in the SAS. You must have done some breaking and entering.'

The smile widened, turned into a grin. 'Okay, I admit it: I suppose I've done my fair share of sneaking around places I shouldn't. That said, when you go in with the SAS you go in hard and fast. You don't worry about being caught because the people that matter have a split second to register you're there, and then they're dead.'

'Oh,' George replied. It was the matter-of-fact way Priest said this that got to her. He was talking about killing the same way other people talk about the weather.

'I haven't done much of this playing detective business, so any pointers . . .'

'It's easy,' George told him. 'Keep your eyes open for anything odd. And before you ask: you'll know "odd" when you see it.'

As they moved through the dimly lit hall, she glanced at the pictures, noting the faces that repeated. The three kids grew older, seemingly at random. There was no solid timeline. A picture from the Eighties here, shoulder pads and *Dynasty* hair – one from the Seventies there, flares and nasty hairstyles. Jones's wife got older, younger, older again. Bernie wasn't in many of the pictures.

This definitely had the feel of a man's house. It was difficult to put her finger on why. There were plenty of feminine touches, but it was as though these had faded into the background. Jones's wife left a couple of years ago, which might explain that. The house had the feel of a museum. There was a sense that time had come to a stand-still when she left.

Nothing in the kitchen; nothing in the lounge.

The study gave George the strongest sense of déjà-vu. The furnishings were different, the light was better, and there was no dust, but it reminded her of Mac's study. It was the sense of order that pervaded the room – there was a place for everything, and everything was in its place. The pens and pencils had separate slots in the desk tidy; the paperclips stuck on the large magnet were all facing the same way. Even the spare pins on the cork notice board were arranged into a battalion at the edge, the ranks standing shoulder to shoulder in neat lines. She went over every square inch, checking for loose floorboards, moving pictures aside looking for hidey-holes. Priest got bored and disappeared after about ten minutes of this. She heard him searching through the lounge, giving it a second look. At least he had the sense not to hurry her along. Now *that* would have really pissed her off. Another ten minutes, and then she admitted defeat. There was nothing here. She headed for the hall, calling for Priest in a loud whisper.

'See anything odd?' George asked as they made their way upstairs. They moved with light feet, careful not to provoke any squeaky floorboards. The house was detached, the nearest neighbour far enough away, however, when you were breaking and entering, there were certain protocols to be followed.

'Nope. How about you?'

'Apart from that chintzy china clock on the bookcase in the lounge, you mean?'

'Yeah, that was a bit much,' Priest agreed.

The spare bedrooms merited a cursory glance. They felt unused and unloved, as though when Mrs Jones left the doors had been sealed. The bathroom was littered with typical boy clutter. Shaving gear, deodorant, shampoo and soap, a towel that had been used a dozen times too many. And that was about it. There was none of the stuff that seemed to breed when there were females living in the house: a hundred different shampoos and conditioners, bottles of brightly coloured potions and lotions. This bathroom cabinet actually closed.

They left the main bedroom till last. The first wardrobe she looked in belonged to Bernie. It was filled with his suits: a different shade of grey for each day of the week. The next wardrobe was completely empty except for a collection of naked hangars. There was something about the empty wardrobe that brought home how lonely Bernie's life must have been. There was a photograph of Mrs Jones on the bedside table. The frame was cheap, but that in itself was telling. Bernie had belonged to MI6's old guard – a stiff upper lip and don't dare show any emotion. He had gone out and bought the frame himself, cut the photo to size, and put it next to the bed. It was the first thing he saw when he awoke; the last thing he saw before going to sleep. Perhaps the last thing he saw full stop.

'See anything odd?' Priest asked.

'Nope,' George said, shaking her head.

'Shall we get going, then?'

'Might as well.' George felt deflated. She'd been sure they'd find something here. What, she didn't know, but she hated going away empty-handed. Sometimes you got lucky; sometimes you didn't. That was the way it went.

They made their way downstairs, stopping in the porch while Priest set the alarm. George had taken the piss out of him when they got here, called him a Boy Scout because he'd thought to get the PIN number for the alarm.

'Can you give me a second?' Priest said. 'There's something I want to check.'

George watched him fiddle with the alarm. A couple of minutes later, and she was starting to get bored. The crunch of gravel outside froze her heart. Tyres on stones. A car. She broke through her paralysis, moved quickly to the door and peered through the spyhole. The view was distorted by the fisheye lens, but there was no getting away from the fact that a police car was coming up the drive.

'Shit,' she hissed. 'The police are here. We've got to go!'

'One second,' Priest whispered. 'I'm almost done.'

'No! No seconds!'

'Okay got it. Come and take a look at this.'

The police were climbing out of the car, slamming their doors shut. It might just be a routine visit. Alternatively, they might have been called in by a neighbour who'd seen a man and woman acting suspiciously around the Jones house. George was veering towards the former. They looked relaxed enough, in no real hurry. Priest grabbed her hand and dragged her across to the alarm box.

'Just look!' he said. 'Does this qualify as odd?'

George glanced at the display and did a double-take.

'We'll go out the back way,' Priest was saying. He darted along the hall his footsteps as light as a leopard, and George rushed after him. She couldn't get over how quietly he moved. They reached the lounge and she heard a key rattle in the lock, the creak of wood coming away from wood. The policemen were inside now, the house's atmosphere displacing to make space for them. Priest pulled the patio door open with the utmost care, making a space just big enough for them to squeeze through. He closed it even more carefully. The house on the left looked empty, and they hopped the fence hoping for the best. George landed in a crouch next to Priest, the grass spongy under her feet. Any second now the spotlights were going to flare, the bullhorn would blare, and the men with the guns would surround them. Priest pointed to the side of the house and broke into a run. George caught up with him at the gate. The screech as it opened was far too loud, and she glanced over the fence half expecting to see the two cops come bursting through the patio doors. And then she was following Priest along the alleyway at the side of the house. George walked down the driveway as though she owned the place. If anyone stopped them now they could pretend to be Jehovah's Witnesses. That tended to be a real conversation killer.

It was only when she reached the anonymous safety of the street that she thought about what she'd seen on the alarm display. The alarm had been switched off for seventeen minutes at 2.03 on Tuesday morning. And *that* definitely qualified as odd.

34

Belmarsh had a definite concentration camp vibe, thought Aston as he followed the guard into the reception room. The only thing missing was an 'abandon hope all ye who enter here' sign above the front gate. The guard motioned for him to stop and told him to wait there a second. The room was small and windowless, with a low ceiling and tight fitting grey walls – a coffin rather than a room. A wave of claustrophobia hit without warning, and for a split second Aston was back in Leicester Square, sinking down the tunnel wall, tears streaming across his cheeks, the dead baby clutched tightly to his chest. The air was rancid and thick and hot, and he was breathing embers. His eyes were burning and he felt his chest tighten, his lungs solidifying. The tunnel walls were closing all around him, getting smaller and smaller, pushing inwards. He curled his body around the baby. It didn't matter that she was dead, he still had to protect her. The walls were touching him now, crushing him. He tried to scream but there was no air to carry the sound . . .

In some ways the memory was more alive than the reality. With each retelling the story acquired extra detail, some of it fictional, some dredged from the dark forgotten corners of his brain, all of it too vivid to handle. What fucked Aston off the most was the way the flashbacks came out of nowhere. He could be doing the most innocuous thing, and before he knew it he would be down in those dark, sweaty, choking tunnels again. When the flashbacks hit, they hit with all the force of a tsunami. Post Traumatic Stress, Katrina had called it, holding out a handful of Prozac while excitedly pencilling a whole series of sessions into her diary. A pain in the fucking arse was what Aston called it.

'Are you okay, detective?'

It took Aston a moment to realise the guard was talking to him. He quickly pulled himself together and reminded himself what was what. He was in Belmarsh, and he was currently playing the role of DI Stuart Bromley, one of Scotland Yard's best. 'Fine,' he said. 'My blood sugar level just took a dip.'

The guard looked at him as though he was speaking a foreign language and indicated he should assume the position. Aston lifted his arms to shoulder level and spread his legs. While he was patted down and wand-waved, he thought about the last one-to-one he'd had with Mac. That had been on a rainy London street, and there hadn't been much talking. On that particular occasion he'd been doing his best to beat Mac to death. Aston walked through the metal detector and was declared good to go. He followed the guard through a door and into a corridor. More doors and corridors passed in a blur, and Aston was reminded of Vauxhall Cross. It was the lack of signs that did it. The guard was reciting the rules in the bored voice of someone who had done this a thousand times. Aston nodded in the appropriate places, not really listening.

He was ushered into another windowless box, this one bigger than the reception room and not quite so claustrophobic. In the middle of the room was a wooden table that had seen better days. It had been graffitied in Biro and there were a dozen black cigarette burns seared into the surface. Aston pulled out one of the red plastic chairs and sat down. The chairs were identical to those he'd used at school, and as uncomfortable as he remembered. The walls were white and there was a fluorescent tube in a wire cage on the ceiling. Minimalism to the extreme. A panic button had been fixed to the wall next to the door and Aston wondered what genius was responsible for that. If it all kicked off how the hell were you supposed to get to the button?

Mac appeared a few minutes later. He was limping, wincing whenever his bad leg went down. It was all so obvious, a pathetic play for sympathy.

Mac made himself comfortable on the other side of the table and held his cuffed hands up. The guard moved forward, rattling through his keys.

'I'd rather the cuffs stayed on,' said Aston.

'Fine by me.' The guard headed for the door, then stopped and turned. 'You shouldn't have any trouble with this one. If you do, hit the alarm and we'll have a crash team down here in seconds.'

The door slammed, and Aston was alone with Mac. He stared at his former boss, studying him, searching for those differences he'd noticed at the Old Bailey. Yes, Mac was thinner, and there were definite streaks of grey in his hair. And yes, the cut was cheap and nasty. But he didn't look as beaten. That's what had first struck Aston, how small and defeated Mac appeared. Now, sitting less than a couple of feet away, Aston could see shades of the arrogant bastard he knew and hated.

Mac was having a good, long stare, too. Aston was aware of those sharp blue eyes picking him apart as if he were a previously undiscovered insect. Being the focal point of Mac's full scrutiny was uncomfortable, but he didn't flinch. Maybe once Mac had some sort of power over him. Not any more. That all ended on a rain splashed street six months ago.

'They asked if I wanted to call my lawyer, but I told them it wasn't necessary. DI Bromley and me go back a long way.' There was the glimmer of a smile playing on Mac's lips. 'So, Aston, to what do I owe this pleasure? You know, I've been waiting months for this little get-together. Didn't you get my invites?'

Aston had. Every other week a message had come through that Mac wanted to see him. He'd binned them all. The only person who thought it might be a good idea was Katrina. She'd muttered some more crap about 'closure' that Aston had filtered out along with the rest of her psychobabble. Aston had no idea how she knew Mac had been in touch. Then again, she was working at Vauxhall Cross; that cloak and dagger stuff was contagious.

'I don't mind you not turning up, but an RSVP would have been the polite thing to do, don't you think?'

Aston felt the anger rising and it was all he could do to control himself. Nothing would give him greater pleasure than wiping the grin off the smug bastard's face. This was the man who'd fucked up his life, who'd used him like a pawn in a game he hadn't asked to be a part of. The man who'd killed his father. Aston took a deep breath and tried to get a handle on his emotions. 'So what does it feel like?' he asked.

'What does what feel like?'

'Well, you know, sitting opposite the person who caught you and not being able to do a thing about it.'

Mac kept quiet, his expression unreadable.

'I wish I'd been there. I'd have paid anything to see your face when you found out the lead canister was empty. Do you realise how close you

233

came to wiping out Vauxhall Cross?' A pause. 'Silly question. Of course you do. I dare say there isn't a day goes by where you don't think about it. Then there are all those long nights to contend with. Does it keep you awake, thinking about what might have been? How many times did you tell me there was no place in the intelligence game for losers? And what happens? You end up the biggest loser of them all.'

A moment of silence, then Mac chuckled and shook his head. 'Come on, Aston, let's get a little perspective. I'm in a Category A prison surrounded by murderers, armed robbers, the worst of the worst. Every day my life is on the line. Do you really think a few words can hurt me? You're going to have to do better than that. A lot better.'

Aston said nothing.

'What do you say we get down to business?' Mac looked as though he was about to slap down a winning hand. 'There's only one reason you'd visit me. You need my help.'

Aston just stared.

'This is killing you, isn't it? Coming to me for help. Okay, spit it out. What do you want?'

A deep breath, then, 'Gary Hathaway has been murdered in Rome.'

Mac shook his head, grinning. 'And what? You think I did it? Considering I'm locked up in here, that would be impressive.'

'Did you know Hathaway?'

'Of course I did.' A flash of annoyance from Mac. 'Please don't insult me by asking stupid questions. I expect more from you than that. So how was he killed? Or is that a Need To Know?'

'We're not sure,' Aston admitted. 'His body hasn't been found.'

'Then how do you know he was murdered?'

'His hand was found. It was clutching a bag containing thirty silver coins.'

'Thirty pieces of silver,' Mac mused. 'Okay, what aren't you telling me?'

'There's been a second murder. Bernie Jones.'

'How was he killed? Or are you missing a body there, too?'

'No, there was a body,' Aston said. 'The pathologist says it was natural causes – a heart attack.'

'And maybe it was. He had a high stress job, was in the right age group . . . a prime candidate for a coronary, if you ask me.'

'Mac, that's bullshit and you know it. What's the golden rule? There are no coincidences, right? *Right?* How often have you told me that?'

'Glad to hear I wasn't wasting my breath.'

'In '84, both Greg Hathaway and Bernie Jones were stationed in Moscow. So were you. Can you think of anything that connects them? Something that might have got them killed?'

Mac shook his head. 'Sorry, I didn't know them that well.'

Aston picked up on the lie straightaway. It wasn't anything Mac did; it was just a feeling. Mac

235

was an expert liar. He definitely knew more than he was letting on. 'Is that a fact?'

'You don't believe me?'

'No.'

'Do you want to know the first thing I learnt when I got here?' Mac wasn't expecting an answer. He'd gone into lecture mode and was using that patronising tone Aston hated. 'You don't get nothing for nothing. True in every aspect of life, but in here it's the number one commandment. Believe me, thou shalt not kill is way down the list. When you don't have much, every little counts. I've seen someone stabbed for half an ounce of tobacco.'

'Get to the point,' said Aston, knowing exactly what that point was.

'It would seem I've got something you want. So the big question is this: What do I get in return?'

And there it was.

'Maybe I can pull a few strings, get you moved to a softer prison.' Even as the words came out, Aston was aware they were inadequate. What was that old saying? Never bullshit a bullshitter?

'Could you? I'd really appreciate that. What have you got in mind? An open prison by the sea! All that fresh air! Wouldn't that be nice! Fuck off, Aston, you don't carry that sort of clout and we both know it!'

'Maybe six months ago, no. But a lot's happened since then.'

'Yeah, right! Been doing a bit of networking

236

have we? So who's on your Christmas card list now? The PM? The Home Secretary? Heath? Come on!'

'So what do you want?'

Mac got up. He pressed his cuffed hands into the table and leant towards Aston. 'Absolutely nothing from you,' he said in a low voice.

Aston kicked his chair away and stood up. He stalked around to Mac's side of the table. 'Sit down,' he whispered.

'Or what?'

Aston kicked Mac's bad leg and watched with satisfaction as he crumpled back into the plastic chair. He swooped in close. 'Now you listen to me. Things have changed. You don't call the shots any more, which means I don't have to take your shit. You know something about Hathaway and Jones, and you're going to tell me.'

'And what if I don't? I suppose you're going to beat it out of me. Who the fuck are you trying to kid, Aston?'

'Tell me,' Aston shouted. He could feel himself losing it. The red mist was rising and he did nothing to push it away. It would be so easy to grab Mac and slam that smarmy face into the tabletop. To keep on banging until his face was a pulped, bloody mess. And how satisfying would that be? How much better would it make him feel?

'No.' Mac looked at him and grinned, taunting him, daring him to react.

Aston turned away, then swung back suddenly.

237

He let loose with a right hook that caught Mac just below the left eye and sent him tumbling to the floor. Not a particularly constructive response, but it felt good. He walked over to the door, and banged to be let out. Mac had pulled himself back into the chair and was rubbing the side of his face with his cuffed hands. The door opened and a guard entered. He took a look around, his gaze lingering on Mac, and asked if everything was all right.

'Everything's fine, Mr Derby,' Mac said.

The guard wasn't convinced, but Aston didn't give a shit. He pushed past him and headed out into the corridor. There was a second guard waiting to escort him back to reception.

'Come again soon,' Mac shouted after him. 'It's been a blast.'

'Fuck you,' Aston muttered under his breath.

35

Seeing Aston again took Mac right back to that night last September where everything was going exactly to plan, and then somehow ended as fucked-up as it could possibly get. It was so easy to dwell on where it went wrong. To go over and over the chain of events that led him here, looking for something he should have done differently. There was nothing to be gained from this – Mac knew that – but when your mind detoured down those dark avenues you'd be as well trying to stop a runaway train. The plan had been a good one. However, it didn't matter how much planning you did, you couldn't cover every single eventuality. Had he underestimated Aston, or did he get lucky? Perhaps it was a little of both.

There was no way he would have missed the bang. Call it vanity, call it what you like, but once you'd lit the blue touch paper, were you really going to shut your eyes? No fucking way. You want to see the fireworks streak through the night;

you want to 'Ooh' and 'Ah' at the pretty colours. And he'd felt safe. He knew how to blend with the shadows, how to *become* a shadow. He hadn't thought he'd get caught. Not for a second.

Mac had planned his getaway to the last detail. There was a ticket on the Eurostar booked under one name; tickets on ferries leaving Holyhead and Dover booked under another two names. He'd even reserved an airline ticket. Easyjet flying from Luton. Not that he ever intended using that one. The name he gave Easyjet was a name MI6 could easily have found . . . then they would have had no option but to contact the police, who, in turn, would have been duty-bound to expend a ton of extra resources increasing security at the airports. And while they were looking the wrong way, he would have snuck out across the water.

Standing outside Vauxhall Cross waiting for the bomb to detonate, he still hadn't been sure which route to take. He'd been veering towards the Eurostar option. It was the quickest way out, and Europe was a hell of a lot bigger than Ireland. Then again, there were plenty of places to hide in Ireland – just ask the IRA. And the security over there wasn't anywhere near as tight as the Government would have you believe. Mac knew that for a fact; he'd seen the CX reports.

He still couldn't understand how it went so wrong – perhaps he never would. He'd covered all the eventualities . . . all except one: Aston. Somehow the Boy Wonder had managed to get one over on him. Aston, for Christ's sake! The stupid little cunt had no idea what he'd started. He was going to pay for putting him in here, pay in ways he couldn't even begin to imagine. He reckoned he'd won, and that was his weakness. Mac had seen it in his eyes – they were sparkling and dancing as if his lottery numbers had come up. He thought he was so clever, well, they'd see how clever he was, wouldn't they? Aston had written him off, and that was big mistake number one. What the hell was he going to do stuck in here? Fucking good question. Mac didn't have much, but he did have time. Lots and lots of time to come up with a fucking good answer. He walked over to the window and grabbed the bars so tightly his knuckles shone. He looked up and whispered his promise to the empty grey sky. 'You got lucky once; you won't get lucky again. Next time I'm going to rip your fucking soul apart.'

36

It took a severe amount of willpower for Jem to bite her lip. The false smile was stretched as far as it would go. Further than one of Tony Blair's, and that took some doing. Next they'd be giving her a little French maid's outfit to wear. Why not go the whole hog? Just because she was the youngest, that didn't mean she should be the tea-girl. She put the coffee down on Priest's desk and he gave a half-hearted thank-you without even looking up. Somehow she stretched her smile an extra millimetre and offered a sincere, heartfelt, 'My pleasure'. The sarcasm went straight over his head. She carried the tray to the big desk. Aston was playing lord and master, sitting in his leather executive chair, rocking back, feet up; George was perched on the edge, looking good in faded jeans and a baggy shirt. Late afternoon sun was slanting through the blinds and making geometric patterns on the carpet.

The downstairs office still had that all-too-new

feel, but it was getting there. The desks were finally starting to look lived in: documents and paper piling up in the trays, a scattering of office flotsam and jetsam washed up on the surfaces. To make the place more user-friendly, George had put up a couple of pictures. Black and white shots of New York in plain wooden frames. The Flatiron building, snowbound and dreamy, was on the wall between the windows. Grand Central Station was behind Aston's desk, beams of light shooting from the windows, the tiny stick figures glowing Lowry in monochrome. There were a couple of snapshots on George's pinboard. Family pics. A bunch of over-stimulated kids at a birthday party – rosy cheeks and lemonade eyes, colour galore; a close-up of a little girl pretending fierceness, her face painted with orange and black tiger stripes. The boys' contribution to the interior decoration had been to clutter the place up, which was to be expected. Chalk that one up to genetics. She put the coffees on the desk. White with one for George; black with two for Aston. She even knew how they took their coffee. How sad was that? Jem dumped the tray on the spare desk and sulked into the empty chair, clutching her own coffee in both hands. Her strop went unnoticed, and that, too, was to be expected.

'So how did it go with Mac?' George was saying.

'Don't ask,' Aston replied. 'It started badly and went downhill from there. The bastard knows something but doesn't want to share.'

'You sure about that?'

'Positive. The problem is we've got nothing to bargain with.'

'You could try torture.'

'I'm not even sure that would work.'

'What's so special about this Mac guy, anyway?' Jem butted in. 'You're acting like he's already won. You should hear yourselves.'

'She's right,' Priest added.

Jem did her best not to glare. She didn't need anyone fighting her battles. 'He's only human. He can't be as bad as you're making out.'

'You wouldn't understand,' Aston said.

'Don't you dare patronise me,' Jem said. 'It's bad enough that you expect me to make your coffee all the time.'

'That's not true.'

'Do you even know where the kettle is?'

'She's got you there,' said George.

'But you do make a good cup of coffee,' Aston pointed out.

'And don't change the subject,' Jem said. 'So, come on, answer the question. What's so special about him?'

'Mac and Paul have – how should I put it? – a history,' said George. 'It's complicated. He used to be Paul's boss—'

'And he was the mastermind behind the Leicester Square bombing,' Jem said. 'Yeah, yeah, I know all that. I've done my homework.' During her first week, she'd gone on an information gathering expedition deep into the heart of Six's computer systems. Her primary motive was to find out more about Aston and George – she wanted to know what she'd got herself involved with here. And then she'd kind of got carried away. She'd found a ton of stuff; it was all in there. To say the media only gave half the story with regards 18/8 was a serious understatement. Try a quarter . . . and that was being generous. Jem enjoyed a good conspiracy theory as much as the next hacker, and this stuff was made from platinum and studded with diamonds. Pure bling! And that wasn't all she'd discovered. She'd dug into places perhaps she shouldn't, and one shock had given way to another. It was amazing the stuff the Government kept to itself. If people knew what was really going on they'd probably never leave their homes. Either that or they'd jump on the first plane and head for the furthest, most deserted island they could find.

'Look,' Jem said to Aston. 'From what I can gather this Mac is a grade A arsehole. You shouldn't let him get to you.'

'She's got a point,' said George.

'Why do I feel like I'm being ganged up on?'

'It's not like that, Paul. We're girls and we know what's best for you.'

'And that's just the way it is,' Jem added.

'Priest,' Aston said, 'help me out here.'

'Sorry, pal, you're on your own.'

'Okay, let's get back on track,' said George. 'Why

don't you have another crack at Mac. I'll go with you this time.'

'You sure?' Aston said.

'Yeah.'

On the surface Aston's question seemed innocent enough, but Jem picked up on an undertone. She had the distinct feeling there was more to this story than had gone into the official reports. Maybe a little more digging was on the cards . . .

'Tomorrow?' Aston asked.

'The sooner the better.'

Aston's mobile went off and he answered with a short 'Yeah?' A pause, then, 'Oh hi, Dr Meyer, thanks for getting back. I was just about to call you.'

Jem listened in, all ears, trying to work out what the score was. And she wasn't the only one. George and Priest were doing the same. Aston wasn't giving much away. There were a few 'Uh-huhs', a couple of 'Yeahs', and that was about it. Meyer was doing the talking and Jem tried to pick up what she was saying. Apart from the odd distorted word crackling out from the back of the phone she couldn't hear much.

'Okay, thanks,' Aston said and flipped the phone shut.

'We're waiting,' said George. She had her listening face on, Jem noticed; eyebrows creeping towards one another, a cute little crease forming between them. Her head was tilted ever so slightly to one side and she was holding her bottom lip between her teeth. Jem caught herself staring and looked away. Behave!

'Well,' said Aston, drawing the word out. 'The good news is Meyer managed to get hold of Jones's body. The undertaker had a backlog, so he was in the freezer. The family weren't happy about Meyer taking the body back for a second look, but they'll get over it.'

'And . . .' George prompted.

For a moment there was only the hum of computer fans and the ticking of the clock. Aston was loving it up there in the spotlight. He had this smug I-know-something-you-don't-know look on his face. It was an expression Jem had seen more than once since she started working for Six. Spies, what were they like?

'If that's the good news,' said Priest, 'what's the bad news?'

'For once there isn't any. Meyer found the needle mark, and it was exactly where you said it would be. In his scalp. What's more, the mark is consistent with the sort of mark left by an EpiPen. Looks like you got it spot on, Priest.'

'What can I say? I must be a genius.'

'Says you,' Jem snorted.

'Okay, you two,' Aston said, 'can we at least try and keep up the pretence of professionalism here?'

'You know what this means,' Jem said. 'We've got to work out who's next.'

'And who says there's going to be a next?'

Jem rolled her eyes as though this was one of the dumbest things she'd ever heard. 'I've seen every slasher pic ever made, okay? Of course there's going to be a next. There always is.'

37

Belmarsh Prison, last November
Mac stood under the jet of water with his eyes
closed. Steam rose all around him and a thousand
hot needles pierced his skin. He rubbed some cheap
shampoo through his hair and then rinsed it out;
scrubbed off the top layer of skin with a bar of
soap that smelled of old tyres. He was almost at
the end of his allotted ten minutes when they
came for him. He heard the voice and pretended
he hadn't. Eyes still closed, he tipped his head
forward and made it look as if he was trying to
get the soap off his back. He tried to work out
how many there were, but all he could hear was
the rush of the water.

'Why did you do it?'

The accent was flawless, shaped by an expensive public school education. Mac opened his eyes
and turned off the shower. When he had arrived,
there were three other cons in the shower room:
an old boy who'd been in Belmarsh forever, a

cocaine dealer, and a double murderer. The main reason Mac had his eyes closed was to give the illusion of privacy. Shower time was precious – for those few brief moments it was possible to convince yourself you were on the outside. The other three were gone now. The shower room had cleared like a Wild West saloon.

Christopher was standing directly in front of him, a man on either side – all three had towels tied around their waists. A fourth man was guarding the door; the youngest of the four, he was constantly looking to the others for guidance, a Bambi expression on his smooth face. None of the men was particularly big, or hard. Individually Mac would have taken any of them on. Even two wouldn't have worried him. Four was a different matter. Prison life had not been kind to Christopher. Up close, he was a shadow of his former self. He'd lost a load of weight, and he hadn't had much to lose in the first place. He looked like an AIDS victim on the final straight. His skin was grey, cheekbones jutting; he was a walking, talking cadaver.

Christopher shook his head. 'What did you think? That we would just let you get away with it?'

Humour had never been Christopher's strong suit, but Mac had never seen him look this serious. His brain spun scenarios, looking for the out. He knew an execution squad when he saw one. 'You know how it is in this business,' he said, playing for time. 'There are no guarantees.'

'You promised us a spectacular, Mac. The Albert Hall in ruins. Thousands dead. Thousands more dying from radiation poisoning. It was the only thing that got me through my first couple of days in prison. I kept imagining what it was going to be like. The fear and awe on people's faces when they realised the might of Allah.'

That had to be a first. Half a dozen sentences before Allah got a look-in. Normally it was Allah this, Allah that, like they were best mates. How was he supposed to explain that the Albert Hall had never been his target? MI6 had done such a good job with the cover-up that even the Area 51 die-hards suspected nothing. If he told him he'd set a bomb off in Vauxhall Cross, Christopher would probably get his mate Allah to smite him on the spot for lying.

'Thirty million pounds we paid you. Thirty million and nothing!' Christopher spat the words out, struggling to keep his voice level and low. 'You've upset a lot of people, Mac. We don't like being lied to. And we don't like being stolen from.'

'Christopher—'

'My name is not Christopher. I am Mohammed al-Fagih, son of Ahmed al-Fagih. And I am proud to call myself a soldier of Islam.'

'Whatever . . . look, you've been playing this game almost as long as me—'

'This is not a game! We're fighting a holy war.'

'Bullshit! Save that crap for the kids you brainwash into strapping bombs to their chests.'

Christopher stepped forward. There was spit shining on his lip, hatred in his' eyes. This was exactly what Mac wanted.

'You don't understand!' Christopher was right in Mac's face now. 'You'll never understand! How can you? You're an infidel!'

From the corner of his eye, Mac saw Christopher's two friends reaching under their towels. Three guesses what was hidden there. Shanks made from toothbrushes were the weapons of choice in Belmarsh. The metal detectors didn't see them, and they killed you as dead as any knife. They were easy to make. Once you'd melted the toothbrush with a lighter, all you needed was time and a stone surface to sharpen it on . . . and there was plenty of both in here.

Without warning, Mac grabbed Christopher's towel and ripped it away. Conditioning took over, and Christopher reached down to cover himself up. Mac saw his opportunity and took it. He stepped behind Christopher and wrapped the towel around his neck. One twist, a second, tightening the makeshift noose. He pulled him close, using him like a shield, and stared the other two down. 'Stay where you are!'

Like he thought, both men were armed with sharpened toothbrushes. One red, one blue. Mac inched towards the door, dragging Christopher with him. He had to get out of the shower room. Once he was back on the landing he'd be safe. Christopher was actually getting some colour in

252

his face. Grey had turned to pink, and was giving way to red. Another thirty seconds and they'd be hitting crimson. He struggled, but Mac held him easily. He was so emaciated it was like wrestling a bag of feathers. Mac nodded to the far corner. 'Over there,' he said to the toothbrush twins. 'You, too,' he told Bambi.

One of the twins turned to Bambi and hissed something in a language Mac didn't understand. *Stay put*, he guessed. Something like that. Bambi was frozen to the spot like a baby deer caught in the headlights. The toothbrush twins moved, positioning themselves between Mac and the exit.

'I said get over there! Now!' If he didn't get control of the situation in the next ten seconds he was fucked. Christopher was trying to say something. Two words, over and over. It took a moment for Mac to work out he was saying 'kill him'.

'Not a good idea,' he told the other three, jerking the towel tighter. 'Come any closer and he dies. Understand?'

They understood, but that didn't stop them closing in. Mac swore to himself and backed away. This was what he'd been worried about. These deluded bastards couldn't wait to get to paradise. No doubt Christopher already had his virgins picked out. A final step backwards, and Mac felt cold tiles against his skin. Christopher was getting heavier, his struggles lessening.

'Back off now and I'll let him go. You can still save him.'

The toothbrush twins ignored Mac, eyes fixed intently on their boss. Mac felt Christopher's head pull forward, and at the last second realised what he was doing. The bastard was nodding. Issuing his final order. What was it with these suicidal fuckers? The '*nooooo*' Mac screamed out was primal. He jerked the towel as tight as it would go and dragged Christopher down into the corner. Too late. The toothbrush twins were on them in a heartbeat, slashing and stabbing. Christopher was absorbing most of their fury, but it was only a matter of time before they got to him. Pushing deeper into the corner, burying himself under Christopher's body, Mac closed his eyes and went foetal. Warm, sticky blood flowed across his face, his skin. He didn't think he'd been hit, but that could be the endorphins talking. He was only vaguely aware of a commotion over by the door. Screws, hopefully, although he figured it was too little too late. All it needed was for one of the twins to get lucky. Snick a major artery or jam one of those shanks between his ribs, and that would be it. Mac felt Christopher go slack and knew it was over for him. He sincerely hoped that paradise turned out to be a lie. The ultimate betrayal by his beloved Allah was exactly what that cunt deserved.

He kept hold of Christopher as long as possible, but there were two of them and only one of him. The body was unceremoniously pulled off, and Mac's eyes snapped open. It took a moment to register what he saw. The twins were dead. One had the blue toothbrush shank sticking out of his chest; the other's head was resting at an unnatural angle. Over by the door, Bambi's big brown eyes were open and unblinking, staring at forever. Harris's bodyguard hunkered down next to him, breathing hard, eyes spinning with psychopathic glee. He looked him over.

'You'll live.'

'Thanks,' Mac said, and meant it.

'Sorry.'

Mac was about to ask what he had to be sorry for. Then it dawned on him that the bodyguard was apologising for what was about to happen. He didn't see the fist move; didn't feel a thing.

38

Aston thumped his glass down on the table – a little harder than he meant – and did a tally. Was this his fifth drink or his sixth? Not that it made much difference. He was a long way from drunk . . . glowing merrily, but still in full control of all his faculties. George was sitting opposite in her own private glow. She was a couple of drinks ahead, and her rosy cheeks were the same shade of red as her scrunchy. Thursday nights were sacrosanct, a tradition dating back to their training days. Drinks followed by a curry followed by more drinks. These days, Aston usually alternated his drinks – JD and Coke, then a straight Coke – it saved things from getting messy. Not tonight. After going head-to-head with Mac he needed a drink. *Really* needed one.

The Roebuck had become their regular because it was so convenient. A five-minute stroll from the office, it was on the opposite side of the canal from Camden's main market, next door to

Starbucks. The pub was a favourite of the stall-holders, colourful characters who still hung on to their hippy roots. Unlike most of the pubs in Camden, The Roebuck hadn't dressed itself up to attract the trendy crowd. Aston reckoned if he suddenly found himself back in the Sixties, nothing would have changed . . . that included the land-lord, who looked like he'd been here since the war.

'You know, I've been thinking about Hathaway and I'm not sure how relevant his gambling problem is.' The bar was packed and George had to speak up to make herself heard.

'Go on.'

'If it had just been Hathaway who was dead, then fair enough. He was owing money to one lot of bad guys, it's not a huge leap to assume he was owing money elsewhere. Basically, he's robbing Peter to pay Paul. Okay, so, he's borrowed money all over the city and someone finally gets fed up asking for it back and tops him. Sounds reasonable enough, right?'

'Perfectly reasonable,' Aston agreed.

'Until you factor in body numero two.'

'And that's where it all goes pear-shaped,' said Aston. 'Someone went to a lot of trouble to make Jones's death look like natural causes. My guess is they don't want the deaths linked.'

'The unspoken assumption here is that the same person killed Hathaway and Jones.'

A girl bumped into Aston's chair and offered a slurred sorry. She was wielding an alcopop bottle

257

– a bright pink concoction that looked like bad medicine – and Aston wondered why she wasn't at home doing her homework. He waited till she'd gone before continuing. 'Of course it was the same person.'

'And you're basing that on what exactly? The MO is completely different. And let's not forget we're talking different countries as well.'

'Not buying,' Aston said. 'Two former MI6 men are murdered within a couple of weeks of each other. Not only that, they worked together. That's way too many coincidences for my liking.'

'I agree with you up to a point. The two murders are linked. Maybe the MOs differ because the killings were carried out by two different assassins.'

'And when exactly did we jump from a single murderer to a consortium of hired killers?'

'You've got to admit it's possible, though.'

'Yeah it's possible,' Aston conceded. 'I'm just not sure how likely it is.'

George picked up her glass and took a hit. 'Okay, what about Jem's slasher movie theory?'

'The slasher movie theory . . .' Aston laughed. 'I like that. Okay, so who's next?'

'The most likely suspect would be someone who was in Moscow at the same time as Hathaway and Jones.'

'Like Mac, you mean.'

'Like Mac,' George agreed.

'Now that would be a loss to mankind.

Unfortunately, I think Mac's as safe in Belmarsh as anywhere. If I know Mac, he's found the biggest bad-ass on the block and is paying him to watch his back.' Aston took a drink, checked the level in his glass then put it down on the table. 'I should have handled him differently today, George.'

'Don't beat yourself up, Paul. We'll have another go at Mac tomorrow. He'll talk.'

'I hope you're right.' Aston checked the time. Almost half past ten and he wasn't ready to call it a night. 'I'm not tired. How about you? Fancy calling a cab and hitting a club? We're not too old to dance the night away.'

'Actually,' George said, letting the word hang there.

Aston felt his eyes narrow, his forehead tighten. 'I'm not sure I like where this is going. The last time someone used that tone of voice I was already in the restaurant. I suppose I should be thankful that she *did* phone me.'

'I'm sorry.' George muttered 'Shit' to herself. 'Look, I thought we weren't doing this Thursday. Remember, something came up for you.'

'But I got out of it.'

'Yeah, and by that point I'd made other arrangements.'

'Ah,' Aston said, 'I see.'

'Don't say it like that.'

'What? I didn't say it like anything.'

'I heard the disapproval in your voice.'

Aston felt himself being pulled into an argument and was powerless to stop the slide. Didn't want to stop the slide. 'Can I ask something? You've been seeing this guy for what? A month? And you haven't mentioned him. Not once. Why?'

'And if I haven't mentioned him, how do you know I've been seeing him for a month? Are you stalking me?'

'He's married!' Aston laughed to himself. 'That's it, isn't it?'

'For your information, no, he's not married.'

George met his eye and Aston realised he'd gone too far. Even if he wanted to, though, there was no going back. 'So why are you meeting him so late?'

'He's been away on business and his flight didn't get in until eight.'

'Convenient . . .'

'Oh, fuck off, Paul!' George drained her glass and stood up. 'I'm going to go now. If I stay any longer I'm going to kill you, or at the very least cause you severe bodily harm.'

Aston watched George squeeze between the punters as she headed for the door. It flapped open, flapped closed, and then she was gone. Well that had been fun . . . not! He drained his glass and headed to the bar for a refill.

39

Belmarsh Prison, last November

One second Mac was in the shower room, the next he was in the Hole, lying naked on the hard slats of the bed and wondering how the hell he'd got there. They'd given him the same cell as before. Same bed, same graffiti, same poxy view. He had no idea how long he'd been unconscious for. Long enough to be carried down here and dumped onto the bed. Five minutes, perhaps ten. That was one hell of a right hook Harris's bodyguard packed. His left cheek was swollen where the punch had landed; the back of his head hurt like a bastard from where it had clattered against the tiles. Apart from the industrial strength headache he seemed all right. And at least he was in one piece. He had a couple of scratches, a bruise or two, all very superficial. It could have been so much worse – mortuary slab worse.

The bright orange prison overalls on the table smelled of dead people. Mac dressed quickly and banged on the door, kept banging until someone came. Politeness didn't get you anywhere down here. Eventually, the hatch slid open and a pair of eyes peered in.

'What is it, Macintosh?'

'I need some aspirins.'

'I'll see what I can do.'

The guard made it sound as though he was doing a huge favour. He wasn't. By now, Mac knew how the system worked. Requests for medication in the Hole tended to be met. Especially downers like Valium. The more docile the cons were, the easier they were to handle. Five minutes later the eyes appeared back in the hatch.

'Here you go.'

The screw chucked a strip of four aspirin into the cell and slammed the hatch shut. Mac didn't recognise the voice, which wasn't unusual. Screws were forever being moved around Belmarsh from one houseblock to another. Then there were the outsiders who were drafted in from other prisons. Mac dry swallowed three aspirins and laid back on the hard slats. Hands behind head, he stared at the scars on the ceiling and waited for the tablets to kick in. It was slowly sinking in how close he'd come to dying back there. If it hadn't been for Harris's bodyguard . . .

The bodyguard just happened to be passing. The right place at the right time, eh? Mac wasn't comfortable with coincidences. What had Harris told him when he got out of the Hole the first time? How he knew everything that went on in here? How nothing happened without his say-so?

Harris had set him up.

He wasn't working with Christopher, though. No way. Christopher wouldn't have given him the time of day. Harris might have controlled Houseblock Four, but he didn't control the Arabs. There was an uneasy truce between the two groups, an unwritten agreement that each would respect the other's space. The way it worked was that they pretended each other didn't exist. Mac suspected Harris had a spy in Christopher's camp. This proved it. Harris had known Christopher was about to make a move, so he had sent his bodyguard along to even out the numbers. Right time, right place. Not a chance. This had 'set up' written all over it.

Which led to a more worrying question. Why? Mac didn't have an answer, but he was sure he'd get one soon enough. Harris had saved his life, which meant he now owed him big-time.

At the hearing the next day, the Governor looked even more stressed than usual. Finding four dead Arabs in your shower room would do that, Mac supposed. All those forms to fill in, all those awkward questions to answer. Mac stuck resolutely to his story: Caught in the crossfire, Your Honour; I was having a shower, minding my own business, next thing I know all hell broke loose; no, I didn't see any faces – there was too much steam, and it all happened so fast; and, no, I didn't recognise any voices – like I said, everything happened too quickly; no, as far as I'm aware there's nobody with a grudge against me; I try and keep myself to myself – all I want is to do my time as quietly as possible. The Governor didn't believe a word, but what could he do? His shoulders sagged a little further as he sentenced Mac to two weeks' solitary confinement.

The first hour crawled by, the other three hundred and thirty-five passed even slower. Prison time was the long time, and time spent in the Hole was the longest of all. Seconds lasted for minutes, minutes for hours, and the days dragged on to eternity. Waiting didn't bother him . . . yeah, that's what Mac used to think. His second spell in the Hole gave him plenty of opportunity to reassess that one. He became obsessed with time. His thoughts were constantly filled with how many hours had passed, which led on to how many hours he still had to go. Nights were the worst. He didn't even have the luxury of sleep to whittle away a few of those long hours. He'd always suffered bouts of insomnia, and this hit with a vengeance. That thousand watt light bulb burning day and night didn't help. On a good night he got a couple of hours, if he was lucky. Mostly, he lay awake staring through the bars at the night sky beyond. Every day those seconds got a little longer, and each and every day those walls crowded in a little bit closer. After two weeks he was living in a matchbox where every minute lasted a year and every hour went on for a decade.

The air on the block was stale and foul – this was air that had passed through hundreds of pairs of lungs, air that was filled with the bitter stink of sweat and pain and despair – however, after two weeks in the Hole, it tasted as fresh and sweet as a mountain breeze. Mac studied his reflection in the scratched plastic shaving mirror, and barely recognised himself. Shaving became a ritual. He wasn't just getting rid of two weeks of fuzz, he was being reborn. He'd been to hell, and now he was on his way back. He lathered up as best he could with the sliver of soap, then gently, almost reverentially, he scraped the blunt disposable razor across his left cheek. He shook the razor in the water then went back for another scrape. It took twenty minutes to do his whole face. When he had finished he stared at his dull reflection for ages, noting the differences. There were a few more lines, and he'd definitely lost weight. He estimated he must have done a year's worth of ageing in the two months he'd been here. What would he look like after a year? After ten years?

Since his last face-to-face with Harris, Mac had done some digging. It was one of the old-timers who'd eventually come up with the goods – the information had cost Mac his tobacco allowance for the next three months, which wasn't any great hardship since he didn't smoke. Scally had survived Belmarsh for fourteen years and was due to be paroled next year. He was in his early fifties but looked ninety. His face reminded Mac of an

Egyptian mummy – skin thick and leathery, cheeks collapsed, eyes sunken. Scally was terminally institutionalised. No family out there, no friends. Mac reckoned he'd last a month on the outside, two at the most. The only thing waiting for him on the other side of those high walls was a shitty rented room and a noose slung over a rafter.

According to Scally, Gordon Harris had been one of the main players in the London underworld. Drugs were his game, everything from hash to heroin. For most of the Eighties and the whole of the Nineties he was untouchable. He had the mansion in Surrey for the family, the playboy penthouse in town for entertaining, the villa in Marbella to ensure his skin stayed the correct shade of orangey-brown. Scotland Yard knew all about him. However, knowing and having enough evidence to nail the bastard were two separate issues. Harris had eventually been brought down by an undercover cop who spent two years working his way up through Harris's organisation. Harris got ten years, and the cop had done a disappearing act. If the rumours were to be believed, there was a million pound price on his head.

Harris had been a kid in the East End when the Krays ruled supreme, and had adopted that whole fucked-up moral code. He came across as civilised . . . until you crossed him. Someone once made the mistake of insulting his date. It happened in a nightclub, all very public. For Harris it was embarrassing and ugly, and there were no two greater sins. The fact she *was* a whore didn't come into it. A month went by, two months. The man was picked up and taken to a deserted warehouse on an industrial estate near Woolwich docks. His hands were bound and attached to a large rusty hook. The chain was tightened until he was standing on tiptoes. He was beaten within an inch of his life, then left there for twenty-four hours to think things over. The next night he was beaten again. On the third night Harris used a chef's blowtorch to melt the man's left eye. This last detail tickled Scally so much, the old-timer almost laughed and choked himself into a coronary.

That afternoon, Mac walked out onto the exercise yard. He felt good; he felt ready. He headed to the place where he'd had his first face-to-face with Harris. And waited. While he waited, he did his usual quick 360, checking where the screws were, noting the position of the cameras. He wondered how long it would take for word to get back to Harris. That question was answered ten minutes later when Harris turned up with his bodyguard in tow.

'Good afternoon, Macintosh.'

'Good afternoon, Mr Harris.'

Mac found the put-on posh accent grating, but didn't let it show. They indulged in some interminable small talk, the sort of nonsense that pissed Mac off no end. He didn't give a fuck about the weather. Some days it was sunny, some days it rained. Deal with it! He smiled and feigned interest, gave all the right answers and made all the right noises.

'Lucky escape you had back there,' Harris said, finally getting down to business.

'It was,' Mac agreed.

'Good job Foster happened to be passing.'

So the bodyguard had a name. 'It was.'

'Very lucky,' Harris said, more to himself than to Mac.

'You didn't intervene out of the goodness of your heart.'

Harris smiled. 'The word is, you've got a whole lot of cash stashed away under a mattress some-where. Eight figures if my information is correct. Possibly nine.'

No way was it nine; that was wishful thinking. Mac said nothing. Let Harris say his piece.

'I was wondering if there's anything you need. If there is, I'm sure we can find mutually accept-able terms.'

That was worth a smile. 'Actually, there is some-thing you can help me with.'

40

The girl sat down in George's still warm seat, lit a roll-up and introduced herself as Max. Whether this was short for Maxine, Aston never found out. Max was in her mid-twenties, and had to be an art student. She had the black clothes, the intensity, the existentialist patter; if she wasn't an art student then she was a trainee anarchist. On a scale of one to ten he would give her a seven. Aston was tempted. A night of wild sex might just be what the doctor ordered. And the girl's body language was screaming out that that was what she wanted. Rampant, animal fucking with no strings attached. Aston made up some lame story and sent her packing. Madness was what it was. Opportunities like this weren't exactly raining from the sky these days. The experience left him with mixed feelings: part flattered, part depressed.

Aston hadn't intended having a six month sabbatical from sex. It just kind of happened. Except that was a lie. Basically, he couldn't deal with intimacy, right now; even the transient intimacy of a casual fuck was too much to handle. Pinpointing the reason was easy; fixing things was harder. There wasn't a day went by when he didn't revisit Leicester Square. Digging through the dirt and rubble in that unbearable heat; the skin being stripped from his hands and fingertips; the soft, loose feel of the dead baby in his arms. On top of that, he'd had the death of his father to deal with. His *real* father. This was a man he'd never known . . . and this stranger had ended up dying in his arms. How fucked up was that? And it was all Mac's fault. It was Mac who'd played those games with his life. Mac who sent him to Leicester Square.

Mac who killed his father.

Aston stayed at The Roebuck until he was physically removed. He wanted to get wasted, craved total oblivion. But he didn't. Instead, he stared into his glass and watched the Coke go flat. Alcohol was something he had to be careful with – that rocky road to ruin was more familiar than he cared to admit. Aston felt stone cold sober when he arrived back at the office. A breath test would have told a different story, but he wasn't driving so it wasn't a problem.

He headed for the kitchen and fixed a coffee. *See Jem*, he thought as he poured boiling water into a mug, *I do know where the bloody kettle is*. Aston carried the steaming coffee mug back through to the main office and settled behind the big desk.

270

He'd left the main lights off and the only illumination came from the screensaver and the moonlight slanting through the blinds. Very Mickey Spillane . . . except Mike Hammer was more likely to bask in the glow of a solitary desk lamp. What the hell was he doing here at this time of night, anyway? There were a hundred answers to that question, but only one contained the truth: his flat was cold, empty and lonely.

And why had he been so horrible to George back at the pub? What the hell had that been about? Taking the piss rather than being happy for her? If there was one person he wished happiness for, it was George. So what if she had a new man, why should that bother him? It was almost as if he'd been jealous, which was ridiculous. They were friends, best buddies, nothing more. Okay, they'd crossed that line once. But only once. And that had been ages ago, way back in training when they'd first met.

Aston took out the pictures of Luke Sanderson – the original from Interpol and the 3D one Jem had played around with. He laid them side by side. So this was the man who'd killed Hathaway. The man who probably murdered Jones as well. Maybe it was the light, but he was seeing something there he hadn't seen before. Uncertain what that something was, Aston picked up the original and tried to look at it with new eyes. The face was vaguely familiar, but was that because he'd been studying it so closely earlier? No, it was more than that.

271

His memory was throwing up a hazy face, one he'd seen recently but couldn't place. Had he seen this person today? Yesterday? During the last week? Maybe he'd passed him on the street and his subconscious had clocked him, something like that. Aston mentally retraced his steps and came up empty-handed. He picked up the doctored image, studied it closely. Still nothing. He could almost see the face. It was like the picture in his head had only been partially developed; a ghost image, undefined and lacking in depth. If he could get that face on to paper maybe he'd have more luck working out where he'd seen it.

It was the wrong side of midnight, but this couldn't wait. He rang Jem's landline and waited for the machine to click in, then hung up. If she was at home she'd be awake now and no doubt wondering who the hell had called. Nobody phoned with good news in the middle of the night. He let her stew for a minute then dialled her mobile. These computer geeks were all the same; if their mobile was more than a foot away they broke out in a rash. She answered on the first ring with a tired hello. In the background, he could hear the girlfriend asking who it was in an anxious whisper.

'Jem, it's Aston.'

'Jesus! Do you have any idea what time it is?'

'Late.'

'What do you want?'

'Well, it's like this. I was trying to do something

272

on the computer, but I've got this message come up on the screen. A fatal exception error, whatever one of those is. I was wondering how to fix it.'

'You're talking about my computer, aren't you?' Jem said, panic rising in her voice. *'Are you fucking with my computer!'*

'Sorry. I'm sure it'll be all right.'

'And who made you the expert?'

Aston heard Jem swearing to herself and grinned.

'Okay,' she said, 'here's what I want you to do. Don't touch a thing. Don't move. Don't breathe. I'll be there as soon as I can.'

The line stayed open long enough for him to hear the girlfriend making her feelings known. He almost felt sorry for Jem. Aston dropped the receiver into the cradle, then tipped back in his chair and put his feet up on the desk. She would be livid when she discovered there was nothing wrong with her computer. He had to smile. The subtle art of manipulation. If he'd pulled rank, she would have told him to piss off and wait till morning. Could this wait till morning? Probably. Could he wait until morning? Probably not. He'd never had much in the way of patience, which no doubt had everything to do with being an only child. Deferred gratification . . . what the fuck was that all about?

Jem turned up twenty minutes later, looking how she always did. Hair a spiky black mess, skin peachy and fresh. There were no signs of fatigue, not even any bags under her eyes. Ah, the bene-fits of youth. Aston had a good idea what he looked like, and it wasn't pretty. His eyes felt scratchy and bloodshot, and there were probably suitcases hanging beneath them. The stink of stale cigar-ettes and old booze clung to his clothing; his five o'clock shadow had long passed the point of designer stubble and was fast approaching wino chic.

'Why are you sitting there in the dark?' Jem spoke sharply, making no attempt to hide her annoyance.

'Waiting for you.'

'Do you have any idea how creepy that makes you sound? Anyway, why aren't you upstairs? I thought I told you not to move, not to breathe etc., etc.'

'Well . . .'

'You weren't fucking with my computer were you?' Jem narrowed her eyes and took a step back. 'You do realise this puts you into a new league of creepy? If this is your idea of a grand seduction scene, I'm not impressed. For starters you're *really* not my type. Secondly, if you don't mind me saying, you look a bit rough.'

'I need your help.'

'And this can't wait till morning? Tell you what, I'm going now and we'll pretend this never happened, eh?'

'Come on,' said Aston as he got up and headed for the hall. 'It'll only take five minutes.'

Upstairs, lured into that twilight world of hi-tech distractions, Jem slowly thawed. She started off in a sulk, but the siren call of the machines was too strong They went back to the original Interpol shot and worked from there, making tiny alteration after tiny alteration. A slightly bigger nose, a smaller nose, more curve to the ears, less curve. Black hair, brown hair, blond. Five minutes stretched to the best part of an hour. Every time Aston thought he had it, he'd check the picture on the screen with the fuzzy image in his head, and it wouldn't quite match. It got to the point where he thought he must be making it up. The face he was searching for was a figment of his imagination. And then suddenly, there it was on the screen.

'That's him.'

'You sure?'

'Positive. Quick, print it out.' Aston wanted that face on paper and in his hand before there was a power cut, or some other disaster. He'd chased this one too hard to lose it now.

Jem loaded a glossy sheet of photo paper into a printer, and thirty seconds later Aston was holding an A4 blow-up of the face. He got up and walked around the room, looking at the picture and grinning to himself. This was beautiful. Absolutely fucking perfect. As the pieces fell into place, it crossed his mind that it might be best if the assassin was allowed to finish his current assignment. He knew exactly where he'd seen the face, knew without a shadow of doubt. It had been that afternoon. At Belmarsh. The killer had been masquerading as a prison guard. Now that took some balls.

'So, is it him?' Jem was asking. 'Or do we have to start over again?'

'It's him all right. What's more, his next target is Mac.'

'You sure?'

'Yeah.'

'So what are you going to do?'

Aston dropped the picture and watched it flutter down onto the desk. His grin widened. 'Now *that* is the million dollar question.'

PART THREE

Smoke And Mirrors

Time shall unfold what plaited cunning hides.
William Shakespeare
(*King Lear* **Act I, Scene i)**

Stopping at each cell in turn, Kestrel slid the hatch open and checked for skin. The cons had been conditioned to sleep with some skin showing: a leg, an arm, part of the face. If there was no skin, then he was supposed to go in and make sure the lump under the blanket wasn't a bundle of clothes or a pillow. The early morning count was all about checking numbers not heartbeats. During the couple of months he'd been here, there had been one midnight escape. A heroin OD. The pathologist reckoned there was a good chance the con had been dead during the 2 a.m. count.

There were two other guards doing the count. He could hear their distant footsteps on the upper tiers, the clank and grind of hatches opening and closing. Kestrel had the ground floor all to himself. Manipulating the rota had been simple; even a schoolkid wouldn't have had much trouble hacking into Belmarsh's computer system. The EpiPen was in his pocket, pressing reassuringly against his leg. There had been no problems smuggling it in – because the pay was so bad, the guards were responsible for bringing more contraband into the prison than the visitors. Even if he had been searched, one look at his medical records would have provided an alibi. As well as a terminally sick mother, the unfortunate Simon Derby was allergic to bee stings. Unless treated immediately with a shot of adrenaline, anaphylactic shock was a killer – the EpiPen was designed to save lives, after all.

Simon Derby had fitted in well at Belmarsh. He didn't rock the boat, just got on with his job. His superiors were pleased with him. The prison system was only one small step from anarchy – overcrowding, understaffing and low moral had taken its toll – so anything that made their life easier was welcome. Derby had trod a fine line with his colleagues. He wasn't looking to make any new best friends; by the same token he didn't want to alienate anyone. During his first week there had been the inevitable invites for after-work drinks, all those curious questions about his past. His poor old dying mum had given him an out on both. The couple of people he'd chosen to divulge this information to had been suitably understanding, and the fact that the invites and questions dried up showed the grapevine inside Belmarsh was as effective as he'd thought.

On the off-chance anyone checked his cover story, he'd set up a phone number that went straight through to an answer machine. Anybody calling would hear the sombre voice of Mr Wallace, the head of Sunny Pines hospice, on the other end of the line. 'I'm out of the office right now but if you leave a name and

280

number . . .' As yet, no-one from the prison authorities had called to see if Simon Derby's dying mother actually existed. If they had, Mr Wallace would have got back to them. In the reassuring tones of a funeral director he would have told them as much of the sad tale as they wanted to hear.

Kestrel peered into a cell, saw an arm, and slid the hatch closed. He moved on to the next cell, his footsteps echoing away into the high roof. Belmarsh was a different world at night. After lights out the prison slowly wound down . . . but it never wound down completely. Even in the empty hours there was sound – snores and grunts, a cry, a random shout – you couldn't have a thousand men crammed together like this without some noise. For most of the cons, dreaming was their only escape; in dreams they got to step beyond the walls and remember what it was like to walk tall and free. For others, the only dreams waiting on the other side of sleep were nightmares; you could hear their moans behind the heavy doors, the occasional scream.

As Kestrel approached the target's cell, he put less weight into his shoes, softening his footsteps. He focused on his breathing, making the exhale twice the length of the inhale, centring himself. The EpiPen was pressing against his leg; it wouldn't come out until he was on the other side of the door. He'd played through this scene a thousand times. Three steps to the bed, then a quick stab with the pen into the skull. The target would be awake by now. But he was old and he wouldn't be difficult to hold. One arm around his chest to stop him struggling; a hand over his mouth to stop him shouting.

Kestrel paused at the door and listened for the other two guards. Good. They were far enough away not to pose a problem. Ever so gently, he slid the hatch open. He half expected a rusty screech, but there wasn't so much as a squeak. He peered in, checking for skin. The target was dead to the world, one leg poking from under the blanket, his back pressed into the wall. Kestrel turned the key in the lock. Again, not even a squeak. Concentrating on his breathing – lengthening the exhale, shortening the inhale – he carefully pushed the door open, his hand already reaching for the EpiPen.

41

Mac had been expecting this from the moment he set eyes on Derby. The disguise wasn't bad – good enough to fool everyone else in here – but Mac wasn't fooled. To pull off a disguise you had to get into those shoes, get right under the skin. You had to believe, and Derby wasn't a believer. In Belmarsh you soon discovered what hopelessness smelt like. That stink was stuck to the cons, to the screws; it was leached into the walls. Derby didn't smell right from the start.

Mac kept completely still as the door slowly opened. Pretending to be asleep. *Believing* it. Derby had to think he controlled the board. He heard the door closing and suppressed a smile. Mistake number one. It was going to take time for Derby's eyes to adjust to the dimness – Mac's night vision was working just fine. The assassin closed in on the bed, moving towards the head. Mac had spent so much time in here, the cell had become an extension of himself; he knew exactly where Derby was down to the nearest inch. Instinct took over and the calmness washed through him. He had run the scenarios, looked at every move the assassin could make and come up with countermoves. He was ready for whatever Derby threw at him. The assassin's footsteps were silky-soft, moving closer. Under the blanket, Mac's hand tensed around the shank. Killing him would be easy. Drag the blade across his femoral artery and he'd be dead in no time, bled out like a stuck pig.

Mac swung his arm and jammed the shank into the assassin's thigh, wrenched it out. He leapt up from the bed and grabbed the assassin. A simple judo throw, and Derby was lying on his front tasting concrete. Mac straddled him, using his weight to pin him down. He pulled the assassin's arm tight behind his back and pressed the shank against his jugular.

'Drop it,' he whispered.

Derby's fingers uncurled and a small plastic tube rolled onto the floor. The pool of blood puddling around his leg glistened darkly in the dim light.

'Okay,' said Mac, 'you've fucked up. You realise that, yeah? Nod if you agree.'

The assassin's head went forward an inch – a gesture Mac interpreted as a nod.

'And you realise I must have a good reason for keeping you alive?'

Another nod.

'And you realise I'll kill you without a second thought if you try anything?'

Another nod.

'Okay here's what's going to happen. I'm going to stand up now. When I tell you to, and not before, you're going to get up and sit on the bed. Understand?'

Another nod.

Picking up the plastic tube, Mac moved to the window and nodded for Derby to stand. The assassin limped over to the bed and sat heavily. Grimacing, he pressed his hand against the leg wound.

'Trousers around your ankles.'

Improvisation was the hallmark of any great performance – those trousers were the next best thing to a set of leg irons. Derby slipped his trousers down and placed a hand on his leg, keeping the pressure on to stem the bleeding. The wound didn't look too bad. He'd live.

'Q and A,' Mac said. 'The rules are simple: I ask the questions, you answer. If I like what I hear, you might walk out of here.'

Derby was in his mid-thirties, anonymous looking, no scars or peculiarities. His black hair was buzzed short – grade one or two – the haircut of choice for most of the screws. He had the bleached skin of someone who spent too much time under artificial lights. The uniform hid his body, but judging by how toned his legs were he was in pretty good shape. Derby's face was a blank mask. His brain was humming, though, searching for the out – Mac had no doubt about that.

'Coulson sent you. Yes or no?' An easy one to get the ball rolling.

No answer.

'Believe me, you really don't want to piss me off.'

'Yes.'

'And you did the hits on Hathaway and Jones?'

'Yes.'

Mac held up the plastic tube. It looked like an off-the-shelf EpiPen, the sort used to treat anaphylactic shock. 'So, what nasties have we got lurking in here?'

'It's adrenaline.'

'Yeah, right.'

'Seriously, it's just adrenaline.'

Mac considered this for a moment, then nodded to himself. Well, that explained Jones's heart attack. Very tidy. He was almost impressed. 'And you decided to take me out the same way?'

A shrug. *If it ain't broke . . .*

'How much did Coulson pay you?'

Derby hesitated and Mac raised an eyebrow, just enough to remind the assassin who was in charge.

'One hundred grand a hit,' he said. 'A two hundred grand bonus for getting all three.'

'So the fact you fucked up with me means you're three hundred grand out of pocket, right?'

'Yes.'

'Okay, here's the deal: I'm going to let you live, and I'm going to pay you half a million to kill someone. Interested?'

'I'm not killing Coulson.'

'And you're in no position to negotiate. Remember: technically speaking I saved your life, which means I own you.' Mac smiled wide and friendly, and Derby stared stony-faced. 'Anyway, who said anything about killing Coulson?'

'I just assumed—'

'And assuming never did anyone any good.'

'Who do you want killed?'

42

'I'm going to take a shot in the dark here, but you're not a happy bunny, are you?'

'Piss off, Paul.' George stomped through the office and slammed into her chair.

'So the early morning wake-up call wasn't appreciated, then?'

'Six o'clock in the morning isn't early, Paul. It's the middle of the fucking night.'

'Think yourself lucky. I almost phoned earlier, then I thought to myself: no, she needs her beauty sleep.'

'Think *yourself* lucky. If you had you *would* be dead by now. The only reason you're still breathing is because I don't have the energy to kill you.'

'Don't you want to know what this is all about? Isn't your curiosity tingling just a little bit?'

'No.'

'Liar.'

Aston pulled out the A4 sized photo from his desk drawer. This incarnation of Luke Sanderson had black hair, grade one short, a few more lines and wrinkles. There was still that air of anonymity, the sense that here was a face you wouldn't give a second look. He carried it over to George and dropped it on her desk. 'Here,' he said, 'what do you think?'

George picked up the picture and took a good look. 'Okay, if it'll stop you bouncing from foot to foot like a kid needing to pee, I'll bite. What's this all about?'

'Meet Simon Derby. At least that's the name he's currently using. For the past couple of months Mr Derby here has been working as a prison guard at Belmarsh.'

'Mac . . . Mac *is* the next target.' George took another long look at the picture. 'You know, we could sit back and do nothing, just let events run their course.'

'Funny,' Aston said. 'That was my first thought. I wouldn't miss him. Not one bit.'

'And the world would be a better place if he accidentally ended up dead.'

'And it would save the taxpayers a fortune if the trial didn't go ahead.'

'So many reasons,' George mused.

'One small problem: we're supposed to be the good guys. Okay, the way I see it, Mac knows something about the murders—'

'—and now we've got something to trade,' George finished.

Aston paced, getting his thoughts in order. 'We'll

give it to him straight. Tell him he's next on the hitlist. If he cooperates, we protect him. If he doesn't, then—'

'Bullshit him, you mean.' George shook her head. 'Not a chance.'

'We can do this.'

'Of course we can, Paul . . . and this time next year we'll be millionaires.'

Aston stopped, put his palms on George's desk and leant towards her. 'George! We *can* do this. But only if we believe we can, and only if we work together. If we go in there tomorrow and give it our best shot, Mac will talk.'

George reached behind and distractedly pulled her ponytail tight. 'Even if we manage to con Mac, that still leaves us with the problem of Simon Derby. What do we do about him?'

Aston smiled. 'All under control. You're not the only one who got an early morning wake-up call. I got Jem to do a little digging and she discovered Derby pulled the graveyard shift yesterday. He finished at six and I got Priest to tail him. We should be hearing from him any second.'

'Someone's been busy. So how much sleep did you get last night?'

'Not much. Anyway, Priest's got the Increment on stand-by. They go in and secure the scene. Then we go in and get first dibs on the questions. Once we've got what we need, we hand Derby over to the police.'

The Increment was a crack Special Forces unit,

the soldiers cherry-picked from the SAS and SBS. Officially the unit didn't exist . . . unofficially, well, that was a different story. MI6 occasionally carried out operations that required some extra military muscle, missions they didn't want to advertise. Black ops and wet work were the Increment's *raison d'être.*

George leant back in her chair. 'Sounds like you've got it all worked out.'

'Well, you know,' Aston said, trying for modesty and missing by a mile.

The phone on the big desk rang and Aston ran across and ripped it from the cradle. Priest gave him Derby's address and he scribbled it down on a yellow Post-it. He hung up and smiled at George. 'Grab your coat. Priest's tracked Derby to a flat in Hendon.'

43

They caught up with Priest in a tatty Ford Transit parked around the corner from Kings Road. Garrety & Son Builders was printed in black lettering on the side of the van. The 'G', 'n' and 'd' had long ago worn away; only the shadow of the letters remained. Aston banged on the back door. One short and two long. The door swung open and Priest's head poked out.

'In quick,' he said. 'You're just in time.'

Aston jumped up and offered his hand to George. She climbed in, and the door closed with a rusty creak and a bang.

'Cosy,' she said, looking around.

The inside of the van was a complete contrast to the outside. As clean as an operating theatre and jam-packed with hi-tech gear. Laptops, radio equipment, and a whole host of gadgets that looked impressive, although what they actually did Aston wasn't sure. Priest was on his own, which was just as well. There was enough space for three midgets – three full grown adults was a squeeze. The Irishman was sitting in the only chair, and wasn't about to vacate any time soon.

'Let me fill you in,' said Priest. 'Number twenty-six is a detached house that's been converted into flats. Three floors, one flat on each floor. I've got two men at the front of the property, two men covering the rear. There's no way Derby can get out. Take a look at this,' he added, pointing to one of the laptops.

The picture on the screen looked like an X-ray of a building. Coloured blobs had been splattered on it at random. Reds mainly, but there were some blues, greens and yellows.

'Infra-red imagery,' Priest explained. He pointed to the red blobs moving around at the top part of the screen. 'Here we've got a family: two young kids, a mum and dad. Probably getting ready for the school run.' He moved his finger to the bottom of the screen. A larger blob of colour was twisting and turning slowly like the goo in a lava lamp. 'And the couple on the ground floor are having some early morning loving.' His finger moved up to the stationary red blob in the centre of the screen. 'This is Derby here. Right now he's fast asleep.'

'I take it you're going to evacuate,' George said.

Priest shook his head. 'We can't afford to spook Derby.'

'What about civilian casualties?'

'Not going to happen,' Priest said. 'Remember,

293

these guys are Special Forces. They're trained to go in hard and fast. Trust me, Derby will be in cuffs before he knows what's hit him.'

'But Derby's going to be armed, and dangerous.'

'And my men aren't?' said Priest. 'George, you worry too much. This is textbook. Take my word for it.'

'I'd feel happier if you evacuated. If any civilians end up dead then we can all kiss our careers goodbye.'

'Can I make a suggestion?' said Priest. 'I'll leave the spying to you guys, and you leave the soldiering to me. Yes, we could evacuate. If we do that, though, Derby gets woken up and barricades himself into the flat and we now have a siege on our hands. Before you know it you've got the police down here. And the fire brigade. And the paramedics. And where they go, the media is sure to follow. Next thing you know it's a breaking news story and you've got a couple of hundred spectators, ice cream vans, burger vans, T-shirt stands, the whole fucking circus.'

'Okay, okay,' said Aston. 'We get the picture.'

'This way it'll be over in two seconds. Take my word for it.'

'Also . . .' Aston waited until he had Priest's full attention. 'You've already cleared this with Heath, haven't you?'

Priest grinned. 'Ask no questions . . .'

'Alpha One and Two in place and ready.' The voice had a Geordie accent and came from somewhere in the roof of the van. Aston looked up, trying to locate the speaker.

'Bravo One and Two in position.' A second voice – Welsh this time.

Priest smiled at George and Aston. 'What do you say we get this show on the road?' He picked up the mic and put it to his mouth. 'Alpha One and Two you have a go. Repeat, you have a go.'

Aston stared at the blobs of red on the laptop screen. The picture had all the charm of a really cheap and cheesy video game, something from the early days when ZX81s and Vic 20s ruled. For what seemed like the longest time, nothing happened. The tension inside the cramped van wound tighter and tighter, quickly moving past unbearable. Aston's skin was prickling and he was aware of every single hair. His heart felt too big for his chest and he could hear the blood whooshing in his ears. The silence was the worst bit. A silence underlined by the hum of machines, and punctuated by the sound of three people occasionally remembering to breathe.

Two new red blobs suddenly appeared on the screen. Alpha One and Two. They merged into one, separated again, merged and separated, working their way fluidly across the screen. On the first floor, they stopped. In his mind's eye, Aston saw the two men as clearly as if they had been standing next to him.

Dressed from head to toe in black, Kevlar body armour and helmets, automatic rifles pressed hard into

295

shoulders. Alpha One lets the gun fall to his side, picks the lock, pushes the door open. He steps aside, rifle up. Locked and loaded. Alpha Two goes in first, Alpha One covering . . .

The Alpha boys were on the move again, merging and separating, moving through the flat, checking the rooms, closing on the bedroom. Aston noticed he was holding his breath and forced out an exhalation. George did the same. Then it was Priest's turn. On the screen, there was only an inch between Derby and the Special Forces men. They separated one last time and Aston could imagine Alpha One tip-toeing across to the bed, while Alpha Two covered, ready to blow a hole in Derby's head if he so much as twitched wrong. On the screen, the red blob closed in on Derby millimetre by slow millimetre.

'Roll over and put your hands where I can see them!' said Geordie.

The voice was so unexpected, George jerked in surprise. Aston rested a reassuring hand on her elbow.

'I said roll over! Hands where I can see them!'

'Come on, do it,' Aston muttered to himself. Geordie wouldn't ask again – asking twice had set an uncomfortable precedent. Seconds later, three dull shots sounded in close succession, the noise muffled by a silencer.

'Target neutralised,' Geordie said without a hint of emotion.

'Shit,' whispered Aston. 'There goes our chance to question him.'

The three of them just looked at each other. There was nothing to add. Aston understood Geordie hadn't had an option. When your life was on the line, you didn't take chances. He'd asked nicely. Twice. Derby hadn't responded, and now he was dead.

'Fuck!' This came from Geordie, the word louder and sharper than any of the gunshots.

'What is it Alpha One?' Priest asked.

'You're not going to believe this. He's not here.'

'Can you repeat that.'

'Sure. The fucker's not here.'

'What!' said Aston, turning on Priest. 'You said he was in there.'

'He was.'

'So where's he gone? People don't just vanish. Not unless they're David fucking Copperfield.'

'Calm down,' said Priest. 'There's got to be a logical explanation.'

'Well we're not going to find it here, are we?' Aston pushed the Transit's back doors open and jumped out. 'Come on! What are you waiting for?'

44

Twenty-six Kings Road was one small step up from a squat. The paintwork on the building's windows and doors was cracked and blistering; the pebbledashing was coming away in chunks revealing the dirty brickwork underneath. Once there had been a front garden, but that was a distant memory now, replaced with a decaying concrete hard-standing that was black and cracked and infested with weeds. The rusting corpse of a Ford Capri hadn't moved for the best part of a century.

'Nice place,' Aston said.

'Yeah, right,' George replied. 'If you're homeless.'

Priest pushed open the creaky gate and made his way up the uneven path. The front door was open and they followed him inside. A pasty face was peering over the security chain of the ground-floor flat, junkie eyes wired and worried. In the background Aston heard a shrill, shrewish voice demanding to know what the fuck was going on.

'Okay, okay. I got it,' the man shouted over his

shoulder. He turned back to Aston. 'So, what's going on? Are you cops?'

'Please go inside, and stay there till we give the all clear.'

'So, you are cops?'

'Please go back into your flat.' Aston stared at the man, daring him to argue.

The door slammed and an argument flared up on the other side of the wood. Aston couldn't make out all the words, but he got the gist. A couple of seconds later there was the sound of a toilet flushing. Aston had to smile. He followed Priest upstairs. The door to the first-floor flat was wide open, and the hallway beyond was damp and dingy. The wallpaper was faded and peeling and splattered with mildew. Some of it had been stripped away, revealing plasterboard. A naked low wattage bulb cast a dull glow.

'Hope your shots are up-to-date,' George muttered as she brought up the rear.

Alpha One and Two were in the bedroom. They were kitted out identically in black combat gear, Heckler and Koch MP5SDs slung behind backs, masks draped on chests. The only major difference was their height: about six inches.

'You've got to see this, mate,' the taller soldier said to Priest. His Geordie accent was even more pronounced than it had been over the radio. He went across to the single bed and whipped the duvet away with a conjurer's flourish. 'Seems someone was expecting company.'

Aston, George and Priest moved in for a closer look. The mannequin was wrapped in an electric blanket and lying on its side, face buried into the wall. There was a bullet hole in the back of the head, another two in a close group in the upper part of the torso. Derby must have been long gone before Priest got the surveillance van in position – that's why they'd only picked up one heat signature in the room. Aston shook his head. Hollywood had a lot to answer for. If the bad guys wanted to know what equipment they were using all they had to do was head down to the nearest Multiplex. It made staying one step ahead almost impossible. Still, that was the nature of the game. The good guys develop a new toy and the bad guys try to find a way to defeat it. That's just the way it was – the way it had always been – and Aston had came to terms with this a long time ago.

'Thought I'd seen everything,' Geordie said, shaking his head. 'The bastard really got us good.'

'He can't just have disappeared,' Priest said. 'I saw him come in.'

'Through here,' Geordie said, and led them to the kitchen.

The window was wide open. Aston peered out, saw the rusty fire escape, saw the garden wilderness, saw the decomposing wooden fence that bordered the next property. Saw it all playing out in his head. Derby must have realised Priest was following him. He'd come back here, stuck the dummy in the bed, switched on the blanket to give a heat signature, then done a runner. But . . .

'What is it, Paul?' George asked. 'You've got that look on your face.'

'Derby had obviously spotted Priest so why did he come back here?' Aston said. 'That doesn't make sense.'

George thought for a moment. 'Because there was something here he needed to do . . . or to get . . . or get rid of, perhaps. Something he didn't want to fall into the wrong hands.'

Aston nodded. 'That's what I think. Okay, you take the lounge and I'll take the bedroom.'

'Anything I can do?' said Priest.

'Check the bathroom.'

'I take it I'm looking for anything *odd*.'

'Got it in one,' said George.

'What was that all about?' Aston whispered to George as they headed out of the kitchen.

'A private joke,' she said, smiling. 'Nothing for you to worry your pretty little head about.'

Back in the bedroom, Aston looked at the mannequin wrapped in the electric blanket and swore to himself. Simon Derby was probably wearing a different face by now; definitely using a different name. They'd been so close to catching him. The only plus was that they'd saved Mac's life – although how much of a plus was that? Derby had almost pulled it off, too. Pretty impressive. Posing as a prison guard like that had required a serious amount of front.

Aston went through the room, checking drawers and cupboards. Underwear, shirts, jeans, a spare uniform. Aside from clothing there were no personal belongings, nothing to give any indication of who Simon Derby was. Except that wasn't quite true, thought Aston. The fact there was only clothing here was telling. Simon Derby was a shell. Nothing more, nothing less.

'Got something odd!' Priest's voice boomed through the flat.

Aston found the Irishman on his hands and knees, poking around in the airing cupboard. He backed out and stood up, brushed the dust away. George appeared at Aston's shoulder. Alpha One and Two weren't far behind.

'Nothing going on in the bathroom, so I thought I'd check out the hall,' said Priest. 'Wasn't anyone else struck by the dimensions of the flat, how it seems bigger on the outside than it is on the inside?'

Now Priest mentioned it, Aston couldn't believe he'd missed that one. He glanced at George, who was also giving herself a mental ticking off.

'It's a two-bedroom flat,' said Priest. 'Only the sneaky bastard's gone and boarded up the door and plastered over it. The new way in is through there,' he added, nodding to the airing cupboard.

Aston crouched down and peered inside. Hidden away at the back was a crude hole bashed through the plasterboard. Priest had dragged away the piece of plywood that had been used to hide

302

the hole, and this was resting against the water tank.

'Anybody got a torch?' Aston called out.

One of the Alpha boys slapped a chunky Maglite into his hand. Which one, Aston couldn't tell – the Increment men all looked the same to him. He clicked on the torch and fired the powerful beam through the hole. There could be all sorts of surprises waiting on the other side – booby traps, mines, broken glass scattered on the floor. It looked okay. Aston searched around with his hand and found an old shoe that had probably been there since the beginning of time. He tossed the shoe through the hole and waited for the bang. Satisfied he wasn't going to be nominated for a Darwin Award any time soon, he fired the beam through the hole and followed it into the room beyond. On the other side, he straightened up and did a quick 360 degrees, the torch cutting selectively through the gloom. The room was about two metres by three metres. There was a small window in one wall with a heavy curtain pinned across it. The opposite wall had a door-shaped hole in it, the back of the plasterboard visible. Derby had ripped out the door and the frame and propped them in a corner out of the way. Aston hit the light switch and another of those naked low wattage bulbs sprang to life. He went over to the desk. There was a computer monitor and keyboard on top, a tower and printer underneath, a document shredder at the side. He lifted the lid off the shredder and peered inside, dipped his hand in and let the confetti run through his fingers. That had been too much to hope for: some nice strips to keep the anal retentives from forensics busy for a while. Aston turned and saw George crawling through the hole.

'Well?' she said.

Aston nodded at the computer. 'We might have struck gold here?'

'Fool's gold more like. I'm betting that's why Derby came back. He wanted to wipe the hard-drive.'

'Even if he has, it's still worth Jem taking a look.'

George was looking around, eyes taking in every square inch.

'What's the verdict?' asked Aston.

'Of the flat in general, or this room in particular?'

'The flat in general.'

'Pretty much the same as yours, I guess. Derby has done a good job of being here but not being here, if you know what I mean.'

Aston thought about the bedroom, and knew exactly what she meant. 'I'm sure a thorough forensic once-over will give a different story. Derby's bound to have left something behind. Nobody can be that careful.'

He crawled back into the hall and flipped open his mobile. Jem answered with a sleepy 'Yeah, what?' He gave her the address, told her to send the names of the current occupiers of the flats to his Blackberry, told her to get over here ASAP to collect Derby's computer. She answered with a sarcastic one-liner that was lost in the static. Aston didn't ask her to repeat it. He flipped the phone shut and dropped it back in his pocket. George crawled from the cupboard, and he helped her to her feet.

'Okay,' Aston said. 'You go and play police-woman and have a chat with the family upstairs. I'll go and have a chat with the druggies down-stairs. My guess is that Derby was the perfect neighbour.'

'Kept himself to himself,' George added. 'You'd hardly know he was there.'

'You never know, though. Maybe he tortured children in the dead of night, held satanic rituals, that sort of thing.'

'We can only hope.'

Aston was at the bottom of the stairs when his Blackberry buzzed. Jem might be a pain in the arse but at least she was efficient. He glanced at the list of names, then hammered on the door, giving it his best cop knock. 'Police! Open up!'

There was no answer. The flat was so quiet he would have suspected it was empty.

'Come on, Stuart! I know you're in there so open the bloody door! I need to ask you a few questions.'

A shuffling behind the wood. The door fell open three inches, stopped by the tarnished brass chain, and Stuart's pasty face appeared. That razor-blade voice piped up in the background, telling him to make sure he saw some ID. 'Okay!' he hollered back. 'I've got it so shut the fuck up!' He turned back to Aston and wiped his runny nose with the back of his hand. 'Let's see your ID, then.'

DI Bromley's identification card did the trick. The door slammed shut and there was a rattle as the chain was shaken loose. Stuart opened the door and stood there blocking the way. His Sid Vicious T-shirt was stained and ripe; the sleeves had been untidily hacked away, exposing stick thin arms. His face was all sharp angles and dark shadows. It wasn't a face you would ever trust.

'What does he want?' The voice cut right through Aston and he wondered how Stuart coped. Maybe it was tolerable when you were permanently medicated.

'If you shut your fucking neck for a second,' Stuart called back, 'maybe I'll find out, eh?'

It crossed Aston's mind that the unflappable DI Bromley would insist on going inside. He would want to interview Stuart in his natural habitat. Talking wouldn't be enough for the detective, he would want the whole picture. Aston could see into the hallway, could smell the rot and damp, and was happy enough to do the interview on the doorstep.

'Is this about the loser upstairs?' Stuart asked.

'What makes you say that?'

'The floors aren't that thick and you lot don't have the lightest feet.'

'That wasn't what I was getting at. What makes you think he's a loser?'

'It's obvious, ain't it? No friends, no girlfriends. Spending all that time on your own can't be healthy.'

And your lifestyle is *healthy*, Aston almost said.

'He's a serial killer, isn't he?' Stuart was saying. 'Man, I knew there was something weird going on there. I've seen all the programmes on Discovery. It's the quiet ones you've got to watch.'

'Did you have any contact with him?'

'What? Like invite him down for a cup of tea?'

No way would Bromley put up with this crap. 'Okay, Stuart,' Aston said in his most reasonable voice. 'Either you start taking me seriously or I'm going to give your address to some of my mates in the drug squad. I'm sure they'd love to pop round for a cup of tea.'

Stuart stared at him, eyes narrowed, face full of contempt. Aston stared right back. It was no contest. Stuart looked away first. He wiped his nose with the back of his hand.

'I'll ask one more time,' Aston said. 'Did you have any contact with him?'

'Not really. We passed each other in the hall, and that was about it. He didn't say hello, I didn't say hello. Why should we? We're from different universes.'

'What do you mean by that?'

'It's obvious, ain't it?'

'If it was, I wouldn't have asked.'

'Well, I can't see them giving me a prison guard's uniform any time soon.'

Aston could feel his patience wearing thin. Time to wrap this up. Stuart didn't know anything. 'So, would you say Derby kept himself to himself?'

'Derby . . . so that was his name. I never knew that.'

'Well?'

'Yeah, he kept himself to himself.'

'Never caused any trouble?'

'That sounds about right.'

'Okay, I've got what I need.'

Stuart hesitated before closing the door. He had the look of someone being torn in two. He couldn't get away from DI Bromley quick enough, but he had to make sure. Aston was expecting the question. 'Your mates from the drugs squad . . .' he began.

'Don't worry about them,' Aston said, then added: 'Well, not this week, at any rate.'

The door slammed shut and Aston smiled to himself. He hadn't been able to resist. Stuart had left himself wide open for that one. What had he expected? He reckoned Stu and the shrew were probably already hitting the property pages. Nothing freaked a junkie out more than the realisation that the cops knew where to find them. They were paranoid enough at the best of times, never mind when they actually had something to be paranoid about. Still smiling, he headed outside for some fresh air.

George caught up with him a couple of minutes later. The family on the top floor had told a similar story. They didn't know anything about the man living below them, hadn't even known his name. He kept himself to himself, they'd said. He was always polite, though, saying hello if they bumped into him on the stairs.

'Ever get the feeling you're chasing ghosts?' George asked.

'All the fucking time,' said Aston.

45

'Relax, George.'

'I am relaxed.'

'Yeah, right,' said Paul. 'If that's relaxed, I'd hate to see you when you're stressed.'

'Okay,' George conceded. 'Perhaps I'm a little tense.' *A little tense!* That was an understatement. As soon as they'd stepped inside Belmarsh, the butterflies in her stomach had turned into wasps. When she last saw Mac, he'd zapped her with a Taser and then strapped some explosives to her stomach. That left an impression on a girl.

'It won't be as bad as you think. It never is.'

'Easy for you to say. It wasn't you he tried to kill.'

'The way I remember it, there were two of us in that bedroom.'

'Yeah, but you could have left any time you wanted.'

'You'd never have forgiven me.'

This almost raised a smile. 'Too right.'

Jem had smoothed the way for this visit. She'd hacked into Belmarsh's computer syste and ticked all the right boxes. So far DI Bromley and DS Sullivan had been given the VIP treatment. As they followed the guard down one anonymous corridor after another, George's sense of unease increased with every step. Seeing Mac again was part of it – a *big* part of it – but being here, in a maximum security prison, breathing the same air as rapists and murderers, wasn't helping. She didn't get spooked easily, but Belmarsh was getting to her. Everything about the place talked of despair and neglect, of dreams lying shattered and dying by the roadside. The institutional grey walls, the overhead fluorescent lights trapped in their wire cages, the sweaty, unclean feel of the place. Even the way the doors squeaked got to her. Belmarsh was like some giant monster, and here she was slowly sliding down its gullet.

'Take it from me,' Paul was saying. 'The stuff going on in your head is a lot worse than the reality. Mac is different now.'

'Different how?'

Paul thought about this. 'It's as if his powers have been taken away.'

'Like Superman after the box of Kryptonite has been opened?'

'Something like that.'

George hoped Paul was right. Those wasps weren't showing any signs of vanishing any time soon. When she thought about Mac it was as

Jekyll and Hyde. There was the Mac who had managed to convince her she was beautiful; who'd wined and dined her; who hadn't taken no for an answer; who'd kept chipping away at her defences until she'd finally agreed to go out with him. The Mac who'd treated her like a princess.

Then there was the Mac who'd tried to kill her.

The guard stopped outside a door that was identical to a dozen other doors they'd passed. He quickly ran through the rules, and they washed over George like the safety announcement at the start of a flight.

'You okay?' Paul whispered.

'Fine.' She found his hand and gave it a squeeze.

The guard pushed the door open and stepped aside to let them through. George followed in Paul's wake. The second she stepped across the threshold, Mac's sharp blue eyes were on her, picking her apart.

'Like buses,' Mac said to Paul. 'I don't see you for months on end, then two visits in two days.' He trained his gaze back on George. 'And to what do I owe this pleasure?'

The rich baritone voice made her shiver – this was the voice that infected her nightmares. George just wanted to get this over and done with, and then get the fuck out of that tiny shoebox of a room as quickly as possible. Back in September, she'd vowed that Mac would never get to her again. A promise that was easier to keep when she wasn't standing in the same room as the sick bastard. Mac was so close she could smell the stale, greasy aroma that surrounded him, a smell she had always associated with poverty. He'd tried to hide it with soap, but hadn't quite managed. She had noticed the same stink on the guard. George forced herself to stay calm. Mac wanted to get under her skin, and he'd only do that if she let him.

'Hello, Mac,' she said as civilly as possible.

'Well,' he said, 'since you're here, why don't you both take a seat?' The cuffs rattled as he waved them towards the two empty chairs on the other side of the table.

'We'd prefer to stand,' said George.

'Anyway, this won't take long,' Paul added.

Mac shrugged. 'Have it your way. No skin off my nose.'

'We've got a proposition to put to you,' said George.

'Here to trade . . . I'm all ears.'

'Tell us about Hathaway and Jones.'

'And what do I get in return?'

'Your life,' said Paul.

46

Mac found it quite amusing really, the two of them standing there like the cats who'd got the cream. He had a good idea where they were going with this. But how much did they know, and how much was speculation?

'Go on.'

'You're next,' Aston said.

Mac feigned bafflement. 'Next?'

'The person who took out Hathaway and Jones is coming after you.'

This was worth a wry chuckle. 'Take a look around, Aston. In case you haven't noticed, I'm in prison. What's he going to do? Pass through the walls? Make himself invisible so the guards can't see him?'

Neither replied, and that silence was worth a thousand confessions. Mac wondered how long they'd known about Derby. Aston hadn't mentioned anything yesterday, so it must be a new development.

'Someone speak,' said Mac, eyes flicking between the two of them. 'My curiosity is killing me here.'

'The way we see it you've got two options,' said George. 'Either you cooperate. In which case we protect you.'

'Or,' Aston added, 'we're going to throw you to the wolves. Take a second to think it over, Mac. But not too long, eh?'

Mac took a second, and a few more for good measure. 'You're bluffing.'

'Prison's a dangerous place, Mac. How safe do you really think you are in here?'

'I've managed to survive so far.'

'Maybe he won't come for you in here,' George put in. 'Your trial starts on Monday. You'll be out in the big, bad world again. Anything could happen out there.'

'Let's see if I've got this right.' Mac looked at them both in turn. 'If I don't cooperate you're going to sit back and do nothing. Not a word to the police, not a word to the prison authorities. Basically, you're going to sling me out on that firing range and paint a big fuck-off target on my forehead.'

'That pretty much covers it,' Aston said.

Mac shook his head. 'Not buying. Know why? Your conscience won't let you do that.'

'I wouldn't be so sure about that.'

Mac detected a hardness in Aston's voice that hadn't been there before. 'Know what? I'm thinking that maybe I'm not on anyone's hitlist. I'm thinking that perhaps this is a story you two have dreamt up to get me talking.'

'Think what you like. It's not me who's going to end up dead.'

'Here's the deal,' said George. 'Cooperate and we will do everything we can to ensure your safety. We'll get your security bumped up to a level that would keep the PM happy.'

'I'll have to think about it.'

'You've got one minute,' Aston said. 'Sixty seconds. Yes or no. If the answer's no, we walk and we won't be back. This is a one-time-only deal.'

A mobile went off and Aston checked his phone. He excused himself and left the room. Mac stared at George long enough to make her uncomfortable, until she turned away.

'I still think about you.'

George's head snapped towards him. For a split second the defences crumbled and she was standing before him completely naked . . . all she ever wanted was to be loved. Her discomfort was exquisite, as delicious as the finest wine.

'Shut up.'

George glared as though he was the devil incarnate. Mac gave his most pleasant smile.

'You're an evil bastard, aren't you?'

'And what's evil?' he asked. 'A giant wave crashes through the Pacific killing hundreds of thousands. Is that the work of a merciful, loving

God? I don't think so. Is it evil? I'll leave that one for you to mull over.'

'Just shut up,' she whispered.

Her voice was light, lacking any real weight. He'd really got under her skin, scratched away at those sensitive places she thought she'd kept so well hidden. Mac stared, but she wouldn't meet his eye. Thirty seconds drifted past, a minute. Aston returned and pulled George into a corner. They conferred in whispers and sign language. Mac tried to tune in, but didn't get much. They turned to face him and he wondered whether this had been stage-managed for his benefit.

'So,' Aston said, 'how does Sir Edward Coulson fit into all this?'

For a split second, Mac acted as if he'd been hit with a surprise slap. As quickly as the mask slipped, it was back up again. Aston noticed, though . . . just like Mac knew he would.

47

Out in the corridor, Aston had pressed the mobile to his ear while Jem filled him in. For once the news was good – maybe things were finally swinging their way. Derby had set a virus loose and the hard-drive was a mess, but Jem had managed to rescue some bits of email and a few other fragments. In cyberspace, Derby used the name Kestrel. No first name, just Kestrel. Obviously that wasn't his real name, but it somehow felt more real than Simon Derby; to Aston, the Derby alias had all the solidity of a phantom. The kestrel was a predator, a killing machine, and Aston could understand the assassin wanting to associate himself with it. Kestrel had been keeping a correspondence going with someone called Spinny. As far as Jem could tell, Spinny was an information broker. The name Edward Coulson had cropped up . . . Sir Eddie Coulson the media magnate. How Sir Eddie fitted into all this was anybody's guess, but instinct told

Aston this was important. So he'd thrown the name at Mac to see how he'd react. And the reaction was more than he could have hoped for. The change in Mac's expression was so fleeting anyone else would have missed it. But Aston had been watching carefully. And Mac had slipped up. Looked like he wasn't invulnerable after all. Perhaps the Kryptonite *was* getting to him.

'What's Edward Coulson got to do with anything?' Mac was saying.

'Nice try,' said Aston.

Mac didn't say anything for a while. He was weighing up his options, and Aston was happy to let him have as much time as he wanted.

'If I go to the Governor and tell him there's someone trying to kill me, he'll just write me off as paranoid. If I tell him there's a killer on the loose in his prison, he'll just agree and tell me that he's got hundreds of them.'

'That's the way I see it,' Aston agreed.

'Got me between a rock and a hard place, don't you?' said Mac.

Aston bit his tongue. It was so tempting to rub Mac's face in it, but this was the most vulnerable part of the negotiation. Aston sensed it could still go either way. One wrong step and Mac would tell them to piss off. However, Aston had the distinct impression Mac wanted to talk. Mac loved having an audience. Any excuse to come across as superior. If he didn't want to talk, he would have dismissed them the second they walked into the room. The lines of communication were still open, and that was promising.

'I want your word that you're going to do all you can to stop this bastard getting to me,' Mac said eventually.

'You've got it,' Aston said. 'So, we've got a deal?'

There was a long silence, then Mac said a very quiet 'Okay'.

Aston flashed a smile at George. They might hit a snake at any second, but for now they were getting ladders. George didn't smile back. She was standing at the edge of the table with a faraway expression on her face. When he told her what Jem had discovered she'd acted as though she couldn't have cared less, which wasn't like her. A breakthrough like this would usually have her turning cartwheels. Something had gone down between George and Mac while he was out of the room, and whatever that something was it hadn't been good.

'This could take a while,' Mac said. 'Maybe you should take a seat.'

Aston looked at George, who shrugged non-committally and sat down. Aston took the other empty chair. Mac had gone into lecture mode. All the signs were there: the chest had puffed up with self-importance, and his voice had taken on that condescending tone Aston loathed. He knew his old boss well enough to keep his mouth shut and let him talk. After all, that's what they'd come here for.

'This all starts with Coulson, but back in the Eighties he was still using his real name: Alistair Forrester. Forrester worked for MI6.'

Mac paused for dramatic effect, and Aston bit back all the questions that had suddenly dropped into his head.

'His background was nothing spectacular.' Mac was talking to Aston and acting as if George wasn't in the room. 'Similar to yours, in fact. A nice middle-class upbringing. Both parents were teachers – his father was headmaster at a grammar school in Newbury. Forrester went to Cambridge where he came to the attention of one of Six's talent spotters. After training he ended up in the Soviet department. Forrester loved being a spy . . . or more accurately, he loved the *idea* of being a spy. For him, it was all about the image. He made sure he got his suits made by the right tailor, drove the right cars, made all the right friends. He was good at networking, brilliant at recruiting, and he was a charming son of a bitch, too.'

Edward Coulson was a regular face on TV, so Aston could see what Mac was getting at. He was an expert at staging events to get maximum publicity. You wanted to hate him for being so successful, but somehow you just couldn't.

'He was a brilliant field agent. Women loved him. In the late Seventies, he had an affair with the wife of one of the top people at the Russian embassy in London. She thought it was love; for him it was business. The information he got was priceless. Of course, this was all hush-hush; there were only a handful of people in on this. And the KGB was oblivious, which was no mean feat.

'In '84, Forrester was posted to Moscow. Bertie Jones was H/MOS and Forrester was his right-hand man . . . and heavily touted to be the next head of station.' Mac paused, and offered a foxy smile. 'Back in those days I was still ambitious. I wanted the Big Chair, and heading up the Moscow station was a big step in the right direction. Forrester was in the way and the simple solution was to take him out.

'Forrester was still cruising on the goodwill he'd created by screwing that diplomat's wife. The more I thought about it, the more suspicious I got. Something smelled wrong. The KGB just weren't that careless. I planted a piece of information in a place only Forrester could find it. Two months later, the same piece of information comes bouncing back courtesy of one of our spies in the KGB. It wasn't enough to hang Forrester, but it was promising. Gary Hathaway was in Moscow at this time as well. He was way down at the bottom of the ladder, but there was no-one else I could use and this was too big a job to do on my own.

'Over the next six months we did a complete number on Forrester. We tracked his movements, discovered where he went, who he went with. We looked into his lifestyle, his finances. Forrester had been careful, but not quite careful enough. To finance the lifestyle befitting the spy he believed himself to be cost money, yet he wasn't in debt. The extra cash had to come from somewhere. And that somewhere was the KGB. I called a meeting with Jones and told him what I'd discovered. To start with he didn't want to hear. Understandable. Even today, all these decades on, the Cambridge Spy Ring casts a long shadow over MI6. Jones didn't need a scandal of this magnitude. It's a career killer. So I gave him an out. Want to know what I did?'

If there was one thing Aston hated more than Mac's patronising lecturer voice, it was his super-cilious smugness. Knowing that Mac would tell him anyway, Aston kept quiet.

'Basically I helped Jones turn a potential shit-storm into one of the greatest intelligence triumphs of the Cold War.

'Of course, Forrester denied everything. I was given the task of breaking him. After three days I had my confession. Forrester was greedy, not stupid. When I told him what I had in mind he practically bit my hand off. For my troubles, I got a pat on the back and a promotion to MOS/1 – Forrester's old job.

'We gave Forrester the codename JUDAS and for the next three years he carried on feeding infor-mation to the Russians. The big difference now was that we were in control of the information the Russians were getting. Also, Forrester was eager to redeem himself and came back with some really good stuff. So, the KGB was fed enough false information to keep them busy for years, and we were able to round up a dozen spies, including one from the upper echelons of the MoD.' Mac paused, a wistful expression on his face as though he was reliving the glory. 'Eventually the Soviets got suspicious. That age old spying dilemma again: if you don't make use of the information, what's the point in having it? The KGB should have worked it out sooner, but Forrester was good. We kept him in play as long as possible. If it had been left to me, I would have let the Soviets round him up and put him in front of the firing squad. Jones wouldn't hear of it. A deal was a deal. Since he was technically in charge of the op, it was his call. Ironic really. If he'd done what I suggested he'd still be alive.

'So, we pulled Forrester out, gave him a new name, paid for a new face, stuck a few quid in a bank account and sent him on his way. That was the last I expected to hear from him. Forrester liked a drink, and I thought he'd dive to the bottom of the nearest bottle. It happens to a lot of ex-spies. When MI6 cuts that cord, it's cut for good. A couple of years later, Edward Coulson as he is now known, turns up. He has a new wife, and not any old wife. Helen Smith-Thomas was one of the richest women in the country. The rest of that story you already know. If you don't, you can find it out easily enough.' A patronising smirk for Aston. 'Four people knew about this. Aside from me, Jones and Hathaway, the only other person in the loop was The Chief. Four people, and three are now dead. The old chief from natural causes; the other two murdered.'

And now Aston understood why Mac had co-operated. To start with, he'd been suspicious, couldn't understand his motive. Mac had to be getting something more than extra protection out of the deal. Now it was obvious. He'd said there were four people in the loop. Not quite correct. There was a fifth: Coulson. For some reason, Coulson had started killing off the people who knew his secret. Mac would be aware of how vulnerable he was, and that was why he had co-operated. There couldn't be any other reason. Basically, he wanted Coulson taken out of play. And he had manipulated Aston into doing the job for him. This left Aston with mixed feelings. Even now, stuck in prison, Mac seemed able to push his buttons. It wasn't right.

'I've kept my side of the deal,' Mac said. 'You'd better keep yours.'

'We will,' Aston said as he got up.

On the long walk back through Belmarsh's anonymous grey corridors, Aston asked George's opinion on what Mac had told them. She was quiet for a long time, long enough for Aston to gear himself up to ask what the matter was. She'd been acting strangely ever since he'd taken the call from Jem. Before he could ask, she answered.

'You know,' she said. 'I think he's telling the truth. I reckon he's been itching to boast about that one for a while.'

'That's my feeling,' Aston said. 'I never thought I'd say this, but for once I'm glad he's such an egotistical wanker.'

48

Edward Coulson settled back on the white leather sofa, a Havana steaming away in one hand, a snifter of Courvoisier XO Imperial in the other, and watched the pretty young thing strip. Gentle music played in the background. Something she'd chosen. The CD was one of Tanya's. A bit too modern for his tastes, but inoffensive enough. Anyway, he wasn't really listening.

The agency was the best in the city, discretion guaranteed. He'd asked for a girl in her late teens, and Suki claimed to be nineteen. A lie he'd let pass because she was absolutely stunning. She had to be at least twenty-two, maybe even mid-twenties. He'd had a hard-on from the second she'd floated from the private elevator. A vision in black silk, stilettos adding another three inches to her height, a hint of the Orient in her features. Her hair was short and boyish, silky black. Suki had taken two steps and stopped dead. A common reaction. One wall of the penthouse was made entirely from glass, the London cityscape laid out as though for his benefit. At night the view was incredible. The Thames winding far below, the London Eye, Westminster, and thousands upon thousands of multicoloured lights twinkling far into the distance. Breathtaking.

The penthouse was as impressive as the view. The elevator opened into the main living area, a large open space with modern sculptures displayed in their own light halos, like museum exhibits. Stylish Impressionist paintings hung on the white walls, professionally positioned to best show them off. Lots of light wood and chrome, a perfect blending of the natural and the manufactured. An impressive staircase swept upwards to the bedrooms. It was the sort of place where, if you had to ask the price, you weren't buying.

Suki was down to her underwear now: a tiny black lace thong and matching bra, hold-up stockings with elaborate patterns around the tops. Her silk dress lay puddled at her feet. Eyes closed, she swayed to the rhythm, her perfectly manicured fingers running across tanned skin. Her left hand slipped under lace, lingered a while. She brought the hand to her mouth and looked him straight in the eye as she slowly licked herself clean. The bra came off next. Coy as a schoolgirl, she flipped the catch, shook it off one shoulder, then the other, and dropped it on top of the dress. Suki placed her right foot onto the coffee table and began unrolling a stocking. Coulson stopped her with a wave of his hand. He took a long pull on his cigar and told her what he wanted. Suki smiled as she pushed the panties over her hips. They fluttered to the floor and she stepped out of them, revealing a small strip of hair that was barely a centimetre wide. She sat on the edge of the coffee table, then reached behind and took a brand new cigar from the humidor.

For the next ten minutes, he watched her do a Monica. Normally, he would have found this entertaining. Not tonight, though. He was distracted, tense. Everything was in place for a wonderfully self-indulgent Friday night: a beautiful girl, good cognac, good cigars. Tanya was at the house in the country, no doubt dreaming up more ways to spend his money. Yet, it wasn't happening. He knew the reason. His thoughts edged towards places he didn't want to go, and he reeled them back into the here and now. Coulson watched Suki, not really seeing her any more, his erection fading.

It had started to go wrong back in November. Why the hell couldn't Hathaway have just let it lie? Stupid, greedy bastard! It happened so long ago. In a different lifetime. But once you've sold your soul, you're never completely free, no matter how much you delude yourself. Coulson had always known this, but had never fully understood the implications. Not until Hathaway contacted him. He had asked for three hundred and fifty grand. Small change, but Coulson was an expert on the mechanics of blackmail. That would be the first instalment. From the moment the money changed hands Hathaway would be a permanent – and unwelcome – addition to his life. Coulson had spent too long getting here, had invested too much time and energy, to let Hathaway screw it up.

Coulson had put the phone down, knowing what he needed to do. The long dead Forrester was able to help. Forrester knew all about black ops and wet work. Arranging an assassination was no real problem. And if you were going to the trouble of arranging one, why not arrange three? The hit on Macintosh was supposed to have taken place last night, but Macintosh was still alive. To make matters worse, Kestrel was incommunicado.

Worry about it later, Coulson told himself. Suki's keening was tugging at his attention. Eyes closed, lost in a world of her own, she came with a holler and a sigh. Whether her orgasm was real or faked, he neither knew nor cared. Suki opened her eyes and smiled. A thin sheen of perspiration was coating her skin. She reached over, plucked the cigar he was smoking from his fingers and dropped it into the brandy. A sizzle as it extinguished. She took the glass from him and placed it on the table, prepared the cigar she'd been using. Even above the stink of tobacco he could smell her pussy. She held out a lighter and he leant into the flame. Then he sat back and smoked a while, admiring her as though she were a priceless work of art.

She didn't flinch under his gaze, just sat there quiet and serene, head swaying gently to the rhythm of the music.

Coulson took one more pull on the cigar and laid it in the ashtray. He ordered Suki over to the window, told her not to turn around. Then he undressed, folding each item carefully and making a neat pile on the sofa. Rubbing himself hard, he tried to ignore his problems. Suki was doing her best to please, so he might as well enjoy what was left of the evening. Coulson put the condom on himself; being this rich, it was prudent to be careful. A single pinprick was all it would take, and a paternity suit was not his idea of fun. He padded over to the window, the wood cool beneath his feet. She was a good girl, knew how to follow orders – there hadn't been so much as a single glance in his direction. He lingered behind her for a moment, savouring the smell of her perfume, the animal smell of her sex. Ever so gently, he pushed her against the window, enjoying that moment when skin connected with cold glass. The way her muscles tensed, rippling then relaxing, was sublime. He parted her legs with the back of his hand and entered her slowly, tenderly. Moving in time with the soft sounds coming from the stereo, he traced the elegant line of her neck with his tongue and forgot about his troubles for a while. And far below, London glittered like a neon-inspired fairy tale.

331

Kestrel had got as far as London Bridge station before realising he was being followed. Big mistake. How long had the tail been there for? Kestrel couldn't say for sure, but if he'd been following him since Belmarsh then that was a serious lapse . . . the second in less than twelve hours. As far as he could tell, there was only one tail. He was good – too good to be a cop. MI6 or MI5 was more likely. Kestrel should have spotted him sooner, but his mind had been elsewhere, mulling over the fucked-up attempt on Macintosh's life. He'd occasionally aborted hits. That was the nature of the profession. Unless everything was one hundred per cent perfect you didn't pull the trigger – you never pulled the trigger and hoped for the best. Being caught out like this was a first. He had seriously underestimated Macintosh and was lucky to be alive. That would never happen again. He'd learnt his lesson, and a harsh lesson it had been. Still, there was a silver lining. The hit Macintosh wanted done was as straightforward as they came. Easy money.

Standing there on the platform, Kestrel had considered

doing a disappearing act – it would be so simple to vanish, never to be seen again. As easily said as done. The problem was the computer back at the flat in Hendon. There were things on the hard-drive that could make life uncomfortable. It needed to be dealt with. If they were already this close, it wasn't going to take them long to discover where he lived. Maybe they already had. While he waited for the train, Kestrel threw together a crude plan. He had to get to the flat as soon as possible and ascertain whether it was being watched. If it wasn't, then he had to get inside and deal with the computer. Shaking off the tail would take too much time; he would just have to work around that problem. Probably best to act as if he hadn't seen him, let him believe he still had the upper hand.

Somehow they'd found out he was working in Belmarsh. From there they would have followed the trail to Simon Derby's personnel file and discovered Derby was currently living in Fulham. The address for that flat was real: the lease short-term, the rent kept up to date. He dropped by once a week to clear the junk mail from the front door and put a fresh pint of milk in the fridge.

Kestrel was convinced the tail wanted to discover where Simon Derby really lived. If they'd just wanted him, they would have taken him outside Belmarsh . . . probably driven up in an armoured car with blackened windows and snatched him from the kerb. Giving up Derby's Hendon flat was no great hardship. In Kestrel's mind Simon Derby was already dead and buried; that particular snakeskin had been discarded. Whether they *found out about the flat now or later made no real difference.*

The short walk from Hendon station was tense, like negotiating a minefield. Working hard to remain inconspicuous, he was aware of everything around him. The tail stayed well back, merging with the rest of the early morning commuter traffic. Kestrel reached Kings Road, his antennae buzzing. Any indication the flat was being watched and he'd keep on walking. Just get the hell out.

But the flat wasn't being watched. Once inside, he headed straight for the airing cupboard and crawled into the spare bedroom. Multi-tasking, he shredded pictures and documents, set the computer virus loose, stripped to his underpants. Quickly to the bedroom, where he arranged the dummy in the bed and switched on the electric blanket. Kestrel got dressed – sweatpants, T-shirt, sweatshirt – and was still pulling his trainers on seconds before he clambered onto the fire escape. He rushed downwards, jumped the last six feet, sprinted through the undergrowth and hopped the fence into the house behind. Green Street ran parallel with Kings Road, identical in almost every respect. Twenty-eight seconds after leaving the flat, he was just another jogger out for an early morning run.

Macintosh had offered £500,000 pounds for the hit. A cool half million. You didn't turn your back on money like that without a good reason. Kestrel had outlined his conditions, and Macintosh had eventually agreed. At midday, Kestrel called the mobile number. The lawyer picked up immediately. Yes, the money was in escrow.

Held in a Swiss bank. Mr Macintosh would not be able to get it back. Yes, subject to the conditions of the agreement between yourself and Mr Macintosh being carried out in full, the money will be transferred to the Cayman Island account you specified. Kestrel had asked for a contact in Switzerland who could verify the money was where the lawyer claimed. The lawyer had hesitated briefly, hummed and hahed, and Kestrel had said nothing. Eventually, the lawyer had parted with the information.

Kestrel had done all he could to ensure he would be paid, and instinct told him Macintosh would honour his side of the bargain. On the whole, clients paid up. He had only been conned once. Driving down the steep hill from his palatial home, that particular client had discovered his brakes weren't working. As anticipated, the airbag saved his life – Kestrel wanted the client to have a few hours where he could really appreciate the gift of life. Later that night, dressed in medical whites and a wig, he sneaked into the client's expensive private room and pumped a syringe full of air into the catheter in the back of his hand. A particularly excruciating way to go.

With Simon Derby dead and buried, Kestrel breathed life into William Cryer; a legend he kept in case of emergencies. William Cryer's documentation was held in a waterproof ziplock bag hidden in a rusting tub of white Dulux gloss in a lock-up garage he'd rented in Wembley. A second tin held a SIG P226 and a silencer. There was a grand in cash in a third tin.

William Cryer used the cash to buy a change of clothes, a black hold-all, and a few odds and sods from B&Q;

335

his documentation was more than adequate to persuade Hertz to part with a two litre Mondeo. By mid-afternoon, Kestrel had put enough miles between himself and London to start to relax. He pulled off the M4 into Chieveley services, and William Cryer's Visa card got him a room at the Travelodge. Using plastic was risky, but paying by cash would have looked more suspicious. The risk was calculated; Cryer would be long dead before anyone came sniffing around the motel. Kestrel set the alarm for seven in the evening and was asleep as soon as his head hit the pillow.

A shower and a shave, and he started to feel human again. He headed to Newbury for dinner, opting for a chain restaurant where he wouldn't be remembered. The food was bland and uninspiring – a carb boost to keep his energy levels up.

Kestrel reached the village in the early hours of Saturday morning and parked in a road off the High Street. Every house was cloaked in darkness; there wasn't a soul about. No lights shirking behind curtains, no curious insomniac eyes peering out into the night. Streetlamps cast an eerie stillness in orange and white. It could have been a ghost town. The cottage was exactly as Macintosh had described it. Even in the charcoal dim of the night Kestrel could see that. The well-kept greys of the garden, the shadowy flower baskets. He could just make out the house name on the plaque: Rose Cottage. A last check to make sure no-one was watching before heading up the small path to the back garden. He placed the hold-all at his feet and teased the lock with a skeleton key. Fifteen seconds and he was in. The SIG in one hand, the bag in the other, he moved silently through the house. A sniff to test the air. The remnants of a lamb dinner lingered, camouflaged by a chemical hit of air freshener. Orange and peach. There were pictures and ornaments everywhere, lace and frills and chintz. The stairs were treacherous. Old and squeaky. Down on hands and knees to disperse his body weight, Kestrel made his way slowly upwards.

He killed the man first. A single head-shot. The woman awoke to the kiss of cold steel against her cheek. He placed a silencing finger to his lips and she turned to her man for reassurance and answers. Saw the dark patch spreading across the pillow. Saw the abattoir mess that was his head. Kestrel was quick to get a hand across her mouth before she woke the whole village. A gag replaced his hand; twine to secure hands and feet. Her old lady eyes were wild with fear, full of tears and mercy pleas. He went into the bag and pulled out a hacksaw, made sure she could see it. Keep her alive for as long as possible. Macintosh had been adamant about that.

49

'Paul, get your lazy arse out of bed!'

George banged on the door, not caring if she woke the neighbours. She knew he'd heard her and was probably lying there with a pillow pulled over his head hoping she would disappear. He'd dragged her out of bed yesterday . . . revenge was sweet. It wasn't particularly early – a little before nine-thirty – but, it was a Saturday morning. She would have still been in bed if it hadn't been for Mother who delighted in giving her an early morning call most Saturdays to remind her it was the Sabbath, and drop a few unsubtle hints that maybe it was time to get back on the straight and narrow. Usually, George took the call on autopilot, grunting at all the appropriate points. Ignoring the phone wasn't an option – Mother kept ringing back till she answered. After one particularly heavy Friday night, she'd unplugged the phone. Bad move. Mother had panicked . . . had even tried her mobile. Convinced that George must have fallen victim to carbon monoxide poisoning, she'd come charging round to make sure she was still alive. Being in the same room as her mother was a trial at the best of times . . . with a raging hangover, well, root canal work was preferable. Mother hadn't phoned this morning, but George had still woken up around the time she usually called. Conditioning was a bitch! She'd lain there tossing and turning for a while, her mind playing with work stuff, before giving up and hitting the shower.

Fist clenched, George hit harder and got a bit of a rhythm going. She stopped for ten seconds, then started again, shouting out the occasional 'Paul' for good measure. Finally, she heard sleepy footsteps padding along the hallway and the door swung open. Without a word, Paul turned and padded back down the hall, buttoning up his shirt with all the awareness of a sleepwalker. George took this as her invitation to come in. She picked up the paper bag in one hand, her briefcase in the other, and kicked the door shut behind her. She found Paul in the kitchen filling the kettle.

'Good morning,' she said breezily. 'And how's my little ray of sunshine?'

'Piss off,' Paul said as he heaped spoons of instant coffee into two mugs.

'But look.' She held up the bag. 'Bagels and cream cheese.'

'And that makes everything all right, does it?'

George found a knife and plates, and prepared the bagels. She carried them through to the lounge and sat down on the leather sofa. Paul appeared thirty seconds later with the coffee.

'And before you say anything,' he said, settling beside her. 'I know it's instant. My coffee-maker's on the blink.'

'Did I say a word?'

'I thought I'd head you off at the pass.'

George bit into her bagel and washed it down with some coffee. The coffee tasted nasty, but she kept quiet. She'd poked and prodded Paul enough for one day. Reaching for the briefcase, she pulled out the background information she'd collected on Coulson and spread the papers on the coffee table. Most of it had come off the Internet; she'd got a lot of it from trawling newspaper and magazine sites. The gaps had been filled in by Jem. The computer expert was a tabloid junkie who main-lined gossip. When it came to the rich and famous, Jem seemed to know everything about everyone. This had surprised George – she'd thought the computer expert would be above all that.

In 1992, Edward Coulson hit the media spot-light like a hyperactive moth. One second nobody had heard of him, the next everyone had. The reason for his rapid ascension was Helen Smith-Thomas, who was widowed and desirable and worth a fortune. Her grandfather had purchased a small local newspaper shortly after the second world war, and one paper had quickly become two. When he died in the mid-Sixties, the Smith-Thomas Newspaper Group was the largest independent newspaper group in the country. Helen's father took over the business and his first move was to buy into TV and radio. Smith-Thomas Senior had been short-sighted on this score. The old man felt that TV and radio were fads . . . they were a newspaper group goddamit, ink was in their blood! Smith-Thomas Junior's major coup was taking the business global, buying on both sides of the Atlantic. He also did a major rebranding job – the Smith-Thomas Newspaper Group became Poseidon Publishing.

Helen was an only child. There had been complications during the pregnancy, and she was two months premature. The doctors' opinion – and Smith-Thomas had trawled Harley Street for a second, third and fourth opinion – was that his wife was lucky to be alive. Another pregnancy was not advisable. Initially, he was disappointed he didn't have a son to take over the family business. Helen, however, turned out to be a Smith-Thomas through and through. Ink flowed in her veins.

At eighteen, Daddy got her a job as a trainee journalist on the *Chepstow Times*. This was the first newspaper her grandfather had bought, a tiny weekly with a circulation of 9,500. By twenty she was news editor; by twenty-three she was editor. That same year she married the Sports Editor, much to her mother's horror. Her father was more laidback; his son-in-law was a journalist, which made him all right. Helen would have been happy staying in Chepstow playing at being a wife and journalist, but her father had other ideas. In her mid-twenties, she went to work at Poseidon Publishing's head office, a twenty-storey block in the centre of London. Working at her father's side, she learnt everything there was to learn about running a multinational publishing empire. On hitting thirty, the ticking of her biological clock became too loud to ignore. The result was Craig.

Eighteen months later, her mother died. She'd never fully recovered from the pregnancy, and had the money to indulge in hypochondria. When she was told she had breast cancer, it was almost as if it was a relief to discover there was actually something wrong. Helen felt strangely unaffected by her mother's death. She'd never been a big part of her life. Three months later, her father suffered a massive stroke. His death hit Helen hard, but she had little time for tears. Poseidon wasn't going to run itself.

Overnight her life changed. This took some getting used to. Open season was called on her private life – rather than being a servant of the media, she became an object of fascination. Her husband couldn't handle it and started drinking too much. One night Helen was awoken by the police to be told he'd wrapped his Ferrari around a lamppost. The autopsy showed his blood-alcohol level was four times the legal limit. The first whisperings that the Smith-Thomas fortune might be cursed started around this time . . . not much to begin with – a lazy paragraph here, a paragraph there – but enough to get the ball rolling.

Helen had a couple of failed relationships before Edward Coulson arrived on the scene. The media were like vultures, and their scrutiny had made it impossible to have a normal relationship. Coulson appeared unfazed by the attention. Three months in, and the media was hinting at wedding bells. The pre-nuptial signed, they got married on Necker Island in a small ceremony away from the media glare and attended by only a handful of close friends. Helen was given away by three-year-old Craig. It seemed that things were finally looking up. Edward was the perfect man for her. He was as interested in Poseidon as she was, and she soon had him working for the family firm.

The curse of the Smith-Thomas's struck again two years later. As an anniversary surprise, Coulson arranged a trip to India. On the third day they were walking through a marketplace when a thief tried to snatch Helen's camera. The old Pentax was only worth a couple of hundred pounds, but in terms of sentimental value it was priceless. She'd bought it herself with her first wage packet. Helen was stabbed as she fought to keep a grip on the Pentax, the blade nicking her heart.

The board had assumed they'd hold the reins until Craig was old enough to take over. However, when the will was read, Coulson was named as acting president; Craig would take over the company on his 21st birthday. The company flourished under Coulson's leadership and was now one of the world's leading media giants. Coulson had houses across the world, a private jet, a yacht, all the trappings of the seriously wealthy. His current girlfriend was Tanya, a former Slovakian air hostess with supermodel looks. Three years ago he had visited Buckingham Palace to receive his knighthood for services to British industry.

Going through this, George remembered what Mac told them. He'd said Coulson was a good field agent, and he hadn't been kidding. Alistair Forrester had been living as Edward Coulson for well over a decade and nobody suspected a thing. Not only that, he had been living as Coulson under the full scrutiny of the media. She could see how he'd pulled it off. Famous people had two lives: the backstory and the afterlife. The afterlife was the current reality, the diamond studded fame and fortune existence that the media sold to the general public. The backstory covered the 'humble beginnings' bit, and it wasn't unheard of for a whole brand new history to be invented. Either there was something to hide, or they wanted to make themselves appear more interesting. The public was really only interested in the afterlife: who they were screwing, how much they were earning, that sort of thing. As long as the backstory sounded like the truth, that was good enough. Looking at Coulson's backstory, George had to smile. Once you knew it was fiction, it was so obvious.

Paul flicked through the papers, picking sheets up at random, glancing at them and then putting them back down. 'I already know most of this,' he said. 'So, tell me, why exactly have you decided to ruin my Saturday morning?'

'Misery loves company,' George said, smiling.

'Are we talking about you or me?'

'Well, you're the one sitting there with a face like thunder.'

'You're not making any new friends here.'

George paused. 'So, what do we know? We know Hathaway and Jones have been murdered. We know Coulson ordered the hits. Not only that, he was a traitor who sold secrets to the Russians. The fact he turned against them after he'd been burnt doesn't count. Once a traitor always a traitor. This is serious shit, Paul. If any of it gets out, Coulson is ruined.'

'Okay, George, here's a question: why kill Hathaway? That doesn't make sense. For years everything's going along fine, why rock the boat by ordering the hit now?'

'I've got a theory. Coulson isn't stupid. He's not going around having people killed for fun. There has to be a bloody good reason.'

'And that bloody good reason would be?'

'I'm speculating here, but what if Hathaway was blackmailing him. Hathaway had a gambling problem, right? By the sounds of it, there were a few nasty individuals in Rome who weren't particularly happy with him. Hathaway approaches

345

Coulson and gives him an ultimatum: hand over the cash or he's going to blab.'

'Okay, but why not stop there? Why kill Jones? Why order the hit on Mac?'

George shrugged.

Paul considered his own question for a moment. 'I suppose he could be tying up the loose ends. Mac said there were four people who knew about JUDAS. If they're all dead then there's nobody to blab.'

'Possible,' George conceded.

'So, we knock on Coulson's door and escort him to the nearest police station, yeah?'

George laughed. 'If only it was that easy.'

'I think you could safely say we've got a distinct lack of hard evidence,' said Paul. 'The testimony of a terrorist, a load of circumstantial evidence, and not a lot else. I can't see Coulson being convicted on the basis of that, can you?'

'Not really. So what are we going to do about it?'

'That's easy,' Paul said. 'We go and find ourselves some hard evidence.'

50

Aston chewed on his bagel and let his mind roam. This was a tricky one. Coulson was guilty, but *proving* that was a different matter. Coulson would get the best lawyers money could buy. Any loophole – no matter how tiny – and the case would be blown out of court. But did they need an actual conviction? Would dragging him through the courts be enough to ruin his reputation? Would that be enough to take him out of the game? An interesting idea, and possible, too. There was one problem. Coulson's reputation might be ruined, but he would still have all that money and power, and the freedom to use them. And he would also have a couple of new names to add to his shitlist. No, if they were going to take him down, they had to make sure he didn't get up again. Somehow they had to get enough evidence to put him away forever. A knock on the door shook him from his thoughts and he flashed a little boy grin at George.

'Go get that, would you?'

'What did your last slave die of?'

Aston grabbed the closest sheet of paper from the coffee table and pretended to read. 'Go on. I'm busy.'

George harrumphed as she got up and walked out of the lounge. Footsteps moving down the hall, the squeak of the front door opening, a plastic 'thank you'. The door thudded shut and George walked back along the hall. She came in with a bemused expression on her face carrying a parcel that was the size of a shoebox. It was wrapped in silver paper with a red bow tied around it. 'It's not your birthday,' George said as she handed it to him, 'which means you must have a secret admirer you haven't told me about.'

Aston took the parcel and froze, every instinct telling him something was wrong. He carefully placed the parcel on the table and got up.

'What is it?' George asked, suddenly concerned.

'Who delivered this?'

'A motorcycle courier. Why?'

'He took the lift?'

'Yeah, I think so.'

Aston was already on his feet and sprinting barefooted for the front door. Out of the flat and along the landing. He crashed into the stairwell and took the stairs two at a time, jumped the last four. George wasn't far behind, shouting for him to wait up. Aston stopped for a moment in the lobby. The lift doors were grinding shut;

the front door slowly falling closed. He barrelled out onto the street. Looked left, looked right. Aston heard the throaty throttle of a big bike and turned towards the sound. A Kawasaki dodged out from behind George's Volkswagen Beetle. The motorcyclist was dressed from head to toe in black leather and wearing a red helmet with white go-faster stripes. Ignoring the grit and gravel digging into his feet, Aston ran into the middle of the street. The Kawasaki kicked up a gear and roared around the corner. 'Shit!' he muttered to himself.

George caught up with him, panting, her crinkly black ponytail bouncing. 'Paul, what's going on?'

Aston didn't answer. He walked back to the pavement, scanning the street as he went, looking for anything suspicious, anyone who looked out of place. Just an ordinary Saturday morning. A man was pushing a pram along the opposite pavement, playing the weekend dad; the woman laughing into her mobile was dragging a dog behind her that looked more rat than canine. Aston stared at the blank windows of the houses on the other side of the street. There was a sniper behind each one, and their high-powered rifles were trained on him and George.

'Got to say, Paul, you're freaking me out a little here.'

'This is all wrong,' Aston muttered, more to himself than George.

'What's all wrong?'

349

He turned to her. 'You're right: it's not my birthday. The problem is that I don't have any secret admirers, either.'

'So who sent the present?'

'I can think of two likely suspects. Mac or Kestrel. But why? That's the bit I don't get.'

Aston started back towards his flat and George grabbed his arm, stopping him in his tracks.

'Okay,' she said, 'let's say this is from Kestrel . . . or Mac. You're just going to walk back in there!'

'Why shouldn't I?'

George sighed. 'You really haven't thought this through have you? What if it's a trap? A parcel bomb? Something like that?'

'It's not a bomb.'

'And you're sure of that?' George raised an eyebrow. 'If you go back in there you're taking a stupid, unnecessary risk.'

'No, I'm taking a calculated risk.'

'A calculated risk! And how exactly do you work that out?'

'Easy, if it is a bomb, it's impractical for it to be on a timer because there's no guarantee it would reach the intended target – that would be us.'

'Maybe it's remote controlled.'

'The fact we're still here disproves that. If it was remote controlled then Kestrel would have been close by. He would have seen the courier come out and pushed the button. Bye-bye us. No, the most obvious method is for it to be triggered when the box is opened. So long as we don't open the box we're okay.'

George didn't look convinced. She tightened her grip on his arm, fingers digging into muscle. 'So you admit it might be a bomb.'

'Don't worry, I'm not going to do anything stupid. Promise.' Aston shook George away and walked back into the old orphanage. She caught up with him at the bottom of the stairwell.

'I don't like this, Paul.'

'Well, wait outside then.'

'Not going to happen . . . and you know it.'

'In that case, let's get going.'

Aston's confidence abandoned him the second he stepped onto the landing and saw the wide open front door. Out on the street, it had been so much easier to be brave. He took a deep breath and walked into the hall, headed straight for the lounge before he bottled it. The box was sitting where he'd left it, surrounded by a scattering of the Coulson printouts. Aston had this crazy urge to pick it up and give it a shake; the box possessed the same fascination as the live rail on the Underground. It looked innocent enough with its big red bow, but it wasn't. Not any more. George had planted the idea that it was a bomb in his head, so that's what it was. Except he knew it wasn't a bomb. Aston's curiosity was killing him. If it wasn't a bomb, what was in there? He reached for the box. Hesitated. Reached out again, and pulled his hand back. It was as though there was an invisible barrier; he could get so close but no further.

'Paul!' George said sharply. 'You promised.'

'It's not a bomb.' Even he could hear the lack of conviction in his voice.

'But you don't know that for sure.'

Aston shook his head and let out a long sigh.

'Thank God for that! Sanity prevails. Can we leave now? Please?'

George didn't wait for an answer. She pulled out her mobile and headed for the hall.

'Who are you calling?' Aston asked as he followed her along the hall.

'Priest. He'll know a thing or two about bombs, right?'

51

The three of them sat squashed into George's little red VW Beetle and waited for the verdict. George and Priest had bagged the front seats; Aston had the rear seats to himself and was stretched out with his feet resting against the door. The floor was littered with discarded burger cartons and a few unidentified objects he didn't want to think about. A yellow smiley-face air freshener hanging from the rearview mirror was doing its best to keep the stale smell at bay. The heater was on low, pushing warm air around them and stopping the windows from misting up.

'I hope your mate knows what he's doing,' George said to Priest. 'If there's a bomb in there and it goes off then we're going to be in the shit. We should have evacuated.'

'Not until we know for sure. Heath's orders.'

'I still think we should have evacuated.'

'Let's wait and see what Benny says. And don't worry . . . he's good. Bloody good.'

Benny was an expert on all things that went bang. A bottle of Famous Grouse had got him out on a Saturday morning. Mate or no mate, putting your life on the line for a bottle of whisky was asking a bit much as far as Aston was concerned. Priest's mobile rang and he flipped it open. He grunted a couple of responses, then flipped it closed.

'It isn't a bomb,' he said. 'However, it would appear someone's got a warped sense of humour.'

'Meaning?' Aston said.

A shrug. 'Your guess is as good as mine. Benny wouldn't say any more.'

By the time they got upstairs, Benny was sitting on the leather sofa nursing a glass of Jack Daniels. Straight by the looks of things, the tumbler three-quarters full. The bomb expert was short and stocky. That he was in his late forties had filled Aston with confidence when they met; to last so long in his profession indicated competence. Benny's nose had been broken more than once, and his grooved face was a testament to a life lived hard. His protective gear was piled in one corner.

Benny nodded to the open box on the coffee table. 'If any of you have a dog, then today's its lucky day,' he said, laughing.

Aston followed George and Priest over to the coffee table and peered into the box. What he saw didn't register at first. *Wouldn't* register. Distantly he heard George saying 'Jesus, that's disgusting!'. Priest was making a joke about how his friend's

354

German Shepherd would love to get his teeth into that. Benny was chuckling. All of that seemed to be happening in some faraway universe. This had to be a joke. No way could it be real. No fucking way! Maybe the hand was made from wax. That was it. This was a joke hand, made from wax. The sort of thing you'd find in Madame Tussauds. Except it wasn't. It looked and smelt real. Aston wanted to look away but couldn't. The box tugged at him, exerting a cruel hypnotic pull. It *was* a shoe box, he saw . . . a shoe box that had once contained a pair of Reebok trainers. The red ribbon lay next to it, the bow still intact; the silver wrapping paper had been removed in one piece. Toilet paper had been screwed up into balls and neatly arranged in the bottom of the box. The paper was peach coloured, and Aston marvelled at the way the brain could track the mundane when everything else was unravelling. It was surreal. He was coming apart at the seams, yet in some ways he was functioning fine, able to note the colour of toilet paper. How screwed up was that? George was speaking to him. There was concern in her voice. She was saying something about him looking pale. Did he want to sit down? No thanks, he heard himself reply, he was okay. Aston stared into the box. The antique ring on the middle finger fascinated him. An engagement ring with a good sized diamond. How many times had he seen this ring? The hand was ivory white, drained of blood, an older woman's hand. The fingers were curled around a small cloth bag – a bag that no doubt contained thirty silver coins. It was this last detail that convinced him the box came from Kestrel. The 'why' was a question for later. Right now, Aston was caught up in the middle of a horror movie, unable to believe what he was seeing because the implications were too horrendous. Kestrel had crudely hacked the hand off above the wrist – splintered parts of the radius and ulna were showing. Aston hoped she'd been dead when this happened, and immediately found himself charging headfirst into a wall of guilt. How could he wish her dead? Aston's legs buckled and he dropped to his knees. He retched once, twice, choking up his partly digested bagel. This couldn't be happening! He wiped his mouth and swallowed back the taste of bile. George had stopped asking questions and was helping him to his feet. She led him to the sofa and made him sit.

'Paul, snap out of it.'

This barely registered; George sounded as if she was calling from the bottom of the ocean. The slap stung his cheek and brought him crashing into the here and now. He looked around, momentarily confused, a stranger in a strange land.

'I know whose hand it is,' he said softly.

52

Paul's face told her all she needed to know. Drained of blood, it was as though he'd aged a century within seconds.

'I know whose hand it is,' he repeated in a dead voice that was stripped bare.

'Whose?' George already knew the answer but needed to hear it from him. It was the only way to make it real.

'My mum's.'

Paul's voice was so quiet, barely a whisper. He stared straight ahead, focusing on nothing. On one of the few occasions Paul had talked about Leicester Square – *really* talked – he'd told her about the walking wounded. He'd described their blank looks, the thousand yard stares, and she thought she'd known what he was getting at. Now she knew exactly. Benny was heading for the door and George didn't blame him. This had all the makings of a major clusterfuck. She pulled Priest to one side, out of earshot.

'I think it's best if you go, too. I can look after Paul.'

'You sure?'

A token argument and they both knew it.

'Yeah, I'll be fine.' She nodded to the box on the table. 'What do we do with that?'

'Put it in the freezer.'

George grimaced. Priest's answer was blunt and pragmatic, however, that didn't make it any less gross. Having a human hand in your freezer . . . it didn't bear thinking about.

'Do you want me to do it?' Priest asked.

'No, I can do it,' she said, a little too quickly, and immediately wished she'd kept her mouth shut.

'Okay, I'll catch you later. If you need anything give me a call.'

George listened for the click of the front door, feeling more alone than she'd ever felt. Paul was in the room, but he might as well have been on the other side of the solar system. She wanted to reach out to him, wanted so much to help him. It wouldn't have done any good, though. He was currently in a place beyond help. She looked away, and her eyes were drawn to the box. Why hadn't she said yes when Priest offered to move it? The answer was simple. Being a woman in MI6 wasn't easy – basically, she didn't want to be seen as weaker than the boys. And how dumb was that? Paul's mum was dead, and she was worried about scoring a few points for the sisters.

Taking a deep breath, George walked over to the coffee table. It was impossible not to look inside, and she felt her stomach lurch. The hand appeared to have been carved from stilton. It was bad enough when she didn't know whose hand it was; the fact it belonged to Paul's mum made it all the more horrific. George knew that relations between Paul and his mother had been strained since he discovered the truth about his father. He'd never forgiven her for keeping quiet all those years . . . and now he never would. That would be a ton of guilt to endure. Before 18/8, George had met Paul's mum a couple of times. Paul had bitched about her – of course – but that was because she was his mum. George had always found her really nice – a damn sight more chilled than her own mother. In the way of mums everywhere, George had sensed she was being eyed up as a potential daughter-in-law. Whether she passed that particular test she wasn't sure. She hadn't been warned off, wasn't aware of any curses having been placed on her, which had to be a good sign.

She carefully picked up the lid, touching it with as little skin as possible, and dropped it onto the box. As the lid fell into place she got a final glimpse of the hand. What distressed her most were the shattered slivers of bone hanging from the wrist. She picked up the box with equal care and carried it through to the kitchen. The freezer section of the fridge was almost empty. Typical bloke – hers was so full, shutting the drawers was impossible. George dropped the box into a drawer and quickly closed the door. She spent the next couple of minutes at the sink scrubbing her hands raw, but no matter how much she scrubbed she couldn't get them to *feel* clean. George flicked on the kettle and made Paul a tea with three sugars; hot, sweet tea for the shock. She carried the mug through to the lounge and put it in Paul's hands. Wrapping his fingers around the mug, she lifted it to his lips and made him drink. Paul let her do this without a word. His face was still blank, his spirit in stasis. A dribble ran down his chin and she wiped it away, dried her damp hand on her jeans. She searched for some words to make him feel better, anything that might help. But what did you say in a situation like this? Empty platitudes were the best she could manage, and they weren't going to help. So she kept quiet and made him sip the tea, feeling so inadequate because her friend was hurting and there was fuck all she could do to take the pain away.

For something to do, George went through to the kitchen and rinsed the mug under the tap. As she swilled the water around the mug she realised Paul wasn't the only one in shock. His was obviously more extreme, but hers was just as real. She stood at the sink and gave herself a mental slap. Told herself to get her act together. She'd be no use to Paul if she went to pieces.

Paul wasn't on the sofa when she got back.

360

George called out his name. No answer. She headed for the hall, thinking he must have gone to the loo. But the door was wide open and the bathroom was empty. 'Paul!' She could hear the worry creeping into her voice, could feel it prickling her heart. 'This isn't funny!' George pushed the bedroom door open, already knowing he wouldn't be there. She ran back into the lounge, looked around for his leather jacket – it had been slung over the back of the sofa, but wasn't there now. George ran to the window and saw her little red Beetle pulling away from the kerb. 'Shit! Shit! Shit!' She grabbed her jacket and headed for the hall, her mobile was already in her hand.

53

Aston had tried phoning his mum a dozen times, but just kept getting the answer machine: 'Sorry we're not here. Leave a message after the beep and we'll get back to you as soon as possible'. Each word was pronounced with the utmost care, as though she were auditioning for a play. The sound of her voice broke his heart. He only tried her mobile once. Like he'd thought, it was switched off.

He parked in the High Street and killed the Beetle's engine. Traffic depending, it usually took an hour and a half to get to Great Bedwyn – today it had taken less than an hour. He had no memory of the journey. His foot had been hard to the floor the whole way, the engine screaming in protest, and it was a miracle he hadn't been stopped for speeding. Aston climbed from the car and gently pushed the door closed. He didn't bother locking it. Couldn't see the point. Willing his feet to keep moving, he walked the hundred yards to her cottage; it felt as though he was wading through quicksand. He paused by the gate. This had never been his home. He'd been brought up in one of the big houses on the edge of the village, the house his stepfather still lived in. His mother had moved here after scandalising the village by having an affair with the lead tenor from the church choir.

Rose Cottage had been built in the days when people were smaller, and everything about it seemed out of scale and ever so slightly odd. The doors were a fraction too low, the windows too small. The chimney leant a little to the left and you could see where some of the roof tiles had been replaced. The garden was well-loved, the flowers just starting to peek through – another week or so and it would be a riot of colour and fragrance.

Aston was last here at Christmas. He'd tried to get out of it, but in the end his mother had managed to twist his arm. Just for Boxing Day, she'd said. It would be so good to see you. Knowing she wouldn't take no for an answer, that she'd resort to increasingly extreme forms of blackmail until he gave in, Aston had agreed to go. And it had been hell. They hadn't known what to say to one another, how to relate. All the old rules were irrelevant. What they needed was to start afresh, draw up a new set of rules, but it was too early for that. He hadn't been able to get away fast enough, and hadn't been back since. There had been a couple of stilted phone calls, the deep silences punctuated with a few tentative words. If he hadn't been so fucking furious, he would have found it sad. His mother wasn't a bad person, she just wasn't the person he thought she was. She should have told him about his father. What had she been thinking, keeping that to herself? George had been generous with her opinions: forgive and forget, life's too short . . . she'd tried them all. And, of course, she was right. But he hadn't been ready for that. His mother hadn't suffered enough. *He* hadn't suffered enough.

And now they would never have the opportunity to make things right.

The cottage appeared deserted. Not a good sign. It was a beautiful March day – a bit chilly but the sun was shimmering brightly in an icy blue sky – the sort of day when his mum should have been pottering around in the garden. Aston walked up the path on feet made from lead. He stopped at the front door and checked for signs of a forced entry. There were some scratches around the lock, but he wasn't sure if these came from a picklock. Aston made his way around the back. Checking the windows. The cottage looked secure.

He could still remember what his mum told him when she gave him the key: 'You know you're welcome here any time.' This was just after the scandal broke. What she'd really been saying was 'can you forgive me?' Except there wasn't anything to forgive. Aston had never been particularly attached to his stepfather; as long as she was happy, that's what mattered. He'd told her this and she'd hugged him fiercely and told him she loved him. Of course, this was back when his mother had still been his mother, back in the days before Robert Macintosh had ripped through his life like a tornado.

Unfortunately the key was at his flat, buried under the rest of the crap in the junk drawer in the kitchen. He'd been in too much of a hurry to get it. Aston took off his leather jacket and wrapped it around a large stone. He punched out the small pane in the back door and reached through to let himself in.

As soon as he stepped inside, he knew it was going to be bad. The air carried the faint smell of a butchers, minus the sawdust. He forced himself to go slow and careful. Downstairs first, checking each room in turn, trying not to disturb anything. Walking through the cottage was like walking through a chocolate box. Welcome to Chintz Central. Every spare surface was home to an ornament; there wasn't an inch of wall space that didn't contain a framed photograph. His face stared out from too many of the photos. An unselfconscious smiling superhero grin at four; gap-toothed at seven; awkward and shy and trying to fit into his body at fourteen. Nothing on the ground floor, so he headed upstairs. The bodies were in the bedroom. Roy had got the better deal. A single bullet in the head. Death would have been instantaneous.

Aston slid down the door and shut his eyes. He banged his fist against his forehead to make the image go away, but no matter how hard he banged it wouldn't leave him. The anger came slowly at first, a trickle that soon turned into a raging torrent. He could hear himself repeating one word over and over 'no!', as though this word had the power to turn back time and undo what had been done here. Tears burned his cheeks; anger consumed his heart. Kestrel might have swung the axe, but he was not responsible for this. There was only one person sick enough to instigate this. Reaching deep, deeper than he'd ever reached, Aston pulled himself together. He wiped away the tears and took out his mobile. Jem picked up on the third ring.

'Jem, it's Aston.' He was surprised at how normal his voice sounded, how calm. 'I need to visit Mac. I don't care what you have to do. Just make it happen.'

Before she could fire off the inevitable whats, whys and wheres, Aston hung up. He got unsteadily to his feet, moving with the stiff limbs of someone who had seen a hundred winters. Before closing the bedroom door, he called the cat over. Sooty looked up at the sound of her name, confused and guilty. She considered him carefully, then sprinted from the room, her tail tickling his leg as she sped past.

Aston stood outside the bedroom for a moment. This was too much to take in, too much to comprehend. He stared like a zombie at the door, the thin layer of wood doing nothing to insulate him from the horror on the other side. The images were already seared into his memory, images that would haunt him till the end of his days. Even with the door closed, he could still see his mum lying in a stinking mix of blood, piss and shit. Still see her pinned to the wooden floor like a butterfly pinned to a board. Still see the tent pegs that had been driven through her feet, the tear marks where she'd pulled against them. Still see the way her left arm finished at the wrist, the jagged bits of bloody bone where the hand had been crudely hacked off.

Still see the cat feasting on her torn flesh.

54

The study was Edward Coulson's haven of sanity in the house; both Tanya and Craig knew better than to come in here. He hadn't got heavy with them – that wasn't his way – he just explained it was important he had his own space. Not that this was any great hardship. Marlborough House was more than big enough for the three of them. Helen's father had bought the mansion in the Seventies. It was a huge rambling Elizabethan wedding cake of a building that cost a fortune to run; but when money's no object, why not indulge? Twenty bedrooms, so many bathrooms he'd lost count, reception rooms all over the place, and outside, fifty acres of rolling parkland. Yes, it was plenty big enough.

Even though Tanya and Craig never came in here, Coulson still locked the door. It was always best to be careful.

Carrying his coffee to the desk, he settled into the worn antique swivel chair. One wall of the study was lined with books he'd never read; framed pictures of him rubbing shoulders with the rich and famous were displayed on another. The desk was Edwardian and made from walnut. When he'd dreamt up Edward Coulson this was the life he'd imagined for him. A life of pampered self-indulgence. With a click of his fingers he could have anything he wanted. In recent years he'd begun to believe that he really was Edward Coulson.

He had used all his MI6 experience to reel Helen in, treating it like any other recruitment. The approach had been made at the opening of an art exhibition. The gallery was too modern, the paintings were atrocious, and the artist was completely coked-up and talking crap to anyone who'd listen. But there was a limitless supply of champagne, and the canapés weren't bad. Recruitment was all about seizing the opportunity, and his opportunity had come in the shape of an octogenarian who was talking to Helen's breasts and boring her half to death. Coulson had swept in, pretending to be a long-lost friend. He took her arm and guided her towards the bar, then spent the next five minutes apologising for being so old-fashioned. They got chatting, and this was where the importance of research came into play. She told him her name and he made out that he didn't know who she was, which went down well. She said he must have been living in the back of beyond, and he said, actually, yes he had. For the past couple of years he had been living in Zambia, helping to run a safari business. Of course, this was the point where she told him how much she loved animals. For the rest of the evening she'd gone into journalist mode, cross-examining him on his experiences in Zambia. By the time they went their separate ways it was Helen who was apologising for giving him the third degree. He laughed it off, then cheekily asked for her number. She hesitated for a second. A playful grin, then she fished a business card from her little black bag. She scribbled her private number on the back and handed it over. Coulson took the card, turned it over, looked at the logo, the company name.

'Poseidon Publishing,' he'd said. 'I didn't realise I was talking to a big shot.'

'Stop it,' she said, but she was smiling.

'President, too. Impressive.'

She'd held up her hands to make him stop. 'If you're not careful, I'm taking the card back.'

Coulson turned the card in his hand and made it disappear. Parlour magic. 'What card?' he said, all innocence.

'How did you do that?'

'I'm afraid I can't tell you.'

'Go on.'

A shake of the head and a smile.

'You know,' she said, 'I've really enjoyed this evening.'

'Even though I didn't recognise you?'

'Especially because of that. You've no idea how nice it is not to be recognised for once.'

This was the first proper confidence she shared with him – the first of many – and it was what he'd been playing for all night. The initial approach was the most crucial part of the recruitment process. Screw that up and you didn't stand a chance. The evening had gone better than he imagined possible.

After hooking Helen, he'd reeled her in carefully. For all her apparent toughness, she was fragile. The deaths of her father and husband had rocked her. Coulson took it slowly, offering friendship first. He had a separate mobile for her calls, so he was always available. He worked hard to ensure the groundwork for the epiphany was in place, gave her all the space she needed to come to the correct decision. When she finally saw the light, he was ready and waiting. Three months had passed since the art exhibition. After dinner at her Chelsea townhouse one evening, she'd taken his hand and asked if he liked her. Of course he liked her, he replied. But do you *like* me, she pressed, leaning into his personal space. He'd matched her move for move, letting her take the lead, making her believe she was in charge. It was important for her to think she was calling the shots. It was Helen who initiated the kiss; Helen who suggested they go upstairs; Helen who slowly undressed him before slipping out of her little black dress; Helen who had climbed on top and fucked him ragged until dawn crept in through the curtains. He had just played along like a shy virgin schoolboy. Eventually she'd drifted into an exhausted sleep. Coulson had stayed awake for a while, watching the soft rise and fall of her breasts, knowing he had her.

He opened the desk drawer and pulled out a bottle of Courvoisier, gave his coffee a boost and took a sip. Shutting his eyes, he settled back into the comfortable old chair. Perhaps the way forward was to do nothing. Hathaway was dead. So was Jones. Dead men didn't talk. The only loose end was Macintosh. He hadn't said anything all these years, why would he now? The problem was that he had no idea if Kestrel had actually made a move on Macintosh – had no idea what had happened there whatsoever. The lack of information was frustrating. Kestrel had contacted him on Wednesday to tell him he was going ahead with the hit. Since then, nothing. With the first two hits there had been emails informing him that 'the package had been delivered'. On this occasion he knew the 'package' had most definitely *not* been delivered, but that was only because he'd kept an eye on the news. Macintosh was behind 18/8; if he was dead the news would be everywhere. Likewise, if there had been an attempt on Macintosh's life, or Kestrel had been caught, that would have been big news, too. The obvious assumption was that Kestrel had aborted the hit. In which case, why had he not been in contact?

Macintosh was always going to be the most difficult hit out of the three. But Kestrel was confident he could do the job. He hadn't specified how he intended to do it, and Coulson hadn't asked.

Another sip of loaded coffee before opening his eyes and facing the world. Coulson switched on his laptop and went to the secure email account he used for his more sensitive transactions. Still nothing from Kestrel. He typed a short message, asking what had happened to the package. A click of the mouse and the words tumbled out into cyberspace.

55

Jem hacked into Belmarsh's computer system, her mind only half on the job. This was about as taxing as the work she'd done for Elite Personnel. The security was a joke and it took all of two seconds to smooth the way for DI Bromley's visit. Now she was in, it was so tempting to cause a little chaos. It would be child's play to start sending prisoners all over the country. Or how about this? Maybe the cons would appreciate a nice steak dinner tomorrow night. So easy to do – all you needed were the right passwords and protocols . . . and she now had both. The old Jem wouldn't have thought twice about doing something like that. Anything for a giggle. But that Jem was a distant memory. The fact she was here on a Saturday proved that. Sitting in the dim of her hi-tech womb, she was struck by the sudden reali-sation that she was one short step away from becoming a full-blown workaholic. Perhaps it was already too late. Kathy had tried to get her to see what was happening, and she had laughed her off with a 'Yeah, that'll be right'. Maybe Kathy had a point. Not that she would be getting any more advice from that quarter. Kathy had finally decided enough was enough. At least she'd had the bottle to do the deed face to face – Jem's favoured method was text.

When Jem got back to her flat last night – late again – Kathy was there, sitting on the sofa. The door key was lying ominously on the table, next to the ruined dinner. Kathy kept it together while she explained her reasons, only cracking when she suggested it might be a good idea if they didn't see each other for a while. Jem's first instinct was to argue, but that wouldn't have been fair. Kathy was right – it wasn't working. Her second instinct was to go to her and give her a hug, but that would just have made things worse. Chances were they would have ended up in bed, and that wouldn't have been fair on either of them. Instead, she had agreed with everything Kathy said. After Kathy left, Jem had just sat there with her knees pulled in to her chest, her arms wrapped around them. She sat like that for fifteen minutes, perhaps longer. Then she'd grabbed her jacket and headed back to the office.

Jem could see where Kathy was coming from. If the roles had been reversed she would have done exactly the same. Probably sooner. She could never accuse Kathy of not trying. If anyone was to blame it was her. Lately her life had been all work, work, work. And the truth of the matter was that she was loving it.

The wail of a war siren came from the work-station in the corner, and Jem hurried over. She crashed into the chair and shuffled the mouse. She'd rescued a couple of email addresses from Kestrel's computer and had tasked this machine with keeping an eye on them. These addresses were supposed to be secure . . . yeah, that'll be the day! Secure on the Internet! If people wanted to kid themselves, then great – it made her life easier.

Someone had logged onto the account of smith888. Jem's fingers flew over the keys as she attempted to follow the trail back through the servers to source. This was more like it. Much more interesting than hacking into a poxy prison system. Another beep, and a box blinked up on the screen. Kestrel had new mail. Jem was torn: carry on chasing smith888 or check the email. Curiosity won. It would take two seconds to see who was contacting Kestrel. A single click and Kestrel's inbox came up. The new message was from none other than smith888. Heart beating double-time, she clicked it open.

why was the package not delivered?

What package? Jem still didn't know who smith888 was. Yes, he was one of Kestrel's clients, but that didn't mean smith888 was Sir Eddie. She didn't really know how hired killers operated, but she figured Kestrel probably had more than one client. She clicked back to the first screen. Smith888 was still online. For how much longer, though? Jem took up the chase again. Whoever smith888 was, he was careful. Backtracking, she followed the trail through the Yahoo servers then onto AOLs. From there she tracked smith888 to an anonymous remailer service in Russia, then bounced across a couple of German servers. The final hurdle – and it wasn't much of a hurdle – was navigating a path through British Telecom's systems. Smith888 thought he was being so clever, but had left a trail that a blind man could follow.

Now she'd reached source, Jem moved with all the caution of a safecracker. She didn't want to spook smith888. Her screen was identical to smith888's; whatever he was seeing, she was seeing. Jem sat back, considering her next move. The Outlook page came up on the screen as smith888 accessed another email account. This looked promising. Watching someone like this was a bit sinister . . . sinister but kind of cool.

Phantom words appeared on the screen slowly, a letter at a time. Smith888 was a two finger typist, uncomfortable with the keyboard. Yet, he/she had managed to weave an intricate trail across the worldwide web. Kestrel's influence? The message was to someone called Adam. Short and sweet, work-related by the looks of it. Smith888 hit enter twice and Jem waited an eternity for him to sign off. The first letter was an 'E', the second a 'd'. Jem didn't need to see any more. Like Aston kept telling her, there were no coincidences in the spy game.

Smith888 was Edward Coulson.

Result.

Jem reached for the nearest phone and hit the speed dial button for Aston's mobile. It rang out. Strange. She'd expected him to answer straight-away. She punched in George's number and it was answered on the first ring. Jem could tell imme-diately that something was very wrong. George usually sounded so perky . . . except before her second coffee of the day, which was understand-able. Now she sounded as though she'd been told she had a week to live.

'What's up?' Jem asked.

'It's Paul.'

That didn't make sense. 'He sounded fine when I spoke to him.'

'When did you speak to him?'

'I don't know. Twenty minutes ago. He wanted me to arrange a visit with Mac.'

'Can you get DS Sullivan put on the list, too?'

'Yeah, no problem. What's going on?'

George didn't reply, and the silence was spiky and uncomfortable. Something was going down here, something bad. Jem couldn't help thinking the worst. She hoped Aston was all right. He wasn't her favourite person in the world, but he was just about tolerable. 'Aston's okay, isn't he?'

'Not really. His mum's been murdered.'

56

An old maroon coloured Jag drove up the aisle between the parked cars and skidded to a stop in front of Aston. The car was all retro lines and elegance, a flashback from the Seventies. George climbed from the passenger side and slammed the door. She looked absolutely furious. Aston didn't give a shit. She stomped over and stood in front of him. Hands on hips and blocking the way. He looked past her at the forbidding walls of Belmarsh on the other side of the car park. Priest was in the driver seat, staying put. Wise man.

'Paul, what the fuck are you playing at? You steal my car and just disappear like that! Do you have any idea how pissed off I am with you.'

'Please get out of my way, George.' Aston's voice was calm but there was a tightness there, like an overwound clock spring.

'This isn't a good idea.'

'If you think you're going to stop me seeing Mac, think again.'

George ran a hand over her hair and tugged her ponytail straight. When she spoke, it was with the soft understanding of an undertaker. 'I saw what happened to your mum. We must have got to Great Bedwyn just after you left. Paul, I'm so sorry.'

'So you understand why I need to talk to Mac.'

'Paul, go home and pour yourself a drink, a dozen drinks. Scream at the walls, curse God, whatever. But please don't go in there. Not yet. You're not in the right frame of mind to deal with Mac.'

'And what does the right frame of mind look like, George?'

'Don't do this. Please.'

Aston studied George's face and saw what she wasn't saying. He smiled but the smile didn't touch the sadness in his eyes. 'You know I'm going in there, don't you?'

She sighed. 'Yeah. And you know I'm going with you. I'm not letting you do this on your own.'

Aston walked around George and headed towards the prison. He heard George's footsteps following, heard Priest start the Jag and do a three point turn. Reception was expecting DI Bromley and DS Sullivan, and they passed through the security checks without any problems.

Back in the tiny interview room for the third time in as many days, Aston stared at the scarred table, glared at the grey walls. George was sitting beside him in one of those uncomfortable red plastic school chairs. She barely registered on his radar. His whole focus was directed towards Mac – all his anger, all his hatred. The bastard was going to pay for what he'd done. What form that payment would take, Aston wasn't sure, but he was going to pay.

Mac kept them waiting for almost an hour. And that was fine with Aston. Let him play his little games. If necessary, he'd wait all day, all fucking weekend if that's what it took. He needed to look Mac in the eye and ask one simple question. Why? The answer wasn't important. What was important were the unspoken words in his eyes. That would tell Aston everything he needed to know. Then what? Earlier, when he hadn't been thinking straight, he'd considered smuggling a knife in. He'd had no doubts whatsoever that he could do it . . . and use it. At the time, he had been running on a high-octane mix of adrenaline and fury – he could do anything. The idea was completely crazy, of course. Like he was going to get a knife into Belmarsh. Past the body searches, through the metal detectors. Not going to happen. So, once he had his confession, what then? Could he kill Mac with his bare hands? Well, there was one way to find out.

Thinking about Mac meant he wasn't thinking about his mum. It didn't seem real – couldn't be real – but it was. There were so many things he needed to say to her. He'd been so hard on her these past six months, had wanted to punish her, had wanted her to suffer. And had that done any good? If he'd been asked that yesterday, he would have said yes. Now he realised how destructive all that anger had been, how misplaced. George had tried to convince him he was being too hard on her. His mum had done the best she could, George argued, and if she'd got it wrong, well, we're all human and entitled to make mistakes. He'd grunted a response that could have been interpreted any which way, thinking what the fuck does she know. In hindsight, Aston realised she knew a fuck of a lot more than he did.

Another five minutes passed without any sign of Mac. George hadn't said a word since they sat down. Aston was aware of the occasional sneaked glance in his general direction; he saw the concern in her eyes. He was glad she was keeping quiet. The mood he was in, anything she said would be the wrong thing. All he needed was an excuse to let rip, to let go of some of his anger. George didn't deserve that. The handle creaked and he turned in the plastic chair. It took a second to register that the man entering the room wasn't Mac.

'Where's Mac?' Aston demanded.

Charles Wainwright ignored him and sat down on the other side of the table. The expensive lawyer pulled his cuffs down . . . not so far that they covered the Rolex Submariner. Up close, his hair seemed even whiter, the colour of innocence and purity.

'Where's—'

The lawyer put a hand up. 'I heard you the first time, young man.' His voice was too big for the cramped confines of the interview room.

Young man! The patronising shit. Aston held on to his self-control, but only just. 'If you heard me, then maybe you could do me the courtesy of answering.'

'Of course,' the lawyer said smoothly. His gaze shifted to take in George as well. 'Mr Macintosh has asked me to come along and represent him at this meeting. He's concerned about the way Mr Aston has been hounding him. However, he wants me to assure you that if you stop now, he won't take the matter any further.'

Aston shook his head, convinced he wasn't hearing right. The fact his cover was blown was the least of it. So Mac had told the lawyer all about DI Bromley. Big deal. But what else had he told him? Aston realised he was going off at a tangent and pulled himself back on course. The main issue here was that the lawyer had threatened him, and that was outrageous . . . absolutely fucking outrageous. There were things he needed to say here, things he should be saying, but the lawyer had broadsided him. George stepped in to help out.

'Mr . . .' she said.

'Wainwright,' the lawyer said.

'In what way has he been hounding him, Mr Wainwright?'

'Where to start,' the lawyer mused. His hands were steepled in front of him, his forefingers playing with his lip. The dirty light of the interview room glinted dully off the gold, blue and silver of the Rolex. 'So far my client has been incredibly patient, however, he has reached the point where he feels enough is enough.'

'I'm sorry, I'm still not following.'

'It's very simple. For three days running now, Mr Aston has been hounding my client—'

'There you go with that wor—' George got that far before Wainwright stopped her with an impatient wave.

'When I'm talking,' he said, 'I'd appreciate it if you didn't interrupt.'

George glared. 'Please go on,' she said pleasantly.

'Yes,' Aston added, 'please go on.'

Wainwright cleared his throat. 'Mr Aston requested a meeting on Thursday and my client was happy to oblige. For old time's sake.'

Old time's sake! Aston bit his tongue.

'When he asked for a second meeting, my client was also happy to oblige.'

'For old time's sake again, I suppose,' said George.

Wainwright ignored her. 'He happened to mention these meetings to me, and I advised him it wasn't in his best interests to be talking to you.'

Aston took a deep breath and pushed his anger

down. The smarmy lawyer was winding him up. No doubt that was his intention. Poke with that stick until he got a reaction. Well, it was working. 'We've got evidence that Macintosh is involved in a murder.' That last word was particularly difficult to get out.

'And when exactly did this *alleged* murder take place?'

'Some time during the last couple of days,' Aston said.

'And you say you've got evidence.' The lawyer looked like an indulgent father discussing the existence of fairies with his four-year-old. 'Exactly what does this evidence consist of?'

Aston hesitated.

'Let me help you out, Mr Aston. You don't have any evidence. I mean, how could my client possibly be involved in a murder? He's in one of the most secure prisons in the country. Has he got magic powers that enable him to fly over the walls? I don't think so. Shall I tell you what this is really about? This is part of an ongoing vendetta. You've been out to get my client since last September. Probably before that.'

The lawyer's voice had risen a couple of decibels, and he was preaching as if he had a jury box of twelve of the good and true to convince. It made Aston sick to the stomach to hear him defending Mac like this. How the hell did he live with himself? Aston was on the other side of the table before he realised what he was doing. He

386

dragged the lawyer to his feet and shoved him against a wall, pinned him there with his forearm. The look on Wainwright's face was worth all the heartache this was going to bring. Aston was vaguely aware that this wasn't a good idea. The noises George was making backed that up. It felt good, though. Wainwright's composure had shattered and he looked terrified. The lawyer spent his life dealing with the worst of the worst, but always at arm's length. This was suddenly all too real.

'Okay, Mr Fucking Hotshot Lawyer,' Aston hissed, 'here's a question for you. How the fuck do you sleep at night?'

He brought his right arm back and made a fist. It was only at the last second that he somehow stopped himself from driving it into the bastard's face. And then heavy hands were pulling him off, and low voices were telling him to calm the fuck down. Aston stepped back and tried to shake the hands away. They weren't letting go. He stared at Wainwright, and the lawyer stared back. Eyes wide with confusion, Wainwright edged towards the open doorway. He stopped when he reached it. Safe in the knowledge he could escape whenever he wanted, he pulled himself back to his full height and recovered his composure.

'I'm going to have you fucking crucified for this, Aston. Do you hear me?'

'I hear you fine,' Aston whispered, holding his gaze.

The lawyer looked away first, then hurried from the interview room as though he couldn't get away fast enough.

57

'How is he?' Priest asked.

'Sleeping,' George replied.

Priest raised an eyebrow.

'Okay, I slipped a little something into a whisky for him. He needed some time-out.'

George had taken Paul's place behind the big desk, both literally and figuratively. For the foreseeable future he was suspended from duty. He was currently tucked up in one of the army cots in the back room, cocooned in a narcotic haze. She wanted him close by so she could keep an eye on him. The frame of mind he was in, there was no telling what he might do. Getting out of Belmarsh had been fun; for an uneasy moment she'd thought Paul was going to end up on the wrong side of the bars. She'd needed all her powers of persuasion to placate the prison authorities. The assistant governor had not been happy. In the end, they'd been shown the door and told not to come back any time soon.

'We should call the police,' she said. 'We can't just leave the bodies there like that.'

'Why not?'

'Because we can't. This is Paul's mum we're talking about.'

'It's not as if she's going anywhere.'

More harsh pragmatism from the Irishman. What he was saying was true, but that didn't make it right. 'Priest, you're not listening! This is Paul's mother!'

'Just for a second let's forget that fact and take the emotion out of the equation. How long do you think it's going to take before the bodies are discovered?'

'That's not the point.'

'It is, and if you think about it, you'll see I'm right. The bodies will be discovered by the end of the day, probably sooner. It's a small village, someone's going to notice they're missing.'

'It's just wrong,' said George.

'Look,' Priest said gently, 'you know how it works. We get the police involved and it's going to get messy. We'll be answering their questions from now until forever. Do you think that's the best use of our time? We should be out there trying to catch the bastard who did this, not stuck in an interview room avoiding a load of awkward questions.'

He was right, but just leaving the bodies there . . . it didn't sit comfortably. 'What about an anonymous tip-off?' George suggested. 'I could pretend to be a friend of Paul's mum. We were supposed to meet for lunch, and when she didn't show up I got worried. Obviously the story needs work, but something along those lines . . .'

Priest considered this. 'You could do it completely anonymously? There would be no way the police could trace it?'

'None whatsoever.' George stood up and Priest waved her back into her seat.

'Before you do that, we need to decide on our next move,' he said.

She slumped back in the chair. 'I hope you've got some ideas, because I'm all out.'

'Not really,' Priest admitted. 'Okay let's look at what we've got. One, there's a hired killer on the loose, and so far he's taken four people out. Two, he was hired by Coulson.'

'Back up,' George said. 'You're oversimplifying. The first two hits were ordered by Coulson, yes. Then we're into a big grey area. Mac was supposed to be target number three. However, he's still alive. Not only that, target number three was actually Paul's mother. What's Coulson's motive for killing her?'

Priest shrugged. 'No idea.'

'That's because he doesn't have one,' George continued. 'Now, Mac, on the other hand, does have a motive. There's a whole load of shit gone down between Mac and Paul. Mac wants to hurt him. Emotionally, physically, any way he can. Arranging to have his mother murdered like this is classic Mac.'

'You're making it sound as if this is all a game to him. He somehow manages to arrange this murder, so he gets fifty bonus points.'

'That's not far off the mark. Mac doesn't think and feel like other people. Remember: he was ultimately responsible for all those people who died at Leicester Square. A death or two means nothing to him.'

'You're saying he's a sociopath?'

'It's as good a label as any.'

'Okay, we've got two problems here. We've got a hired killer on the loose who needs rounding up.'

'And then there's Coulson,' George said. 'We know he's guilty, but right now we don't have a single thing that would stand up in court. So what do we do?'

Priest thought about this for a moment. 'Maybe there is a way,' he said, a sly grin spreading slowly across his face.

'Let's hear it then.'

While Priest outlined his plan, George listened with an increasing sense of disbelief. She gave him a whole minute before she'd heard enough. 'No,' she said. 'There's absolutely no way I'll authorise this.'

'Why not?'

'Where do you want me to start? How about the fact she's not a trained agent? Oh, then there's the lack of experience. So there you go: two good reasons to be going on with.'

'It's a sound plan.'

'In theory, maybe. However, the reality is that it's not going to happen. I will not put her life at risk.'

'Okay,' Priest said, 'if you've got a better idea let's hear it.'

'You know what really pisses me off?'

George and Priest turned towards the voice. Jem was sitting on the edge of a desk on the other side of the room. She hopped off and headed over to George.

'What really pisses me off is when people talk about you like you're not there. It drives me nuts. *She's* got a name, you know.' Jem stopped in front of George's desk. 'It's a good plan . . . what's more, in case you haven't noticed, it's the only one we've got.'

'No,' George said.

'I can do this.' Jem looked so small and vulnerable. Like a kid pleading to be allowed up late to watch a scary film.

'The answer's still no.'

'Please.'

'It would be completely irresponsible.'

Jem smirked. 'And that would be a problem how?'

'I won't let you do this.'

Priest moved next to Jem. 'It's not like she'll be on her own, George. I'll be there to back her up. The first sign of trouble and she's out of there.'

'And that's supposed to make me feel better.

Whichever way you look it's too dangerous, Priest.'

Jem laughed out loud, surprising George. This was no laughing matter. 'Of course it's dangerous. If I wanted a safe job I'd still be working for that stupid agency.'

'Easy to say when we're sat around talking like this, but it's totally different out there in the field. At the end of the day you're a computer jockey, not a field agent.'

'You don't have to wrap me up in cotton wool. I know how dangerous this is.'

'No, you don't.'

Jem hesitated and bit her bottom lip. She stared George straight in the eye. When she spoke, she sounded older. 'You know, when I started this job all I cared about was the money. This was my Golden Ticket, my way out of the shit. But it's not like that any more. I love this job. And do you know what I love most? The idea that what I do might actually make a difference. Before you say no again, think about this: yes, it's dangerous, but I *can* do it. You've got to believe that.' She let loose a little lopsided smile. 'What's more, out of the three of us, I'm the only one who can pull this off. Priest in a pair of stilettos . . . I don't think so.'

George looked at Jem, weighing up the pros and cons. This was her call, and it was a call she didn't want to make. She'd be more than happy for Paul to make this decision, but that wasn't

394

going to happen. 'Okay.' The word was barely audible, carried on a gentle exhalation. 'But you do exactly what I tell you. Understand? No arguments. If I decide to pull you out, then you're out of there. No questions asked.'

Jem's smile stretched into a grin. 'Deal!'

It could work, George told herself, trying to justify her decision. She wondered who she was kidding. In some respects the choice had made itself, but that didn't make it sit any easier. Like Jem said: they were all out of options. They needed to get Coulson on his own, away from the hangers-on and the bodyguards. This way, he was doing the hard work. George couldn't see he'd want an audience while he was 'entertaining'.

'Right,' she said. 'We've got work to do. A lot of work.'

58

Jem's stomach crashed into her shoes as she watched George emerge from The Cube. Suddenly, this didn't seem like such a good idea. Why the hell had she argued herself into this situation? Her mouth had fallen open, and all that apple pie crap had spilled out. Making a difference! Yeah right! Craziness to the nth degree was what it was! Kathy always said her motormouth would get her into trouble one of day. Looked like she was right. Again. Yeah, she liked this job, but enough to put her life on the line? No way. So why had she done it? George stopped in front of her – looking confident and cool and gorgeous – and Jem had her answer. This was all about impressing George . . . and how crazy was that?

'Heath's given us the green light,' George said. 'He's going to pull some strings at GCHQ and get a tap on Coulson's phones. You can still back out if you want.'

The voice in Jem's head said, 'Yes, please'; the

voice coming from her mouth said, 'No way.' The mock bravado was so obvious to her, so fake.

'We could be in for a long wait.'

'It's okay. I've seen enough cop shows to know the score with a stake-out. Lots of junk food, gallons of coffee to stay awake, and being stuck in a car with a partner you can't stand . . .'

The call transcript came through less than two hours later. The three of them were in the downstairs office, where George and Priest were giving her a crash course in fieldwork. Jem read the transcript and her mouth went dry; all the blood sank into her feet. She placed it carefully on the desk.

'You all right?' George said.

'Fine.' It was an effort to sound normal.

This wasn't happening, Jem told herself. Not yet, anyway. It was too soon. Coulson had called Serendipity on one of his mobiles and requested a girl for Sunday night. He had asked for Suki – presumably one of his favourites – and signed off by specifying that she should turn up at the usual time and place . . . wherever and whenever that was.

Jem hurried upstairs and hit the computers. It took less than two seconds to hack into Serendipity's system; when you could do the Pentagon, a whorehouse was simplicity itself. It was all in there: contact details for the girls, records on each punter's preferences. Going through the latter almost raised a smile. The things people got up to. Compared to some, Coulson's kinks were harmless. He was a control freak, liked to be on top, liked them young – that was about it. Jem printed out the details and took them down to George. Suki's real name was Susan Rayburn. She had a place in Chelsea, so she was obviously doing all right for herself. George sent Priest off to check Suki out. Jem saw the move for what it was straightaway. An excuse to get her on her own.

'Last chance to back out. If you do, I'll understand.'

'I'll be fine.'

George gave her a look. It was the sort of look that burrowed under your skin and sought out your secret places.

'What?'

'Priest's gone now, you can stop the big brave act. How do you really feel about all this?'

Jem considered lying, but only for a second. 'How do you think I feel? I'm shitting myself.'

'Good. It's the fear that keeps you sharp . . . and staying sharp keeps you alive.'

'You want the truth? I wish you were doing this. You're the spy. You're trained for this.'

'I'd swap places, but I can't.' George laughed. 'Too old, too Jewish, and nowhere near pretty enough.'

'Of course you're pretty enough,' Jem said and almost blushed. She hurried on, hoping George hadn't noticed. 'And you're not too old. You're what? Thirty?'

'Close enough,' George admitted, 'but that's still

398

way too old. Coulson prefers them young, remember. The younger the better. I'm way out of the running.'

'Then I'm too old, too.'

'No you're not. The right clothes and some make-up and you'll easily pass for eighteen.'

Jem sighed. 'Looks like I'm doing this then.'

'Looks that way,' George agreed.

Now they had a deadline, the crash course in fieldwork intensified. They had a little over twenty-four hours to go. A day wasn't long enough – nowhere near long enough. A week would be good . . . a month would be better. George went through the dos and don'ts, the whys and where-fores, and then it was down to the nitty-gritty. The name came first. Until this op was over, she had to forget all about Jem the computer expert; from here on, she was Amber the high class hooker. In some respects this was the easy bit – while playing in cyberspace she often took on new identities. They were up early on Sunday morning, trawling Camden market for suitable clothes for Amber. Elegantly slutty was the theme, designer labels a must. Girly shopping trips weren't Jem's idea of a good time; however, George made it fun. For a while, she almost forgot why they were doing this. They got back to the office laden down with bags full of designer knock-offs, and reality came crashing in on her. Sitting there staring at the pile of clothes, she'd seriously considered bottling it. But it was too late for that now.

Early Sunday afternoon, Aston appeared upstairs. He sneaked in so quietly neither Jem nor George noticed him at first. How long he'd been standing there was anyone's guess. His face was unshaven and there was a stale smell surrounding him. He looked completely broken, a hollow man. Most disturbing were his eyes. They were completely blank, the emptiness stretching far into the distance. A chemical stare. In a dead voice Aston had asked what he could do to help. It was heartbreaking; he looked so lost. George told him they had everything under control and he should go back to bed. He argued half-heartedly, then gave up and went downstairs. Jem had tried to catch George's eye, a ton of questions needing answers, but she wouldn't look at her.

Jem had caught the whispers about what happened at Belmarsh. Aston had lost it big-time, by the sound of it. Attacking that lawyer . . . not one of his smartest moves. She couldn't begin to imagine the stress he was under. Jem didn't get on particularly well with her own mother – dear old mum didn't approve of her lifestyle choices, although she was slowly getting better. If anything happened to her, though, Jem would be devastated. If – heaven forbid – she was murdered, well, how the hell did you begin to deal with that one? Jem hated to admit it, but she was actually concerned about Aston. And George was worried sick. Jem had picked up on some weird shit going on between those two. The sooner they fucked the better. Of course, that wouldn't happen because they worked together, which was mad. If two people were meant to be together then they should be. Jem's own feelings for George didn't come into the equation. That was just a crush, no different from a teenage girl drooling over a pop star. Then there was the fact that George was one hundred per cent straight. It was fun to daydream, though, and if you're going to indulge in fantasies you could do a lot worse than a doomed love story based on unrequited love.

And now it was Sunday evening and she was riding in Priest's Jag, off to meet her doom, wearing ridiculous clothes and feeling like a freak. Walking in heels was a bitch! Why the hell did women put themselves through this torture? They'd eventually decided on the little black dress. A classic, you couldn't go far wrong with the little black dress. The underwear was a joke. Who the fuck in their right mind wore stockings and suspenders nowadays? Uncomfortable and impractical was what they were. A bloody nightmare. And she'd never been a fan of thongs, never mind lace ones. Jem had jokingly argued that Amber might be more comfortable in big pants and combat trousers but George had vetoed this; she didn't think Coulson was a big pants sort of guy. Speeding along the side of the Thames, she kept catching glances of herself in the rear-view mirror. The stranger in the war paint looked like her, but it was disconcerting to say the least.

Her biggest concern was that she'd just be getting into the whole act and Suki would turn up. That would be a complete headfuck. If that happened she was convinced she'd go to pieces. George would have handled it, though, somehow talked her way out. But she wasn't George. Priest and George had assured her Suki wouldn't turn up. Someone from Serendipity – George putting on a posh voice – had called Suki to cancel. By all accounts, she was glad to have a night off. A visit by the vice squad to Serendipity's offices had also been arranged, so checking up on Suki would be way down on their priority list. Jem wasn't convinced. Worry was in her nature, and she could see a million things that could go wrong. Priest parked his old Jag outside a tall tower that appeared to be made entirely of glass. It rose high into the night sky, shining silver in the moonlight. Jem's heart doubled in speed. This was it. No going back.

'You'll be fine,' Priest said.

'Easy for you to say.'

'You're wired, so I can hear everything that's going on. Any problems and I'll be there in less than ten seconds.'

'Less than ten seconds?'

'That's a promise,' he said. 'You look gorgeous, by the way.'

Jem ignored the compliment and got out of the car. She leant back in before closing the door. 'Less than ten seconds. You promise.'

'And I always keep my promises.'

With a shake of her head, Jem turned and headed for the entrance. She moved almost gracefully in the heels, glad that George had made her put in all that practice.

59

Coulson was under no illusions about his feelings for Tanya and love didn't come into the equation. He certainly lusted after her – and who wouldn't with a body like that? – but she could be too much. The constant demands, the whining. Was it worth it? He did wonder. Paying for sex was so much less complicated. The act of love reduced to a business transaction. Yes, that made life simpler. Still, Tanya served a purpose. As photogenic as a supermodel, she really looked the business draped on his arm. The media were suckers for a good love story, however the principal characters had to look the part. When it came to deception, image was everything.

Then there was the boy to contend with. Craig was well into his teens now. On the plus side, teenage boys had the communication skills of a Neanderthal, so at least they didn't have to talk much. Playing stepdad was a role he had to continually work at. And Craig was getting closer and closer to the magic number: twenty-one. Coulson still hadn't decided what to do about that. Getting rid of both of mother and son together would have appeared suspicious, so he'd opted to deal with them separately. After Helen was murdered he had taken on the role of Craig's mentor, grooming him to be Poseidon's next President, safe in the knowledge that that would never happen. Like a lot of rich kids, Craig was into extreme sports. Skiing and snowboarding, in particular. Thinking about it – and he'd thought about it a lot – there were definite possibilities there.

Weekends at Marlborough House could be painful. It needed to be done, though. Some quality time with the little lady and the boy for the sake of appearances. Tanya loved it up there in Hertfordshire, which had surprised him. When they first met, she'd been a real party girl. Now, as long as she got down to the city once every week or two, she was happy. Tanya had even taken up horse-riding. She'd tried to persuade him to have a go, but it wasn't going to happen. As far as Coulson was concerned, horses were only good for betting on. Mind you, Tanya did look good in jodhpurs.

It was always a relief to get back to the penthouse. This was where he felt most at home. High above London, the city stretched out before him as far as the eye could see. He finished his brandy and turned away from the panoramic window, went to the study and fired up the laptop. He accessed the account he used for communicating with Kestrel, expecting it to be empty. There was one unread message in the Inbox:

Checked the logistics for the last job. Can't see how it can be done. Arrange the final instalment for the previous two jobs ASAP.

Coulson swore under his breath. Kestrel owed him an explanation. He said he could do the hit on Macintosh, and he'd screwed up. And now he had the cheek to demand money. Coulson considered withholding the payment. But it was only a hundred grand, and it probably wasn't wise to piss off a hired killer. Despite being a Sunday night, it took only ten minutes to arrange the payment. The banks he used didn't operate on high street hours.

He shut the computer down and checked his watch. Perfect timing. Suki should be here any minute. He'd enjoyed her on Friday night. Eventually. She'd turned out to be the perfect distraction . . . and Christ could he do with a distraction now. So what the hell was he going to do about Macintosh? Paying him off wasn't an option. If the rumours were correct, he wasn't short of a few quid. Killing him was still the only solution. Dead men didn't talk. It was as simple as that.

And what was Kestrel going on about? Arranging for someone to be killed in prison shouldn't be that difficult. A bunch of murderers locked up together, surely someone would be willing to do it. So, why hadn't Kestrel thought of that? He'd obviously overestimated the assassin's abilities. No, the best idea was to wipe his hands of Kestrel and go find someone to do the job properly.

A buzzer sounded and Coulson made his way to the elevator. The face on the monitor wasn't Suki's, which pissed him off. The agency should have informed him they were sending someone else. He buzzed her up anyway. Settling down on the sofa, he crossed his legs and waited for her to arrive. Who knows? Maybe she'd be okay. Most of the girls the agency sent were pretty good. And some – like Suki – were exceptional.

The elevator doors concertinaed open and the girl stepped out. Well, she was pretty enough. The body was less curvy than he liked – a Kate Moss body – but he could live with that. She looked at him and smiled. Nice smile. Good teeth. She walked over, heels tapping on wood. Strange. That was the point most girls caught the view and stopped dead. This one hadn't noticed. She was focused completely on him, oblivious to her surroundings. Jesus Christ, this was all he needed. They'd sent him a fucking rookie!

'What's your name?' he asked.

'Amber.'

'Okay, Amber, there's the bar over there. How about you fix us a couple of drinks.'

The girl answered with another smile and

floated over to the bar. Coulson watched her go, enjoying the way her hips moved. Hopefully what she lacked in experience she'd make up for in enthusiasm.

60

For the umpteenth time, Jem told herself to relax. She was in over her head here, everything happening way too fast. So much for all that crap about how time slows down during moments of high stress, how it crawls to virtually a standstill so you can take everything in. Coulson must be able to see through her. How could he not? So far she'd managed to get one word out. One single word. Amber. And she'd almost fucked that up. Her real name had been on the tip of her tongue, and it was only at the last second she'd managed the switch. He must have heard the tremor in her voice. How could he miss it? No, this wasn't going well at all. As she walked across the vast apartment her fingers found the unfamiliar ring on her left hand, and it took all her willpower to pull them away. Playing with the ring would make her look nervous. Nervous! That was a laugh. She'd never felt more nervous in her life, more uncomfortable in her own skin. George had made her go through the plan again and again, and she went through it in her head now, hoping that would calm her down. That's what George told her to do. You planned and trained until it became second nature; you wanted your moves to be grounded in reaction rather than thought. But her movements felt as wooden as a puppet, and she was overanalysing everything. Even the simple act of walking was a trauma. And that was simplicity in itself. Left foot then right foot, left then right. She'd been doing that every day for over twenty years, and now she felt as unsteady as a toddler. Somehow, she reached the bar. Like the rest of the apartment it was ultramodern and reeked of money, all chrome and polished wood. There was every drink imaginable, the bottles lined up with an obsessive compulsive's attention to detail. A straight brandy for Coulson; an industrial sized double with Coke for her. George had warned her to go easy on the booze. Fuck that! A little Dutch courage was exactly what she needed. She glanced over at Coulson. He was snipping the end off a cigar. More importantly, he wasn't looking at her. She wouldn't get a better opportunity. Jem's left hand floated momentarily over Coulson's glass. A flick of the ring, and the pill tumbled out. She'd practised this move a hundred times, but she was still all fingers and thumbs as if she'd never done it before. Or maybe that was just how it felt. Perhaps she was coming across as cool as ice. Yeah right! Another glance at Coulson. He was lighting the fat cigar now, leaning into the flame, sucking and puffing. A deep breath. Jem picked up the two glasses. Fighting the urge to gulp, she took a sip from hers. The alcohol burned her throat, making her feel better. She *could* do this. No way was she going to let George down. She was Amber. Confident and gorgeous. The best in the business. She turned and smiled at Coulson, then walked slowly – and seductively, she hoped – towards him. The huge sofa had swallowed him up. He had his feet on the coffee table. The cigar looked obscene, like a big brown cock. The image flashed up in her mind without warning and she bit back a laugh, knowing if she started she'd never stop. Nervous laughter was like that; the more you tried to contain it, the more it flooded out. Jem stopped in front of the sofa and held out the balloon glass. His eyes were all over her, examining her from tip to toe as if she were a piece of meat, an object to be owned rather than a person. It made her skin crawl and she hoped her contempt didn't show. In his own time, he took the balloon glass and lifted it to his lips, paused, brought his hand down again. Jem realised she was staring at the glass and forced herself to look at his face. It was a lived-in face, handsome in its own way. Up close she could see the evidence of age, lines and wrinkles that she hadn't noticed in the glossies. She'd seen the pictures of his girl-friend. Tanya was drop dead gorgeous and the reason she was with a man old enough to be her father was obvious. Money was one hell of an incentive. A question with a less obvious answer was why the hell Coulson paid for sex when he had someone like Tanya in his bed. Jem didn't get it. Then again, she'd given up trying to understand men years ago. Coulson lifted his glass again. This time it got as far as his lips before he brought it down. He patted the empty space on the sofa and told her to sit. Why couldn't he just drink the fucking drink! What the hell was he playing at? She lowered herself onto the sofa, careful to keep her legs together; it had been a while since she'd worn a skirt. Coulson leant forward and put the glass on the table. Jem watched its progress with a sinking heart. He shuffled closer and she could smell him: cigars and alcohol and after-shave, the aroma of success. The cigar was burning away between his fingers, the smoke stinging her eyes. His arm snaked around her shoulders and it was all she could do not to puke. This was too much. He was going to make a move, and she had no idea how to deal with it. He came closer, and now she could smell the faint whiff of garlic on his breath. Jem closed her eyes, wishing herself anywhere but here. Something warm moved towards her left cheek. The heat quickly intensi-fied, climbing higher, moving closer. She opened her eyes and found herself staring at the red hot glow of his cigar, the tip no more than an inch away. And then it was half an inch away. She

412

started to struggle but it was no use. She might have screamed, probably did. And then, merciful darkness descended.

61

'Priest, what the fuck is going on?' George shouted into the mic. 'Come on! Speak to me!' A blood-curdling scream had filled the earphones, then ten seconds later the sound feed died. If anything had happened to her . . . George didn't finish the thought. This was neither the time nor place for blame.

'I'm on it.'

'Where are you?'

'The maintenance stairwell. Another dozen flights to go.'

'Just hurry, okay?'

'Going as fast as I can.'

There was a sound behind her, and she turned to see Paul silhouetted in the doorway. Great! Just what she needed. He stepped into the hi-tech gloom, head turning this way and that, as though he was seeing it all for the first time. She felt guilty for keeping him medicated, but it was the only way. He was a liability at the moment, too emotional to be of any real use; the stunt at Belmarsh proved that beyond a shadow of a doubt.

'Hey, Paul, how you feeling?'

He answered with a shrug that meant everything and nothing.

'Why don't you go back to bed then, eh?'

'I've been in bed all day. I need to move a bit.'

His voice had the flat inflections of a long-term asylum inmate, and the guilt bit hard at George. She'd done this to him. What sort of friend was she? He needed looking after, and what had she done? Drugged him and hidden him away in a dark room in the hope that the problem would disappear. It wasn't right.

'What's happening?' Paul asked.

'Nothing.'

'Did someone just scream?'

Shit! He'd heard that. Paul came over to her chair and she caught the odour of sour sweat and sickness. And he was sick, she supposed. Heartsick.

'No.'

'I'm sure I heard a scream.'

'You must have imagined it.' That was the thing with lying: you started with a small lie, then just kept piling more and more on top.

He looked confused for a moment. 'Yeah, that must have been it.'

'Why don't you go back to bed? I'll be down in a bit to keep you company.'

'That'd be good.'

415

She watched over her shoulder as Paul shuffled out of the room. He'd been a mess after Leicester Square, but nothing compared to this. And now she had Jem to worry about, too. What had she been thinking? Jem was cocky enough for fieldwork but she just didn't have the experience. And now she was in deep shit and it was all her fault. *Don't even go there*, George told herself. All that mattered right now was getting the computer expert back in one piece.

'Priest,' she said into the mic. 'Status?'

'Almost in position.'

They'd laughed about needing a plan B. Said it sounded like something out of an old black and white movie, a rainy Sunday afternoon special. It didn't seem funny now. George studied the monitor. Jem had gone through this a dozen times. All she had to do was a couple of mouse clicks. That's how fucked up this had all got. It should be Jem here doing the computer stuff. It should be her in Coulson's penthouse doing the spy stuff. And Paul should be calling the shots. It was like the whole world had gone mad.

'Okay,' Priest said. 'I'm ready. Let's roll.'

62

Coulson slapped the girl till she came round. He had wanted to scare her, but not this much. She flapped back into consciousness, arms flailing, reaching for her face, her eyes. Let her work it out for herself. She half scrabbled, half crawled into the corner of the sofa, made herself as small as possible, knees tucked into her chest. She blinked in light, and seemed surprised that both eyes were working.

'What's your name?' he asked.

'Amber.' She held his gaze for a whole two seconds before looking away.

'Let's try again, shall we? What's your name?'

'Amber.'

'Your real name, please.' He reached for the balloon of brandy and held it under his nose, appreciating the aroma. 'My guess is Rohypnol. Tasteless and odourless.' He slowly tipped the glass, watched the brandy splash onto the wooden floor.

'Once more: what's your name?'

'Jem.'

'Doesn't sound like a real name to me.'

'It's short for Jemima.'

'Okay, Jemima, now how about you tell me what you're doing here?'

'The escort agency sent me. Serendipity.'

Coulson moved closer and she cowered deeper into the corner of the sofa. He reached out and gently stroked her cheek. She tried to turn her head away, but there was nowhere to turn to. Coulson grabbed the girl's throat and squeezed, watched her eyes bulge. She was easy to hold; there was nothing of her. 'If you're a hooker, I'm a saint. For a start, most hookers aren't wired. You made one crucial mistake. Want to know what it was?' A grin while he reaffirmed his grip on her throat. 'You didn't ask me what I wanted to drink. Now, not only did you bring me a brandy, you brought me Courvoisier XO Imperial, which just so happens to be one of my favourites. What was I supposed to think? That you're a mind reader? Now, I'm going to let go and you're going to start answering my questions. Nod once if you understand.'

The girl's face was moving through various shades of red. She nodded and he let go. He gave her a minute while she coughed and spluttered and got her breath back.

'Who are you working for?'

'MI6.'

He gave her a pointed look. 'You wouldn't lie to me?'

A frantic shake of the head. Her pixie face was wet with tears. She didn't look like a spy. Then again, what did a spy look like? Six were really scraping the bottom of the barrel these days. Didn't they bother with training any more?

'I'm not lying,' she said. 'Honest.'

'So what happens after you drug me?' The girl hesitated, and that was answer enough. 'That's when the big guns get here, right?'

A nod.

Suddenly the lights went out. And it wasn't just the lights in the penthouse; a sizeable chunk of the city had plunged into darkness.

'Ah,' Coulson said. 'My guess is that's them now.'

63

Ten fucking seconds, he'd said. Well, that had to be the longest ten seconds ever. Moonlight and sodium leached in through the panoramic window, carving graphite shadows. Coulson was a few feet away, a grey shadow amongst all the other shadows. He didn't seem particularly concerned. He was just sitting there, legs crossed, calm as anything. George had found the right buttons to press. Thank God. During the last five minutes Jem had lived a thousand lifetimes. She'd been so sure Coulson was going to burn her eye out. It was the look on his face that convinced her. Jem, an aficionado of the slasher pic, knew a psycho when she saw one. But this wasn't some fantasy blasted up onto the silver screen, this had actually been happening. She'd seen the glowing end of the cigar coming closer, and the fear was unlike anything she'd ever experienced. There was only so much stress the body and brain could take before it shut down. She had gone way past that point with inevitable consequences. She'd never passed out before; had never considered herself the fainting type. A man-shaped shadow was moving across the room. The night vision goggles gave him a peculiar profile.

'Keep your hands where I can see them, Coulson,' Priest called out. 'Don't give me an excuse.'

'You can put the gun down. I'm not armed, and I'm not going to do anything stupid.'

'Let me be the judge of that. Jem, are you all right?'

'More or less,' she said in a voice she barely recognised.

Priest's hand moved up to his throat mic. 'You hear that, George? Our girl's fine. Hit the lights on the count of three. One . . . two . . . three . . .'

The hidden halogens flared, revealing Priest. The goggles dangled from one hand; he held a snub-nosed automatic submachine gun in the other. His finger was curled around the trigger, the barrel pointing at Coulson's chest. A modern sculpture sat on the pedestal beside Priest. The loose collection of marble curves inferred a dancer . . . if you squinted. Jem kicked off her heels and stood up on unsteady feet. The chances of making it more than two steps in those shoes was zilch. She glared down at Coulson, then slapped him across the face. In the cathedral-like space of the penthouse the stinging blow echoed like a gunshot. Coulson's head snapped to one side. Slowly, he faced front.

He stroked his reddening cheek and smiled at Jem. She slapped him again, harder this time, then walked over to Priest on trembling legs, the sound of her heartbeat filling her ears.

'Ten seconds! No way was that ten fucking seconds!'

Priest gave a loose smile. 'Maybe it was closer to twenty.'

'Twenty! And the rest!'

'What happened to your neck?'

Jem motioned to Coulson. 'He's what happened.'

'Is that right?' Priest said.

'Just trying to get some answers.'

'So when I ask my questions, you won't mind if I get a bit rough?'

A 'whatever' shrug from the multi-millionaire.

Priest pressed his throat mic. 'The situation's under control, George. We'll be back at base in fifteen.' He turned to Coulson. 'You can either go without a fuss, or I carry you out unconscious. The choice is yours, although I know which I'd prefer.'

64

The windows of the downstairs office were covered, freezing time; it could have been day outside, could have been night. There were three of them in the office. Coulson was blindfolded in a chair with George sitting opposite; Priest was hovering in the background, just itching to play bad cop. She'd set out the ground rules to Priest in advance: this was her show.

'I don't suppose there's any point asking for a lawyer and a phone call?'

George looked into the familiar face, studied the body language. There were no signs of stress whatsoever. Coulson had been dragged from his penthouse in the middle of the night, blindfolded and driven halfway across the city . . . surely he must be feeling a little uncomfortable. But that was the old school for you. Coulson was a Cold War survivor. And not just any survivor. He'd betrayed his country, betrayed the Russians; not only had he survived to tell those particular tales, he'd ended up rich. That was no mean feat. George made a mental note – whatever happened, she would not underestimate Coulson.

'If I'm not getting a lawyer, the least you can do is let me take off the blindfold.'

The engaging smile filled with neat white teeth was made all the more disarming by the dimples. *No*, she thought, *it would be a mistake to let your guard down with this man even for a second.* 'You can take it off,' she said.

'Thank you.'

Coulson reached behind and worked the knot. He folded the blindfold neatly and laid it on the arm of the chair. 'Would you like me to say a few words so you can get the correct recording level?'

'What makes you think we're recording this?'

Coulson just looked. George fought the blush rising in her cheeks and wished Paul was here. Interrogations were so much easier when he was around.

'Okay,' Coulson said, 'you've gone to all this trouble to get me here. I suppose the pertinent question is: what can I help MI6 with today?'

George was aware of Priest moving behind her. Coulson was following the Irishman with his eyes. 'Does the name Alistair Forrester mean anything to you?'

Coulson's attention snapped back to George. 'I think we can dispense with the softly, softly approach. Unless Six has gone completely to the dogs, I'm happy to accept that you know exactly who I am.'

There was that self-confidence again, a confidence bordering on arrogance. It made George edgy. Nobody should be this relaxed. Coulson was acting as though he had an ace up his sleeve. A bluff, or did he actually have one?

'Tell me about Greg Hathaway,' George said.

'Hathaway, Hathaway,' he said, making a big deal out of searching his memory. 'Ah yes. Raving poofter with a weakness for drinking and gambling.'

'Why did you have him killed?'

'That's some accusation.'

'We know you arranged the hit.'

'You *know*,' Coulson said. 'I hope you've got evidence to back that up.'

George didn't see the point in lying – Coulson would have spotted it in a heartbeat. 'We'll get the evidence.'

'And then what? The big trial? A full-on media extravaganza? And after I'm found guilty they'll throw away the key, I suppose. You're not giving me much of an incentive to cooperate, are you?'

'When this goes to court, you'll be ruined.'

'Is that right?'

'That doesn't worry you?'

'Not in the slightest,' Coulson said. 'And why would that be, do you think?'

Condescending prick, George thought, but she could see where he was going. There was an ace up his sleeve, after all.

'This will never go to court,' Coulson continued. 'And the reason?'

'Because MI6 won't let it,' Priest said quietly from behind.

A slow handclap from Coulson. 'Bravo! If I'm dragged through the courts, do you think I'm going to go quietly? Not a hope in hell. And that's why you'll never see me at the Old Bailey any time soon. I know where too many bodies are buried. So, give me one good reason why I should help you out.'

George met his gaze. One good reason, that's what it always came down to. For some it was money, for others it was belief. Sometimes you used pain, sometimes the threat of pain was enough. There was always a lever. What was Coulson's? 'You miss it, don't you?'

'Miss what?'

'The game. There you are, you've got the houses, the cars, more money than you could spend in a hundred lifetimes. And it's so boring, isn't it? Back in Moscow, you must have thought you were so bloody clever. You were selling secrets to the KGB and we didn't have a clue. And then that went pear-shaped, so what do you do? You sell the Russians out. That must have been such a buzz. Getting one over on the mighty KGB.' George gave a charming smile of her own. 'Come on, Coulson, admit it.'

'You think I miss the bad old days?'

'I do, actually.'

Coulson chuckled. 'The ridiculous thing is that in some ways you're right. Don't get me wrong I wouldn't trade my current lifestyle for anything. But occasionally . . . well, occasionally you get nostalgic.'

'Hathaway was blackmailing you, wasn't he?' Priest said.

'No,' Coulson said. 'He *attempted* to blackmail me. Big difference. You could ask him to explain that difference. Unfortunately, he's dead.'

'And you arranged the hit?'

Coulson considered this. 'There's no getting away from the fact that my life is simpler with him out of the way, is there?'

'What about Jones?' George asked.

Another long pause. 'Wasn't it Benjamin Franklin who said three people can keep a secret so long as two of them are dead? When Hathaway crawled from the woodwork, I realised it was time to tidy up the loose ends.'

'One thing I don't understand: why did you have Hazel Aston killed?' George watched Coulson carefully, studying his reaction.

'Who?'

'Hazel Aston.'

A shrug. 'Sorry, I've no idea what you're talking about.'

Coulson was telling the truth, which meant Mac was definitely responsible for that one. 'And then there's Mac,' George said. 'What went wrong?'

'What makes you think anything went wrong?'

'He's still alive. Kestrel must be losing his touch.'

'Just picked that name out of the hat, did we?'

'How do you contact Kestrel?'

'So, this is where we get to the crux, is it? You want Kestrel.'

'And you're going to help us get him.'

'Am I?'

'You're right: MI6 would never allow you to step inside a courtroom.' George waited until she had Coulson's full attention. She couldn't resist a small victory smile. There was always a lever, and she'd just found Coulson's. 'However, we can make your life hell. Imagine what it would be like. Your phones tapped, followed everywhere you go, Big Brother watching 24/7. That would cramp your style, wouldn't it?'

'Is that a threat?'

'Oh, yes.'

'And if I tell you what you want to know?'

'Then as far as I'm concerned we've got no further business together, and I wish you a long and healthy life.'

Coulson paused, considering. 'I've never met Kestrel,' he said eventually. 'We communicate via the Internet . . .'

65

'Thoughts?' said George She was upstairs with Priest and Jem; Paul was conspicuous by his absence. She'd looked in on him on the way up and he was sound asleep. The computer expert was still a bit strung out from her earlier trauma – face pale, eyes wary and older – but she'd live. She kept glancing over at the monitor, at Coulson. He was sitting there staring into the never-never, legs crossed and looking more relaxed than ever. George knew from personal experience that it would take time for Jem to get this into perspective, to squash it down into an appropriate-sized box.

'I reckon he's telling the truth,' said Priest. 'Maybe not the whole truth, but he's definitely not lying.'

'I agree,' George said.

'And what Coulson said helps fills in the blanks.' Jem said. 'The email address he gave corresponds with some of the fragments I got off Kestrel's computer. Now we've got a complete address, we can contact him. That could be useful.'

'Okay, is there anything else we need from Coulson?'

Priest shook his head. 'You pretty much covered everything.'

'Jem?'

'I've got what I need.'

'Okay, Priest, you'd better take him home.'

Jem stared at George in disbelief. 'What! You're letting him go! Please tell me you're joking.' Her face flicked from confusion to anger and back again. 'You're not joking, are you? You're just planning to let the bastard go!'

George glanced at Priest and saw he was happy to let her field this one. Jem was owed an explanation. Unfortunately, it was up to her to give it. Time for a lesson on how the world really worked.

'Jem, like I've said before, in this business there are a lot of grey areas.'

'This one seems pretty black and white. Coulson hired a killer. Four people are dead. I'm no lawyer, but that sounds a lot like conspiracy to murder.'

'If only it was that simple.'

'It is that simple.'

'I wish it was.' Jem was furious, and George didn't blame her. 'MI6 can't afford another scandal at the moment. We're still reeling from 18/8. That one hit us hard. Coulson knows that, and if we bring him in he's going to play on it mercilessly. How do you think it's going to look if it got out

430

that Coulson was selling secrets to the Russians in the middle of the Cold War? The media is just looking for an excuse to hang MI6. Any excuse will do.'

'So, this is political. That's what you're saying, right?'

'That about sums it up.'

'And what I just watched was Coulson selling Kestrel out to save his sorry ass. MI6 might not have the person responsible, but at least they've got someone to blame.'

George shrugged. 'Sorry Jem, that's just the way it is. Nothing I can do to change that; nothing anyone can do.'

'That's so fucked up!'

'Yes, it is,' George agreed. 'You can't win them all. Sometimes you've got to make do with a draw.'

'And that's fucked up, too.'

Jem got up and stomped to the door. George made to follow, but Priest placed a hand on her arm.

'Let her go,' he said. 'She needs space to work it out for herself.'

George shook her head. 'She's right, you know. It is fucked up.'

'No arguments here,' said Priest. 'So, what's next?'

It was a question she'd been toying with. She was pretty sure Priest wasn't going to like her answer. 'I'm thinking that Coulson might want to employ Kestrel for one last hit.'

Priest raised an eyebrow. 'Okay, I'll bite. Who's the target?'

'I am,' George said.

'And how does that work?'

'We contact Kestrel and offer him a silly amount of money . . . quarter of a million should do it. We'll use Coulson's email address so it looks like the request has come from him. Kestrel heads to my place in the middle of the night, armed with one of those adrenaline filled syringes. As soon as he steps through the door you're there with the Increment to take him down. Sound like a plan?'

Priest shook his head. 'One problem: Kestrel's going to want half the money up front. Don't know about you, but, yeah, I've got a hundred and twenty-five grand tucked away under my mattress for a rainy day.'

George smiled. 'I thought you could go and speak nicely to your mate Heath.'

'And you reckon he's going to give me the money just like that?'

'Yeah, I reckon . . . but only if you ask nicely.'

66

The journey from cell to van took half an hour.
All those checks and searches to go through, all
those doors. As Mac was bundled inside, he caught
a tantalising glimpse of azure. He stopped for a
second and tasted free air, then he was being
pushed forward again and getting told to move.
The van doors slammed shut, locking him in with
the grey and the gloom. Curtis was a big black
guy with a real don't-fuck-with-me demeanour,
an attitude backed up with hardware: a gun, a
retractable baton, Taser and mace. Mac had seen
him on the block. Curtis was mid-forties, his body
trim and tight – a man familiar with the inside of
a gym. He cuffed Mac to the steel pole and told
him to take a seat. The prison guard was polite,
experienced enough to know that winding the
cons up gained nothing. The van pulled away, the
driver taking it nice and steady. Behind, Mac heard
the roar of the motorcycle escort. He knew when
they'd arrived the media smelled blood and it had

got them salivating. Mac could imagine what it was like out there: paparazzi fighting each other for the best positions; one or two breaking from the pack and running alongside the van, holding their cameras at arm's length and firing off shots of the blackened windows; the police trying in vain to keep them back. The noise faded and the van rolled to a gentle stop.

Court Two was packed, everyone wanting a glimpse of the monster. Curtis escorted Mac up to the dock and told him to sit; the guard took his seat in the corner, right next to the big red panic button. The dock was in the middle of the court and Mac could feel hostile eyes all around him. The public peering down from the gallery; the press staring daggers into the back of his head. Wainwright was off to his left. His hair was whiter than usual, somehow brighter. High above, Mac saw that bright blue sky through the glass ceiling. He inhaled deeply and his nose filled with the scent of old wood and centuries of justice.

The suit Wainwright had chosen for him was a good one. Nothing too flashy, though – they had an uphill struggle as it was without alienating any jurors. If the Crown Prosecution Service had their way, Mac reckoned he'd be wearing bright orange prison overalls right now, ankles shackled with irons, wrists cuffed. No way would the CPS want the jury to view him as anything but guilty. Wainwright had coached him on what to say, how to act. They had a whole host of signs and signals worked out. A scratch of the nose indicated a witness was lying, a tweak of the ear meant they were telling the truth – the lexicon of body language redefined.

Judge Charles Staunton appeared in his best robes and wig, and the room rustled and coughed into silence. He took his seat and looked around the court like a king surveying his kingdom. His face was ancient and leathery, the nose sharp enough to spike paper.

The case outlined by the prosecutor was simple: Mac was guilty as hell, end of story. Six foot tall and looking like your favourite grandfather, he put on a good show for the jury, strutting and preening, confidence oozing from his pores. Think of the families of the victims, he urged in a smooth, deep voice. Think what they're going through, how their lives have been ripped apart. And spare a thought for the victims. Can any of us imagine what it was like down there? That bomb going off, flesh and bone ripped apart. The dark, the panic, the confusion. By the time he wrapped up, the jury was hanging on his every word.

Then it was Wainwright's turn. He got up and told the jury that, with all due respect, the prosecutor was talking nonsense, exaggerating for the sake of sensationalism. Time and again, he drove home the point that they needed to be a hundred per cent certain of his client's guilt before convicting him. Ninety-nine per cent wasn't good enough, ninety-nine point nine per cent wasn't good enough. It had to be a hundred per cent or nothing. He thanked the jury for listening and took his seat. Judge Staunton called time out for lunch.

When he reappeared after lunch, Judge Staunton had the smugness of a man well-fed and watered. Rosy-cheeked and misty eyed, he glanced over at the accused. Mac held his gaze, kept staring until the Judge looked away. The afternoon droned on as the first witness took the stand. Mac wasn't really listening. He had a quick look-around, and liked what he saw. Everyone seemed relaxed. And why shouldn't they be? Wainwright got up to cross-examine, and Mac did another surreptitious 360 degrees. Still looking good. Heavy eyes all round, even a yawn or two. Those couple of hours after lunch were dead time. After eating, it was only natural to want a nap. And it was warm in the court, which enhanced the soporific effect. A juror's head nodded slowly forward, then abruptly nodded upwards again. Mac glanced at Curtis's watch.

Ten minutes till showtime.

To be truly believable, a deception needed to evolve slowly. Feeding someone a lie and pretending it was the truth rarely worked. Leading people into the lie, giving them enough information so they felt compelled to fill in the blanks, well, that was a different story. When you had a

vested interest, you were more likely to believe
. . . you *wanted* to believe.

Mac held his breath for a while, pushing his
heart rate up and getting some colour into his face.
He waited until Wainwright glanced in his direction, then reached for his glass of water with a
shaky hand. The lawyer knew all about the blinding
headaches he'd been getting for the past month or
so. They knew all about them in Belmarsh's hospital
unit, too. Not that they'd been much help. The
extent of their sympathy was a couple of aspirins.
'I'm sure it's nothing,' he'd told Wainwright.
'Probably just the stress.' The lawyer wasn't
buying. He was currently in the process of arranging
a visit to a proper hospital where a proper doctor
could give him some proper tests. Mac argued it
wasn't necessary, they were just headaches, he was
sure there was nothing sinister going on up there.
Wainwright rarely lost an argument.

Two minutes to go.

Mac held his breath again – this time he didn't
need to reach for the water glass. Wainwright was
watching him closely, looking concerned. Mac
waved him away, giving him the old trooper act.
He had the lawyer hook, line and sinker. Keeping
a poker face, Mac counted off the seconds.

There was one weak point with his plan, and
that was Harris. The drug dealer had made all sorts
of promises and Mac just hoped he'd deliver on
them. He was confident he would. The last time
they'd talked, a couple of days ago, Harris had

assured him everything was in place. 'Everything?' Mac had asked. Harris had said yes and Mac believed him. It all came down to that fucked-up Kray Twin morality code . . . that and the fact he was paying Harris three million pounds to make this happen.

He heard the thud a few seconds before he felt it. The courtroom froze – nobody dared move. Behind him, the whispering had already begun. He picked out one word being whispered over and over, a word guaranteed to strike fear into the heart of any Londoner.

Bomb.

The exodus began with the journalists, the panic quickly spreading to the public gallery. Suddenly everyone was up and moving. Judge Staunton banged his gavel in a futile attempt to restore order, the sound lost in the uproar. The clerk stretched up on tiptoes and beckoned for his attention, gave him a story. With a swish of his robes Judge Staunton was gone, disappearing through a back door. The court was emptying fast, everyone heading for the exits, a confused crush of terrified people. Wainwright fought the tide, pushing through the crowd, making for the dock. He climbed inside and demanded to know what the hell was going on. Curtis was talking urgently into his radio, and shushed him with an impatient wave. The guard clipped the radio back onto his belt.

'A bomb's gone off in the pub across the road. We want Macintosh back in Belmarsh immediately.' The guard turned to Mac. 'On your feet.'

The three of them headed down the steep stairs to the cells. Mac waited until the last step before collapsing. He crumpled into a heap and let his left side go slack – a performance worthy of a pat on the back from Stanislavski himself. Wainwright and Curtis sank down beside him, one on either side. They tried to help him up, but he was a dead weight. Working together, the two men flipped him over. Mac heard Wainwright take a sharp breath.

'Oh Jesus, he's had a stroke.' There was a ton of concern in the lawyer's voice; no doubt he was calculating how much money he stood to lose if his meal ticket died. 'Robert, can you hear me?' he shouted. 'Robert!'

Mac just lay there in his broken body, pretending not to hear a damn thing. A stroke. Well, what else was the lawyer going to think after he'd planted all those seeds? That he was acting? The arguing started, the outcome a foregone conclusion. This was what he was really paying Wainwright for . . . this was the lawyer's moment to shine.

'We've got to get him to a hospital,' Wainwright said. 'St Bart's is just across the road.'

'No way,' Curtis replied. 'They don't have the facilities to deal with a Cat A prisoner. We need to get him back to Belmarsh. The hospital staff there are more than qualified to deal with this.'

'That's going to take too long. The sooner he gets treatment, the more chance he'll survive.'

'Security has got to come first.'

'And what the hell is he going to do? Look at him, for Christ's sake!'

'Security comes first,' Curtis repeated, standing firm.

'Okay, but if he dies I'm holding you personally responsible.' The lawyer hammered each word out making sure Curtis completely understood the consequences. Wainwright in full flow was a force to be reckoned with. 'You'll be filling in paperwork from now until the end of time, do you hear me? You won't even be able to get a job as a security guard when I'm through with you.'

Two seconds later, Curtis was calling St Bart's for an ambulance.

While they waited, Wainwright did his best to make Mac comfortable. The lawyer didn't know the first thing about First Aid, but Mac wasn't about to register a complaint. The paramedics arrived, calm voiced and reassuring. They man-handled the patient onto a gurney, pulled a blanket over him. Then they were off and running, moving fast. The gurney bumped into the back of the ambulance with a thump and a rattle.

'There isn't room for both of you,' said one of the medics. He had a strong East End accent; someone born within earshot of the Bow Bells rather than a Mockney. Mac could imagine the looks passing between Wainwright and Curtis. Neither would want to let him out of their sight.

'Don't even think it,' Curtis said.

'I'm going,' Wainwright said.

'No fucking way! Sending him out there with no security. It isn't going to happen.'

'I am going with my client!' Wainwright's voice was shaking with Old Testament doom. 'Anyway, in case you haven't noticed, he's comatose. What's he going to do? Even if by some miracle, he *did* regain consciousness, the streets are crawling with police. It's not as if he's going to be escaping any time soon. Who do you think we're dealing with here? Harry Houdini?'

'Not the point. Either I go with him, or we wait here until a police escort arrives. Your choice.'

'He needs to get to a hospital! Now!'

'Gentlemen,' said the medic. The voice of reason. Mac could imagine Wainwright and Curtis stopping dead in their tracks, could see them turning and glaring at the paramedic. 'This goes against protocol – and it'll be a squeeze – but since Bart's is only across the road, I'll take you both. But you need to get in here right now. Okay?'

A scrabbling of feet on metal, and then the door slammed shut. It *was* a tight squeeze, and Mac was reminded of prison. There were too many people sharing too small a space, everyone stealing each other's air. Wainwright's aftershave was heavy and expensive, and clawed at his throat. They turned into Newgate Street and Mac became aware of the commotion outside: sirens, shouts, panic, all the noise you'd associate with a major terrorist incident. He could imagine what it was like out there. Police everywhere, fire engines . . . and, of course, dozens and dozens of ambulances.

In his mind's eye, Mac saw the route the ambulance was taking. Crawling along Newgate Street, dodging the police and firefighters and paramedics, swerving around the emergency vehicles.

Instead of turning into Giltspur Street, they carried on towards Holborn.

'What the fuck!' Curtis said, each word an explosion of shock.

Mac opened his eyes. The paramedic was five-five with a crewcut, hard eyes, and a face more used to scowling than laughing. He was holding a Heckler and Koch P7 to Curtis's head, the silencer digging in hard enough to crease the guard's skin. Wainwright was just sitting there slack-jawed, miles out of his depth. Mac reached under the blanket for the gun the paramedics had left him. A silenced Glock 17. The ambulance slowed to a stop. Probably a police barricade. Mac pointed the gun at the lawyer and motioned with his fore-finger for him to keep quiet. He wasn't worried about Wainwright; the lawyer was practically wetting himself. Curtis was a different matter. The guard's eyes were searching wildly; he had the look of someone about to do something stupid and heroic. Mac could taste freedom – he had got this far, no way was he just going to stand back and let it all turn to shit. He aimed for the guard's heart and squeezed the trigger. The paramedic caught Curtis and gave Mac a what-the-fuck look.

Up front, the driver was negotiating with a cop, giving him some bullshit about an RTA he needed to get to. The partition was closed so the cop couldn't see into the back. Wainwright knew to keep quiet, knew that his only chance of getting out of this alive was to cooperate one hundred per cent . . . ninety-nine per cent wouldn't do it, ninety-nine point nine per cent wouldn't, either. His face was snow white, even whiter than his hair. The ambulance rolled forward and slowly picked up speed. Mac shook the blanket away and stood up. He stepped up to the lawyer.

'Couldn't have done it without you.' Mac smiled at Wainwright, then pumped two bullets into his head.

67

George took the stairs two at a time. She slammed into a chair and rolled up next to Jem. BBC News 24 was on one screen, Sky News on another, CNN on another. The pictures were more or less the same – the only real difference was the camera angles. Details were sketchy, but the reporters were managing to stretch out what little information they had. A bomb had gone off in a pub near the Old Bailey, that much they agreed on. The police had evacuated, and the area was now cordoned off; the emergency services were making the right noises. All the news channels were in agreement that this was a terrorist attack. The Old Bailey was a monument to truth and justice. This had al-Qa'eda written all over it. They couldn't say how many had been injured and killed, but as soon as they had more information . . .

George caught a movement behind her and turned around. Paul was standing there looking dazed and confused. Tomorrow, she promised herself. As soon as Kestrel was behind bars, she'd sort Paul out. Get him off the Valium and get his head straight. It was all about prioritising. They had an opportunity to catch Kestrel and it would be crazy not to take it. This justification did nothing whatsoever to ease her guilt. Paul came over and glanced at the screen.

'How are you feeling?' George asked.

'Numb.'

That was his standard response at the moment; it was the same response he'd hidden behind when his father had been murdered. Jesus, that had to be harsh. Both parents murdered in two separate incidents. Her heart went out to him; it was simply too much for one person to deal with. George reached for his hand and gave it a reassuring squeeze. She followed his gaze to the screens.

'There's been a terrorist attack near the Old Bailey,' George explained.

'Oh,' was all he had to say on the subject, and that one syllable showed how bad it had got. The old Paul would have been firing off questions, wanting to know all the details. This doppelgänger didn't give a shit. It looked like Paul but it sure as hell didn't act like him. At that moment, George realised she'd give anything to have her old friend back.

'I think I'm going to lie down for a bit,' he said.

'Yeah, you do that. I'll look in on you later.' George let go of his hand and watched him shuffle out.

445

'God, he's in a bad way,' Jem said when he'd gone. 'If you ask me, he's heading for a nervous breakdown.'

'No-one *was* asking you!' George snapped.

'Hey, sorry, just saying.'

'Well think before you just say in future, okay?'

'Whatever . . . look, I said I was sorry.'

George shrugged off the apology. Jem was young, and that was as good an excuse as any. For the next twenty minutes they watched in silence while the TV reporters tried to piece it all together. There was a burst of Scissor Sisters from George's pocket and she fished out her mobile. She checked the number, but didn't recognise it, said a cautious hello.

'I know you still work for MI6, so let's save ourselves a load of time and grief and get that one out the way right from the start.'

George placed the no-bullshit voice immediately. Detective Superintendent Harry Fielding from the Met's Anti-Terrorist Branch. She and Paul had worked with Fielding last September, although saying they worked together stretched the definition. They had tolerated one another's existence. But only just, and only because they'd been ordered to. 'And good afternoon to you, Detective Fielding,' she said. 'Considering what's going on at the Old Bailey, I take it this isn't a social chat.'

'It wasn't a terrorist attack,' Fielding said.

'That's not what the media are saying.'

'They don't have a fucking clue.'

446

'If it's not a terrorist attack, what's going on?'

'It was a distraction. Macintosh has escaped.'

The silence that followed was as long as any George had ever known. It all made perfect sense. Create a diversion and then, when everyone was looking the wrong way, you've got all the time and space you need. It was similar to a magician using sleight-of-hand to bamboozle the audience. There was a precedent here, too. Mac had used the same tactic last September.

Then the implications hit home and George felt the ground sway beneath her. Mac was on the loose again. That was bad enough, but it got worse. She didn't care what anyone said, Mac wasn't going to be caught any time soon. He'd got careless once and that wouldn't happen again. How much damage was he going to cause? How many more innocent people were going to die? Of course, there was always the possibility that he would just disappear. Even as George had this thought she realised it was just wishful thinking.

'How could you let him get away?' she said.

'Let's get something straight. *We* didn't let him get away. Macintosh was the responsibility of the court and the prison service. If you want to point fingers, then that's where you should start.'

'What happened?'

Fielding dodged the question. 'We know you and Aston visited Macintosh on Friday. We know Aston went to see him the day before. We want to know why.'

'And I'll be happy to help in any way I can as soon as you tell me exactly what happened.'

A sigh. 'Still as pig-headed as ever.'

'You call it pig-headed, I call it curious.'

'Bear in mind we're still piecing this together.'

'I'll take whatever you've got.'

'Okay, at 3.41 this afternoon there was an explosion at The Chambers. The pub is across the road from the Old Bailey and they look after tourists' bags for three quid a shot . . . a policy they'll no doubt be reviewing. Ten people dead, another fifty injured – the pub is a write-off. Of course, the media are screaming out that al-Qa'eda is responsible, and on the surface that's exactly what it looks like. Another terrorist spectacular. But I wasn't convinced. It just didn't *feel* like an al-Qa'eda attack to me. Then we found the ambulance and it all began to make sense.'

'The ambulance?'

'Last anyone heard of Macintosh, he'd fallen ill – a stroke or a heart attack or something. He was shipped to St Bart's, but with everything else going on nobody thought to check with Bart's to see if he arrived. And the hospital was on full alert, waiting for the casualties to start flooding in, so their minds were elsewhere. The ambulance was found abandoned in Hammersmith with two bodies in the back. Charles Wainwright, Macintosh's lawyer; and Leonard Curtis, a guard from Belmarsh. The guard was shot in the heart and the lawyer took two in the head.'

448

'What about the paramedics?'

'No sign of them. The lack of corpses led us to believe they were working with Macintosh – there's no way he could have pulled this off on his own. Forensics are checking the ambulance for prints as we speak, so fingers crossed.'

'What about the ambulance? I'm guessing it was stolen from St Bart's.'

'They haven't reported any missing, so we think it was probably bought at auction. We're looking into that. Okay, your turn.'

George opted for an economical version of the truth, parting with enough information so Fielding felt he was getting something. She mentioned Jones, figuring the detective would already be aware of the MI6 man's murder. Just a routine in-house investigation, she told him. They'd gone to see Mac because he'd worked with Jones in the past.

'And was there a link?' the detective asked.

'Unfortunately, no,' George lied.

'Mmm,' Fielding said. 'One other thing: I don't suppose you've seen Aston lately. His phone is switched off and we need to speak to him. Urgently.'

'Why?'

'His mother's been murdered.'

George said nothing.

'I might be wrong,' Fielding continued, 'but I'm guessing that's old news to you. According to our forensics people someone – or to be more accurate, three someones – got to the murder scene before them. They were pretty pissed off to say the least, muttered something about a herd of rampaging wildebeest.'

'When I see Paul, I'll get him to contact you.'

'Please do. And one more thing: I get the strongest feeling I've only got half the story here. Mind you, that's the feeling I generally get when I talk to you people from the other side of the river. I think we need a face-to-face, don't you?'

'Today's going to be tricky.'

'For you and me both,' Fielding agreed. 'Tomorrow then. And do me a favour. See if you can track Aston down. I *really* want to talk to him.'

The line went dead and George put the mobile away. Mac was on the loose again. She wasn't looking forward to passing that one on to Paul. The old Paul would have gone ballistic. There was no telling what effect it would have on the new Paul. The news would probably push him deeper into his shell. George sighed, feeling tired and useless and so old. Inch by inch, he was slipping further away, and she didn't have a clue how to get him back.

It was getting late in the day, but the Internet café was humming with activity. Most of the customers were foreigners – there were lots of Eastern Europeans, quite a few Asians. Kestrel sipped his coffee, and kept one eye on all the comings and goings. So far he had been left alone and he saw no reason for that to change. Most of the customers had their heads down, typing – he certainly wasn't doing anything to invite conversation. He'd taken up residence on a machine near the back. Right next to the emergency exit. Always make sure you've got an escape route. He had almost turned the job down. It was the money that motivated him in the end. Coulson had put a quarter of a million pounds on the table, and you didn't say no to money like that without a good reason. The job was straightforward enough. In a lot of respects it was similar to the hit on the old woman, and that hadn't caused any problems.

Coulson had specified the job should be carried out au naturel. *No big statements, just a peaceful slipping away into the long goodnight. Remembering how Jones*

451

had gone – panicking and clutching at his chest, crashing from the bed and crawling along the floor – Kestrel couldn't promise peaceful. However, he would do all he could to ensure it looked as natural as possible. It wasn't unheard of for thirtysomethings to suffer heart attacks. A tragedy to die so young, but not unheard of.

This was going to be his last job for a while. He'd got two hundred grand from Coulson for the first two hits; five hundred grand from Macintosh for bumping off the old lady. And now this, another two hundred and fifty grand for what amounted to a few hours' work. Add it all up and he was only fifty grand short of a million. Not bad, not bad at all. There had been no bartering. A quarter of a million pounds was nothing to Coulson. Kestrel hadn't decided where he was going to go yet. Possibly the West Indies. Or Hawaii. He'd rent a little place on the beach and catch up on his reading. Kestrel reckoned he could manage six months before getting bored. Six months to recharge and reassess. Those bumper paydays were proof he had hit the big time, and he needed to decide how to capitalise on this.

He was going to wait until two. The target lived in a flat on their own. If there was a bed partner, it wouldn't be the end of the world. Collateral damage was a professional hazard. The old woman's husband was a prime example of that. He'd been in the wrong place at the wrong time and now he was dead. Shit happened. Unfortunately that would put paid to the hit looking like an accident. Unless . . . a fire, maybe. That would be tragic. And it could so easily be made to look like an accident. It was worth considering.

Hawaii. Definitely. That was about as far away from England as you could get. Before he changed his mind, Kestrel logged onto lastminute.com and booked a flight. He paid using a false credit card; he'd worry about accommodation when he got there. Kestrel clicked the confirm button and leant back in the chair. He closed his eyes for a moment and conjured up images of perfect blue skies and endless golden beaches. He could almost taste the salt in the air.

68

George got home around eight and did her best to have a normal evening. If Kestrel was watching, he needed to buy into the illusion that it was business as usual. She heated up a tasteless microwave meal, forced half of it down and scraped the leftovers into the bin. Then, because it was what she always did, she took a shower. Bad idea. All she could think about was Janet Leigh being hacked to death in *Psycho*. It was the quickest shower ever. No languishing under the hot water while the worries of the day melted away – just in and out, and a quick scrub dry with the towel. It was crazy. Kestrel wasn't going to get anywhere near her; Priest would make sure of that. But who said fear was rational? In her mind she could see the front door being kicked in, hear the slow, deliberate footsteps coming down the hall, the creak of the bedroom doorhandle. And then Kestrel would be standing in the doorway pointing a gun at her. A pull of the trigger and that would be that. Game over.

A vivid imagination could be a curse and a blessing.

She thought she would feel better – safer – when she got to bed. There was an extra wall between her and Kestrel, an extra door. If anything, she felt more vulnerable. Part of the problem was that she was in her pyjamas – she was one thin layer away from naked, and had never felt so exposed. It crossed her mind to get up and dress. Ridiculous. A pair of jeans and a T-shirt were not going to stop a bullet any more than her PJs. Now, if the T-shirt had been made from Kevlar, that might have been a different story.

Priest had insisted she was armed. The can of mace and the Taser were within easy reach. There for her peace of mind . . . or so Priest had said. She almost asked why she needed them – if he did his job then she shouldn't, right? She hadn't asked because she didn't want to hear the answer. Her imagination was already torturing her enough as it was.

She lay in bed, staring at the ceiling. There was the occasional glance at the bedside clock to confirm that, yes, time *was* standing still. Priest was only seconds away, but George had never felt more alone. And it wasn't just Priest out there watching her back. Four of his mates from the Increment were within whistling distance. Home was where you should feel safest. You shouldn't be worrying about someone breaking in and blowing your brains out. As she lay there, she could feel her speeding heart, hear the blood rushing through her ears. It was the waiting that was the killer. Kestrel could make his move in the next couple of minutes, the next hour, any time. Not that he was going to get anywhere near her, she reminded herself. And did that make her feel any better? Any less twitchy? Did it fuck.

The numbers on the clock slowly closed in on two, and George started convincing herself it wasn't going to happen. Maybe Kestrel had been spooked, or maybe he'd decided to do it tomorrow night. Perhaps a quarter of a million didn't outweigh the risk, and he'd decided to abort. And then, as if she didn't have enough to worry about, she started worrying about Paul. And the more she worried, the more she convinced herself there was a reason to worry. Telling herself she was being stupid, she grabbed her mobile from the bedside table. Jem answered on the third ring, pissed off and bored and wanting to know when it was all going to kick off. George ignored her whinging and told her to go downstairs and check on Paul.

'Why bother? He's stoned off his box. He's not going anywhere.'

'Just do it.' George sighed and hung up.

When her mobile went a couple of minutes later, it was so loud her heart stopped. The phone flashed brightly on the bedside table and she just stared at it, paralysed, unable to pick it up.

Shit, there was something wrong with Paul!

Or maybe it was Priest phoning to say Kestrel had made his move and he was now face first in the dirt with a couple of SAS men pinning him down.

Or perhaps Kestrel had slipped through, and all she had to do was hold him off for a couple of minutes . . . they'd be there as soon as they could.

George broke free of her paralysis and grabbed the phone. She flicked it open and checked the caller ID. Jem launched in without so much as a hi. 'Aston's gone,' she said.

'What do you mean gone!' George's voice spiralled up through the registers, anger and dread infecting every syllable. *'Gone where?'*

'I think he's gone after Kestrel,' Jem said. 'And it gets worse.'

'Worse! How can this possibly get any worse?'

'He's taken one of the Glocks with him.'

69

To be truly believable, a deception needs to evolve slowly.

Aston could remember where he'd been when Mac delivered this lecture. It had been a slow Friday afternoon, not much happening. Mac had poked his head around the office door and told Aston to grab his jacket. They'd headed into the city and found a pub, settled in for the long haul. The reason this day stuck in his mind was because Mac actually paid for the first round. His old boss had been in a talkative mood, happy to go wandering down Memory Lane – he could almost have passed as a normal human being. And then it was lesson time . . . *always* lesson time.

Mac was right. Feeding someone a lie and pretending it was the truth rarely worked. Leading people into the lie was the only way. Give them just enough information, and they'll feel compelled to fill in the rest themselves. It worked like a charm. George wanted to believe he was an emotional wreck, which meant she'd already done the hard work. All he needed to do was supply the evidence to support this. Acting distraught wasn't a problem because that was how he felt; there wasn't any acting involved. The relationship with his mother was a complicated one, but, at the end of the day, she was his mum. She'd changed his nappies, raised him, done her best to teach him right from wrong. When he'd had night-mares she comforted him; when he fell out of trees or came off his bike or tripped up and skinned his knees, she wiped away the tears. Because that's what mothers did. For all her faults, she had tried her best. She certainly didn't deserve to die how she did. No-one deserved that.

Acting stoned was easy, too. You stare blankly into the middle distance and mumble your sentences, shuffle your feet when you walk, job done. The Valium had ended up down the toilet. All of it. He didn't need that shit to function. He wanted to feel, *needed* to feel. Right now, the pain and anger were the only things keeping him going. Whatever happened, he was going to have a face-to-face with Kestrel – he needed to look the bastard in the eye. And then he was going to settle up.

Everyone had written him off, which made it easy to keep tabs on what was going down. He would have expected George to be more careful. But why should she? He was practically a zombie; the next stop on the line was the Alice in Wonderland ward. And they were all on the same

459

side. There was no reason for any of them to watch what they were saying or doing when he was about. He'd been hovering on the stairs when George got the call from Fielding about Mac's escape; he'd been eavesdropping in the kitchen when they put together their plan to trap Kestrel. Hi-tech gadgets had their place, but all a spy really needed was his eyes and ears . . . another one of Mac's little lessons.

The plan they'd put together was a workable one. George had uncovered some dirt on Coulson and was blackmailing him. As a result, the multi-millionaire wanted her out of the way, and quickly. If the hit was carried out within twenty-four hours, Kestrel would get a quarter of a million; with each passing day the fee dropped by fifty grand. They wanted to hurry Kestrel into action, and greed was always a good incentive. Of course, the story hadn't been presented so bluntly. The assassin was given just enough information, and then left to fill in the blanks. Heath had given the green light, and arranged for half the money to be deposited in an anonymous Swiss bank account.

Aston waited until everyone was busy upstairs before making his move. It took less than thirty seconds to log into Kestrel's account; George had left the password on a yellow Post-it stuck to her computer monitor. His luck was in. Kestrel hadn't checked his mail. Aston deleted the email Jem had sent. The one he sent in its place was identical apart from two details: the name and address of the target. Then he'd headed back to bed, back into the illusion of Valium-inspired blandness. And nobody was any the wiser.

George left around seven; Priest left much earlier. It crossed Aston's mind that Jem might be a problem. He considered tying her up, but that wouldn't have worked. George and Priest would need to liaise with her, and if she was suddenly incommunicado that would raise suspicions. On the plus side, Jem was upstairs, no doubt lost in her own little bubble. She acted as though he didn't exist at the best of times, so she probably wouldn't even notice he was gone. Before leaving, Aston arranged the pillows and duvet to make it look like there was someone in the bed. It wouldn't pass a close inspection, but it was the best he could do. He took a Glock from the office safe. The one with the silencer. The gun felt good in his hand. Righteous. Satisfied he had covered as many bases as possible, Aston headed for the street. Like Mac had told him more than once: You do what you can to limit the odds, but there comes a point where you have to say fuck it, and just go for it.

70

The flat felt neglected, which was no surprise since he hadn't been here for a few days. Except that wasn't the whole story. It had actually felt this way since George moved out back in October. Dusty and unloved, it was missing a woman's touch. Aston noticed the smell straightaway – musty and stale – and realised this was what Kestrel would notice first. He found a rusting can of polish and an air freshener under the sink, and used them to make the place smell more user-friendly. The Maglite was in the junk drawer in the kitchen . . . and, miracle of miracles, the batteries still had some juice in them.

In case Kestrel had the flat under surveillance, Aston left the lounge light on until midnight. Time enough to watch some telly and have a nightcap before heading for bed – in his mind he was measuring this out as an ordinary day. From there he'd gone into the bathroom. The light stayed on for a couple of minutes, long enough to clean his teeth and take a piss. Finally to the bedroom. He figured

462

thirty seconds of light would be enough there. It had been another tough day at the office and all he wanted was to hit the hay.

Aston stood in the bedroom while his night vision kicked in. A dim yellow-orange light was creeping around the edge of the curtains. Occasionally the headlights of a passing car stirred the shadows – dark angles opened and closed; lines stretched and shrank and then settled again. Kestrel wouldn't want to advertise his existence by flicking on lights or using a torch. Would he be wearing night vision goggles? Possibly. Aston picked his way carefully through the charcoal dark. The best place to stage an ambush was the lounge. He left the door ajar, angled at sixty degrees to the wall, and pressed himself into the gap. All that was left to do now was wait.

One o'clock came and went. Time had ceased to have any real meaning. He didn't know how this would turn out, didn't really care. It would end how it ended. He had stopped caring when the realisation that he was responsible for his mum's death had hit home. If only Devlin had approached someone else. If only he hadn't gone along to that interview at 3 Carlton Gardens. If only he hadn't done so bloody well in training. If only he hadn't gone to work for Mac.

Mac.

And that was the problem, wasn't it? The all-seeing, all-knowing Mac had been pulling his strings from the word go. If he hadn't hooked him in like that, he would have found some other way. The ever-resourceful Mac, who was out there some-where right now. On the loose and free to cause all manner of chaos and suffering. They'd underesti-mated him, and that was a mistake you only made once with Mac. There were two people dead tonight who should still be alive; two families who were dealing with the grief of losing a loved one. And Aston knew only too well about that sort of grief.

He should have killed Mac on that rainy London street all those lifetimes ago; should have taken him out when he had the chance. That was one mistake he would not make again. Aston had no doubt that Kestrel would strike tonight. The others thought money was the incentive. They were wrong. Kestrel killed because he enjoyed it. What he did to his mum proved that. He could have killed her quickly, like he'd killed Roy. Instead, he'd drawn it out, made her suffer. Kestrel was a sadist. Killing was a drug to him, as addictive as crack. Tonight, he had an opportunity to indulge, and he would take it. Wedged into the crack behind the door, the night breathing all around him, Aston made a vow to himself: whatever happened, the assassin would not live to see the new day.

In the dark, every sound sharpened and became more distinct. The beat of his heart; the fridge purring and clicking; the old orphanage moving and settling; the dulled sounds of the street beyond the double glazing.

He heard the scratching at the front door, metal on metal.

Heard the click of the lock giving way.

Heard the scrape of the door opening.

Heard the footsteps in the hall, each one lighter than air.

Aston picked up the faint sound of Kestrel's breathing. Each breath was deliberate – long, slow, measured – the sound getting louder as the assassin came closer. Aston loosened his fingers then tensed them again, reaffirming his grip on the Glock. In his mind's eye, he saw Kestrel following his gun along the hall, placing each foot with infinite care. The assassin stopped at the open doorway, and Aston was convinced he was going to come in. He pressed himself deeper into the wall and held his breath, the plywood door the only barrier between them. Adrenaline flooded through his body, readying him for the fight. The gentle squeak of a shoe rubbing against wood – a sound so invisible he thought he imagined it – and then Kestrel's footsteps were moving away, his breathing growing thinner as he carried on down the hall.

Aston did a slow count to three then stepped into the hallway. Kestrel was only six feet away. The assassin sensed a presence behind him and spun around. Aston raised the torch and flicked the switch, aiming for the goggles. The powerful beam cut like a laser, catching Kestrel by surprise. Without a moment's hesitation, Aston aimed the Glock and squeezed the trigger. Kestrel dropped his gun and crumpled to the floor. One hand reached up to rip the goggles off, the other clutched his thigh. The tendons and veins in his neck were as tight as violin strings, and he was inhaling short, stuttering gulps of air. His face was haunted and desperate. Aston kicked the gun out of reach, far enough so it wouldn't be a temptation. Biting back the pain, Kestrel looked at the blood seeping between his fingers. Slowly he lifted his head and locked eyes with Aston. There was enough light spilling from the torch to make the whites glow. Aston stared, looking for answers. The question came out in a voice he didn't recognise.

'Why?'

Kestrel grinned, and that was answer enough. He raised the gun and aimed between the assassin's eyes. Hands rock steady, his finger tightened on the trigger. At the last second he caught sight of his silhouette in the hall mirror and froze. He wanted to fire, wanted to keep on firing until the Glock clicked empty. But the silhouette demanded his attention. His reflection was featureless, a sheet of darkness cut into a man shape. The emptiness stretched to infinity – there was no substance, no emotion. Was this what he had become? Was this what Mac has turned him into? Aston lowered the gun. He might be many things, but he wasn't a murderer.

A rattlesnake movement on the floor and he glanced down. Too late. Kestrel lashed out with his leg and caught him behind the knees. He went down hard, hands scrabbling to break his fall, the Glock slipping from his fingers. Kestrel jumped on top and pinned him down. For someone who'd just taken a bullet, the assassin was moving too fluidly. Aston realised his mistake, realised it might be the last mistake he ever made. *Should've taken more time when I aimed.* The bullet must only have clipped Kestrel – just a flesh wound. What was it Mac always told him about assuming? Aston had a split second where he wished he had blown the assassin's head off when he had the chance, and then he was fighting for his life. He thrashed and struggled but it made no difference. Kestrel's grin widened. The fucker was actually enjoying this, getting off on the fact he had Aston right where he wanted. He was using one hand to hold him now, and Aston still couldn't move. Kestrel produced the EpiPen and made sure Aston saw exactly what it was. Made sure he understood the implications. Panic gripped him and it took all his willpower to squash it down. Think. Think. *THINK!* He remembered the self-defence classes he had taken during training; remembered George flipping an instructor twice her size. A long shot, but it was the only shot he had. Aston let his body go slack. It was all about timing now. Kestrel was looking at the top of his head, figuring out the best place to stick the needle in. Every part of Aston was screaming to fight, but somehow he managed to keep still. Wait wait wait. Kestrel made a decision, and reached out with the EpiPen. He tilted forward, changing his centre of balance, lifting his weight off Aston's chest. This was it. Now or never. Summoning every ounce of strength he possessed, giving it everything he had, Aston put in an almighty buck. In that same instant, he twisted his left shoulder

467

forward. Unbalanced, arms flailing, Kestrel thudded headfirst into the wall, hitting it with a thump. Aston was dimly aware of something giving way in his back, but the adrenaline masked the pain. He scrabbled away from the assassin. Saw the EpiPen, saw the Glock. The EpiPen was closer. He lunged for it, grabbed it. Remembering what Priest said, Aston jammed the EpiPen into the assassin's skull.

For a second, Kestrel just stared at Aston in horrified disbelief. Neither of them moved, neither breathed; time had ground to a complete standstill. The assassin rubbed his scalp, looking confused, looking as though he couldn't believe this had happened. Then he staggered to his feet and started bouncing along the walls towards the front door. He managed half a dozen steps before collapsing to his knees, hands pressed against the left side of his chest. Aston walked over slowly. The agony on Kestrel's face was real. This was no act. A tear fell, followed by another, and Aston was surprised by this. Tears of regret or tears of pain? Kestrel was trying to speak, but couldn't. There was no oxygen getting into his lungs, no air to carry his final words. And what were those final words? A plea for forgiveness or a condemned man's rant filled with curses and obscenities? Kestrel tried one last time, the veins and muscles on his neck bursting through the skin, and then he tipped forward.

Aston just stood there for a while, his attention fixed on the dead man at his feet. He guessed he should check for a pulse. Just to be sure. But what was the point? Kestrel looked dead. More to the point, he smelled dead. Aston had been exposed to too much death, but this was the first time he had caused it. Staring at the dead assassin, he figured he should feel something, anything, but emotionally he was running on empty. Surely that was wrong. He'd killed the person who murdered his mother. Wasn't this the payback he wanted? The revenge he'd craved? So why did it feel as though nothing had changed? Then again, maybe that was it. Maybe the problem was that nothing *had* changed. His mother was still dead, and there wasn't anything he could do to bring her back.

Adrian Hart was hidden in a clear plastic waterproof bag in the cistern – passport, full documentation, wig and glasses. Aston tipped the bag into a hold-all, slung some clothes on top, and left the flat without looking back. Walking quickly but not too quickly, he crossed the street and merged with the shadows at the corner. The cavalry arrived a couple of minutes later, hurtling in from the other end of the street, just as he knew they would. Priest's Jag led the way; a BMW X5 with tinted windows wasn't far behind. Aston watched George jump from the Jag and run towards the converted orphanage as though her feet were on fire – she was so focused on getting inside she didn't notice the lone figure hiding at the far end of the street. 'See you around,' Aston whispered as she crashed through the front door. He sank deeper into the shadows, then, like a wisp of smoke curling into the breeze, he was gone.

Epilogue

Edward Coulson pushed his nose into the balloon glass and inhaled deeply. To call *L'Esprit de Courvoisier* a brandy would be like calling a McLaren F1 a runaround – at almost £3000 a bottle this was the most expensive and exclusive cognac in the world. He sipped and savoured, gazing out of the panoramic window at the London skyline twinkling far into the distance. It was good to be home. A whole weekend of Craig and Tanya was enough to test the patience of a saint. Still, it could have been worse. Craig was as talkative as ever, and had given him a wide berth. And Tanya had been horny as hell. That happened every once in a while. She'd just want to fuck and fuck and fuck. For a man heading towards his twilight years, Coulson knew he possessed an impressive libido – men half his age would have difficulty keeping up – but he struggled when Tanya was in one of those moods. Thank the Lord for Viagra. He took another sip of the *Courvoisier* and allowed himself a smile as he remembered what they'd got up to that afternoon. Tanya was athletic and graceful, and Jesus what a body! He'd forgotten that position existed, forgotten how much fun it was. But, boy, was he going to ache tomorrow.

Almost a week had passed since Macintosh's escape. Thinking about it now, Coulson considered the escape a blessing. It was funny how things worked themselves out. Jones and Hathaway were dead, so they wouldn't be talking. And Macintosh would be keeping a very low profile – it was unlikely he would cause problems, at least in the short term. In the long term, well, it might be an idea to go looking for him. Nothing high profile, just a couple of discreet enquiries. Offer a few quid here, a few quid there, see what crawled out of the woodwork. If he left Macintosh alone, chances were Macintosh would leave him alone. But he couldn't be certain of that, and Coulson wanted certainties. Another sip. A deep, contended sigh. Life was good. Not perfect, but good. He was at an age where he knew 'perfect' didn't exist. That was an ideal chased by younger men with too much energy and too little common sense. Feeling every single one of his fifty-eight years, he put the glass down on the coffee table and shut his eyes . . . just for a second or two.

The bite wasn't bad, but it was enough to wake him. A mosquito, perhaps? A spider? Rubbing the spot in his scalp where he'd been bitten, he opened his eyes, and found himself staring at Priest.

471

'I thought our business was finished.' All things considered, Coulson thought his recovery was pretty good. He sounded relaxed and confident, in control. Priest had taken him by surprise but he'd be buggered if he was going to let it show.

'Not quite.' The soft Irish accent was lilting and friendly, but the eyes were those of a soldier – eyes acquainted with death.

'What do you want?' Coulson decided to play along. He knew a negotiation when he saw one. Priest had dug up some dirt and this was his crude attempt at blackmail. He'd agree with his demands, get rid of him, and then he'd have him hunted down and killed. Who the hell did he think he was?

'You made a mistake going after Hathaway and Jones. Six always looks after its own. You of all people should know that.'

Coulson opened his mouth to say something, but his words were stolen away by a sudden sharp stabbing pain in his chest. That first stab was quickly followed by another, and another, each worse than the one before. The pain was immense and all-consuming, agony unlike anything he'd ever experienced. He couldn't breathe; every nerve ending was on fire. Coulson tried to stand and toppled forward. His flailing arm caught the balloon glass, sending it crashing to the floor where it shattered into pieces. There was a loud thud as his head clattered against hard wood. Paralysed with pain and fighting for breath, he just lay there, shards of glass jagging into his cheek. The smell of spilt *L'Esprit de Courvoisier* filled his nose and he could feel the dampness seeping through his shirt. A shadow fell over him and he turned his head towards it. He had just long enough to consider that this might not be blackmail, that maybe he'd read the situation all wrong. The image he took to the grave was of Priest staring down at him. The Irishman was holding something in his hand. It looked like some sort of syringe.

David Saunders's shoes fitted Mac perfectly; he was more than comfortable in this particular skin. Saunders was a righteous guy, trustworthy, someone you wouldn't have any reservations about doing business with. One look and you knew he had a wife tucked away at home, that they'd been happily married forever. It wouldn't surprise you to discover they were High School sweethearts. Nor would it surprise you to learn there were a couple of kids in the equation – a son and a daughter – and that those kids had grown up to be perfectly normal. No drug problems in the Saunders household. No teenage pregnancy scandals. No eating disorders. Everything just, well, normal. And you wouldn't have a problem buying into this myth because it was a crazy old world out there and it was reassuring to know that small pockets of normality did actually exist.

Mac had last stepped into Saunders's shoes four

years ago. He had flown to Dublin and spent an afternoon establishing his Get Out Of Jail Free card. The journey had been a complicated one. He'd travelled by Eurostar to Paris then caught a flight to Zürich. Only when he was a hundred per cent sure he wasn't being tailed did he board the plane to Ireland.

Dublin was one of his favourite cities. Vibrant, alive, and a great place to hide. The bank had been around for centuries; it was housed in a sturdy granite building that looked like a court-house and inspired confidence. Mac had chosen this bank because it was one of those institutions that prided itself on customer anonymity. It didn't even have a name – you either knew it was there or you didn't.

Siobhan was looking after David Saunders today, and doing a grand job. She had black hair and the greenest cat's eyes; the most delicate skin and a voice like music. Early thirties. A good age. Old enough to have shaken off most of those youthful anxieties – young enough so there was still some bounce left in the skin. Mac had been inside for six months, and all he wanted to do was grab hold and fuck her into a coma. Behave, he told himself. What would Mrs Saunders say?

Mac followed Siobhan down the stairs, deeper and deeper and deeper. She led him through a well-lit maze of corridors into a room that was empty apart from a conveyor belt and a retinal scanner. Mac watched Siobhan press her face into the black plastic moulding, fascinated by the gentle pulse in her neck. She stood aside and indicated he should do the same. Eyes wide open, Mac followed her lead. The computer said yes, and there was a distant buzz of well-oiled machinery. Thirty seconds later, the conveyor belt started up. The stainless steel safety deposit box arrived within moments, stopping right in front of him.

Mac picked up the box and Siobhan led him to a small side annexe. This room was completely white – walls, ceiling, floor, desk and chair – bleached of all character. The lighting wouldn't have been out of place in an operating theatre. There were no cameras. Siobhan pointed to a button on the wall and told him to buzz when he was finished. Mac waited until the door was closed before lifting the lid.

Inside were bundles of hundred dollar bills, a million in cold, hard cash. The dollar was truly the international currency – ask any drug dealer. The green contrasted pleasingly with all the white. Mac placed the black leather briefcase on the desk, and carefully stacked the bundles of notes inside. There were a couple of passports in the bottom of the box: one Australian, one American. They were works of art, the legends fully supported. And, best of all, they had never been used. MI6, MI5, the CIA, the NSA, nobody knew about these two aliases. Mac lifted out the wallet folder and laid it on top of the money. The lid went back onto the empty box and he

clicked the briefcase shut. Mac glanced at the
Rolex Submariner – it was too ostentatious for
his tastes, not quite as classy as the Tag, but it
would do for now. His flight left at two . . . plenty
of time. He buzzed for the lovely Siobhan to come
and get him.

'Anything else we can help you with today, Mr
Saunders?' Siobhan asked as she led him back
through the maze.

'Actually, since you ask, there is one thing. I
know it's a bit cheeky, but I don't suppose you've
got a computer I can use. You see, I need to send
an email and my laptop's on the blink. And don't
you just hate those Internet cafés . . . ?'

'I know exactly what you mean. Dreadful
places. Computers are a wonderful invention . . .
but only when they work, eh?' Siobhan's smile
bordered on the flirtatious.

'That's the truth.' The smile Mac flashed back
was friendly enough, but there was nothing
remotely flirtatious about it because that was the
sort of guy David Saunders was.

A week without so much as a word from Paul,
and all the signs were pointing to him having gone
for good. They'd arrived at his flat, guns drawn,
charging in to save the day. All six of them: George,
Priest and four of his mates from the Increment.
The second George saw the corpse in the hallway
she knew it was too late. A quick once-over of
the flat confirmed her worst fears. Paul was gone.

The ports and airports were alerted: name, details and the most up-to-date picture she could find. They got a hit almost immediately. Paul Aston had bought a ticket for a flight from Heathrow to Athens, leaving at 7 a.m. George had demanded – and got – the full cooperation of the authorities at Heathrow. Of course, Paul hadn't shown. The flight eventually left two hours late with a whole load of pissed-off passengers, and one empty seat. It had been too good to be true. Too easy. He'd paid for the ticket with a credit card, for Christ's sake. But it was their only lead and she had to follow it up. Which he would have known. And while she'd been looking the wrong way, he'd quietly slipped out of the country. Over the next couple of days they pieced together some of Paul's movements. In the early hours of Tuesday morning he'd done a tour of hole-in-the-wall machines. He'd stretched his overdrafts to breaking point and collected as much money as the computers would let him have. And then the trail had gone cold.

George knew that, lately, she had been a complete bitch. She'd been working every hour God sent, and a few more besides, working herself into the ground. She had followed up every single lead – not that there had been many of those – anything that even looked remotely like a lead. That she was clutching at straws was obvious to everyone. She had seen the way Priest and Jem looked at her. They hadn't tried to stop her, though, realising it was best that she kept busy.

Even if she wanted to, she couldn't let this go. Paul was out there, hurting; there was no telling what he might do. She had ruled out suicide. He was acting too logically for that . . . and they would have found the body by now. So what the hell was he doing? Where the fuck was he?

God, she missed him so much.

It was like a bereavement. Or a break-up. Okay, he could be an annoying shit sometimes, but that's what happened in a close relationship. You got to know each other too well; it was only natural to wind each other up. And they had spent so much time together – more time than most married couples. Day in, day out at work, often in high pressure situations. It was a wonder they hadn't killed one another. So why the fuck hadn't he got in touch to let her know he was all right? He must realise she'd be worried sick. If he wanted space, if that's what this was all about, then he could have as much fucking space as he needed. All she wanted was to know he was okay. Was that too much to ask?

The reaction of the police would have been comical if the situation hadn't been such a tragedy. They had actually managed to convince themselves Paul was a serial killer! They'd been okay with the idea that he had killed Kestrel in self-defence until they found the hand in the freezer. After that, their little imaginations had gone wild, dreaming up all sorts of scenarios. Paul's saviour had come in the unlikely form of Detective

Superintendent Fielding. The bullet-headed detective had waded in and put everyone straight. Of course, there would be a price to pay, and Fielding made sure George was aware of this.

There had been a couple of developments on the Mac front. Fielding had been right about the paramedics – they were working with Mac. One set of prints in the ambulance had belonged to Kevin Turner, a known associate of Gordon Harris. George hadn't heard of Harris, but Fielding filled her in. Harris was a face in the London underworld, a big-time drug dealer who was currently serving a ten stretch. The detective had given her three guesses which prison. George only needed one.

The good news – if you could call it that – was that Paul wouldn't face any charges. Heath and the I/Ops department had worked overtime to get this one hushed up, pulling more strings than a hyperactive puppeteer. There was no link between the murders in Great Bedwyn and Kestrel's death – and nor would there ever be. The murders in Great Bedwyn were the result of a burglary that went wrong . . . and Kestrel's death never happened. That was that. End of story.

'Don't tell me you've been here all night.'

George looked up, blinking her bleary eyes, and saw a hazy Jem floating on the other side of the big desk. She was using Paul's desk because it somehow made her feel closer to him. 'No, I haven't been here all night. I woke up early and couldn't get back to sleep, so I decided to come in. I thought I'd try and make myself useful.'

'Well you look like you've pulled another all-nighter. You look like shit.'

'Thanks. Just what a girl needs to hear.'

'I didn't mean it like that.' A pause. 'I'm worried about you, that's all.'

'Well, don't be.'

'He'll turn up.'

'That's the thing, Jem. He won't just turn up. We need to find him.'

'You know, sometimes the best way to find something is to stop looking for it.'

George almost laughed. 'And where did you get that from? A fortune cookie?'

'Hey, only trying to help.'

'I know. And I'm a cranky bitch who's drinking way too much coffee and getting far too little sleep.'

'Look, I've got work to do.' Jem paused on her way out. 'By the way, did you hear what happened to Coulson?'

'Yeah, I saw it on the news.'

'The bastard got everything he deserved. Maybe there is a God after all.'

The computer expert smiled sweetly then disappeared through the door. George went to make another coffee – her fourth of the day and counting. When she got back there was a message from Jem on her computer.

cum up quick sumt u need 2 c

'Sumt' had obviously got Jem's knickers in a twist, and George doubted it was anything important. What the hell? It wasn't as if she had much else to do. She dragged herself from her seat and headed upstairs.

'You'll need to sit down for this.' Jem spun an empty chair around for her.

'No dramatics, please,' George said. 'I'm really not in the mood. Just get to the point, eh?'

'Sit!'

George sat with a sigh.

'Take a look.'

Jem flicked the mouse and clicked it once. An email flashed up on the screen. Unimaginatively, it had come from John Smith. As George read the simple one line message, the temperature in the room seemed to plummet.

'I've been keeping an eye on Aston's email accounts,' said Jem. 'This came through this morning. I'm guessing it's from Mac.'

'What can you tell me about it? And I want facts, not guesses.'

'It was sent at 9:16 this morning to Aston's secure MI6 account. I've traced its origin to a wireless data network that covers most of Europe . . . of course, we're talking wireless here so that could be anywhere in Europe. Mind you, it wouldn't help us if we did know where it was, Mac could

481

have connected to the network from anywhere.' Jem shrugged and shook her head. 'And that's about it, I'm afraid.'

George nodded, unable to take her eyes from the screen. She had to find Paul before Mac did. That was more important now than ever. The message was only three words long, but those three words were a challenge, a promise and a threat all rolled into one:

watch your back

Paul Aston stared out of the Greyhound's window at the bleak Texan landscape. The sunblasted sand shimmered all the way to the horizon where three tall towers of knobbly rock reached out of the ground like skeleton fingers. Mini-tornadoes of dust spiralled up on the wind, dancing and romancing. He had spread himself across the seat to keep the other passengers away. The last thing he wanted was anyone getting up close and personal and giving him their life story. Everything about his body language said 'leave me alone, please'. The emphasis was on that 'please'. Too much fuck-off-and-die and he'd be remembered. What he was playing for was a level of isolation where people were happy to respect his space.

Countless miles rolled off into the past; countless miles stretched far into the future.

Aston pulled the Boston Red Sox baseball cap down over his eyes, and shifted around to get comfortable . . . or as comfortable as he could get on the cheap seat. He pretended to sleep for a while – one more reason to be left alone. The iPod he'd picked up at Heathrow was another reason. The earplugs were in, but the only thing coming out of them was silence; he wanted all his senses fully functioning. Nobody would know that, of course. Not unless they got up close, closer than was acceptable.

Killing Kestrel, Mac's escape, his mother's murder . . . it felt as though it had happened so long ago. In fact, only ten days had passed. After hitting the cash machines, he had gone to Heathrow. Yes, he could have gone to a smaller airport – Bristol or Birmingham or Luton – or even one of the seaports, but he didn't see the point in sneaking around. Either his disguise would work or it wouldn't. The wig had cost a small fortune and was made from real hair. Heavy framed glasses gave his face a different shape. You lived and died by the details.

He had walked into the departure lounge like he owned the world – when you acted like you belonged, you tended to get left alone. Using a credit card registered to an electronic ghost, he bought a ticket to Dublin. He checked the departures board and calculated when the heaviest flow of passengers would be hitting security. Two and a half hours later he was queuing up for the X-ray machine. He'd already decided which machine he wanted. The woman guard on the left had the aura of someone who'd do anything to get ahead – it was getting on for six in the morning and she looked ready to jog to the moon and back. He moved up to the front of the queue, and for a heart-stopping moment it looked like he was going to get her. Not good. She was just finishing up with a family of three and any second now she was going to wave him over. Aston bent down and fiddled with his shoelace. He told the businessman standing behind him to go on ahead. When he stood up again, the businessman was being wand-waved with all the intensity of an internal exam. The guard manning the machine on the right called Aston across and gave him a cursory once-over. This was someone who really didn't give a shit. Aston dumped his bag on the X-ray machine and was pointed in the direction of the metal detector. The guard had barely looked at him. The flight itself was routine; there were no problems with disembarking. As far as the computers were concerned, he was Adrian Hart.

The next night, he went through it all again. This time, Adrian Hart flew Delta to Atlanta. If you can't retain your anonymity in the world's busiest airport, where can you? Aston was on edge the whole way. Post 9/11, America's airport security had really been tightened up. He needn't have worried. The immigration official he picked out to stamp his visa waiver form was as lethargic as the guard back at Heathrow.

He always bought two Greyhound tickets for

two different destinations, deciding at the last second which one to use. North or South? East or West? Seattle or Miami? Overkill probably, but caution had been imprinted into his DNA. And so far, so good. He wasn't being followed. The next hurdle would be to stay in one place for a few days – his money belt was getting lighter; he needed funds. Aston wasn't quite ready for that yet. Another couple of days, and he would have to. But for now he was happy to stay on the road. He preferred to keep moving.

Mac rarely intruded on his thoughts. Maybe one day, he'd turn a street corner and come face-to-face with his old boss. If that happened, he'd deal with him. Aston had no intention of hunting the fucker down . . . not this week, at any rate.

It hurt too much to think about George, so he tried not to.

For a while, he must have slept because he awoke with a start, momentarily disorientated. He had dreamt he was in a brightly lit white room with no windows and no doors. The room was small, no more than six feet by six feet; if he stretched up he could brush the ceiling with his fingertips. It was bigger than a coffin, but no less claustrophobic. He had banged to be let out, screamed himself hoarse, scratched at the walls until his nails tore away and his fingers bled. Realising no-one was coming, he had squeezed deep into one of the corners and wrapped himself up into a ball.

485

Aston glanced out of the window, getting his bearings. Far in the distance, he could see the tall glass and steel skyline of Dallas glimmering like some modern day Oz. When he turned around there was a black girl standing by his seat watching him, a pretty little thing of about four or five wearing a sunshine yellow dress. She had neat cornrow braids and a smile jam-packed with sparkling white teeth. The girl was staring with that complete lack of self-consciousness only the very young or the very old can get away with. Aston pulled out his earphones and smiled at her.

'My name's Celia.'

'Hi Celia.' His American accent was still a little rusty, but it was getting there.

'Did you have a bad dream?'

He nodded.

'My mom says that bad dreams can't hurt you. My mom says that if you close your eyes and count to ten the bad dreams will blow away.'

'Your mom must be a very clever woman.'

Celia turned and pointed towards the back of the bus. 'She's over there.'

Aston followed the finger and saw a tall black woman walking down the aisle. The woman was pretending to be angry. 'Uh-oh, I think she might be looking for you.'

Without another word, Celia made a cheeky face and ran off up the aisle. Straight into the arms of Mom, who scooped her into a hug and mouthed a 'sorry'. Aston waved the apology away. He watched mother and daughter move hand-in-hand towards the back of the bus. Celia was talking nineteen to the dozen, telling her mom all about it – looked like Mom had her hands full with that little bundle of energy.

Dallas was no closer than it had been a couple of minutes ago. If anything, it looked further away. Aston closed his eyes and counted to ten. When he opened them, the view hadn't changed. Nothing had changed. He snorted a humourless little half-laugh. That would have been far too easy. So what now? Another anonymous city to lose himself in, another night in a crappy no-star hotel, and then another bus journey to fuck knows where, that's what. Depressing didn't even begin to cover it. Aston put his earphones back in and pulled the Red Sox cap down over his face. He settled into his seat, acre upon acre of tarmac rumbling away under the heavy wheels. With the sound of the road filling his ears, he closed his eyes and tried to escape from the world.